To my son, who continues to inspire me each and every day.

Sylvia Townsend

Out of Time

AUSTIN MACAULEY PUBLISHERS™

LONDON · CAMBRIDGE · NEW YORK · SHARJAH

A CIP catalogue record for this title is available from the British Library.

ISBN 9781787102385 (Paperback)
ISBN 9781787102392 (E-Book)

www.austinmacauley.com

First Published (2018)
Austin Macauley Publishers Ltd.
25 Canada Square
Canary Wharf
London
E14 5LQ

Acknowledgments

By far the simplest part of completing this novel was the writing of it.
The most difficult was taking it from first draft to first print.
There are a multitude of people who have helped me along the way. Here they are, in order of appearance:

First, and always, my son, my greatest supporter. His unconditional belief in me is what got me here.
John and Pat Zieman and all of my co-workers at Mortgage Depot gave me their blessing to go off on a one-year sabbatical, and graciously took care of business while I was away.
Other friends and family away from home were Martine, Philippe and Sarah Galibert; Issy, Norbert and Lucas Sarrobert; Kyla, John and Jordan Stevens; Jill, Jim and Alli Stewart; Roz Morgan Shaw and Andy Shaw. You created a space for me to get to know the culture, live the joie to vivre and write freely. You could never fully understand what you have all meant to me.
Next my editor, Sherry Hinman (www.thewriteangle.ca) who had the magical ability of critiquing my work without ever making me feel criticized. She didn't rest until it was 'perfect'. I still don't know how you did it.
The long list of friends can only be presented alphabetically, as it is an impossible task to try to determine whose support impacted me in each way, but all played a pivotal role:
Riviere Bedard, Amy Biddeson, Ali Burke, Jessica Grant, Denise le Moyne de Martigny, Stephanie Lotwis, Pat

McDermid, Jan Martens, Jess Newton, Mary Jane O'Byrne, Samm Port, Kate Scott-Moncrieff, Dave Suddaby, Lindsay Thompson, Maureen Wright.

To my mother, my siblings and my nieces and nephews, who individually supported me in their own way. Your love and patience have meant the world to me. I wish my father were still here so we could have commiserated, but I know he's still paying attention, so 'thanks, Dad'.

The Well Red Book Club (The Finest Book Club Ever) – Rita Chand, Colleen Creighton, Laurie Klassen, Michelle Loewen, Vickie Milne, Karina Perkins, Nikki Sieben, Nikko Snow and Shannon Tong – whose encouragement and unwavering belief in me gave me the push I needed to see this thing through. What an incredible group of women, friends and fellow book lovers.
Kate, Neil, Liam and Sam Scott-Moncrieff – my second family – have infinite ways of supporting my son and me. And a special thanks for bravely taking your young family to France for a year, and paving the way for us.

Thanks to Jessica Grant for her medical insights and guidance, in addition to her friendship and constant encouragement.

To Amy Biddeson, who continues to enthusiastically support me all of these years.

Denise, my dear friend. You always know just what I need to help me move forward in life. A push. A pull. A laugh. You always hold me in the best light, even through the darkest times.

Last but definitely not least, the artistes extraordinaire – my dream team – who took the images out of my mind and translated them into the perfect cover, layout and design:
The Photo Shoot Team:
Putting together this novel cover took courage, patience, talent, vision and a bit of crazy. Thanks for capturing exactly what I wanted. And for making the process unforgettable!
Amy Biddeson, Director, Friend, Confidante Brian Pridham, Photographer / Magic Maker Danielle Bennett, Stylist and Design

Heather Bretschneider, Model and Design - the perfect Isabel

Cover Design and Layout (post-photo production): Adam and Maria Lawson
Chase Theory I Creative
www.chasetheory.com
Working with both of you has been an absolute pleasure. Your artistic insights astound me, and the final results delight me. You have taken everything I envisioned and turned it into something so much more. Incroyable!

To Langham Court Theatre, Victoria, BC for costume rentals.

Prologue

"Wake up! Wake up!" Someone was shaking her violently and she fought her aggressor through her sleepy stupor. Her dreams started to become hazy and yet the feelings were still so clear. So intense. The place was strange to her, but there was a man—a beautiful man—she thought through her fog, and she fought to hold on to his image. She detested being woken in this shocking way, especially from such a dream as the one she'd been having.

"What is it? And it had better be life or death because you have disturbed the most amazing dream, you ninny." Her maid was always in a state of urgency. Everything was a crisis or a drama and she doubted this would be any different.

"He is here. He is here. Get up and get dressed. He's here and you are not ready. Oh, *mon Dieu*, what is he going to think? Look at you— you're a wreck." Paulette was frantically trying to rouse Isabel and drag the covers from her warm limbs while scanning the room for a presentable dress.

"*Who* is here?" Now Isabel was getting irritated and started tugging back the covers, teasing her maidservant to the point of breaking.

"*Le Duc de Veauville,* you lazy folle."

"*Georges* is here? *Now?* Oh, *mon Dieu*, but he does not have an appointment. I need to get dressed. Hurry—fetch my blue gown. No, not that one," she hissed. "The other, hanging on the armoire. Look at my hair. Arghhhh, this cannot be happening. What is he doing here?" Now both women were rushing around the elegant boudoir in a comic rhythm, a dance they had obviously practiced many times before. Isabel pulled the dress over her head and as it dropped in place, she spun around with her back to Paulette. Snatching a jeweled comb from her vanity she started arranging her long loose tresses in one stack atop her head, all the while tilting forward so Paulette could tighten her corset.

1

As she reached for her velvet slippers with the jeweled buckles and sapphire settings that matched the comb, Paulette held up her stockings and garter and shoved Isabel onto the bed. In that moment, they heard the nearing footsteps on the stairs leading to the adjoining salon and looked at each other with raised eyebrows. "No time," they mouthed in unison, and Isabel let out the giggle she'd been trying to stifle. Paulette looked horrified, as if to say, this is *not* funny at all, but Isabel continued the rest of the preparations with her little smirk in place.

She glanced into the oval cheval mirror and gave a slight grimace at her reflection. "It will have to do," she said under her breath, intending her thoughts to remain for her own musings. But hearing them, Paulette quickly reassured her that she was beautiful as always and everything would be fine. *Vraiment.*

They gave each other a quick embrace, careful not to rumple Isabel's dress, and then scurried through the secret door that led to the far end of the *chambre*. As the door clicked back in place they heard the rapping of the main double doors to the *chambre* where she met her clients. Paulette bustled over, glanced back at her mistress, took one deep breath and calmly opened the doors...

Part I

Chapter 1

Marc could feel the stirrings of disappointment rising up from his belly to his throat, bringing him back to his childhood. Where was Nate? What was keeping him so long? Nate was late for everything, so he was not surprised. Only disappointed. This was a moment he wanted to share with his brother. He felt both anticipation for Nate's possible interest and the pleasure of an opportunity to gloat. He knew he was more excited about the latter but didn't care. It was not often he was in a position like this and he was going to savor the moment.

The unspoken rivalry had always existed between them. Being the first born by three years, Nathan still walked around with a silver spoon in his mouth. The relationship they shared had been strained at best, in Marc's opinion. "The gospel according to Marc," Nate was always saying, as their versions were often so vastly different.

Nathan held his own resentments but because of his aloof nature it wouldn't have occurred to him to feel jealous or inferior. His way of seeing life didn't have space for that. An easy perspective when you're the one at the top, leaving Marc to struggle between loving his arrogant brother and detesting everything about him. Not unlike what he was feeling now. And his brother's resentment was unfounded. The fact that he had been born later, 'stealing' what was left of their parents' affections wasn't his fault and he wished Nate would stop blaming him and get over it.

He looked up from his signing table and reveled in the scene. The floor-to-ceiling windows of the newly converted brownstone looked out over the city lights of the coastal city of Victoria as they glittered in the misty air. The Book Cellar was the latest trendy literary wine bar and tonight it was packed with the 'who's who' of Victorian life, all there to celebrate their newest neighborhood success. Marc had attended many such soirées in the past, but for the first time in his life, he was the star attraction.

Like Nate, he had started his working career with their father. There was an expectation for both of them to participate and excel in the financial world. Marc strayed into the field of stocks and bonds and became quite proficient at predicting the market. His sixth sense was something his clients joked about but didn't take too seriously. Like him, they did well by his sometimes obscure choices, leaving Nate and his father—both so conservative in nature—baffled. But two years ago he hung up his license. He figured he had enough socked away that he could coast comfortably for awhile, and decided to embark on a 'fruitless endeavor'—a phrase coined by his father—to follow his passion for writing. His parents were gallivanting around Europe and therefore unable to come tonight. Marc suspected the timing was deliberate as Philippe Bouchard was not a man who liked to be proven wrong, not even by his own son.

He wondered about the likelihood of Nathan sauntering in this evening and twisting the spotlight toward himself. High, he suspected. It would be subtle. So subtle that he was likely the only one who would notice. And possibly Sabine. That girl had Nate's number, and the more he watched them interact the more he was willing to bet on the short-lived duration of their relationship. What did she *see* in him? What did anyone? When you were as self-centered as Nathan, there was no room for anyone else. Subtle or not, he refused to give this night over to his brother. "God, I have to start standing up for myself," he muttered, as he scratched his signature into yet another book.

"I'm sorry?" With typical Canadian politeness, a woman was looking directly down at the top of his head, eyes wide in anticipation, obviously not sure what he had said, but almost desperate to glean some morsel of personalized attention from the latest writing success.

"I was just saying how hot it was in here, and that I'd like to stand up for awhile and get a drink." What an idiot. He wasn't sure if she'd bought it but he was new to this type of social setting and it was the best recovery he could make.

"Let me get you something from the bar. It looks like you've been doing this for ages and you could use a break. I'm about to head there anyway. Can I grab you something?"

Yup, she bought it, and her flustered manner suggested hook, line and sinker, but a drink would hit the spot and she did have lovely eyes. A bit young for his taste, but lovely eyes all the same. And a voluptuous shape, so rare when the entire female population seemed to be starving themselves.

He looked over the queue of people, all of them waiting to say a few words to him, waiting to give their critique, their praise. It was a long line. "A scotch on ice would be superb—thanks for offering. I don't know if or when I'll be able to sneak away. What was your name? I'm about to sign your copy."

"It's Chloé, with an accent. Oh, of course you'd know that, being French and all. Sorry. What a dumb thing to say." She blushed and looked down at the floor, incensed at her dim-witted comment.

But he was quick to put her at ease. "No, not at all. My father's family is French but I don't speak a word of it. Well, a few words here and there. I did know about the accent, though, from the perfume." He gave her one of his charming smiles and a slightly mischievous look, which had the immediate effect of removing the embarrassed tension from her body.

She smiled warmly in return. "Thanks for that. I felt like such an idiot. I'll be back shortly." And she pivoted on the spot, heading off through the crowd in search of a drink. Nice smile, too, he thought. And legs.

His eyes darted around the room once more for his brother. *Oh, grow up.* This time, he made sure it really was said silently. He didn't want a repeat of what had just happened. People would start to think he was losing his mind, especially after reading the book. It got a bit twisted in parts.

The plot revolved around a courtesan and her lover—a wealthy and renowned businessman—and how he unexpectedly falls deeply in love with her despite her lowly station in life. As it was set in France in the 1700s, Marc was able to dig up some of the family history and base the book loosely on his own roots but without—God forbid—defaming any of the pristine characters of the actual members of the Bouchard family. *Now if that story could actually be told. Talk about an instant best-seller of intrigue and derangement.* The tidbits he'd gathered from family members over the years made his book sound like it belonged in the nursery rhyme section in comparison. Maybe next time he'd tackle the real story of their self-righteous history. His stomach lurched just thinking about it.

Drawn out of his thoughts by some unknown sense, he looked up from his task to see Sabine shuffling through the crowd. Her delicate hand was raised in a gesture of "We're here." Her expression said, "Sorry we're so late," and was followed by a quick sideways glance, eyes up to heaven and then behind her to Nathan. Then she smiled and he smiled back, an understanding between them that words need not express. Nate's head popped up amongst the crowd and he had both hands up in the pathetic victim's stance of "I couldn't help it. Really, it wasn't my fault." Marc despised weak victim attitudes. Just once, he'd like Nate to sincerely apologize, tell him the truth. The real reason he was late was because his brother's book signing was not that important to him, or not more important than sending out the last-minute emails at his oh-so-important job, or whatever it was that kept Marc wondering half the evening why he never rated as even moderately significant in his brother's world.

"Sorry we're late, little brother. Wow, nice crowd. I think I'll grab a flute of champagne and mingle. Anyone else?" Marc was used to brushing off Nate's behavior and getting on with his life. This was his big night—one of his life's defining moments—and Nate could shove it up his ass.

He smiled at them both, nonchalantly replied, "No thanks," and looked back to Sabine, who stood in front of him, holding his book against her chest like a small child with her favorite bedtime story. *She's so sweet. And has such bad taste in men.*

"Look at you, Marc. You did it. You really did it. I couldn't be happier for you and can't think of anyone who deserves it more. Except me, of course." Her laugh was sincere and full of joy. She really did mean what she said, but the intent wasn't spiteful in any way at all. Just her own basic truth.

"Thanks, Sabine. And I couldn't be happier for myself, either." It felt a little awkward on his lips but he was willing to try her approach as it felt good sharing with someone who wouldn't judge him for it. Sabine and Marc had been developing a close friendship ever since Nate introduced them. There was no spark between them, nor any underlying desire for intimacy. Theirs was simply and quite profoundly a true friendship built on common values and altruistic ideals.

Sabine was really Nate's first decent girlfriend, which partially excused his lack of ability to treat her as she deserved, but Marc was still alone in the world and besides always having female companionship, no one had marked his life deeply enough to develop something long-term. He often contemplated whether he needed to put more effort in up front to *see* if the relationship could go deeper. That was his logic talking, though, and his heart—which had always won the argument so far—disagreed. So at thirty-nine he was still alone, but thankfully, not yet cynical.

His scotch arrived, hand delivered by the woman with the nice eyes. Sabine turned around to see who it was and almost jumped into the woman's arms. "Chloé. What are you doing here? And more importantly, what happened to my advice *never* to buy a strange man a drink?"

Chloé just smirked. "It's an open bar and I wasn't sure of the ruling on that, so I thought I'd risk it. And what are *you* doing here, if I might ask? I thought you had a hot date."

"I did. I do. Nathan's over getting us champagne. At least that's what he led me to believe ten minutes ago. Marc is Nate's brother, but I see you've already met. Marc, Chloé is my assistant, although partner would be a better term, but the partner who has to do all the boring stuff so that I can do all the fun stuff. Wouldn't that just about describe your position, Chlo?"

Chloé had been Sabine's assistant for almost eight years. She had no desire to become a financial planner like Sabine, but enjoyed the day-to-day challenges of the investment world. She knew she was part of her boss's success, although she respected her enough to know that Sabine would be successful no matter what was placed in her path. She was quite simply destined to do well. Her passion for her work showed through and she'd been at it long enough that her clientele came back to her time and time again, also referring many of their friends and family. Chloé's greatest strength was her efficiency—it had to be, to keep up with Sabine's needs—and she shared Sabine's genuine interest for their clients. Their rapport went deeper than a mere business relationship, though. Chloé was indispensable to Sabine and they both knew it. Did she play that to her advantage? No need. She was given all of the privileges she could ever want, including a higher-than-average salary for her position.

"She's always making herself out to be the ogre, and honestly, she only becomes ogre-esque later in the day. Unless she hasn't had enough coffee, and then it can be in the morning as well, but that doesn't happen often, thank *God*."

"Ha, ha, ha. *Très drôle.*" The atmosphere relaxed noticeably and Marc and Chloé, who had been casting inquiring glances back and forth, instantly became more interested once they had Sabine as their common ground.

In that moment, Nate slid in behind Sabine, reached over her shoulder while leaning into her body and handed her a glass of bubbly. "Did you miss me, love?" He always seemed to use words that deflected the focus from his behavior. Instead of, "Sorry it took so long," it was always something else. 'Sorry' was not a word he used often.

"Oh, you're back. Thanks for the champagne. We were just discussing how the four of us were all connected by different threads."

"Fascinating. Speaking of threads, did you see that guy's suit? It must have cost a fortune. Probably his own personal tailor, or maybe he has them flown in from London. It's cut perfectly. I'll have to ask him. Will you excuse me? I'm just going to find some nibblies. I'm starving..." And he was off on another schmoozing mission.

The three remaining each held different expressions with a common theme. They were trying unsuccessfully to hold their emotions back through a pasted tight smile. Sabine's was irritation. Chloé's, complete surprise. And Marc's, simple anger, considerably more intense than Sabine's. None of them voiced the underlying feelings and Chloé broke the trance with her usual grace and humor. "Speaking of threads," she quipped, laying it on so no one missed the snub, "I do find it intriguing how we *are* all connected and didn't know it until this moment. Marc, you and I could have met ten minutes earlier and for the rest of our lives we would never have known each other past our first impressions. And you," looking over to Sabine, "know Marc only through his brother. What if you and Nathan weren't dating? Would you still have met Marc?"

It wasn't the best time for Sabine's mind to wander off in the direction of not dating Nathan. She was fed up with his selfishness and if she were completely honest with herself, the problem would be obvious, that they were two such different people. There was nothing wrong with the way he was. Some women would find him charming, but to her, that depth she was longing for just wasn't there. She gave Chloé a knowing look and Marc pretended not to notice, but of course he'd known his brother his whole life and knew Nate would need to change his ways drastically to hold on to Sabine for the long haul.

To them both, she simply shrugged and said, "I don't know, but what I do know is that life has a way of bringing things to you whether you've planned for them or not. So yes, I do think Marc and I would have connected, with or without his brother. We've become such close friends in such a short time. I can't imagine that not *ever* happening, can you?"

Marc shook his head. "No way, kiddo. The only thing Nathan has done is prevented me from going for you first." Chloé's eyes widened and Sabine lowered her eyes coyly, while showing a hint of a smile. Sabine loved to play this innocent game with him, as they had talked out this issue shortly after they met and agreed their connection wasn't sexual. Their friendship possessed a rare freedom that most mixed-gender friendships couldn't have, mostly due to Nate's ever-looming presence. In that way they were both grateful to him, although in this moment they were both loathe to admit it.

Chloé stood on the sidelines, trying to determine if something was happening here that she had missed earlier. They were looking intently at each other, and then simultaneously burst into laughter, making Chloé painfully aware that their little ruse had worked and she'd fallen for it. "Great party trick." Her sarcasm deliberately laced her response but didn't hide her quirky smile.

"Isn't it? We do that one quite a lot, don't we, Bean? We have others, if you'd like to see them, too."

"I'm sure you do, but I think it will lose its effectiveness with more than one, wouldn't you agree, *Bean*?"

Chloé enjoyed that type of humor, even when it was at her expense. "Where did *Bean* come from, anyway?"

"My niece Sophie named me 'Bean' when she was first learning to talk. When my brother would greet me at the door, he'd turn to Sophie with great excitement and announce, 'It's Sabine.' Of course little Sophie heard, 'It's a bean.' My brother thought it was hilarious, as did the rest of my family, friends, neighbors and distant relations. You get the picture. It just stuck. Even now, when people act like five-year-olds they like to call me that." Sabine gave Marc a mock sneer and he sheepishly grinned back.

Nathan was back from his rounds and wanting to nose back into the tight circle, which he sensed was more intimate and private than he liked. He felt Marc upstaging him with his ever-so-interested listening approach. No wonder people loved talking to him. Who wouldn't? *I should try it sometime.* But he knew that day would never come. For Nathan, that would be giving up too much. His deep, dark secret self needed to stay secret, especially from his biggest rival.

"The turnout's amazing, Marc. Well done. I knew you'd knock out a best-seller, even when you had your doubts. You've always had such an effortless talent when it comes to writing."

"High praise, coming from you, bro." He wasn't sure whether he'd just heard praise or one of those well-executed backhanded compliments his brother was so skilled at delivering. He always appeared to be sincere, so why did Marc question his motives every time he did or said something nice? He knew it was one of two things. Either his sharply-honed intuition was telling him his brother was full of it, or his deep-rooted paranoia was acting up again. At this point, he wasn't ready to rule out either possibility. "Thanks, I think…" he said, subtly covering both angles.

"Don't mention it." Nate's response tipped the scales drastically toward Marc's intuition. He was starting to feel that uneasy pit in his stomach again. This is what he was afraid would happen tonight. Nothing deliberate or obvious. Nate would simply take over the space with his presence and, in a stealth-like fashion, start taking Marc's success down, notch by notch. The saddest part was that Nate didn't realize he was doing it. It was unconscious and unintentional but it cut just as deeply. They'd been dancing this passive/aggressive dance since they were young children—probably since the moment Marc arrived to share his brother's glory. Nathan didn't like to share—most children don't—but it was a characteristic he'd never quite grown out of.

Marc was mulling it over, trying to shed some light on a solution. Not for Nathan's sake, but so he could find some peace within himself. For him, sharing was a selfless act, a giving up of something that held personal meaning and importance. Without that ability, people became so self-absorbed and tight with their affection that they would never be able to give or receive. He couldn't help feeling a pang of sympathy for the poor guy. What a way to go through life. *Stop it, or he'll pounce on me again when he senses my vulnerability.*

All these thoughts were circling around in his head as they had many times, but something about this night, this moment, felt different. Marc was an overnight success. He had amazing friends and although he wasn't closely involved with anyone he had no shortage of dates. He had a lot to be grateful for, and as ideal as Nate's life seemed on the outside, Marc was starting to see the thin veneer that was barely keeping his brother's pain at bay. Why else would he be so cunning and thoughtless? Most people who knew Nate considered him to be big-hearted, but it appeared to Marc that sincerity was lacking and this was all part of his act. Hmm. Maybe he was the one who was finally learning to deflect his brother's abuses. *Enough psycho-babble. I want to get back to this night. My night.* He eased his thoughts back to the present, where his brother was still dominating the conversation.

"How much longer are you going to be stuck here, Marc? Will you be able to slip away for a drink with the three of us, that is if you'd like to join us, Chloé?" Nathan was obviously getting bored with the scene. He'd done everything he enjoyed doing and spoken to everyone he'd tagged when they first arrived. Now it was time to wrap it up.

Marc took a slow, deep breath, recalling his thoughts about Nate's pathetic life—not much compassion there, so keep breathing—and when he was ready to comment without words laced with anger, he answered. "I'm not feeling like I'm stuck here at all, as this evening was organized, promoted and pushed onto my friends and family for *me*. So, you go ahead. I don't expect you to stick it out, but this may be the only time in my life I can look around a crowded room and know that every single person is here because of something I did. Something I created. It's a big deal." And then more lightly to Nathan, "It's a bit like when you got caught smoking pot in university and *you* looked around that crowded courtroom and knew everyone was there because of something *you* had done. Can you understand now what this means to me?"

Nathan took the jab with good humor, as he caught a glimpse into a side of his brother he didn't often see, and it finally dawned on him that Marc really was a success in his own right. "Maybe I should read the book after all," was his underhanded comment, evening the score, and both brothers knew there was truth in that statement. "Shall we go?" Nate gently rested one arm on Sabine's shoulder and the other on Chloé's, and waited for confirmation.

Chloé was the first to respond. "I think I'll stick around for awhile. I've only had one glass of this divine champagne and there are a few people I haven't spoken to yet that I haven't seen in ages. We've been monopolizing your time, Marc, and I'm sure there are other groupies who would like to have their chance at meeting you. Now that I've got *my* autograph, I think I'll mingle. Sabine, hon, see you Tuesday. Nate, a pleasure. Marc, much success. I know I'll love the book. Sabine raves about it. And look around you. *They* love you."

Marc knew she was sincere and he actually felt a glow from her words. *How simple we humans are. It doesn't take much to make us tick.* "Thanks, Chloé. It's been a pleasure, and I hope we cross paths again."

"Oh, you will," piped in Sabine. "You're both invited to Nate's birthday dinner next Thursday, remember?"

"Ah, yes, the event that shall not be missed. See you all there, and thanks for coming tonight. It meant a lot to me." Marc leaned over to kiss Sabine's cheek, patted Nate on the back and offered his hand to Chloé. "Till Thursday, then."

"Can't wait." His grip was strong and his hand warm and she searched his eyes for any sign of attraction. She wondered if he was nervous.

Chloé smiled her fullest smile, did a 180 and headed off toward the other guests.

When Marc opened the door to his character home near the beach, he carried out the routine he'd created to wind down from a hectic work schedule or a stressful encounter. He wandered over to the floor-to-ceiling French doors, opened them wide and walked the five steps to the edge of his verandah. He leaned his arms lightly on the rail and looked out over the sights of the city and the water in the distance. Coming out here, breathing the night air, listening to the stillness around him all put Marc into an almost meditative state and he came to rely on these few moments as essential to his well-being. Even tonight, after a successful evening filled with friends, celebration and promises for an abundant future, his nightly ritual allowed him to absorb the events and integrate them into his being. After only a minute or two, a calm enveloped him. He'd learned the hard way that if he skipped his nightly gaze, his sleep would be restless and he would wake up feeling as if something was unfinished and unsettled.

The next thing he did, which wasn't a nightly ritual at all, was head back inside where two bottles were awaiting him in the wine cooler: one, a bottle of Cristal, which he had purchased in the event of a successful evening, and the other, a bottle of his favorite and very expensive scotch, which he'd laid to chill beside the first in case the whole thing turned out to be a flop. He did it as a joke to himself, but he also knew that at the end of tonight he'd be opening one of them and they were a reminder of how life could go either way and it wasn't necessarily something significant that would determine the final outcome.

He ripped the metallic wrapping from the champagne and gently loosened the cork, reveling in the indulgence of knowing he would only be having a glass or two and then pitching the rest out, as it would quickly lose its bubbly luster. Or he might whip together a champagne sorbet from a recipe he'd wanted to try. It would be a nice way to recall the evening over the next few weeks as he nibbled on his creation with fresh berries or chocolate. Working in the kitchen always had a relaxing effect on him and as wonderful as this day had been, his stress levels put him on edge. He'd had no idea how much of a toll it took to be the center of attention, all eyes on you, expecting you to have the wittiest responses ready, and never repeated. His agent had warned him, but it's not something one can really prepare for. The glamour of fame quickly lost its pull and he felt a stab of empathy for those who truly possessed it. Most people there tonight wouldn't recognize me tomorrow, he realized. They might remember my novel and the party and some of the famous guests who were there. But me? Unlikely. And he was happy to know that he would be able to carry on as he had been, grateful for his anonymity but also thrilled to have had his 15 minutes of fame.

As he set his flute on the counter and swept the room with a quick glance, he felt content. Not complete, but definitely content. The one missing piece was a life partner. They could come home together, rehash the evening, and laugh at his many faux pas. Share the highlights and high praise from unknown admirers, pick apart the hors d'œuvres and then define the ingredients so they could recreate them at home. Now his evenings could only end in monologue and it felt like his life was being lived in 2-D instead of 3. Without having truly experienced the other, he still felt his life had an almost lifeless quality. His many flings and short-term relationships had left him bored and frustrated. It took so much energy to meet someone and then suss out whether they were worth pursuing, and if they weren't, what role would they play in his life, if any? Dating a lawyer because he needed legal advice didn't suit his sense of morality, nor did sleeping with someone with no intention of seeing her again. Unless, of course, in a rare alignment of the planets both parties were on the same page, and then the evening could be whatever it became, with no regrets or expectations on either side. But that was a rare occurrence and had only happened twice in his lifetime. In fact, looking back, he was pretty sure one of those didn't count, as there was a hostile undercurrent when they next met. Once in a lifetime would be a more apt description, and he'd already had his.

On nights like this, when everything in life was in perfect balance and the challenges were all being worked out, he liked to imagine himself with someone. What would that look like? Or feel like? Would it ever be possible to have a relationship and share a profound level of connection? And then his favorite game; *Maybe she was there tonight. Maybe we brushed sleeves, or even spoke. Did I look into anyone's eyes and feel a spark of recognition?*

It all felt a bit contrived, but there was still a part of him that believed that by holding the image of her, clearly and with strong intention, she would be out there somewhere and he wouldn't let her out of his mental grasp. Because if he did, somehow that would jeopardize his chance of finding her. Maybe he was just being superstitious. It didn't matter, though, as it felt good to leave the cynicism to his brother.

On the other side of town, in a luxury high-rise on the inner harbor, Nathan and Sabine were deep in conversation, and similar thoughts were flitting through Sabine's head. She couldn't help it. She couldn't stop them. Tonight was another example of how incredibly wrong this man was for her. What kept her hanging on for more? Was she a glutton for punishment? Was it low self-esteem? Bad taste in men? All of the above. Whenever she got involved with someone, within a short time his traits—evident from the first glass of wine—kept playing over and over like an old album with a scratch. It was becoming almost humorous. But unfortunately there were two real lives in this comedy and neither of them would be walking away unscathed.

"What the hell were you thinking back there? That poor young woman serving us was *not* —despite your strong beliefs otherwise—a peon of society put on this earth to serve you and only you, and to take your abuses. She's probably a struggling law student with twice your IQ, and I hope she gets the opportunity to sue your ass some day. You can be *such* a jerk." Even though it was Nate's apartment, Sabine stormed over to the fridge to open the bottle of scotch that she always had on hand.

"Me, a jerk? Who's being the jerk now? What happened to defending your partner and showing a bit of support? That bitch spilled my drink and almost ruined my jacket." Nate was fuming and pacing around the spacious living room with his arms flailing while he ranted. "And then you had the audacity to laugh, along with everyone else at the table. It was embarrassing and humiliating and I can't believe you're taking her side."

"The only embarrassment was your behavior. No wonder we all laughed. You were acting like a toddler having a tantrum. What is it about you that expects perfection in everyone around you and yet you deliver mediocrity?" They'd had this conversation before, but never this elevated. She was on the verge of making a permanent departure and they both knew it.

"Mediocrity? Is that what you think of me? That I'm some substandard *three* dressed up as a *nine*?" Nate's pout was not having the desired effect and he was starting to panic.

Sabine took a long pull on the scotch, let the warmth of it settle into her gut, and then took one deep breath before answering. "We're not talking about you, the person. We're talking about your behavior. It's not the same thing." Her voice had a softened quality, like the wind had been knocked out of her sails and she was struggling just to drift through this argument. She looked directly at Nathan as she spoke, no longer angry or even surprised. He looked like a little boy who had just been reprimanded and now he needed to recover some ground so he wouldn't feel badly about himself. Such a typical reaction carried over from a childhood fraught with neglect and indifference. Sabine knew his parents well enough to recognize the cool, detached affection often found amongst the very wealthy who chose to have children out of family obligation and not from parental instinct and longing. *We are all a product of our childhood.* The sadness continued to seep into her bones as she spoke her next phrase.

"Nathan." She didn't use his full name unless she was furious, and he knew where she was going by her subtle tone. "I can see that this evening has upset us both, for different reasons, but with the same end result. Personally, this is not how I want to spend my Friday evenings. I have enough personal growth to get through without trying to take on yours. Especially when I don't see you delving in on your own to sort out some of your inner demons. You may be perfectly happy living your life from a place of blame, where none of the responsibility lies on your shoulders. I can see how that may seem easier than facing some deep, personal truth. But I can't do it and have no more strength to try to pull you over to the other side. It only works when you're a willing participant, which you are not. Neither way is right or wrong, but they're so different, we'll never be able to find middle ground."

She'd wanted to express this thought for some time, and she continued, in spite of his obvious discomfort and premonition of where this was heading. "If I live my life from a place of 'everything that happens to me is, in some way, my creation, and therefore my responsibility,' and you live yours from 'nothing that happens to me is my fault,' then guess what? Everything that goes on between us will always be my fault. It's tedious and imbalanced and I refuse to live my life that way. You have *everything* going for you—*everything*. But without this seemingly insignificant piece, it's not enough for me." She placed her empty glass gently into the sink and walked toward the door.

"Sabine. Please, you can't be serious. You can't end *us* based on a technicality of where responsibility lies. It's absurd and it seems almost as if you're looking for an excuse to end things." He paused to collect his thoughts and then without warning his eyes flew open with rage. "Is there someone else? I *knew* it. It's my brother, isn't it? I can't believe you would do this to me. I can't believe *he* would." Nathan started to shake with rage.

Sabine felt his anger as she debated over her next words. "There is no one else, and there never was. Think about what you just said. And did. This epitomizes my point perfectly." Without another word she picked up her wrap from the sofa and quietly walked out the door.

As she drove back to her place, she contemplated her life and her relationships. What was it about her that attracted men like Nathan Bouchard? Although she would be turning 30 this year, she wasn't even close to working through the stack of emotional baggage left over from her childhood. Her small-town-girl life was pretty normal, as was her family, but 'normal' and 'family' used together was an oxymoron. The simple outsider's perspective can make a childhood appear idyllic, and yet the emotional subtleties were what formed her life. Why weren't children given some guidance to deal with the chaos of growing up? Why didn't her parents sit her down when she was four and explain that life was going to get complicated quickly and that was just part of the ride, so hold on tight. But don't get all caught up in it, because it's just that: a *ride*. Even her search for love was based on her impression of her parents' love for each other from a child's eyes. It felt like her ideals around love were still grossly immature. *Well, that would explain Nate.*

By the time she arrived at her condo across the bay, she was completely spent. She knew she wouldn't be able to sleep, so she made herself some tea and picked up Marc's book, freshly signed. She rubbed the inscription lightly with her thumb, remembering his kindness. His gentleness. She needed this book tonight for the perfect distraction from the age-old argument she'd had with Nathan. Instead of dwelling on thoughts and regrets, she instead revisited all of the things in her life she was grateful for: her work, Chloé, Marc, her niece and family, her home. She stripped out of her clothes, flung them over her favorite Bérgère chair, pulled her silk charmeuse slip over her head and slid into bed. She was surrounded by comfortable luxury and knew she'd only be able to read a few pages before she'd fall asleep. To her pleasant surprise, the opening had her entranced. She was proud of Marc and grateful for the distraction his book was unwittingly giving her. She started to get into the characters' lives and then fell, with heavy lids, into a deep, dream-filled sleep.

Part II

Chapter II

"Bonjour, Duc de Veauville. How nice to see you, as usual." Paulette slowly opened the doors and Georges pushed past her, his eyes searching the room until they landed on Isabel, who was sitting by the window, reading a book of prose. She had the appearance of boredom, as if she had been there for hours and was relieved by the distraction of some company. Paulette was once more impressed by Isabel's ability to move from chaos to tranquility in a heartbeat, which, judging from her own pounding heart, was not a long span of time. She glanced down at her mistress's feet to see them tucked discreetly beneath her gown, hiding her stockingless, garterless legs.

"Oh, Georges, what a pleasant surprise. I was just saying to Paulette how it has been so quiet here without you stopping by and why it might be that I have not seen you for so long, *mon chéri*." She caught Paulette's look, as Georges was now standing between the two women and could not see the maid's expression. Paulette had her eyes to the sky and one hand to her forehead, as if about to swoon. Georges caught the exchange and glanced back only to see Paulette smile, tugging one of her stray curls and tucking it back into the pins around her head. The smile she returned was one of curiosity; 'What are you looking at me for? I am just the maid?' In that same moment, Isabel put her embroidered hanky to her mouth and lightly coughed. Paulette caught the laugh, but fortunately Georges completely missed it, now heading over to her with a look of concern on his face.

"Are you alright, *ma chérie*? I rushed over here as soon as I heard you were ailing. My footman heard from Gaston's valet that he had seen you out last night and you didn't look well."

Isabel glanced at Paulette with an almost imperceptible nod, dismissing her. Paulette's look was, 'Are you sure?' and with an even slighter nod from Isabel indicating 'Yes,' she quietly opened the main door and slipped out, leaving the two alone in the *chambre*.

Isabel weakly stood up and held out her arms for an embrace, leaning her head slightly onto Georges' lapel. "Oh, *mon chéri*, it has been the most dreadful week. I have been *worried* about you. You have not been by. Is it something I have said or done? Please tell me, what is it?" Before he recognized her diversion tactic for what it was, he was apologizing for his negligence and absence and starting in on a tirade of his abhorring week.

"You would not believe what the ministers have been arguing about, *chérie*. They just go 'round and 'round, getting nowhere and talking about the same issues over and over. Does anyone really care *who* takes over the position from Monsieur le Bouviac? Any of the candidates are qualified, and it is not like any of them need the pension. And then they come running to me to whine and complain about how so-and-so is incompetent, and so-and-so deserves the position, and on and on. I have been going to private meetings, sometimes until dawn, and each one has proved to be futile. Futile. I am desolé, *ma chérie*. I have hardly slept a wink."

"Oh, my poor love." And she stroked his hair lovingly, coaxing him over to the chair he so loved, designed from the earlier Louis XIV style that was now considered passé. Style was so fickle, changing with every king. Distracted by her furniture and whether or not she needed to contemplate updating some things, she didn't hear a word he said, and knew it didn't matter. She was skilled in the art of listening and could follow any conversation, interjecting with just the right nod, gesture or comment, but if asked to recount what was discussed, she could not recall a word. Except the names, of course. She always paid close attention to whom he was talking about, and obviously some of the content filtered in as she seemed to know a lot of details about many different people. But she had learned that most people did not want you to understand what they were talking about (Georges would say, "How could she, anyway? She is only a woman."). They simply wanted you to understand them. None of the rest was important. In that regard, Isabel was a master of her craft and men were drawn to her. For that same reason woman tended to hate her. And her unusual beauty fanned those flames all the more.

Her eyes were her most alluring feature. Amber, they glinted with flecks of gold and had a cat-like appearance. They were captivating and men tended to stare, hoping for her to catch their gaze. But her shyness gave her the false appearance of being aloof, far off the mark of her true character. Her porcelain skin seemed delicate, and yet she could be tough as nails. She was cunning without being malicious, which kept men intrigued. She was a contradiction in many ways, adding to the allure.

Paulette entered the room with a tray of wine. The elegant carafe and two tiny hand-cut crystal glasses circled a vase of fresh cut roses. Her abilities as Isabel's trusted aide continued to amaze her, but of course she did not let on to Paulette. Roses were Georges' favorite flower and he smiled at Isabel knowingly, as if she had arranged every detail. The tray was set on the tiny table between them and two glasses were poured, only halfway to the top. It was their private signal, one of many, that said he wouldn't be able to stay long. Obviously Isabel had another engagement and she would need to rush through this meeting while giving her guest the impression that *he* was the one that needed to rush off as she urged him to stay longer. Another useful talent, and one on which she regularly relied.

As one of the city's most desired courtesans, Isabel's life was hectic and often exhausting, requiring a set of complex skills outside of the boudoir as well as within. Isabel knew no other life, since her parents had died of tuberculosis when she was only thirteen. She was one of the fortunate ones, found by Madame de Rouler and taken in without question. Her family had been poor, leaving nothing behind, so when Isabel faced her future she knew she had only two options: beg for money on the streets, or earn money on the streets. She knew even if she chose the former it would inevitably lead to the latter. Madame de Rouler had a reputation for fairness, so Isabel deliberately set up outside Madame's *maison*, hoping to be spotted.

For several days she waited, neither begging nor approaching the passersby. She was dirty and hungry and cold, but kept her head high and confidence up, at least by all appearances. Inside, she was quivering with dread. Even if she were taken in, would this now be her life? Was it any worse than the life of poverty she faced without her parents? These were questions that would only be answered with time, or not at all, and she continued keeping vigil, imagining Madame coming out of the main door onto the street, seeing her there, looking lost but capable. Every time the doors opened she would glance up with hope, and every night she would curl up in the corner, disappointed, but not defeated. People would drop crusts of bread on her blanket, or sometimes a chunk of meat, and the season was wet enough that there was ample water dripping from the rooftops. But fall was fast approaching and she knew she would not survive the winter if her fate continued in this way.

From a small window on the third floor, Madame watched the young girl. Although she had a soft heart, she was a formidable businesswoman and knew if this girl broke under the strain she would never make it in the courtesan world nor in the world into which she had been abandoned. After three days, she was confident the girl would survive but her curiosity got the better of her and she wondered how long she could keep up the ruse. Four days went by. Then five. Finally, on the morning of the sixth day, Madame went out the front door and approached her next protégée. Isabel looked her directly in the eyes, held out her scrawny little hand and spoke the first of many words to the woman who would soon become her mentor and friend.

"Bonjour, Madame. Je m'appelle Isabel la Fontaine. Je suis enchanté." It was only a brief introduction, but Madame de Rouler was taken aback by the authority in her young voice. She knew what a struggle it must have been to stay upright and speak with such clarity and intensity after the week she had spent on the streets. Madame did not take her proffered hand, as it was covered in grime and God knows what else, but she looked kindly at Isabel, held one arm out in the direction of the door, and placed her other gently on Isabel's shoulder, indicating that they should both head into the *maison*. Once inside, two young girls put Isabel's arms through theirs and only then did she collapse with exhaustion while they both struggled to get her upstairs into what would be her room in her new home. She would recall fragments of the next three days but it would remain mostly a blur. There was a scalding tub where she was soaked, prodded and scrubbed. She knew how painful it had been only from the raw skin it left, still healing a week later.

Her malnutrition and lack of sleep had weakened her to the point of collapse. She went in and out of sleep and heard faint whispering and talking. The smell of broth, gentle hands spoon-feeding her, crusts of bread dipped in, then more broth. And an anise tea that she would always associate with that time. She slept in a fevered state the first night and, once the fever broke, dipped into a deep and dream-filled sleep. Ghosts of the past. Fears of the future. It was less than two weeks since her parents had died, along with so many others taken by that tragic disease that swept through and annihilated so many cities.

Isabel slowly opened her eyes, peeking out from her drowsy lids. A set of bright brown eyes was staring down at her, only a hand's width away from her face. She closed them again, not quite ready to face the world. She felt as though she'd slept for a lifetime, and in a way, she had.

"Is she awake?" one whispered in an anxious tone.

"I don't know. I can't tell yet. I think so," another voice responded. They chattered back and forth in hushed tones until Isabel could no longer keep up the ruse.

"I'm awake," she mumbled, and opened her eyes fully to see two young girls jump back, startled by their patient, whom they'd grown to know solely in her sleeping state. They both felt a little shy and uncertain of what to say. They'd been talking non-stop while she slept, asking her questions, telling her about her new home, and divulging deep secrets about themselves that they knew she wouldn't remember. Now, here she was, ready to deal with the next step, and their silly game came to an abrupt end as they remembered the horror she would be facing.

"You've been asleep for a long time. Three whole days, in fact. I'm Lauren and this is Paulette. You're in *la Maison de Rouler* and *Madame de Rouler* would like to speak to you when you're able. Would you like to sit up?" Her voice was gentle and Isabel felt the kindness through her words. Having been oblivious to the full extent of this girl's actions, she guessed she had shown her immense kindness during her semi-conscious slumber.

"Oui, merci." With four arms, they slowly raised Isabel to a sitting position. She swayed slightly and her head felt woozy.

Lauren spoke the words to Paulette she had hoped to hear: "Go tell Madame she will *not* be speaking with her today." The other girl smiled, curtsied and spun around so quickly Isabel felt a touch of vertigo. Everything felt hazy, as if a fog still settled on her brain. She mouthed "merci" to Lauren, leaned her head back into the soft pillows and promptly closed her eyes. "Are you alright?" Lauren queried. "Can I get you something? Some water, perhaps, or some wine with water? Are you hungry?"

"No. Thank you, though. I think I'd just like to sit like this for a few minutes. Try to get my bearings." She was starting to regain clear consciousness, and with that, memories. Tragic ones fraught with death and loss and loneliness. Before she could stop herself, her eyes welled with tears and by closing them, the tears escaped down the sides of her face, dripping onto the front and shoulders of her nightie. She didn't want to cry. She needed to be strong. She was thirteen-years-old, for God's sake. No longer a child. And for that matter, she'd been running her household for years, ever since her Mama had been sick. I will *not* cry. I will *not*. She felt a light warm touch on her cheek as the back of

25

Lauren's hand brushed the tears away from one cheek, and then the other.

"*Ma petite sœur.* It's okay. You can cry. You need to cry so you can wash away all of that sorrow you've been holding. Just let it all wash away." And she leaned over and took Isabel into her arms. "That's it, let it all out. It is okay, *ma petite*. Shhhh, shhhhh, shhhhh. That's it. You are safe now."

And with those words, Isabel's reserves crumbled and she broke down, sobbing in torrents, sometimes gasping for breath, sometimes with short tiny sobs until finally her breathing started to return to a steady rhythm and the flow of tears slowed. She felt mildly embarrassed until she looked at Lauren and Lauren looked back with nothing but compassion and understanding that diminished Isabel's self-consciousness and allowed her to release the last of her unshed tears.

"Je m'excuse…"

But Lauren cut her off. "Uh, uh, uh. *Non, non.* No apologies, *d'accord*? Do not even *think* about feeling badly for feeling badly. There will be no such silliness here, comprends?"

"Oui, I understand. I… I… I want to say, thank you—for everything. I do not exactly know what you and the other girl have done but I have an idea that you have not been sleeping nearly as much as I have these past few days." She attempted a thin smile with her words. "And for all of that, I am grateful."

"No need for thanks. We will get it out of your hide once you are well enough." For a moment Isabel was not sure if the other girl was serious, as she said it with such a grave expression, but then she let loose a smile and both girls felt the beginnings of their friendship. "You need to be a great actress in our line of work, as you will see. I had you there, did I not?" Lauren was still chuckling at her attempt at lightening the moment, and Isabel nodded her agreement.

"Brava. Brava," and she raised her hands together in the air as if to clap, but they fell back on her lap and both girls broke into laughter at her feeble attempt.

"No theatre for you, young lady, until you are able to stand up and give a girl the ovation she deserves. But now, I must take my leave and go check in with the other girls and then Madame. I will be back in a few minutes but I will send Paulette—she was here earlier—to see you as soon as I leave. Will you be okay while I am gone? It will only be a few minutes, I promise."

"Do not worry about me any more, Lauren. I am fine. At least I will be soon enough. I have come through the worst and will be dealing with the sorrow for some time. But my head is clearer and I'm starting to feel hungry. A good sign, n'est-ce pas?"

"A good sign and I'll send some food back with Paulette," Lauren agreed. "*A bientôt.*"

"*A bientôt.*" And as Lauren quietly closed the door behind her, Isabel closed her eyes and slept again.

For the next few days Isabel would go in and out of sleep, waking always to find either Lauren or Paulette at her side. Each day she felt stronger but a fatigue had settled into her bones and Madame was concerned that the girl had caught the White Plague as well, her fever and persistent cough common symptoms of the disease. The girls watched her closely, and they knew to be cautious around her and report any changes. But generally her health improved each day and at the end of the first week Isabel asked to see Madame.

"Are you sure?" asked Lauren. "She is a patient woman and will wait until you are ready."

"I am ready now," was her reply, and both girls knew it was true. Putting if off any longer would only be delaying the inevitable, and the unknown was causing more stress on the young girl's mind than what she would actually be facing. "Please, Lauren. You have been so kind, but could I ask one more thing of you? I would like to borrow a day dress if I could, and have some help with my hair. The first impression I gave Madame was not my most flattering, if you remember." Her shy smile was almost apologetic, although by now she had seen Lauren's heart and knew this would be no imposition.

"*Ah, bien sûr, mon amie.* Best to be prepared, for sure. Paulette, go get my blue robe. The one with the cream overlay and silver stitching." And then to Isabel, "I think it will fit you perfectly, and will pull out the color of your eyes. It may be a bit tight in the bodice, but it will do nicely, I think."

Together the three of them primped and primed more that she had ever done in her short life. They decided to put her hair up in the back, but leave a few loose tendrils to fall over her face, giving it a natural look, despite the hour or so it took to arrange. The dress was a little short but as she had no shoes that fit, her stocking feet would have to do, and the effect was charming instead of contrived. No makeup, no perfumes or oils. Her natural buffed and polished skin and hair would give the best impression, the girls assured her. Madame had asked to see her at three that afternoon and it was already just ten short minutes away.

"Look her straight in the eye when she speaks to you," cautioned Lauren.

"And do not fidget," added Paulette.

"Yes, she detests fidgeting, or biting your nails, or twirling your hair," Lauren affirmed. "Stand as still as you can, with your hands folded in front," she continued. "But if you need to sit, just ask her. Fainting again will not make a good second impression, I should think." She squeezed Isabel's hand in assurance. "You will be fine, you'll see. And when you are done, excuse yourself and then run back here and tell us *everything, d'accord?*"

"*D'accord.*" Isabel held out her other hand to Paulette in thanks, released them both and then brought her hands silently together as if in prayer, eyes up to the heavens. "Oh Lord," she began, and the other two looked at her, wide-eyed with surprise, waiting to see where this would lead. "That is all I remember of my prayers," she said, and she giggled with joy as she saw their sighs of relief, knowing she had duped them both. She bowed low before sauntering to the door, swaying her hips in an exaggerated gait as she went.

Another girl was waiting outside Isabel's bedroom door to escort her to Madame's private *bureau*. The walk was a confusing journey down hallways, down stairs, around corners, down more hallways and then down a long wide passage where a light shone under the door at the far end. The girl rapped lightly, and then opened without waiting, allowing enough space for Isabel to slide in. The door silently closed behind her, with no chance for her to say thank you or goodbye. The room was bright and airy, which surprised Isabel, as most of the passageway had been dark and a bit damp. This room looked out onto a spacious courtyard below, with flowers blooming and even an apple tree, bending under the weight of its fall bounty. She brought her focus back to settle on Madame de Rouler and waited for her to speak the first words.

"You look so different from our first meeting. Are you, in fact, Isabel la Fontaine?"

Isabel wasn't sure if she was teasing her or asking a serious question, so she replied with certainty. "Oui, Madame. C'est moi, Isabel la Fontaine. The young girl you took in from the street last week."

"Forgive me for my surprised manner. Your recovery is, how do you say, miraculous. I am most pleased. For you, of course, my dear." *And also for you*, Isabel thought, trying to keep her cynical thoughts from revealing themselves on her face.

"Yes, and for me, too, of course," was Madame's reply, not giving away a hint of catching Isabel's thoughts, but she realized in that moment that she must be careful. This woman held her future in her hands and not much got by her; of that Isabel was already aware. Whether it was Madame's strong intuition or her ability to read people, or possibly both, Isabel knew in that instant that there were no secrets in this house and to attempt to have them would be folly.

"*Alors*, I see that my girls have been taking good care of you. The color is back in your skin and you have put on weight. Good girl. And now, I am sure you would like to get settled into your new life here and start taking steps to put your old life behind you. I will go over the house rules and expectations and we will take it from there, *d'accord*?" Isabel knew that no reply was necessary. She continued to stand in front of Madame with folded hands, listening attentively. When she said something that Isabel didn't understand or did not quite hear, she would start to scrunch her eyebrows just the tiniest bit and Madame would insert a new word, or change the phrase, without missing a beat. In this way, Isabel began to learn to modify her facial expressions in the subtlest ways.

The rules were straightforward and strict but she could see their necessity. There were seven courtesans and five maidservants in all, so with a dozen women under one roof, plus the rest of the staff (all women except for Josef, the manservant and girls' protector) keeping unwelcomed men out was essential for everyone's well-being. She knew Lauren, Paulette and Lisette, but had only heard of Marie and Sylvie, whom Lisette talked about incessantly because of all they did for her when she first arrived. Louise was the only maidservant she knew nothing about, and she was told she would meet Janine, Adèle and Colette this evening at dinner. There were three other courtesans; Thérèse, Henriette and Amélie were all at the country house and expected back in a few days.

The expectations of her were next, she sensed, and Isabel started to feel nauseous. She kept the interested expression on her face, but small beads of perspiration started to collect on her brow. Madame walked over and swung open both windows, and then turned to the cabinet to pour them each a glass of water. "It is warmer than expected today, is it not?" And that was all she said. Her responses were automatic, with no questions necessary. She picked up on every nuance and bodily change and took her cues from that. Most would not notice she was doing anything, but Isabel was aware of the level of concentration required to be able to accommodate every single change without asking a question or making the other person feel awkward. She was developing a great respect for this woman, her patron, her savior. Mixed in with that was a healthy dose of fear.

"Now we come to our mutual arrangement. And when I say 'mutual,' I mean that literally. I will tell you how this *maison* has been managing for over 100 years. Not by me of course." A sly smile—the first one of the meeting—curled onto her thin lips. "But by my predecessors, and myself in turn. I will first tell you two things that may surprise you, but will also give you immediate relief, as I am sure your curiosity has been piqued. I give strict instructions to everyone in the house to discuss *nothing* of our inner workings until after I have had a chance to explain everything in the way I choose. After this meeting, they will come running to you, I am sure, asking what I said, and giving you their version of it all. That is perfectly fine, so you can relax in the knowing that, after our meeting, you will have the full support of the girls." The relief showed visibly on Isabel's face and body, and she took her first deep breath since entering the room.

"You will begin your role here as housemaid, helping the girls where it is required, being available to do small tasks for the running of the household, but mostly getting to know the workings of the *maison* and the general etiquette required for its flawless operation. This is no small task and one you will be required to take seriously. One mistake and you are out on the street. No second chances. Period.

"When you feel you are ready, and only then, you will move into the role of maidservant and be responsible for the care of one or two girls. There is an interwoven bond that will develop among you that can never be severed, except through leaving the house or by death. You cannot imagine such a strong bond, but mark my words, even if you marry some day, or fall in love—God forbid—this bond will be different. The connection is like no other found on Earth and I expect you to treat it with reverence, as some day you will be relying on someone not unlike yourself to make your life bliss, or total hell.

"But I digress. I'm sure you would like to know when you will be meeting your first client, in an intimate way, that is?"

"I would like to know, yes. I feel I need some time to prepare, but it would help me to know what is expected." Isabel bit the inside of her lip, hoping Madame would not notice, and tasted the metallic flavor of blood. The distraction helped but it was not enough to ward off the inevitable. She almost felt like Madame was drawing it out, to see if she would squirm, so she refused to give her the satisfaction. When Madame still did not reply, she raised her eyebrows in a question Madame certainly could not miss. *So?* They intimated, though no word crossed her lips.

Madame gave her a look of slight irritation, as if she had been caught out of her little game and now needed to get back to the business at hand, but what she said next almost knocked Isabel flat on her derrière. "When you are ready you will come to me and ask to begin, and not before." She paused until she saw the words had sunk in. "Understood?" Madame was enjoying this, as a multitude of expressions flitted across Isabel's face and she completely lost her composure.

Taking it to the extreme, which was a bad habit she had developed as a young child when she was trying to get her mama's attention, she asked, "What you are saying is if I want to spend the next 20 years as a maidservant (assuming I don't get tossed out for bad behavior), I could wait that long to come to you before I said, 'Okay, I am now ready. If I could just get some henna for my gray hair, I would like to get started.' And that would be acceptable?"

"My dear Isabel, sarcasm does not become you and I would suggest you curtail it for your thoughts alone. And you would do well to eliminate it entirely. But in answer to your question, yes. You will come to me and tell me when you are ready, as I said. Not before. Understood?"

And she did, clearly and completely. "Madame, I am not sure if what I am about to do is appropriate, but…" She took two quick steps up to her and planted an abrupt kiss on each cheek, and murmured, "Merci, Madame. Merci." Then she stepped back, curtsied low and skipped toward the door. With her hand on the handle, she heard a sharp voice behind her.

"Isabel?"

"Oui, Madame?" She realized immediately her error in leaving without being dismissed, and her face dropped heavily in anticipation of the reprimand, before turning to face Madame.

"That will be all. You are excused." Her face was stern but Isabel was certain she detected a glint in her eyes that resembled laughter. She curtsied again, more deeply and with more maturity, and turned the handle before slipping out into the darkened corridor. She had no idea where she was or how she would get back but she knew that in that moment it did not matter. She was *free*. And she was the luckiest girl on Earth.

Chapter III

The next few weeks brought a host of challenges for Isabel, who was doing everything in her power to please everyone, including the two girls, Janine and Adèle, who were infamous for being in a perpetual state of dissatisfaction. Being the new girl always added the extra pressure of being perfect, and these two played on her vulnerability until Madame called her aside one morning. Isabel was devastated to think that she had done something to anger her. The phrase, "No second chances, no second chances" had worn a groove in her thoughts and the fear kept her paranoia at such a high state that she was starting to imagine trouble where there was none.

"Isabel, I would like to talk to you about something important."

Oh God, please no. Not now, not me. Madame always had a stern look about her and this morning was no different. Isabel was learning to read her moods, but Madame was still the master and far out of Isabel's league if she sensed she was being analyzed. All the same, Isabel started to relax and sensed the danger lay elsewhere in the house. With relief, she followed Madame into an adjoining corridor, out of earshot of the other girls.

"You have been here for three months now, n'est-ce pas?"

"It will be four next week, Madame." Isabel wasn't trying to be confrontational. She knew Madame well enough that accuracy was expected in all instances and this type of detail was important to her.

"Yes, four. Of course. My mistake. And in those four months would you say you have kept your end of the bargain, or our agreement, I should say?"

"Why, yes, of course." She did not know where this was going and knew her look of confusion was readily portrayed.

"Do you know everyone here is living under the same rules? The same expectations? The same agreement?"

"I was not aware of that but it would make no sense any other way." Isabel was still cautious but incapable of answering with anything except her usual blunt honesty, then paying the price later, as necessary.

"Well observed. This is why I want to remind you that this system works infallibly and as long as you stay true to your side of the bargain, if others are *not* playing by the rules it will not affect you. Do you understand?"

"I am not sure I want to be so bold as to say that I do."

"Fair enough." Madame continued to explain, but without any malice or condescension. "I have been watching you—now, do not look at me like that. You have no need to feel singled out, my girl. You know I watch everyone all of the time—and what I was saying is that I appreciate the efforts you have been making in support of the other girls and the operation of the *maison*. Take this as a warning, though. Sometimes in life, no matter how much you play by the rules you cannot win the game when others around you cheat. Their behavior cannot affect yours. Remember, the rules are what make the game, not the outcome. Do not stray from that focus no matter what others around you are doing. That is all I have to say on the matter." With a slight nod, she turned and headed back down the long corridor to her *bureau*.

Three days later, Isabel knew exactly what Madame had meant and was relieved that she had heeded her advice. Outside of business hours and outside of the *règles du jeu,* two of the girls—the two who had been atrocious to Isabel— decided to make a go of it on their own. The rules were designed to keep the girls safe while simultaneously ensuring the house got its fair share of the fee. But they had made small requests of her to lie and cover their absences. At the time she did not understand nor did she play along, but they were both smart girls and most times Isabel's innocence and naïveté convinced her that they were doing nothing wrong, simply wanting a bit of freedom. Their excuses were always plausible and Isabel's first response was always to believe. The girls knew this and started using her as their choice ally, but it quickly escalated. She did not threaten to say anything but she was clear that she would not do or say anything that went against the house, so they began to ridicule and taunt her. The more she resisted their antics, the more malicious they became. She sensed Madame's warning pertained to this situation but she could not be sure.

Madame summoned everyone into the large salon on the first level. Isabel looked up to see the *gendarmes* walk in and her stomach clenched. Madame welcomed the two men warmly with *bisous*, one on each cheek.

"We have not seen you in some time, Monsieur," she whispered in one of their ears as she gently kissed his cheek.

"I know, Madame. *Je suis désolé.* My wife has been, shall we say, more attentive than usual and it has been difficult to get away," he subtly whispered into her ear as the second kiss was planted.

"And you, Monsieur, I do not think we have had the pleasure. You are welcome any time." Madame spoke as if she had just been introduced to her son's best friend and the world relaxed in her presence.

"And now," gathering the attention of the group, "we must get to the business at hand. Most of you already know that Janine and Adèle were found this morning on the streets of St. Michel in a gravely injured state." A few gasps escaped, including one from Isabel, so many had not yet heard the news after all. Madame waited for the room to settle down. "Janine is at Hôpital Bicètre and we cannot be assured that she will survive the night. Adèle, however, sustained minor injuries and is presently in my care. The two gentlemen," she said with unmasked anger, "are in the custody of the police, and we are trying to get evidence to convict them both. So if anyone knows of any specific information that was shared by these two girls it is imperative that you come forth and share it with the police, and with me, of course. If both girls survive, and I pray that they do, they will be out on the street immediately. I will *not* allow anyone or any*thing* to put this house and its occupants at risk, which these girls have blatantly done. It is reprehensible and undermines everything we are about. When men are shown no limits, their behavior becomes reckless. Do not forget that—under *any* circumstances. That is all."

They were quickly dismissed to go about their day, but everyone continued to mill about, speculating on what had happened the night before and what would now happen to the two girls. Isabel felt a wave of relief, as these two girls had been the only black mark on her otherwise untainted life. Her only regret for them was that their lives were burdened by these challenges and even though they had good hearts it would take an immense shift to change the direction of their lives. She understood now why Madame had a policy of no second chances, as she felt they were futile. Your first steps show your true colors and if you break from that there is always the danger of continuing on that same misdirected path. These two didn't possess the foundational code of ethics that ruled both Isabel's and *la Maison*'s world.

This one event had a significant impact on Isabel's life and it was the turning point for a shift in her thoughts that would eventually lead her along her own life path. She could not stop thinking about the difference between her and Adèle. She did not get to know her well personally, as Adèle tended to be closed about her past and her family. But all the girls in *la Maison* gossiped amongst themselves—not in a malicious way, but as a way of staying connected and in tune with each other's comings and goings. Every tidbit of information was added to the bank, which would develop into a picture that would continue to become more detailed over time. From an insignificant comment such as, "My father would be *furious* if I did that," added to another, "…when he wasn't drunk, that is," plus, "I could not wait to move to Paris," would be combined to make up an often accurate account of another's life. The father in question was a raging drunk who abused his daughter until she finally ran away. More often than not, this was the typical family life for a young French girl, and in Adèle's case the picture got worse as more detail was unveiled.

Isabel's life had been different. It had a more tranquil quality that was not common in such a poor household. But her father took an optimistic view on life and despite his heavy burden, he approached each day as a blessing. He loved his wife dearly and she, him. They had met when they were both young and had fallen instantly in love. As neither had come from 'good families'—such an inaccurate description in their case, but one that depicted anyone who wasn't poor—their parents did not resist their match, as they were both healthy, lived in the same village and would enhance the families' lives more than detract from them.

Her mother came from a long history of poverty and did not know differently, so she, too, had made the best of what she had been given. What else was there to do? It was a logical approach to a simple life and one that was passed on to Isabel. Their love for their daughter was natural and genuine, and Isabel was surrounded by her parents' acceptance since birth. Even when her mother became gravely ill and her health steadily declined until the fatal disease finally took her, she continued to treat Isabel with love and respect and still appreciated her meagre life, as if to say*, 'It was the will of God, and who am I to question His will?'* They weren't a devout family by the country's standard, but God had been woven into their lives along with the rising of bread or the sowing of the fields. He was a part of their daily lives that was never questioned or discussed. They gave thanks each day and that one simple act was what kept the hardships in their rightful place.

These were the facts of life, the challenges that were placed at their feet that needed to be conquered and overcome. Isabel remembered the first time she asked, "Pourquoi, Papa?" His answer had always stayed with her: "Isabel, *ma petite chérie*, asking the question *why* is a futile exercise that will bring more tragedy to your life than anything else on this Earth. *Why* is the opposite of *trust*, and when you live your life from a place of trust instead of always questioning *why*, it is from that place and no other that you will find peace."

When she looked at Adèle's life, it wasn't the question *why* that she was interested in, but *how*. How is a life determined? If Isabel and Adèle had been switched at birth, would Isabel's life look like Adèle's and hers like Isabel's own? Are people's characters created by life's challenges or are they born with a pre-determined set of experiences and no matter what family one is born into, those experiences will come to pass? What about if Adèle had a sister? Same family, same circumstances, different attitude and choices made. Is it really that simple? By shifting one's attitude, can a person make her life different? Isabel just could not believe that she would do the things Adèle did no matter how difficult her life had been. But maybe that was her naïveté talking. She had never been neglected or denied love, so how could she begin to understand what drove Adèle to do the things she did. But she felt sure there was something inherent there. Something that must have existed before.

The more she mulled these ideas over in her head, the more resolute her fixation became on adjusting her attitude when her circumstances seemed overwhelming. Her parents' death was still a fresh memory and the pain was never far from the surface of her emotions. She would often feel the tears welling up and would struggle to keep them from cascading down her cheeks. A part of her was afraid that once the dam was unlocked, there would always be a steady flow, and her control would be lost. But each day brought her closer to acceptance, and her father's words were a constant beacon to her thoughts, bringing them back in line. "…it is from that place, and no other that you will find peace." That place of trust. She was determined to live her life from that place no matter what was set before her.

If time heals all wounds then Isabel was well on her way to a near-complete recovery. A full year had passed since her parents' death. Four full seasons with all the holidays and birthdays of the past. She felt she had reached a milestone with her grief as her year of *firsts* was now behind her. It had been a difficult year, not only because of her parents' tragic ending. Janine, the girl who had risked everything with Adèle to have a better life, sadly lost the gamble and died in hospital two days after they found her. Adèle disappeared without a word.

Some happy events took place as well. One of the girls fell in love, got pregnant (or got pregnant and then fell in love—they were never sure, nor did anyone care) and ran off to get married, with Madame's blessing, of course. A new girl, Colette, came to live in the house and took over as housemaid. Isabel had long ago left that post behind except to help when necessary. She had been working as Lisette's maidservant after the first three months and they had developed a close partnership that rivaled the best in the house. Paulette, the other nursemaid who was there when she first opened her eyes one year ago, was older than Isabel but wasn't assigned to a specific girl. They all came to Paulette for help and advice as there was an unspoken understanding that she would never become one of them, so there were no feelings of competition. She was lovely in her own way but didn't carry herself with enough confidence to ever succeed as a courtesan. At fifteen, her mannerisms were still silly and she didn't take anything too seriously. Ideal qualities for a maidservant but ineffective when it came to attracting the attention of the elite. She was also perfectly happy in her role and had no lofty goals to ever change it. Isabel on the other hand, was another story.

Chapter IV

September was drawing to a close and Madame was working on her accounts for month end. It had been a lucrative summer and she was now preparing for a quieter season when travel became more limited because of weather, and parties more infrequent. She was distracted and looking out the window at the fallen fruit scattered on the courtyard when she was startled out of her reverie by a rapping on the door. "Oui?"

"Madame, c'est moi, Isabel," she heard in muffled tones. "May I come in, please?"

"*Mais oui, ma fille. Entrez.*" Madame's rules for the girls were clear. If they knocked before entering they would gain admittance, sometimes only for a moment, to be told to return at another more suitable time. But if they neglected to give her that courtesy, their entrance in future would only be obtained by a pre-set meeting time. Isabel had never forgotten to knock and Madame was pleased for the distraction. "What may I do for you, *ma chérie?* Is there something you need that is not being provided, perhaps?" This was her method of paving the way, to put the girls at ease. When they knocked on her door it was invariably to ask for something they wanted that was out of the realm of their normal comforts. She found it also shortened the conversation by cutting through the small talk and going directly to the point.

"Madame, I have no needs that are not already provided, for which I am truly grateful. What I came to discuss with you is my future. Our future. I have come to tell you that I am now ready for the next step." Isabel's gaze was steady and her breathing stayed even. It took Madame a few moments to grasp the meaning of her words and when she did, she was shocked.

"But *ma petite*, you are so young. Only fourteen. You cannot possibly be ready. Next spring would be better, when the new season is about to

38

begin and we can arrange for a grand launch and announce your début to all of Paris. It will be a huge fête, and…"

But Isabel cut in by repeating, "Madame, I am ready. I started my flow six months ago. I have been working side by side with the finest courtesan in Paris. Lisette has proved to be a worthy teacher and is much like an older sister to me. She has been grooming me for this day and I know in my heart I am prepared."

"So, Lisette agrees with your decision?" Madame's look was skeptical.

"Oh, Madame, she does not know. I came to you first." Isabel had a moment of doubt when she wondered if Lisette would possibly *not* be supportive of her change of roles. She would no longer be Lisette's assistant, a position she had finely honed to a precise art. They would be working side by side now and although it was never spoken aloud they would be in direct competition with each other, sharing the same men. All men wanted to try the new girl and that would include some long-term clients of Lisette's. She had not thought this part through and was questioning her choice when Madame broke into her thoughts.

"This decision has nothing to do with Lisette and you did the right thing by coming to me first. She loves you, Isabel, like the friend and sister you have become, and she will support whatever you decide regardless of the effect it will have on her. You would do the same for her, would you not?"

"*Bien sûr, Madame.*"

"I assume you have given this much thought?"

"*Oui, Madame.*"

"And you have no hesitation with your decision?"

"No, Madame."

"*Alors*, as you wish. We will start preparations immediately." She started jotting down a few notes on the paper on her desk, dabbing her quill in and out of the tiny ink well that was always kept full. Isabel stood still for a moment, wondering how to couch her next request. She had her mouth open to speak when Madame looked up from her writing to add, "One more thing. I feel Paulette needs a more elevated position. I am assigning her to be your personal maidservant. Do you think the two of you can become a professional team between all of the giggling and teasing? Hmm?"

"Oh, *oui,* Madame. *Oui.*" Her final request remained unsaid as her heart leapt with joy at having her desires fulfilled.

"*Va t'en! Va t'en!* We have much work to do. Go fetch the tailor and send Lisette to me, please. Not a word, *d'accord?* We must keep this between us until Lisette and Paulette know. Go on, then. Go." She waved her hands at Isabel in a dismissive way, but her eyes were sparkling with what looked to be both humor and pride.

Isabel's remorse set in immediately after she closed Madame's door. She was petrified at what this next step meant but had begun to realize that she would never really be ready to take it.

Ever since her blood started to flow those short months ago she had started the painful process of waiting and knew the sooner she made the transition the sooner the waiting would end. She would face her fears instead of putting them off and that is exactly what she had done. But oh, the fear. How was she going to become someone's competent lover when she had never even been kissed by a man? She had never seen a man naked but the comments flying around the house implied that it was horrid. See? This is exactly why she needed to get it over with. Stop this mind chatter that would drive her crazy if she let it. *Enough.* She took a slow, deep breath, closed her eyes and imagined a truly magical experience. Her lover would be kind and gentle and honored to be with her, guiding her through each step. After, she would know she was changed. She would be a woman, *enfin.* Complete. Those are the thoughts she held as she drifted back to reality and headed toward her *chambre.* Everything will be fine. Everything will be fine. Everything will be fine, she chanted silently, and through this affirmation, she felt better.

The house was buzzing with activity. Once Lisette was calmed by Madame's words and assurances she became fully supportive of Isabel's launch. Paulette, too, could not be happier. She would miss being the girl everyone sought out, but she loved Isabel like no other and would proudly dedicate her life to her success and well-being. The rest of the group was mixed. Never before had a girl been so young. Fourteen was usually the earliest Madame would consider the transition, but neither could anyone ever recall anyone asking. There was excitement mixed with the odd tinge of jealousy but it was light and well meant. "She is so beautiful. Of course she is ready so young. I would be too if I had her porcelain skin, or full bosom, or luscious lips, or auburn tresses." There was an abundance of things to be jealous of but mostly they were happy for her and wanted her to succeed. Isabel had always been kind to each of them, which fostered a natural reciprocation.

The couturier was the first to be enlisted from the outside world and was sworn to secrecy. Madame Sévigné's reputation for her quality and cut of dress was unsurpassed, as was her discretion in matters of *la Maison.* Isabel would require an entire wardrobe but first the necessary clothes would be made for her first night. The couturier had some creative suggestions and Isabel began to enjoy the attention being thrust upon her.

Clients had admired Isabel on many occasions when they wandered past her while in *la Maison*. Madame decided she would create a stir like no other. It would need to be divulged quietly with great strategy in order for her to pull it off. There would be whisperings around the city and the anticipation would mount. It was a rare occurrence for the *Maison de Rouler* to present a virgin, and never one so young or becoming as Isabel. Madame would take full advantage of the situation, enlarging her purse and the coffers of the house, but more importantly, setting the stage for Isabel's beginning, for her life. And Madame took that responsibility seriously. It must be perfect and she must become the talk of Paris. If she missed this opportunity, Isabel would forever scramble to climb the courtesan ladder, which was full of mean and bitter woman who would do anything to rise in power and status. *La Maison de Rouler* was not the only *maison* in Paris. It was one of the most reputable but many of the houses turned out girls who were quite formidable. There were only so many wealthy elite men in the city and all the courtesans sought the same prize: exclusivity with one of these men, and then many other lesser types on the side. That was the game and both sides knew the rules.

Madame was a master player and well respected for her honesty, fairness and quality of stock. It was a harsh reality but the courtesan's life was bought and sold to the highest bidder and rarely did they have a say in the outcome. Unless, of course, they rose to the upper echelons of their specialized society. There were always three or four girls at one time who monopolized the game, who could pick and choose their pawns instead of the other way around. That was what Madame intended to manifest for Isabel. It was a rare prize with hundreds of courtesans and prostitutes throughout Paris vying for it, but Isabel had all the makings of someone who could become one of the select few.

Who would be the first to come upon this juicy secret? Would it be le Comte d'Ambroise, or de Siméon? Perhaps le Duc de Veauville? The word would spread quickly as the nature of secrets seemed to compel people to share them. Within a day or two they would be clambering at her door. She decided to rely on her staff to execute the plan. Discretely calling Paulette into her *bureau*, she closed the door behind her. They spoke briefly and in hushed tones about the best candidate to first receive the announcement. It would be critical not to offend anyone, so for this reason they agreed it must be le Duc de Veauville, as he was closest to the king. Sending an invitation to the king directly would be offensive, as he had a wife, and although there were many reported mistresses, they were only discussed privately and not meant for public knowledge. Though Madame knew the information would reach the king's ears and he would consider it seriously. That could prove disastrous for Isabel, but life had its own way of unfolding and Madame could only do so much to secure her protégée's future.

She wrote a note on elegant parchment in her flowing hand, folded it and sealed it, handing it to Paulette with these instructions. "You must ensure this reaches le Duc's eyes alone, *ma fille*. Take it there now and ask to be admitted to him directly. This is not the kind of note that can go astray or fall into the wrong hands. His privacy must be protected, so do not, under any circumstances, place it in anyone else's hands but his own, comprends? If they will not admit you, ask them to relay that Madame de Rouler has important information for him and to please come as soon as is convenient. *D'accord?*" They were both standing by the door and Madame thought she heard a faint rustle as she turned the handle to give Paulette her leave. But the corridor was clear, with no sign of anyone about. "*Vas y,* Paulette. And report back to me as soon as you return."

The young girl walked purposefully through the winding halls of the *grande maison* past the *chambres* of the other girls and toward the back stairs that were used only for the staff, the privacy of the girls and some of their special clients. Madame's carriage was ready for her and Paulette pulled her hood up over her head, looked both left and right, and mounted the steps to the carriage.

Back in her *bureau*, a feline smile spread across Madame's face. These walls had ears and she knew the first step in her plan had succeeded. Le Duc would be the second person to hear of Isabel's début. Le Comte de Siméon, the first. The maid, who Madame knew had been listening outside the door, was a close friend of the Comte's scullery maid and she was an unknown participant in many secrets that intentionally flowed back and forth between the two maisons. Had she known, the effectiveness would evaporate and she would need to be let go, as Madame could not tolerate such insolence. But for two years it had been a guaranteed exchange of information and she had relied on her indiscretion on many important occasions. The Comte was one of their most esteemed clients as well as Madame's close friend. He was party to the little ruse and would know immediately that he had been chosen as the first to be told. He would feel honored and obliged to

Madame for yet another favor she had bestowed upon him. He was a man of honor, one who always returned a favor.

At almost the exact same time another servant would be betraying his master's confidences and the Comte d'Ambroise would have the secret divulged to him, swearing he would not talk of it with anyone. It was through this underground network of staff serving the French upper class that all news was circulated. It was a delicate game that needed to be played with precision, as the myriad of possibilities and outcomes, as well as the timing were most critical. If le Duc thought for a moment he was not the first approached there would be hell to pay and Isabel would suffer for it.

When Paulette returned a mere two hours later, the talk on the street was already in full swing and she knew the delivery of her note was only a small part of her mission. This was one of the qualities Madame honored most in this young girl. She had an uncanny ability to play out this type of scenario to its limit and then judge accordingly, with great precision, what to say to whom, and when. From the carriage driver to the shopkeeper on the way home where she stopped for a comfit, to the first words she spoke to the maid who had started the dominoes falling in the first place. "You cannot *imagine* what we saw on the way back from le Duc de Veauville. *Mon Dieu*, it was terrible…" And in this way, she did not obviously divulge the contents of the note, but she did confirm that it had been delivered, causing another ripple to cascade back out on the streets. Madame was waiting casually in the main salon overseeing Isabel's fitting with Madame Sévigné, who had been working with Isabel on her outfit since first thing that morning. As Paulette approached, she gave a low curtsy of acknowledgement to Madame, followed by a wink and a broad smile. Without breaking the flow of her stride she continued in the direction of her *chambre*.

Earlier that morning, Madame had discussed with Isabel how things would be played, so she would be aware and also so she could ask any questions before Madame started the wheels in motion. Madame sensed a tinge of excitement as they discussed what the bidding would entail. She wasn't sure if Isabel had momentarily forgotten what they were bidding for, or if the idea of so much attention and money about to be placed at her feet was too alluring to ignore. Whatever the cause, she was pleased with the result and relieved to see how well Isabel was handling it. With those thoughts in mind, she held out both hands to Isabel, looked into her bright young eyes and asked lovingly, "How are you doing, *ma chérie*? It has been a hectic day and this is only the beginning. How are you managing? Do you need anything?" They spoke freely in front of Madame Sévigné, who was pretending not to listen but had Madame's absolute trust and knew she was free to partake in the conversation if she so chose. She had been dressing the girls for most of her lifetime, and Madame was one her oldest and dearest friends. Besides which, the secret was already out and there was no stopping it now. Anything the couturier could share, once she left the *maison*, would already be old news. The entire city would be talking about it, and embellished versions of what was about to take place would start trickling back to them momentarily.

Everyone in the *maison* had the strictest instructions not to disturb Madame for the rest of the evening. She was completely *indisponible* for anyone or anything—except the king, of course—as the joke went. "On second thought, not even for him," she said with a grand flourish of her arm. She said it in jest but also knew there was a slight possibility his carriage would arrive and she would have to sneak out the back door so she would *not* be there if he called. She was expecting one or two persistent inquiries tonight and by putting them off until morning it would help escalate the whole affair. She watched the scene transpire from her darkened room with one window overlooking the street.

Not surprisingly, the first to arrive was le Duc, who was quite insistent that he be granted an audience immediately. He even glanced up at Madame's window and she lurched back in surprise but quickly remembered that she could not be seen. (They had done many tests from this position, at all times of the day and night, to assure her of that.) She stepped back to her post, smiling at his audacity, surprised at his knowledge of her habit of watching, hidden, from the window. The poor maid who had started the whole mess in the first place was beside herself. No matter what she said he would not leave and at one point he thrust his booted foot into the open door and refused to remove it, even after she attempted once again to close the door. At that precise moment a carriage from the couturier's *maison* pulled up and the coachman jumped down and strode purposefully over to the door.

"I have a message for Mademoiselle Isabel. *Il est très important, s'il vous plaît.*" Le Duc casually pulled his foot closer to his body to avoid the embarrassment of being seen in that compromising position, and leaned against the outside wall. The maid, not knowing the protocol, left the door ajar and rushed off in pursuit of Isabel. She found her at the top of the stairs, walking casually across the grand foyer, and handed the card to her without a hint of leaving until it had been read. Isabel opened the card and mouthed the message half to herself, half aloud, "*Je suis désolé*, but I will be later than expected this evening. The dresses will be delivered in two days. Signed, Madame." Isabel sighed, thanked the maid and turned to go back to her *chambre*. Le Duc, having nudged the door open a little further, and the messenger, who was waiting patiently for a response, took in the entire scene.

"*Mon Dieu*, she is beautiful," le Duc said in a breathy whisper.

"Oui, Monsieur," was all the response that was expected of the messenger but he, too, took in her exceptional grace and beauty and once more in his long life felt regret for not being a wealthy man.

The maid returned, almost forgetting her visitors, and said with a touch of annoyance, "*Vraiment,* Monsieur. She is not here. I will tell her you stopped by with an important message and that you would like to see her in the morning. Now, is there anything else I can do for you this evening?"

"No, that will be all. *À demain.*" Both men turned to leave and heard her reply.

"Tomorrow, then," but didn't see her roll her eyes to the heavens, dreading what tomorrow would surely bring.

Madame had to chuckle. Men were such gullible creatures. *People* were, in fact, as the maid played her part unknowingly for the second time that day. Madame Sévigné had come up with the idea earlier while they were discussing the difficulty of keeping the wolves at bay. She had one of her sons dress as a street urchin and stand on the corner, just up from Madame's. The carriage was parked on the next street, out of view of the *maison*. As soon as her son noticed le Duc's arrival, he signaled to the coach. They waited for two or three minutes until it was obvious the situation was getting heated, and the second signal came, indicating for the carriage to arrive with the messenger. It was executed perfectly, but really, it had been such a simple plan. Now le Duc could leave, satisfied in knowing that no one else would get to Madame before morning. The maid was a bit confused as she swore she saw Madame going into her *bureau* earlier that afternoon and not come out. But never mind. It was a big house and she could not hope to keep track of all of the comings and goings of the entire house. She brushed the thought aside and started hatching a way to go out on a special errand so she could deliver the latest update to her friend at *la Maison* de Comte de Siméon.

There was a quiet rap on the door, followed by three more in equal succession. Isabel slid in the back way just as Madame was pouring two glasses of Armagnac. "Come in, my child. Or shall I say, Mademoiselle?"

Isabel couldn't contain her excitement and rushed over to give Madame a kiss on each cheek before starting into her account of what happened. "Oh, Madame, it was *too* funny. Everyone did exactly as you

45

had said—you are clever, Madame—and it was as if they were acting out parts in a play you had written. Even the look on the maid's face when she saw me at the top of the stairs—*incroyable*. I almost had to laugh but maintained a far-off look as you had instructed, and I'm sure the coincidence rang true. And le Duc. Mon Dieu, he is not very handsome, n'est-ce pas? And so old. But persistent, n'est-ce pas? Sticking his foot in the door. I was watching it all from behind the long drapes at the top of the stairs. Even the messenger looked shocked, although he was in on it, too, wasn't he?" She stopped and took a breath and caught Madame's smile. "What's so funny? Why are you laughing?" And they both let out a giggle, like two children.

"Shhhhh. I'm not here, remember," Madame said in a hushed tone, which made them laugh even more. "You were perfect tonight and le Duc is quite smitten. He got a glimpse of you, *ma chérie*, that he shall not soon forget."

"Do you think so? Do you think it will be him? I mean, the one that… you know, the person I will…," she stammered. "The winner?"

"Well said, Isabel. The highest bidder will definitely be the winner and the prize is like no other. You are a special young woman and what you are doing cannot be undone. You understand this, don't you? Once the choice has been made, it will affect you for the rest of your life." She handed Isabel the glass of brandy, and lifted her glass before she made a toast. "This brandy signifies your transition into womanhood and I am honored to share it with you. I am going to offer you some on the night of your first encounter, if you so choose, as it will help relax and warm you. But for tonight, enjoy this moment. To your success and adornment."

"To my success. *Merci, Madame, pour tout.* Everything you have done for me has created whatever success I may experience, now and in the future. You have given me a life like no other and have saved me from certain destruction. So, I toast you. To *you,* Madame."

"*À nous.*"

"Yes, to us," and Isabel raised her glass and clinked Madame's a third time. Then, needing to move on to something less serious, she said, "Mmm. I like this drink very much. What was its name?" They continued to sip on their brandy, counting their blessings as they did, each of them including the other at the top of the list.

Chapter V

The dawn broke with a bright red sun, a sure sign that winter was fast approaching. The colors of the sunrise covered the sky as the dusty carts and carriages changed the shades to brilliant oranges and reds. There was a nip in the air that had only just arrived and the trees, so recently full and green had all but lost their leaves, now scattered around the streets, already beginning to decompose with the fall rains. The streets were still quiet but inside *la Maison de Rouler*, lights cast their glow from windows on every floor.

There was a palpable energy in the air. Everyone anticipated that something was about to happen but had no clear idea of what it was or how it would unfold. The servants all knew it would mean more work and stress for them, especially in light of the previous night's incident with le Duc, but their promised bonuses helped them join in the spirit of things. Isabel felt a nervous excitement at the base of her stomach that had started as soon as she woke, long before the sun, and had been mounting ever since. Lisette and Paulette were excited for Isabel, and Isabel for Paulette for her new position. It was Madame who spent the night in a state of restless thought, weighing the options and possible outcomes depending on who would be involved. She knew there could be only one victor and the rest would be disappointed and in some cases, angry. She had decided there was only one fair way to handle the men, and now it was simply a matter of waiting.

The carriages started to arrive at the earliest possible calling hour and everyone began milling in and heading toward the grand salon on the first floor at the top of the sprawling staircase. A party-like atmosphere developed as the men helped themselves to coffee, fresh rolls, and wine. Most of these men knew each other well and they talked amiably about their estates, the current unrest with the king and church, their wives, their mistresses. But they were all unsure as to the protocol of what was expected of them. Viscount Viennois saw Paulette approach and asked the whereabouts of Madame. She turned to the group to give her reply, "Madame will be here shortly. She's asked me to make sure you're comfortable while you wait, so please be patient as there are a few details she's still working out. This was all most unexpected and we apologize for the désordre…" It was an all-out lie on both counts, and most everyone knew it, but that was all she offered and she continued on her mission, leaving the group more curious than before.

As promised, they didn't have long to wait before Madame's presence was felt as she approached the salon. "*Messieurs*, I am so sorry to have kept you waiting. We have a rather delicate situation on our hands, one that this house has not seen for some time, and certainly not ever with someone so, how do you say, pure?" Her voice had a devilish tone to match her coy smile. The men laughed politely. "I am most embarrassed, as I had wanted to make poor Isabel's début as smooth as possible as she is so young. But alas, the secret is out and there is no taking back what is already known, *n'est-ce pas*? *Alors*, as there is only one Isabel and many of you, here is my proposition.

"For each man in this room—or his representative in some cases, I see—you will have one chance to put forth one bid." The room erupted in a disconcerted growl. Comments were spoken, and shouted around: "*C'est impossible.*" or "*Non*, that cannot be." "It's not fair; I was here first." "*Non*, I was."

And on it went, until, "Silence. I will not have this disruption in *ma maison* and you are all free to leave if you do not like the arrangement, *comprenez-vous*? Now then, the bids will be sealed and I will be the only one to see them. You will have until this evening to present them to me here at the house, as I know some of you will need to give it some thought, or talk to those you represent. Please understand I have found myself with no easy solution. I think you will agree this is the only way."

"When can we see her?" one man boldly put forth, voicing the question on everyone's mind.

"She is not a horse, Monsieur. I am sorry if some of you have not had the privilege of meeting Isabel but I will not parade her around to be judged and prodded. She is a virgin, *c'est tout*. And she will be treated with the respect and dignity she deserves. If you happen to have the winning bid, you will meet her then. You will be free to converse with her—with me in attendance, of course—and if at that time you do not feel your money would be well spent I will free you of your obligation and contact the next highest bidder, and so on. But for those of you who have met her, I am sure you already realize the unlikelihood of that occurrence, *c'est vrai?*" She paused for maximum effect before delivering the *piece de resistance*. "The highest bidder will be granted one night, from dusk till dawn." Murmurings went around the room at such an unusual offer. "That is more than generous, *non?*" Many of the men nodded in agreement. "Now, are there any further questions? *Non? Bon.* I will see you back here this evening, if you so desire. I bid you all a good day."

The men did not leave immediately, as they all wanted to get some indication of where the others' hearts—and more importantly, pocketbooks—lay. Madame made her way back through the rooms behind the salon and stood by one of the doors that opened onto the room where the men stood mingling. It was easy to hear their comments and she listened intently for any clues of what to expect. But there was nothing forthcoming. Every comment was negative: "I won't partake in this bidding as this whole charade is ridiculous," or, "How can one night be worth all of this aggravation and expense?" and then, "I think we should all agree not to participate."

Comte de Siméon laughed out loud. "Listen to all of you. Not participate? You must be joking. If you are not, all the better for me. Personally, I am going to leave this room and sell off everything I own to guarantee my success, because I wouldn't miss this for the world. Not participate? Ha! I think most of you wouldn't know what to do with her if you had her. That's what's got you so scared. This is too *drôle.* Gentlemen, please excuse me. I must leave you, as I have an auction to organize." He skipped off down the stairs, laughing to himself all the way out the door.

"Who was that?" Isabel asked Madame, who also stood waiting in the room.

"That was my friend Comte de Siméon. He is on our side, Isabel. We had a little chat this morning before everyone arrived and he said he would rally our cause. He really just likes to stir up the men and I think he's done a fine job. Look at them. They don't know what to do now."

"Prepare for an auction, perhaps?" she said, giggling. She was enjoying the game and had overcome most of her anxiety. *How bad could it really be? One man, one night. Whatever it is—whoever it is—I can get through one night.* It was with this attitude that she approached the rest of the week leading up to her fateful evening.

That day proved to be busy, and passed quickly for everyone involved. The big night would be five nights hence and there was much to do. The *chambre* needed to be completely redone, as most of the men had seen many of the *chambres* with different girls and this one had to be new and unlike anything they'd ever experienced. They had chosen an Arabian theme and were busy acquiring silks and beads and other props—anything that resembled that exotic land that few had seen. Madame had many contacts in the shipping world and she had already contacted them to start collecting their wares. It was a risqué idea but Isabel had wanted to dress like an Arabian harem dancer. Tonight was the night that the highest bidder would be awarded his prize but he wouldn't gain possession of her for five days. Although the details of tonight's outcome were unknown, they all knew what the result would be. Only two small details were missing: who and how much. Those two missing pieces would dictate, to some degree, the details of the plan but ultimately most of the work could be done without having that information in advance.

Madame was sitting at an ornate Louis XIV *escritoire* in her public *bureau* near the bottom of the stairs of the main entrance when the first knock came. Paulette waited a half minute before opening the door. A footman of Comte d'Ambroise stood holding a fine card with silver scrolling on the top. The bottom showed his silver seal, so elegant in its design, and so distinct compared to the more common red wax seals.

Paulette escorted him to Madame's office, rapping lightly on the door before letting herself in.

"Madame," as he handed the card to Paulette, who then handed it directly to her.

"Merci, Monsieur," was her simple reply. And that was that. The rest of the evening passed in a similar fashion. A few of the messengers attempted to glean some information as to how much was expected and one made the slip of accidentally showing he had two envelopes in hopes that he could make a better decision depending on her answer. "Give me the higher of the two, Monsieur. It will almost surely be too low still, I'm afraid, knowing the donor as I do," she said. This was half under her breath, but the messenger also heard and both knew the truth in her words.

It was almost midnight when the last card was delivered. Madame debated whether to wait until morning but she knew she was fooling herself as she couldn't possibly wait another minute and had already struggled not to peek throughout the evening. She had promised the men they would be for her eyes only and she was happy to honor that, as the thought of Isabel having to go through reading the cards, the comments, the amounts—it would be too much.

She bid the girls good night, leaving Isabel to the last. "Good night, *ma petite*. Come see me in the morning and we'll celebrate your success over *un café. Bonne nuit.*"

"*Bonne nuit,*" Isabel replied, and her exhausted form padded off to bed with the others.

Madame took the stack of cards—27 in all—and headed for her boudoir, where she put on her nightgown, poured herself a large glass of brandy, lit a few extra candles and began sifting through them. Once she was settled into her favorite chair, as a game, she stacked the cards in the order she thought they would play out, with the lowest bidder on top, graduating to the highest on the bottom. The first 15 were relatively easy to predict, but the last 12 were more difficult and she mulled the process over for some time before her analysis was complete. The first one was the most exciting, as she really had no idea what had transpired and it was thrilling to know she had such a large collective amount of money on her lap. Not that she could cash it all in. In fact, it was a bit sad that only one could be utilized, but now she was just being greedy, and, not taking these thoughts seriously, she got on with the game.

"Madame," she read, "I would be honored to spend an evening with Mademoiselle Isabel and would be willing to offer 45 francs for the privilege. I ask that you please consider my offer and notify me at my residence on Rue de Lyon. Yours, Vicomte d'Orange." The next one was only 25 francs. "Hmm, I misjudged you, you sly snake," she said, and tossed it on the table with the other one. The following five ranged between 25 and 100, all reasonable offers and in any other circumstance, very generous indeed. She placed them on the table with the others and picked up the next one in the stack.

My Dear Madame,

I know I will have no hope in procuring Mlle Isabel's first night, as the company you keep is far beyond my station. But permit me to request that my bid (in the amount of 150 francs), although not high enough for the first, be for the second evening. I have seen Mlle Isabel on more than one occasion and feel an honorable meeting, albeit not the much-coveted début, would be better suited after the fanfare has subsided and real life begins to unfold.

Yours most sincerely,
Monsieur François de Bérgère

What a kind and generous man, she thought. Madame was deeply touched by his letter and placed it to one side. One hundred and fifty francs. A lofty sum, but she knew it wouldn't be near enough, as she hadn't even started into the final dozen. This man had planted a seed for an idea that was germinating into something quite lovely. She decided in that moment that no matter what, he would earn the second meeting whether or not he had second highest bid. But what about third and fourth position, or fifth and sixth? She would contemplate this possibility as it may be a way to capitalize on all of these generous bidders.

There were a lot more cards to get through and it was already taking more time than she anticipated, so she took the next one from the stack and placed it onto the pile. No surprises here and her guesses had proven to be quite accurate so far. By the time she got to 20 she was on her second set of candles and her third glass of Armagnac. *What were some of these men thinking?* The 21st was the second one this evening that piqued her interest. Monsieur le Blanc had a proposal. He would like to offer 200 francs for her début and in addition, have her become his mistress with a guaranteed yearly stipend of 500 francs, plus a spending allowance to be negotiated until either party chose to end the agreement but with a guaranteed time from Monsieur of five years. Hmm, interesting idea and one she would need to discuss with Isabel. We could argue the bid to include the five years' stipend plus the upfront fee, putting him far ahead of all the others. If it were something she wanted then the amount, seeing as it was open-ended, could be construed to be much higher if an argument was ever required. Monsieur le Blanc was an educated man. *Not too many quirks, if I remember correctly. I must make a note to find out more about his personal habits before considering an agreement like this. And I thought a simple evening of checks and balances was in order.* Higher to the right; lower to the left, and so on, until the biggest number stood alone on her right.

She started up again with twenty-two, and then twenty-three and twenty-four. No surprises again, although the numbers, when considered alone, were staggering. She'd had no idea it would escalate to this. And now the final three. Who would it be? Who would ante up and show their true colors? Madame was hoping for Comte de Siméon, not only because they were friends, but because he would be gentle and kind to Isabel and would make the experience as enjoyable as possible and most definitely enjoyable for him. He had a joie de vivre that rivaled that of most men and he was a sought-after dinner companion and guest because of his ability to enjoy any and every moment. She read the three seals with a knowing glance. They were on her top three list: le Comte de Siméon, le Duc de Veauville, and—thankfully, not King Louis as that would be disastrous—a man she knew little of but was aware of due to his immense wealth. She opened le Comte's first, as she expected it to be the lowest of the three. Five hundred francs—*Mon Dieu*—with a note that he expected it to be used for new linens as the last night he'd spent there, they had been a bit tatty on the edges. Such a comic. She really loved this man as a good friend and hoped it was enough. Sadly, le Duc had offered double his bid at 1,000 francs. That was more than some Frenchmen earned in a lifetime and it was more money than one of her girls would earn in one year, let alone one night. Astounding, yet thrilling at the same time. She had a sense that the third envelope was the wild card of the evening.

Monsieur Armand du Preix was looking at Isabel as a man who must possess her. It was not a loving feeling, more of an animal's attraction to its prey. He was well respected in the city, so Madame had no concerns for what he might do to her (she had no tolerance whatsoever for deviant behavior) but there was a quality to him that she hadn't seen in too many men. She opened the card slowly, wondering if she had won the small bet she had made with herself. What she saw made her suck in her breath and rendered her unable to do anything but stare: *Two thousand francs*—an unfathomable amount of money. It made her hair stand on end. That kind of power and wealth must be kept under control or it would wreak havoc on those who possess it or could be possessed by it.

Monsieur du Preix was the victor and, without a doubt, was already tasting his victory. This was obviously a man who liked to win. Who *needed* to win. Le Duc would be furious but Madame would be happy to see him take second position for once. A bit of humble pie would do him good. There was a new rival in town, one to take note of. "I wonder how Isabel will react?" she pondered.

It had been a long, grueling day. The Armagnac was having its desired effect and she started to feel drowsy. She felt at last she could sleep, although these next few days would be no less chaotic. The anticipation of tonight had caused her a surfeit of stress and now that it was finalized she gathered up the cards, tossed them into the drawer, turned the key and placed the key on its chain, which hung at all times around the tie-back of the heavy brocade drapes, folded discreetly into the seam that had been sewn for this purpose. No one knew of its whereabouts and the letters would stay permanently out of the reach of prying eyes. Anything put to paper could have damning results if used in a manner that broke the writer's trust and privacy, and Madame was scrupulously careful in these matters. With these precautions in place, she slipped under her down quilt and gazed up at the ceiling above her

53

bed, watermarked and cracked with age, but otherwise plain and calming. *If you are listening, God*, she silently prayed, *if you are, in fact even there at all, thank you for this day. Thank you, on Isabel's behalf. I am eternally grateful. Amen.* And she drifted into a deep stupor.

Chapter VI

"Who is it? Who won? Who is the victor? Tell me, please. *Who?*" Isabel was beside herself with excitement. She was acting her young fourteen years, not the wise, mature courtesan she had been portrayed as to the entire city these last few days. "*Madame? Please. Who is it? I must know.*"

"Well, if you *must* know, I guess I'll have to tell you then, won't I?" The answer would be revealed soon enough. What was a minute or two more? "It is…" and she paused for effect, "someone who was here last night."

"Yes, I *know* that. Who?"

"It is…someone who has…"

"…a big fat belly? It is le Duc, is it not? I *know* it is le Duc," Isabel interjected, without allowing Madame to finish.

"Well, if you *know* then I guess you do not need to hear it from me, do you?" Madame now sported a mischievous grin.

"It is *not* le Duc? Really?" She looked to Madame, who was slowly shaking her head. "But then who?"

"You have two more guesses, and then that is all you get."

"Madame, you cannot be serious. Okay, two guesses. Hmm. If it is not le Duc, who was my first choice—well, not exactly my *first* choice…" and she slid in a little grin—"then it must be… le Comte. Le Comte de Siméon? I heard his little speech and he must have run home and sold everything to win. It is le Comte, then?" But Madame slowly shook her head again. Now Isabel was enjoying the game and had forgotten her impatience as she focused on the challenge at hand. "Ah, too bad. I liked le Comte. He seems so nice. *Old*, but nice."

"Everyone is old compared to you, *ma chérie*. Now, one more guess. Look around the room in your mind. Who was the most intent on winning? Did you notice anyone that stood out from the crowd?"

"Well, yes, I did." A slight blush rose to her cheeks as she recalled. "I am not sure of his name, but I think it was Berge—no, Bérgère. Monsieur Bérgère. Is it he, Madame? Please, that is enough torture. Is it?" Madame saw in that moment that Isabel hoped it was. She also knew that Isabel already knew his name, and her hesitation was to try to throw her off. It was brought to Madame's attention early that morning that Isabel had been making discreet inquiries as to who he was.

"I am saddened to say that it was not he, although I have news regarding Monsieur Bérgère that will make you feel much better. But not now—after. I must first divulge the victor so you can relax and I can get on with my day." Madame could see that young Isabel was torn as she was now so curious about Monsieur Bérgère she almost lost complete interest in her suitor, but she composed herself and gave Madame an expectant look, so she continued. "It is a Monsieur du Preix. He was in the salon yesterday morning. Do you not recall? He had a night-blue velvet jacket with jeweled cuffs—large jeweled cuffs, and dark hair and eyes. Quite attractive, actually."

"I think I do remember him. He did not say much, did he, but he was quite handsome, for being so…"

"…old. Yes, I know. In spite of his age, he is quite attractive. And wealthy, I might add. Would you like to know how much of his wealth he is willing to lay down for you, *ma petite*, if you don't mind the play on words? It is a rather large sum, so be prepared to be surprised." Madame was watching Isabel with a mother's eyes, but there was little reaction or interest at play.

"Yes, please. Do tell," she said, bringing her thoughts back to the task at hand.

"It was in the amount of…" She was still grappling with the sum "…two thousand francs." The room was completely silent. Not a single breath. Not a stir.

When Isabel finally spoke, she was horrified. "Oh, Madame, no, this cannot be. This is not real. It is too much, *vraiment*. I cannot believe it. How can I even begin to imagine sharing a bed with a man—for my first time, no less—with *no* experience or finesse, with *nothing* to offer— for *two…thousand… francs?*" She slumped down in the chair like a rag doll, arms loosely hanging at her sides, head bent low, her face devoid of expression.

Madame crouched down in front of her, skirts haphazardly dragging on the floor in every direction. Raising her hand, she gently held it to Isabel's chin, cupping it. "Isabel," she said in the quietest voice, "look at me. Look at me," she said a little more sternly the second time.

"Isabel, you will not likely understand the events of these last few days, nor the next, for many years to come, but I assure you, you will grow to understand the value of this night you are offering, the importance of the game, and the impact on the players, both for the winner and the losers. Do not try to understand it now. But do you trust me, *chérie*?"

"Oui, Madame," came her faint reply, as she tried to will her tears to keep from flowing.

"Then carry on as planned, without any more thoughts to our silly game. We have much to prepare. There is much you still do not know, and Lisette and I will both be guiding you in the ways of the boudoir before your début, so although you think you know nothing, it is only that you do not realize all you have learned from being around the girls in the house. And in four days, you will know more about the art of loving than most women in the whole city of Paris learn in their lifetimes. Just ask some of the men that come in through these doors to talk about their wives." That brought a slight smile to Isabel's lips, so Madame continued in the same vein. "This event will determine the outcome of your life and I could not have asked for a better result. The excitement caused, and the sense of loss soon to be felt by the other twenty-six men from the competition will leave them with an urgency to try to meet you that will likely carry you through the next few years of your young life. With much planning and forethought you will be set up for life, Isabel, and be able to dictate who you want and when. Women in this profession dream of this possibility but few ever achieve it. Now, let us put this part behind us and move on to the next. Are you not still curious about Monsieur Bérgère?" she asked with a devious twinkle in her eyes.

"Monsieur Bérgère? Oh, I almost forgot. Yes, please tell me your good news. I think a bit of good news will cheer me up, *n'est-ce pas?*" Isabel was starting to feel better and the color had returned to her cheeks.

"Okay, I will tell you now," she began in a conspiratorial tone. "But you and I—and the Monsieur, of course—are the only ones that can ever know, *comprends*? Ever."

"*Oui, je comprends*. Now what is it? I have played enough of your silly games today." And on cue, Madame leaned forward and began to whisper his generous offer and the details of her secret plan.

François de Bérgère had more intelligence than money, and he was counting on the former to formalize a contract with the charming Isabel. Although he was young and relatively new to the courtesan world, he had been with enough women to know that she was one of a kind. How did she become a courtesan? How did anyone? He had four sisters and couldn't fathom the prospect. And yet, this enticing beauty was up for auction. It was so degrading. And he had to have her. Not for her sake—although he would like to pretend he was doing this for her—but for his. He was embarrassed to admit that he was mad for her.

Monsieur de Bérgère was a nondescript man, with average features and moderate dress. He carried himself well and wore the latest fashion, but he had always been the type of man to be 'forgettable' at a dinner party or soirée. He put on most of his impressions intentionally, as he found—in the business world, at least—that being subtle paid huge dividends. He had been questioning that approach with *la Mademoiselle* and second-guessing his strategy. He would partially have to rely on Isabel's mutual attraction, or her alleged attraction. Could he be so naïve as to be caught in an act? He dearly hoped not, and was counting on her to help in his conquest. In spite of his painstaking methods, he had many obstacles to overcome, not the least of which was Monsieur du Preix.

Once Madame had given the crushing blow to le Duc in person, she set out to tell Monsieur du Preix of his victory and to discuss terms of payment—to be delivered in advance, of course—and offer the option to meet with Isabel prior to their arranged night if he so desired. He arrived later that morning and was ushered into Madame's *bureau* on the main floor.

"That will not be necessary, Madame de Rouler. I have seen all I need to see and I feel the prize is well worth the price."

Such confidence, such certainty. Madame was compelled to ask the question burning on her lips. "Monsieur, if I may be so bold as to ask…?"

"How any man in his right mind could justify paying 2,000 francs for one night with a whore?" He knew this was the question that would be on everyone's mind, not just Madame's.

"Well yes, in fact, that is it, although I would have chosen a different word from the crude one you have used, Monsieur." This was a reprimand, and from what Monsieur du Preix knew of Madame, was not to be taken lightly. She had the power to forfeit the game at her whim, and her dedication and protective ways with her courtesans was unrivaled by anyone he'd ever met.

"I do apologize, Madame. I am most used to having these conversations in the company of uncouth men and my manners have been utterly lost to me in this moment. If I may, I will answer your question and hopefully put your mind at ease. But I will also ask for your discretion, as I have not taken this little game of yours lightly and I plan to use it to my full advantage without deterring from your house or Mademoiselle Isabel in any way, of course. In fact, I feel I have just upped the ante, and as importantly, the tariff in your business, which will benefit your *Maison* for years to come."

"Yes, I agree. The ripple effect did not escape my gaze nor was it absent from the planning. But you can be assured of my utmost discretion, Monsieur. If you know nothing of my reputation in that regard then you must simply look upon the success of my *Maison* and recall the faces in the room yesterday to know that whatever we speak of here today will not leave this room."

"Thank you, Madame, but your reassurances are not necessary as I did my own enquiries before I embarked on this rather expensive journey," he added with a playful smile that showed no hint of sarcasm, "and your reputation in this matter is without flaw. So, let me continue. There is the obvious enticement of spending a full night with an untouched virgin that I cannot deny. She is lovelier than I would have hoped. But I decided to jump on this opportunity, shall we say, before I ever saw your divine Isabel. You see, I am relatively new to Paris, and therefore, unknown. I have spent these last few years abroad, securing my holdings in ports as far as China. My company has established a powerful import/export trade, and my wealth is guaranteed for many of my future generations to come. But what does one need to create future generations, Madame?"

"A wife."

"Yes, a wife. *Exactement.* And in order to acquire—I believe I can use that word in your presence, as we both know that is the way of the world here—in order to acquire a wife one must have position and wealth. I, sadly, have only one of those requirements. My line is not flawed but neither is it *bleu* and in order for me to secure the business partnerships I need for my ambitious plans and therefore my success, I need to be one of the few that overcomes the barrier of blood by entering the arena with such wealth and power so that it may be discretely overlooked."

"I see your dilemma and it is one I have often fought hard to change, with some success, I might add. Do you have your sights set on a particular 'acquisition'?"

Monsieur du Preix noticed Madame's tone and began to warm to her. She had intelligence and a forthright attitude. A rare combination in anyone, and he had yet to encounter it in a woman. Yet, here it was, sitting elegantly before him. "Yes, I do, Madame. Maybe she is someone you know. Le Duc de Veauville's daughter, Juliette." A wide grin spread across his face.

"You *knew* le Duc was first in line for Isabel's début and you still went after it, knowing you would win, all the while having your sights set on his daughter? Oh, this is too rich. Wait, I need a minute to see what your game is," and within a few short seconds, the dawning of it struck and she laughed out loud. "Bravo, Monsieur. Bravo. This could be the most fun I've had in some time, that is, if you allow me play along," she pried, coyly.

"I think I've met my soul mate, Madame. If you had royalty in your veins to match your large purse I would get down on one knee in this moment and demand your hand in marriage. Sadly, your purse is not what I need but I am duly impressed. I have heard much about the infamous Madame de Rouler but the praise has paled in comparison to the flesh I see before me."

"Monsieur, if I thought for a moment this wasn't also part of your little ruse, I might blush," she said, and the co-conspirators looked at each other with renewed respect.

Chapter VII

Monsieur's plan was obvious to anyone who cared to watch, and one of the oldest ever played. He knew le Duc's daughter to be willful and extremely defiant. She was seventeen and not yet married but not for lack of offers. Her father had tried, unsuccessfully, to arrange three marriages to date and she had refused all three for varying reasons, but the underlying speculation was that she did *not* have to do what her father asked of her. Le Duc had a soft spot for his youngest child and only daughter, who resembled his strong-willed wife to a fault. There had been an informal agreement that if she had not found a suitable husband by her 18th birthday she would agree to marry whomever her father chose. She had a full nine months—ample time in a city teeming with men—but she was being too particular, according to her father, and he doubted she would beat him to the finish line.

As always, he underestimated the women in his life and she was, even now, considering a risqué choice, but with a little convincing, a good one. Armand du Preix had met Juliette on three occasions. The first was a ball held every spring at le Duc's own country house. Monsieur du Preix had been invited by association through his business dealings with Comte Laronde. Le Duc had been introduced to Monsieur du Preix at one of their meetings and when the Comte accepted le Duc's invitation to the ball, he had inquired about the possibility of Monsieur joining the party. The more the merrier, was le Duc's attitude and he had been made most welcome. They had a long discussion about the infringement of the church on the state and how their pious hands were spreading further and further afield, making it increasingly difficult to conduct day-to-day business. It was a heated and stimulating discussion where both discovered, to their pleasure and surprise, that they sat on the same side of the controversial fence. At one point, Armand looked out to the dancing mass and saw a young woman eyeing him. She continued to brazenly stare and instead of holding her gaze in a flirting manner, he looked away and continued with his conversation with le Duc. He was curious to know her and was enlightened shortly thereafter when she approached them both and leaned in to le Duc to kiss his cheek.

"*Bonsoir, Papa.*" Then turning to him, "Monsieur," she said staring him in the eye, and then tossing her head in deference back to her father.

"Mademoiselle," he responded, with equal disinterest. "Je m'excuse, Duc de Veauville, but I must go see Chevalier Bertrand. Enchanté, Mademoiselle," and he strode over to where le Chevalier was standing with a group of shared business associates. He felt her eyes follow him and knew she wasn't accustomed to being ignored, which pleased him. Hmm. A bit haughty for his taste but a lovely figure and intelligent wit, he sensed. I must play this one out with great caution. Later on that evening, le Duc approached him again, with a stunning woman on his arm, obviously his wife, *la Duchesse.*

"Ah, Duc de Veauville. This must be another of your lovely daughters, *non?*" His face was set in a serious tone but his eyes were smiling, as were hers.

"Merci, Monsieur, but sadly, *non*, I am his wife, Claire. We have only one daughter whom you met earlier. My husband has been speaking highly of you and your ideas for a possible enterprise together. I would be most interested to hear more."

"Your husband is most gracious, Duchesse de Veauville, and his ingenuity will take him far in this world, with or without my assistance." She was probably the most beautiful woman he had ever laid eyes on and he was having trouble focusing on her words. Her eyes were a brilliant green with black flecks scattered randomly around her large pupils and her intelligence was obvious but he could tell she attached little importance to it for the benefit of the male world that dominated her. She was also taking him in and seemed pleased with what she saw. His features were not obviously handsome when separated one from the other but together they made him an admirable site and his obvious class and style enhanced his overall appearance. Clothes do not necessarily make the man but in many instances they do much to enhance character and station and Monsieur needed all of the help he could get, as the climb up the social ladder was what he was after. *La Duchesse* was obviously intrigued by this stranger in her home and after he parted to freshen his wine she made discreet inquiries to her husband, couched as general questions so as not to arouse his suspicions. Later, when Juliette approached, she asked the same benign questions and *la*

Duchesse knew he had caught her daughter's interest, a rare event indeed. He would have an uphill battle with le Duc, no doubt, but he seemed worthy of the challenge, if she placed any stock on first impressions.

Du Preix made an effort to avoid the Veauville family for the rest of the evening, as eagerness would be his undoing. He met many interesting men, potential business contacts and social connections, and paid special attention to other unattached women in the crowd, being careful to avoid wives and mistresses. He needed to be the perfect guest, with no hint of deviance or dalliance. Before approaching any of the young women he would first enquire to ensure their eligibility. In this way, whenever Juliette or Claire and le Duc saw him he was certain to have a young girl laughing and blushing, utterly mesmerized by his charm.

His second encounter with Juliette occurred only three days later, and he was quite sure it was no coincidence. He was seated at a large dinner gathering at the house of Duc Gaston, whose son had just returned from the Americas and was vibrant with tales of savages and adventure. Du Preix was entranced by his travels and then amused to see Juliette sitting at the far end of the table looking not in the direction of the host's son, but at him. He gave her a false smile, indicating clearly he had barely recognized her let alone wanted to have this interesting conversation interrupted by her distraction, and then casually looked back at the young man. She really was not good at this game and he was starting to enjoy seeing her pout when she realized her usual flirtations were not affecting Monsieur at all.

The third meeting was two nights ago, when the Martignys invited him to their home along with a dozen or so other guests for Saturday dinner and cards. It was his first invitation from them and he knew things could go one way or the other, so he took meticulous care in dressing, arranged for his carriage to arrive fashionably late with a flourish of haste showing he had obviously come from something important but wouldn't want to miss this evening for anything. He knew most of the guests, although one or two he merely recognized and they had never been formally introduced.

He was placed next to Juliette's brother Charles, who was a surprisingly interesting dinner companion, and the two men chatted like old friends. Now and then Juliette would worm her way into the discussion and du Preix would listen attentively and ask questions, giving no indication of his earlier disinterest and standoffish behavior. His responses were well thought out and courteous and his questions were probing in a way that made her feel respected and intelligent, a rare happening in male company. He started to find her quite attractive in more than physical appearance and enjoyed her ramblings and antics but also noticed her perceptivity and insight. But just as quickly, he turned it off and went back to Charles, leaving Juliette confused as to whether he was merely being polite or if she had actually sensed some interest on his part. Pulling away had the desired effect of drawing her to him and she didn't stop to ask herself whether she found him attractive or not, as she was being swept into his circle, and her strong desire to have him was being magnified by his withdrawal.

His plan was working as he knew it would on someone so young and naïve. It wasn't done without heart, rather just as a method of speeding up something that would have naturally occurred eventually. He didn't have the luxury of time nor position, and he also knew he had only one chance to win her affections or all would be lost and possibly most other potentials in the city, as his reputation would be tarnished extensively if she turned him away.

He and le Duc had become acquaintances, where each was genuinely pleased to encounter the other on the street or at a social gathering. He knew how much le Duc wanted the young virgin for his prize (although *why* was anyone's guess, when he could have the lovely Claire any time he wanted) and le Duc seemed at first surprised to meet du Preix at Madame's *maison* on the morning of the bidding. Once he got over his initial shock, he was embarrassed when he realized du Preix would want to be there along with all of the other wealthy men of Paris and the region. Isabel was a beautiful young woman. Who wouldn't want to bed her? He might have been even more surprised had du Preix not shown an interest. The two men exchanged a few words, with le Duc ending by saying, "I shall enjoy this conquest very much, my dear friend."

To which du Preix slyly replied, "*Bien sûr.* Whoever wins the bid will enjoy her very much. Very much indeed," and the two men shared the private joke, le Duc assuming du Preix was agreeing and du Preix laughing at the slight deception involving his new friend.

When le Duc learned he had lost to someone else he was furious, but when he learned it was du Preix he was outraged. He went ranting throughout the house, swearing and dragging his foe's name down with every slam of his fist. When asked what had happened, of course he could give no reply as it would implicate him as well, and this angered him even more. Claire and Juliette did not know what to make of it, but the gears began to turn in Juliette's young head and in the dawning of the next day, not recognizing a connection, she finally made her choice. Du Preix would be her husband whether her father liked it or not.

Madame refused to tell him the amount of the winning bid but gave le Duc the impression that it was a close race, which seemed to soften his mood slightly. At this point she had not yet been made privy to du Preix's intentions but now, looking back, the entire plan unfolded before her and she appreciated his strategy and wished the best for him. The two were still discussing his plan when he leaned in closer to Madame and said, with great seriousness, "There is something you could do to help this situation along." Madame's face suggested, 'yes, go ahead' so he continued. "I would like to offer to withdraw my bid and allow le Duc to match it."

"*Mais,* Monsieur, that would not be possible. I cannot do that as it would not be fair play. Truly, *je suis désolé.*"

"No, Madame, please let me finish. I would like to *offer* but I would understand if you had to *refuse* me for any reason," and he let the thought linger.

"Ahhh," she replied, as his intentions were made clear. "As I said, Monsieur, thank you for your gracious considerations for le Duc but I am sorry I cannot accept. It would not be fair play after all and would ruin my reputation. Even if you and le Duc were the only ones party to it, I could not take the chance. I'm afraid you are bound by your offer, so please do not make this difficult on any of us."

"Certainly, Madame. I at least wanted to make the attempt, as I feel terrible about le Duc. *Terrible.* But, alas, I understand your position and will honor my original offer. *Comprenez-vous?*"

"Oui, Monsieur, I understand perfectly. I will talk to him as soon as our meeting ends."

Being embroiled in many of her clients' complex lives took a lot of Madame's energy. It was only mid-morning and now another errand would take her away from her own duties. As there was a lot of money on the line she would do what was necessary, as she always did. And since this money was coming from the man before her, it was a small request and one she could easily accommodate. As they stood up for Armand to take his leave, he brushed her cheek with a kiss that lingered longer than necessary and whispered his heartfelt thanks in her ear.

"It has been my sincere pleasure, Monsieur. *Au revoir.*"

"*Au revoir, Madame. À bientôt, j'espère.*"

Chapter VIII

As she could not go to see le Duc directly, her footman delivered a card to his home requesting his presence as soon as was convenient, and readied her office, and herself, for yet another meeting. The house was slow to rise that morning as the last few days of excitement had exhausted most everyone, including Isabel, who was just now stumbling around looking for something to eat while stifling a yawn and rubbing her eyes.

"After you've washed and dressed and eaten, of course, I would like you and Lisette to come to my *bureau*. It is time to start on your lessons as there are only four days left and we have much ground to cover." Turning to the maid, she asked, "Have there been any deliveries yet this morning? We're still waiting for the props for the room, and what about Madame Sévigné—has anything arrived from her? She had hoped to have a first fitting for the undergarments of your costume."

"Nothing yet, Madame, but you did receive a card from a Monsieur Bérgère and it is on the desk by the door. Would you like to see it now? We always place your cards there, Madame. I'm surprised you did not grab it when you first came in. It is unlike you." The maid tsk-tsked, as if to say "you are slipping," but Madame's steely gaze brought it to a halt.

"Aren't you going to see what it says, Madame?" Isabel asked with a note of persistence.

"Ah, yes, of course. I'll do that right now. Isabel, would you follow me please? There's something else we need to discuss." The two of them headed toward the grand staircase leading up to Madame's private *bureau*, Isabel almost skipping after her. "Control yourself, girl. We're almost there, and in the meantime, all the girls are watching you. Do you not want to show them a certain level of maturity? Or would you like them all to believe you're still a *bébé*, running off to play with your dolls, hmm?"

"You know I never in my life played with dolls. Hmph. I am not a *bébé*. I am a sophisticated young woman who is casually and calmly following you to your office to discuss important adult things." And before Madame realized what had happened, Isabel ran up beside her, snatched the thick white card from her fingers and raced down the hall in her stocking feet, laughing and taunting Madame by waving the card in the air and twirling it around mischievously. Madame picked up the pace and reached her office door just after Isabel, who was now smiling and panting and had a pink glow to her cheeks.

"You would not dare," Madame queried, enjoying Isabel's antics immensely. She was due for a look at the lighter side of life and Isabel was the perfect remedy to mellow out the seriousness that had been pervading her and the others all week.

"I am hoping I will not have to, but perhaps this," she continued to flutter it under her nose, "is what you wished to discuss."

"Perhaps it is," she replied, with an uncommitted glance.

"I *knew* it. Please hurry. I cannot wait to see what he has said."

Madame had almost forgotten about the second place winner and how she had promised to inform him of her decision. She had explained to Isabel what he requested and Isabel was excited and expressed her desired to grant his request. Madame slit open the seal and read the short note aloud:

My Dear Madame,
I have, through a reliable source, discovered that M. du P. has won the esteemed honor of Mlle's début, for which I was sorely disappointed, but not surprised. Please allow me to remind you of my interest in this matter and if appropriate, pass on my regrets and hopes to Mlle I.
Yours, F. B.

"I admire this man, Isabel. I truly wish things had turned out differently and we had been able to choose Monsieur Bérgère for your first meeting. I want to tell you something that may be difficult to understand or believe but in times like this I rely on it as my truth and it gets me through difficult times.

"Although it is impossible to see why what is happening is actually the best possible thing that could happen, I would like to assure you that there is a grand plan here. Oh no, not mine. That is not what I meant. A bigger life plan that we may not understand at this moment but that often makes itself clearer in time. Monsieur Bérgère is obviously drawn to you as I sense you are to him. And yet Monsieur du Preix is the one who will give you your first intimate encounter, one that will shape you and even partially define you. 'Why?' you might ask…"

"No, Madame, that is a question I have learned not to ask. My father taught me that the 'whys' will eventually show themselves but only when they are ready and it is in the 'hows' and 'whats' that are the questions worthy of my thoughts'. Sorry for interrupting. Please, continue."

"That's good, Isabel, as that simple rule will guide you well. In this situation it must be difficult, but the rules are the same. I would even suggest that the bigger the challenge, the more the rule fits. It is this trusting that allows us to get to the next step with the least amount of pain. Resistance is pain, Isabel, and this may be a time when you are asked to do something you do not want to do, or feel you should do, or any other resistances—many of which are valid—that will cause you undue pain and nothing more.

"Monsieur du Preix is a businessman and for him this is a business transaction. Have you had a chance to talk to Lisette in detail on the physical process and what to expect?"

"Oui, Madame. We stayed up late last night, giggling and whispering until the wee hours." So far Madame was not impressed by her report, but she allowed her to continue. "That is why I am so tired this morning. She told me all about what a man likes to do, most of which I already knew from living so close to the girls. I have to admit it horrifies me, and it is so hard to imagine anyone wanting to do that. But after some talking, she helped me realize that this was their way and in time I would make it my way, too, as she has and as all women do in varying degrees."

"She took her responsibility seriously, Madame. Do not worry about that." I am sure I am well versed in what I must do and most everything that I might expect. Although I have never seen a man's, well, a man naked, the description she gave was so awful that I think anything I see in real life must be better. She did it to make me laugh but also I think to prepare me for something she knew I would have no way of preparing for. The unknown is what I am usually most afraid of and I have been fretting and allowing my imagination to go wild since the day I walked through your front door. But this morning when I arose and thought back to everything she said, I realized that men are all little boys in bigger bodies and there is nothing unusual or unnatural about their desires. I am sure I will grow accustomed to them in time, don't you think?"

68

Madame was visibly relieved and nodded her ascent. "*Oui*, Isabel. *Très bon. Alors,* shall we get back to Monsieur du Preix? His reasons for winning this bid are private and not necessary for you to understand. The 'why' in this case will be left unanswered. But they are important reasons to him and I want us to honor that by delivering on what we have promised. And that is you, *ma chérie*: pure, unadulterated and virginal. Lisette was asked to give you information regarding the male sex, its shape, its tendencies, the man himself and his habits and quirks. But she was not meant to tutor you on the fine art of lovemaking. Was she true to her word?"

"*Oui,* Madame. She said she was not allowed to tell me a thing about what I should do and she agreed it was better that way, anyway. I am just to relax and follow Monsieur's lead and any instructions or directions. Is that correct?"

"Yes, it is. Well done, both of you. Your innocence is what has played on these men's minds and it would be wrong to tamper with that. This will be, in fact, your first time and many a maiden goes into her first experience knowing nothing of what is involved, and she survives, often quite contentedly. You are engaging in this as a life choice but there can also be much pleasure in it. But I would not expect too much for your first. Most women don't.

"Which brings me back to your second match. Now, *he* may be the one to bring you much pleasure, so patience, *ma chérie*. And even more importantly, the first time will be behind you and all of the fears and nervousness will have passed. See? Now we can both understand the perfection in the order of your experience. First, Monsieur du Preix will be the one to help you overcome your fears and then Monsieur Bérgère can be the one who will teach you. The more I think about it, the more I'm relieved Monsieur du Preix won the match. We couldn't have made a better choice if it had been ours to make."

Chapter IX

The night of the *event of the season* had finally arrived. All of the preparations, all of the organization had finally come together beautifully and Madame's *maison* had never looked finer. She had taken this opportunity to do a top-to-bottom cleaning and updating of all of the rooms in the house. The wood shone, the floors glistened and the glass and mirrors reflected the candlelight, creating a warm, soft and inviting atmosphere. The Monsieur was to arrive at nine that night and it was already half past eight. A calm settled around the house and Madame took one last tour before approaching Isabel's personal *chambre*. She rapped lightly on the door and was greeted by Paulette, who opened it with a grand sweeping gesture.

"Welcome, Madame," and her arm flung open to her side as she bowed low, almost touching her head to her knees. She couldn't suppress her smile completely, but as Madame was now looking at the top of her head, she thought she might not notice. The slight shaking of her shoulders gave her laughter away and Madame joined in the game by curtsying back and keeping her head bowed low. "*Merci à vous, Mademoiselle.* I am honored by your presence." She slowly lifted her head and the sight before her took her breath away.

"*Mon Dieu*, Isabel. Look at you. I have never seen anything so lovely. You could be a Princess—of Arabia, perhaps." Madame's eyes shone with pleasure as she took in the details of her newest courtesan, who had become like a daughter to her.

"Oh, Madame, please. You exaggerate, as usual." But Isabel was pleased nonetheless by her high praise. There was no time for further talking as they all heard the carriage wheels approaching on the cobblestone street below.

"*Vite, vite.* Are you ready? He has arrived."

Isabel replied quietly, chin up, with a resigned gesture. "Oui, Madame. I am ready."

"Alors, you will wait here until Monsieur has been settled in the special *chambre* adjoining this one. I will knock twice, like this," and she tapped the desk two times quickly with her knuckles. "That will be the signal for you to use the secret door, which enters the back of the *chambre* where the Monsieur will be waiting. *D'accord?*" Madame was starting to feel anxious and was speaking quickly. They had gone over this several times already, so when Isabel just smiled, Madame knew she was being overprotective, hoping in some way that would make it easier for the young girl. But when she looked at Isabel, she saw wisdom there that many grown women never came to possess, and her heart filled with warmth and love. The two women embraced, pulling away finally when Madame felt the tingle of tears trying to spring forward. She held Isabel with extended arms, looking at her one last time, and with her final words, "*Bon courage*," she turned and walked back out into the hall, silently closing the door as she went.

She arrived at the foot of the stairs just as the front door was opened to admit Monsieur du Preix. At first, Madame did not recognize him. He handed his *manteau* to her valet and underneath he was dressed like a peasant. His loose flowing chemise was made with the softest linen, with full sleeves that tied at the wrists. It had fine leather laces that crossed at the front, but they, too, hung loosely, exposing his neck and part of his chest. His pants were also tied and his well-worn supple leather boots came over them at the knees, wrapped in more leather strapping. The effect was casual and comfortable, and yet still elegant. He had a flair for fashion that challenged the day's attire and stretched the imagination to its limits.

"*Je m'excuse, Madame.* I hope you do not mind. I thought it would be more relaxing for *la Mademoiselle* than if I wore my usual coat, waistcoat, stockings, garters and fourteen other things that may detract from the activities. We only have twelve hours, after all."

Madame's smile was full, and her relief evident. She did not know this man well and felt more comfortable that he had considered Isabel and would do what he could, within limits, to take care of her tonight. "It is *parfait*, Monsieur. I could not have chosen better. Perhaps there is more to this evening for you than simply a business opportunity, hmm?" she teased.

"Perhaps. One must make the best of every situation and I intend to make this a memorable evening on all counts. Shall we go?"

"*Bien sûr*. I will take you to your *chambre* to ensure you are comfortable. Josef will be stationed outside the door for the duration of the evening, should you require anything else. The door is thick, Monsieur," she said, picking up on his disappointment at his loss of some semblance of privacy, "and you will have to open it to get his attention, but he will be there, I assure you." She led him up the main staircase, anticipation mounting with each step. They turned at the grand foyer at the top and slowly walked along the dimly lit hall until they reached the last door. "Ah *bon*, here we are."

They both hesitated for a moment as if to fully grasp what was about to take place, before Madame placed both hands on the double doors, pushing them open to near darkness.

It took a moment for his eyes to adjust and gradually images started to appear, the first one being an intimidating man with a large scabbard slung at his side. Armand stepped back in alarm until Madame introduced him as Josef. There were candles casting a soft light around the room, gradually allowing him to see that Josef was bare chested with a bright sash tied at his waist and ballooned pants tied at the ankles, his bare feet protruding from below the gathered hem. The scabbard reflected beams of light onto the walls and ceiling. He wore a turban and had dark menacing eyes, but he smiled at Monsieur, indicating they were on the same side.

The three stood facing a rich velvet curtain of midnight blue, hung loosely to pool on the flagstone floor. Madame indicated that he should follow her toward it, where she deftly found the opening, pulling one side over while Josef pulled the other to reveal an entrance to another *chambre*. "*Voilà. Entrez, Monsieur.* Welcome to your harem."

His eyes popped open in surprise. In all of his many travels he had never been to Persia or Arabia, but had heard many tales of the immense tapestries, silk cushions, mirrored tables—it was all there before him as if he had entered another time, another country, another world. He turned his head slowly, taking in the vast detail of what lay before him. That must be a hookah pipe in the corner, he mused, and wondered if it was functioning and ready for their use or only for display. The room was draped in silks and embroidered fabrics, gathered somehow from the ceiling and then tied at four corners, creating the illusion of a luxurious tent. His eyes wandered over to the far corner of the room where a canopied bed stood alone, gauzy fabric flowing around all four sides, piled high with every imaginable form of cushion. The floor was scattered with massive cushions as well, although he noticed a comfortable table and two chairs, set with glasses, a carafe of wine and bite-size morsels of a variety of foods, mostly unrecognizable but with a delectable smell, and he was confident the taste would be equally exotic. "Madame, you have outdone yourself. It is *incroyable*, truly. *Merci bien*." His words were genuine and she knew the hard work and expense had been worth it. Seeing his reaction also told her his expectations had been exceeded beyond measure and it boded well for a successful evening.

"It has been my pleasure, Monsieur du Preix. Please, sit." She gestured to the chair facing the curtains where they had entered. "We will leave you now, but again, if you need anything…" She backed toward the curtain and disappeared into the darkness, Josef close behind.

It was a full ten minutes that he was kept waiting, wondering, anticipating. Madame had deliberately delayed things to give him a chance to take in his surroundings, get comfortable and also look around so he was familiar with everything that had been placed in the room for their pleasure and convenience. He paced around at first, realizing she had thought of everything and more, and was looking forward to trying out some of the props, many of which he had never seen or used. It could be fun, depending on Mademoiselle's mood, or highly embarrassing. *We'll see*, he thought, and he settled back into the chair to wait.

A few more minutes passed before he heard a rustling coming from the corner over his left shoulder. He had expected her to enter from the curtained doorway, and at first he wasn't sure who she was. Perhaps another one of Madame's minions bringing wine or more food.

She entered the *chambre* carrying a small tray and as she slowly approached, his recognition became absolute as he gazed in wonder at this vision before him. Her hair was piled high on her head with loose curls and tendrils cascading around her face. A headband interwoven with coins held her hair aloft around her radiant face, her dark kohl eyes demurely looking first to him through a sheer veil, and then downward with each step as she advanced closer. Her ankles and waist tinkled as she walked, bands of coins dangling from both. She was wrapped in a silk robe of the softest aquamarine, draped loosely around her body and a tie made of twisted bands of silk in a darker hue of the same mysterious color. It was sheer with an almost diaphanous shine and occasionally he caught a glimpse of something shimmering underneath. On her neck hung strands of coins that jingled in tempo to the belt and anklet. Her arms were completely bare, except where the robe caught at two points on each shoulder, and on her left arm a silver serpent wound its way from elbow to shoulder. He had never seen a woman so enticingly revealed while still fully clothed.

On her tray lay one tiny jug placed at its center, and his astute eyes took in that it was not shaking in the least. *A good sign.* He took a breath in that moment, the first full one, he realized, since she had entered the *chambre.* She was exquisite and surreal and he felt the first stirrings in his loins.

As she looked down at him she said in a subservient whisper, "Master, I am at your service." Oh, *mon Dieu,* he was done for, and if this was only the beginning he didn't know how he would carry out his drawn-out plan. He was taken aback by her brazen words, said so perfectly, so innocently, and was compelled to leap to his feet, knock the tray from her delicate hands and take her right there in that instant on the sumptuous furs scattered on the floor amidst the many cushions.

She saw the animalistic look in his eye and, imperceptibly, hers opened in surprise, but she quickly recovered and was now smiling provocatively. 'Do it' her eyes were saying. 'I dare you.'

My, my, this one has courage. He quickly adjusted his tack with this new discovery, and began to sort out this new challenge. Thoughts raced through his mind, and his blood was pumping to all the extremities of his body. He started to feel a flush in his face and neck and realized he needed to slow the pace.

He had arrogantly anticipated a whimpering little girl with a beautiful tight body and bubbly mannerisms spurred from nervousness and fear. Instead, he encountered a goddess of serenity and finesse that was in complete control of her emotions. He had been right on one account. Her tight young body was glaringly obvious and he needed to pull himself out of his trance and take his eyes away from her breasts—oh, such lovely breasts—and look into her eyes to sense what she was really feeling. It was also the only way he could pull his thoughts and eyes from the distraction of her.

"Please, come join me at the table. Let's sit and enjoy this fine wine Madame has left for us." He gestured for her to set down her tray and sit down in the deep chair opposite his. He picked up the carafe and tilted it in the direction of her glass, raising his eyebrows at the same time, "*En-veux tu?*"

"*Oui, merci.* I would like some very much." She skillfully unhooked one side of her veil so that it cascaded down her shoulder, revealing her glowing skin from forehead to chest.

He poured a half glass for each of them, set down the carafe and raised his glass. "A toast: To the most exquisite goddess I have ever met, and a memorable evening for us both."

Isabel smiled genuinely for the first time since she arrived and a hint of relief played on her face. "To a memorable evening," and they raised their glasses to drink.

The warmth of the wine settled in her belly and she closed her eyes, took two slow breaths to calm her nerves and then opened them to find *le Monsieur* staring at her.

"*Alors*, my beauty, what am I going to do with you this evening, hmm?"

"Whatever you wish, Monsieur. At least that is my understanding," and it was said in jest with a sly smile turning up at the corners of her mouth.

"Witty *and* beautiful—a dangerous combination, *n'est-ce pas*? I think I will need to pay close attention to your every move this evening, Mademoiselle. And, please, no more 'Monsieur.' My name is Armand and you may call me by my Christian name for this evening. But I should like to call you Mademoiselle. Now, please tell me before I die of curiosity—what have you brought in the pewter jug? My guess is it is not wine, but you held it with such purpose. Is it something to drink?"

"No, Mons—, Armand, it is an exotic oil imported from Arabia and it is used to rub into the skin for relaxation and, ah, sensuality, I believe. I truly have no idea other than that. It does have a divine scent, though. Would you like to smell it? Or shall I rub some on your feet? I read somewhere that lovers do that for each other and it is meant to be, ahm, relaxing."

"On the feet, heh? It is a curious custom, but one I will not quickly discount. Perhaps a little later in the evening we can explore that if we get bored with each other."

"Oh Monsieur Armand, I truly hope that does not happen. I would be deeply ashamed and so sorry for you."

"Mademoiselle, I am only teasing. And as of this moment you must promise me that you will stop worrying about my needs. I assure you I will be well taken care of. How can I not? Most of what happens for a man happens in his head," he said, tapping two fingers to his temple, realizing too late this innocent girl likely didn't need the distinction made between the two. "When his senses are aroused, he is aroused. Look around you. Imagine what it is like for me to look at you. My senses are already well looked after so anything from here on will be in glorious excess for me. Do you understand?"

"No, really I do not. How can I? This is all so new and unknown to me. I have never even spoken to a man before tonight. Not in a private fashion. If I were not so nervous I could find it all quite comical. But I will trust your words and promise not to worry about you anymore." She raised her tiny hand and held it to her breast as if giving an oath.

"Perfect. I only have one more rather delicate item I want to discuss with you before we move from the practical to the more personal. I am sure Madame has made you aware of what is going to happen this evening, from a physical standpoint, but I would like to apologize in advance for the pain I will surely cause you. There is always a certain amount of pain and discomfort for a young virgin and I must also say truthfully that you are so stunningly beautiful I am not sure I will be able to keep myself from ravaging you at some point tonight."

"It is alright, Monsieur. I am well prepared for that and understand it will pass quickly. I also grew up in the countryside and most certainly sustained injuries much greater than this one could ever be. Now look who is worrying." Her resignation had diminished and she began to get into the spirit of the evening. Her hope was to please Monsieur beyond his expectations while still being able to maintain some sense of composure.

Armand was impressed with her mature response and satisfied with their progress so far but he knew that he needed to keep Isabel relaxed and preoccupied in order for the evening to continue to go smoothly. They had each finished a glass of wine, which was enough to relax his young beauty, but did nothing for him. Just as well, as he knew wine to be a great inhibitor of performance if taken in excess, and he had a long arduous night ahead of him.

"*Alors*, tell me about your life in the country, before you met Madame. What was it like?" She was close enough for him to touch her without having to move or stand so he reached over and grazed her hand with his own, stroking it lightly as she held the stem of her wine glass. She started at first at his touch but then forced herself to relax, setting her empty wine glass on the table. He listened intently, all the while stroking her hand ever so gently. Casually pushing the glasses to the side of the table he stroked her hand while brushing his fingertips gently along the top of her wrist, ever so slowly, in a distracted manner. She started reminiscing about her life and recalling certain seasons or funny antics she got into with her friends, going on to describe the lifestyle there, her home, the landscape. She was enjoying his languid touch and continued to reveal small fragments of her life. Their chairs were facing each other at an angle with the table positioned slightly back (more of Madame's planning, no doubt) and in one quiet motion Armand reached over the table with his other hand to latch onto one stray tendril of her hair and started twirling it absently between his nimble fingers, still lightly stroking her wrist and forearm with his other hand. Her words were flowing easily and her face was serene and relaxed. He gently brushed his other fingers along the side of her neck as if by accident while still twirling the tendril of her silky strands. One twirl of the hair, one long brush along her neck with his deft fingers. One twirl, one long brush in a rhythmic pattern, each stroke leading lower down her neck and closer to her breasts. Twist, stroke. Twist, stroke. Isabel was not oblivious to his actions but rather detached from them, allowing the relaxing motion to soothe her as she continued to recount her short life history.

She was enjoying the sensation and starting to feel a warmth creeping quietly throughout her body. As she continued with her reverie, Armand moved his hand from her forearm to her tendrils in one deft move, leaving the other one free to roam further afield. Her eyes flitted open and closed as her words took on a hypnotic quality. Armand's britches were bulging with anticipation, a driving force of pressure. His skilled hands continued to brush stroke her skin, and as he traveled along her porcelain neck he lightly skimmed his fingers in a wide arc, brushing just past her nipples. A gasp escaped Isabel's lips and he now had her attention. She continued to talk but was looking at him with a hint of surprise as he continued his rhythmic dance along her skin, stroking gently along the curve of her collarbone. His next stroke hit its mark and he tugged gently on her hair while his fingers rested firmly on her nipple. He looked squarely into her eyes to see dark pools about to spill over, not with tears but with an intensity of unexpected wonder. He stopped briefly in that position and then ever so gently started rubbing her nipple in small, slow circles, over and over, touching the tip randomly, sending shivers down her spine.

Isabel was now fully present. Fully alert. Her story had stopped abruptly and she was searching Armand's eyes for what she should do. "Shhh," was his throaty reply, kissing his two fingertips and placing them gently on her swollen lips. "Just relax and don't fight it. Don't question anything. Just relax…" came the whisper in her ear as he leaned over, nipping her ear lobe gently. A sharp twinge shot through her body. What she had always referred to as her secret place was now feeling a throbbing sensation that was new and not unwelcome.

Armand's position needed changing as he was half standing, half sitting, and what he wanted to happen next would require more space.

From a leaning position, he slowly stood, facing Isabel, and held out his hands to pull her to her feet. They were now facing each other and Armand started to slowly unravel her sheer costume, deliberately rubbing and brushing against all parts of her as he loosened the ties and unwrapped the cording. Her robe had fallen open and by placing both hands on her shoulders and using only his index fingers he slipped it off, sending it cascading to the floor. What he saw before him took his breath away. The silk slip was so sheer, and her delicate and erect nipples were protruding through the fabric, bringing his manhood toward them like a magnet. He gripped her shoulders firmly and closed his eyes, taking a deep breath, and then another.

She was startled by his actions but he assured her he needed to slow down to take in her beauty. She smiled, trusting him and feeling ready for whatever was to follow. He dropped his arms and held out one hand to lead her to the corner of the *chambre* where the bed, draped in silk, lay in readiment. Keeping his eyes locked on hers, he unlaced and kicked off his boots and stood before the gauzy canopy, pulling her open hand down to his bulging groin. He let out a groan to let her know his wanting was strong, and he pressed her hand tightly to him, barely managing to suppress his desire.

With her silk sheath still on, he motioned her to the bed and climbed in beside her, propping himself on his elbow, leaving his other arm free. Starting with her inner calf, he lightly stroked her skin in an up-and-down motion, lifting the hem of her shift higher and higher with each stroke. Her breathing was starting to become shallow and he was encouraged to go higher, stroking her with long, undulating strokes.

He stopped abruptly. "I'll be right back—don't move." And in quick, long strides he raced back to where they had been sitting, grabbed the jug of oil and returned, four seconds at most having elapsed. Sitting on the edge of the bed, Isabel watching his every move in the soft candlelight, he raised the decanter, tipping it over his open palm until a few drops of the exotic oil dropped onto his fingertips. With his other hand, he placed the oil on the bedside table and returned to his previous position. He proceeded to hook his thumb under the edge of her shift and slowly dragged it up her leg until it gathered around her tiny waist, revealing her wiry mound of pubic hair, which glistened in the candle's glow. With his other hand he slid his oily fingers down to rest on her outer labia, and there he stopped. She took in a quick breath and involuntarily tilted her pelvis toward him.

He stayed in that position for several long seconds, watching her intently while she returned his stare. With his slick fingers, he slowly

78

began to stroke her, naturally following the curve of her pubis into the crevasse of her labia, rubbing her up and down in a smooth stroking motion. His fingers were slick from the oil and a slight pressure caused enough friction for her to feel—for the first time in her life—a sexual pleasure that she could never have imagined. She moaned audibly, incapable now of stopping herself, and her eyes became sultry as she continued to roll back and forth with a slight tilt of her pelvis. Each time she raised herself up, he slid deeper into her core, back and forth, back and forth, each time penetrating further, his thumb still resting on her mound, gently playing with her pubic hair.

He knew she did not have long before she would go over the edge, and he had to slow things down. The stroking stopped just long enough for him to untie the laces on his britches and with one quick motion, pull them off and throw them onto the floor beside the bed. They were now both completely naked from the waist down and he needed her to feel his throbbing sex. He wanted her to know what he was about and what he was shortly going to thrust into her. He guided her hand toward him, never taking his eyes from hers, and had her grip his manhood as he pressed his hand firmly over hers, forcing her to follow his motions, squeezing, pulling, up, down. Faster now. He was so ready—had been since she walked into the room—but he needed to slow himself down as well.

Before she knew what he was doing, he placed both hands on her wrists and slid down between her legs, pushing his tongue gently into the dark recesses of her body, bringing a moan of shock and pleasure from her lips. She was now beginning to thrash around and he gently nipped her clitoris sending her into jolts of pleasant spasms. In one fluid motion he slid his tongue up along her belly, hesitating briefly to suckle her one breast, and then the other. He was now poised perfectly between her open legs, and by continuing to slide his well-oiled fingers in and out, he kept her ready and wanting. In one practiced move, he placed his erect shaft where his fingers had been and gently probed, in and out, in and out, slowly at first, entering her gradually but not fully, using all the self control he could muster.

She hardly knew what was happening as his fingers had been there one moment, then his tongue. What was there now? Armand was doing his best to keep a steady rhythm going without too much thrust, as he knew he would soon break her hymen and he wanted to savor the moment as long as possible. But he would not be able to hang on much longer, nor would she. She was throbbing with ecstasy and his control was weakening with each thrust.

Isabel was writhing with an unknown pleasure and felt she was going to burst. She was panting like a dog and thrashing her head back and forth like a mad woman. She thought there was something wrong with her, but she felt so good, and when she looked into Armand's eyes she knew this was what the throes of passion were about. She could feel her secret places throbbing and she placed her hands on his buttocks, pulling him in closer to her. That broke all of his resolve and he thrust into her with all of his length and passion and she let out a blood-curdling scream. The pain was piercing and brought tears to her eyes, yet the pleasure kept intensifying. "Are you okay, *ma chérie?*"

"Yes. Please. Don't. Stop. Please," a sharp intake of breath between each word, and with that he released his control and allowed himself to go into his instinctual thrusting, with Isabel meeting him at the threshold. As soon as he felt her peaking, he would stop suddenly and allow her pleasure to mount, just to pick up the pace again. She was going mad with desire but each time he would stop. Her passion was spiraling upward and she was now completely out of control. Armand sensed neither of them could postpone it any longer. He sped up his thrusting and she met his rhythm until they were pounding into each other while she thrashed about wildly. He could feel her climax and pushed her farther, farther. He would not be able to hold on much longer.

Suddenly, Isabel's body went wild, gripping Armand's buttocks, thrusting her hips toward him, thrashing her body in spasms. Her screams could be heard out into the corridor but he was sure even Josef wouldn't be responding to them. That was the end for him and his final thrusts were a frenzy that surprised even him. He barely made a sound, but the excitement he felt was near bliss. He gradually slowed his pace until she stopped her writhing, when she flung both her arms to her side as her body went limp. Her eyes were closed but her thoughts flitted through her head. When she had regained semi-consciousness, she looked at Armand and smiled. "I think I love you, Armand."

"No, *ma chérie*. It is not love you feel, but lust. A nice, healthy lust, and you would be wise never to forget it." But Armand was pleased, nonetheless. They lay there, spent, for some time before Armand got up to fetch the wine. He propped the pillows up against the wall, poured them each a small glass and managed to get Isabel to sit up. His concern for her was real but did not surpass their bargain and almost at once he started caressing her and arousing her once more. This time she knew what to expect and he slowly touched her all over her magnificent body, giving her the chance to learn things about herself that many women never learn in their entire lives.

The rest of the night was spent in playful lovemaking. Isabel didn't know why she had been so scared and couldn't understand what all the fuss was about. She voiced this to her lover, who laughed wholeheartedly at her fresh and untainted perspective. She was the perfect virginal lover without the panic-stricken demeanor. She was curious and interested and vocal and quick to express her shock at the tales Armand shared about some of his more bizarre encounters. At one point, when she had been taunting him innocently and he was playing the villain, he grabbed her wrists, pushed her face down on the bed and took her from behind. Isabel's surprise was evident as was her mounting excitement as she got a small taste of the games people played. Armand's intentions were mostly self-serving, but he also wanted to play with Isabel in a safe environment and expose her to some of the experiences she would encounter in her future. When dawn broke they were both spent and had fallen asleep on opposite sides of the bed, he, sprawled out with one leg hanging over the edge, and she, curled up in a ball, knees to chest, still one foot in the cradle. Madame had Josef check in on them at nine, the official end, but they were both sound asleep so she gave strict instructions that they not be disturbed.

Armand emerged first, around one o'clock. He was fully dressed, his chemise tied tight. "Bonjour, Madame. I am sorry for the late hour. We both slept late. But thank you for the café. We will be in touch." With that, he nodded, put on his *manteau* when it was held out to him, and went out the door where his carriage had been waiting since the early hours of the morning.

Madame looked questioningly at Josef. "Was everything okay? I thought you said they seemed to enjoy the evening, *tous les deux*. He seemed so aloof, wouldn't you agree?"

"*Oui*, Madame, but I assure you, everything is fine. Wait until you talk to Isabel and she will confirm my impressions." Josef was cognizant of Monsieur du Preix's need to be professional but he had heard the evening's antics, in spite of the thick door, and was confident Isabel would have nothing but positive feedback for Madame.

Chapter X

Isabel woke, stretched lazily and slowly opened her eyes to the light-filled room. Someone had come in and opened the curtains while she lay sleeping and when she first woke up she couldn't place where she was. Then she recognized the silk canopy, which looked transformed in the sunlight, and her memories flooded back.

The next thing she noticed was how sore her body was. Her private regions were swollen, and the skin around them felt bruised. There were traces of blood strewn across the sheets and she had a moment of panic until she remembered Lisette's tutorial on virginal sheets and about how, still to this day, newlywed husbands check the sheets to ensure their brides were pure on their wedding night. *I'm sure it didn't go unnoticed by Armand, either.* She felt a bit irritated at the prospect but then sloughed it off and rolled over to finally get out of bed. She grabbed the robe that had been laid out for her, most likely by Joseph, and slipped it on.

Then she noticed on the nightstand a card in simple white propped up beside the burned down candle. Like a cat, she leapt for it and jumped back onto the bed like the young girl she was, flat on her stomach, legs bent and crossing each other, elbows propped up so she could read the message. The hand was an elegant script and it said, simply:

Ma chérie,
You were worth every franc. À bientôt, j'espère.
A.

She chose not to be insulted. After all, she was a courtesan now and was paid to perform this very act, and she knew it had been written with the intent to compliment her. It was an extravagant one at that and she, too, hoped to see him again—soon.

There was a knock at the door and Madame entered in time to see Isabel on the bed with the card lightly gripped between her fingers. She tilted her head over to Madame but didn't give any indication that she was going to stand, so Madame walked over and sat down beside her, laying her hand gently on her back. Tears filled Isabel's eyes and she held her smile with great strain. "*Chérie*, what has he done to you? Tell me and I will go fetch him *immédiatement*. Tell me, child."

"No, no, Madame. It is not that. I suddenly felt sadness for what will no longer be, that is all. No, Armand was… *wonderful*," and her voice had a dreamy quality which put one part of Madame's mind at ease but instantly sent up a red flag in another.

"*Armand?* He is *Armand* to you now? My, my, you are on close terms for having known him for such a short time."

"Madame, *please*. Spending 12 hours with someone in this situation is not exactly what I would consider *short*. Have you ever spent 12 straight hours with a man you barely knew?" Madame's mind flitted back to a few occasions but she kept her eyes steady, giving no indication of her ability to relate one way or the other. "In bed, no less? You get to know someone quickly, let me tell you."

"*Bien sûr, Isabel*. I am happy to know the experience was not too difficult. Will you share with me what he wrote in the card?" In place of an answer, she handed it to her and grinned while Madame scanned the short note. Her reply was generous and heartfelt, "Brava, Mademoiselle. You have done well to impress such a distinguished gentleman. You were put under enormous pressure and I am impressed by how you rose to the challenge."

"*Merci, Madame*. And Monsieur as well, *n'est-ce pas?*" and she broke into fits of laughter at her own play on words.

"*Mon Dieu*, you girls and your dirty minds. God, give me strength." She stood up to take her leave and waved her arm at the door. "You, too. Up, up. *On y va*. We've got work to do, you lazy little sloth." And she reached over and swatted her lightly on her bottom.

"Work? More work? I thought I *was* working!"

"Yes, I know, but there are things to prepare. Purchases to be made. A party doesn't happen all by itself, you know."

"A *party?* When? I didn't know anything about a party." She jumped from the bed and was to the door two strides before Madame. She turned the handle, opened the door and Madame slid right past her, looking back over her shoulder with her eyebrows raised.

"How can you expect to know anything when you spend all day in bed, hmm?" Madame quickened her pace and Isabel started chasing her down the corridor, bouncing around with excitement. "Come on, then. First things first. Let's get you into a hot bath. You'll need a good scrubbing and a nice, long soak. Paulette? Paulette? Where is that girl when you need her?" They headed off to the bath, Madame searching for Paulette, who would be the one bathing Isabel, not as a street urchin this time, but as a courtesan. This part of the ritual was of utmost importance and must be done with great care and attention. The douching was particularly important to ensure no unwanted pregnancies occurred and this ritual was performed after every sexual encounter, no exceptions. "Ah, there you are. You two head to the bath. I'm sure Isabel can't wait to fill you in on all the details of her evening. Remember, no gossiping—this is only between the two of you, *comprenez-vous?*"

"Of course, Madame," the girls answered in unison. And then to each other, "Come on. Let's go."

Paulette had been waiting impatiently all morning and was about to burst. "So, what was it like? Tell me."

And then a loud, "*Shhhhhh.*" from Madame, as the girls giggled and whispered, scurrying down the hall toward the back stairs that would take them down to the bathing room.

Isabel's début had been unique because of who she was, and the special circumstances surrounding her virginity. Madame was always working on new and innovative ways to present her girls and this had been a huge success. But Isabel had still not been officially launched to the male community at large. In fact, many of the men who had placed bids on her début evening had never met her. Madame always liked to host a soirée, where the men could mingle with the girls and the girls could have a social evening and a chance to practice their skills in a social setting at the same time. Mostly, it was a chance to expose the girls to prospective clients, while simultaneously giving them an evening of frivolity and fun.

Only the courtesans of the *maison* were allowed to attend, for obvious reasons. Men, when told something was not available to them invariably had to have it and she was not willing to put any of the girls, like Paulette —who had no desire or inclination to become a courtesan—at risk. If she knew one of the maidservants wanted to head in that direction it was often a perfect opportunity to subtly place her in the room, serving drinks or delivering an 'important' message. More often than not, she would receive the enquiry, "Madame, who was *that* girl?" and then Madame could say, "Oh no, Monsieur. She is not a working girl. No, you couldn't possibly," and so on, in that same fashion. The man would go after the unattainable and succeed, and

Madame's new protégée would slip into the courtesan world effortlessly. Everyone was happy, and the men were none the wiser.

But not at this party. Isabel would still be the main attraction and these *fêtes* always generated new interest in her *maison*. This was often the only way for the men to get to know them, as the girls did not travel in the same social circles. Madame would be available to take bookings and schedule meetings and 'arrangements,' when a gentleman wanted to set up a girl on a permanent basis so she would become his mistress, entitling him to certain rights he normally wouldn't have. Avoiding having to get in line for an appointment was one of the reasons many men took on a girl as a mistress. They abhorred having to wait and most had enough money to have had little experience in waiting. Everyone in the house had strict instructions to say the girl in question "was out" or "was not available" or "was unwell" or sometimes, when necessary, "had her monthlies" which usually was enough to send them away. But they *never* said "she is with someone else at the moment." Nonetheless, many men recognized a carriage discreetly parked around the corner or saw a dark shape sneaking out the alley from the back door, and whatever excuse was given, they knew she was with, or had just been with, another man and that idea repulsed them.

For these reasons the party would be an important event and one that took careful planning and preparation. They had just spent the last two weeks in the same mode, and Madame was tired and would prefer to rest on her laurels for a couple of weeks. But the launch must happen on the heels of last night or the fervor of the moment would be lost. The party would be held this coming Saturday and all of the girls would require new gowns. Barely enough time for Madame Sévigné to prepare them all but there would be a hefty bonus in it for her and she would pull in extra help, as she always did, to ensure they would be ready on time. Thankfully, the house had already been 'spit and polished' and would only require a quick dusting and floor washing on Saturday morning. The food and drinks would need to be arranged and this time she would hire the *traiteur*, Monsieur Chartre, who was renowned for his delicate hors d'œuvres and heavenly desserts. He was expensive, but money would not be an issue for the next several years if she planned things right, which she always did. Planning is what made her house the success it was, and she was well prepared to go into her old age with enough money to keep her comfortable for many years, if necessary. Oh yes, and she would need to talk to Isabel about money as well. They hadn't had a chance to discuss her share, and Madame insisted on explaining the ways of money in depth, including investment ideas and methods of saving, before she would give any of them even a single sol. She reminded herself that she needed to do that soon before it would become one of those details that got swept away with other more important issues.

Several rooms and two corridors that headed in opposite directions to each end of the *maison* surrounded the grand salon. Madame had arranged for the men to gather together once again, and all had been offered a beverage and an enticing selection of hors d'œuvres, as expected. They were quite comfortable mingling with each other, and all had hoped for a little chat with Monsieur du Preix, who had not yet arrived. The girls were waiting behind the doors of the adjoining rooms in twos and when the bells struck nine they were to enter the room silently and quickly so as to arrive simultaneously, with as little announcement as possible. As most of the men were gathered close to the center when the girls finally joined them, they immediately began talking to each other in quiet voices and it took the men a few moments to notice they were in the room. All of them looked surprised. In this way, one girl was not presented more favorably than another and the men had equal chance to approach them as well.

Lisette and Isabel were standing on the far right of the salon, chatting amiably beside a table laden with food and drinks. Each had a crystal goblet of wine in her hand, partially consumed, and they gave the impression they had been talking like this for some time. Lisette and Isabel had had an in-depth conversation about this evening, as Madame had warned them both about how much attention Isabel would likely receive. So they had a chance to get comfortable with the idea; for Lisette, she would be giving up the limelight to her friend, and many of her regulars would pass her over. For Isabel, she would have attention lavished on her, something to which she was unaccustomed. Lisette's role would become more that of an assistant, only for this evening, and it was paramount that she portray no ill feelings toward her rival so the men could be put at ease in their company.

As soon as he saw Isabel, le Duc de Veauville almost leapt from his place in the room to land within a short stance from the two women. Others were not far behind but he had the choice position and felt to some degree he had earned it after losing so bitterly to Monsieur du Preix. "*Mesdemoiselles*, how utterly stunning you both look this evening. Mademoiselle Isabel, I don't believe we have been formally introduced. Le Duc de Veauville, *à votre service.*" And he bowed elegantly before her. Before either had a chance to respond, he rose and spoke to Lisette with equal interest. "And Mademoiselle Lisette, I have never seen you look so beautiful before tonight. Is that a new gown, perhaps?"

Both girls smiled warmly at his flattery and Lisette was the first to speak. "Duc de Veauville, you become more charming with each meeting. May I introduce my *good* friend and confidante," with a little wink, added slyly in his direction, "Mademoiselle Isabel, newly arrived, shall we say, at *la Maison*. She knows few people in this big city and none in this room so I know you will do whatever you can to make her comfortable, *non?*"

"*Surement, Mesdemoiselles*. You can count on me, and I would be happy to do my part for you, Mademoiselle Isabel. I shall talk to Madame to see what would be the most suitable way for me to assist you." In this way, he openly told Lisette that he would be passing her by for the moment in pursuit of this new attraction in the house, while also informing Isabel of his attentions.

The evening continued in this way for all the girls. They had been given strict instructions not to discuss times or terms with any of the men, even where there were already previous arrangements or long-standing relationships in place. The men had also been told most clearly that Madame would be available that evening and throughout the next day or two to make appointments and arrangements with the girls. No one in that room intended to wait past this evening to meet with her, though, as they knew most of the girls would be booked well in advance after tonight, especially the guest of honor.

Le Duc was seen heading down the grand staircase, which led to Madame's more public *bureau* on the main floor, conveniently placed beside the front entry. He was nearly to the bottom of the stairs when her door opened and Monsieur Bérgère exited, kissing Madame's hand warmly with his thanks. As the valet handed him his cape, he turned to see le Duc standing askance, nodded politely and left through the front door. Madame took in the scene in one glance, motioned for le Duc to follow her into her *bureau* (quietly asking the valet that they not be disturbed) and walked the few steps to the two comfortable chairs half facing each other in front of the roaring fire.

"How good of you to come this evening, Duc de Veauville. Can I offer you an Armagnac or a glass of one of my best reds? *Non? Alors*, tell me, what can I do for you this evening?"

She knew very well what she could do for him, but he spoke his desires out loud nonetheless. "Madame, I have just had the privilege of meeting Mademoiselle Isabel in person and she is even lovelier than I had first thought. I would like to make an arrangement with her that

87

would suit all of our needs. I was thinking of something on a more regular basis, say, with a five-year commitment and the usual compensation plus, ah, twenty percent?" He had obviously given this a lot of thought and Madame was more than pleased with his offer. But what she said next took him aback for the second time in two weeks.

"*Je suis désolé*, Duc de Veauville, but alas that will not be possible. An arrangement has already been made with another gentleman. Fortunately for you, though," and le Duc's ears perked up, "his is not an exclusive contract, merely one of regularity, which Isabel has agreed to. So, except for the pre-arranged times for him, she will be available and you will be pleased to learn that the times are quite generous, in fact."

"*Merde*," he shouted as he slammed his fist into her solid oak table, shaking the carafe holding the amber liquid and knocking one of the delicate goblets on its side. "How can this be? Unless it was Monsieur Bérgère, whom I just saw leaving. I assume he is the gentleman in question. Do you mean to tell me that had I come ten minutes earlier, I would have got my wish?"

"I am not at liberty to say one way or the other information regarding our other clients. I can only say that indeed, yes, you have missed the opportunity. You know the rules. They have always been and always will be 'first come, first served.' It can be no other way, Duc de Veauville. Truly, I am sorry for your loss. Has Lisette not been a satisfactory companion to you? Perhaps one of the other girls…?"

"I will book the remainder of her time, then. Monsieur Bérgère and I will have to share her, but I am confident my purse will easily outweigh his, so the competition will not be overly challenging, I'm afraid," he said, as he guffawed at his brilliant plan.

"Duc de Veauville, have you already forgotten? There is only one commitment allowed per girl for this exact reason? I will not have them competed for like animals. One commitment, and the rest of the time is to be divided between other patrons, with one guaranteed meeting per week, unless, of course, there is more time available. But only *after* everyone has had their chance to meet with her. Some things in life do not always go to the highest bidder, Duc, and except for last week's event, this *Maison* has abided strictly by that approach. It protects both rich and poor equally, Duc de Veauville. You know what would happen if we didn't control this part of things. Estates and assets would be sold off in the half the country to ensure someone would get his girl, not unlike what happened with Isabel's début. I learned my lesson well by that and I am sorry you were the one to feel the brunt of it. It was not my intention to create animosity between you and your fellow men, nor with our *Maison*. But we must deal with what we have, and what we have are a few weekly spots available for the next several years, if you like. Friday evenings used to suit you well. Is that still the case? Would you like me to mark you down for Fridays, then?"

"What days are *not* available?" He was determined to get control of this situation but Madame was not having it.

"You know very well that is confidential information. Now, I have told you about Fridays, and if that does not suit, you may give me your best choice. If it conflicts, I will tell you, of course, but if it does not, you will have to decide between your choice and Friday evenings, or none at all. Do not push me too far, Duc de Veauville. This must be maintained as a mutually beneficial arrangement and if the scales ever tip too far in either direction I will not hesitate to end this amicable arrangement. *Comprenez-vous?*"

"Of course, Madame. I am sorry for my insolence. No disrespect was intended and I would like to accept Friday evenings, to commence immediately, of course. As well, I shall be keeping my Wednesday mornings with Lisette. She warms my heart, that girl."

"Only your heart, Duc?" she asked playfully, hoping the difficulty in the meeting had passed so she could continue with other requests.

"Ah, yes. More than my heart, rest assured. I will take your leave, Madame, and head back upstairs, if you don't mind. The food is exquisite and there are a few other beauties I haven't spent much time with. Perhaps there is someone else who will give Isabel a run for her money, *non?*"

"Perhaps, Duc de Veauville. And certainly, enjoy yourself. Take as much time as you like."

They both stood and walked toward the door and then into the foyer together. Three other men were milling outside as he left and visible relief showed on his face. "*Bonne chance*," he said with a smile to the small group, and then headed up the winding staircase to the festivities above.

The men were given numbered cards in order of their appearance, which allowed them to continue mingling instead of waiting at the door. One of the staff would approach the next one in line until the last number was called and the final meetings arranged. The three men were obviously next and hoped that by standing ready it might make their chances better. As well, by befriending the persons in front of them, they might take some consideration of them while they were snapping up all of the choice slots. It was human nature, though, to be impatient with the waiting, which is why these three found themselves outside Madame's door.

"Messieurs, welcome to *la Maison*. Viscount Viennois, I believe you are next?" He nodded to his two new friends and followed her back into her office. The two men left outside were regulars to the house, but not well-known to each other. One continued the conversation in a conspiratorial tone. "Did you hear the sum offered for Isabel's début? I heard it was over 1,000 francs, and that is directly from Duc de Veauville, who is none too pleased. *Incroyable*. For one night. I hope she was worth it."

"I'm sure she was," the man responded. "Did you see her? She is magnifique. Come on—hurry up in there. And leave some time for us, you hear?" The two men joked with each other but his words were said only half in jest.

The evening was well on its way when Monsieur du Preix finally took the stairs to the salon, head held high but displaying no air of smugness. He spotted Isabel out of the corner of his eye and in that moment she looked up and right at him. They both smiled, she shyly, he brashly, and strolled toward each other, meeting near the center of the room. By now, the other guests had all but stopped their chatter and waited with anticipation to see what the two would do. Isabel proffered her hand and he brought it lightly to his lips, kissing it ever so gently and lingering there for longer than was appropriate in higher social circles, while bending his knee into a deep bow. "Mademoiselle, how good it is to see you again," he said with a wink and a smile and a sideways glance to the group now crowded around. Isabel blushed but kept her composure and gave him a tiny curtsy in return. There was an eruption of applause, whereby Isabel curtsied to the approving crowd and Monsieur du Preix held his hand toward her in a gesture of acknowledgment to the star attraction. She was at first nonplussed but then recognized the humor in the crowd and her slight embarrassment turned to gladness when she looked into the men's faces of near awe. By now, everyone was enjoying the little game and Monsieur du Preix, who was aware of the night's proceedings, asked the crowd, "Tell me, please, who has the highest number in the room?"

He heard a man across the room shout, "It is me, I believe: number 39."

"Then I shall take 40," he announced, and then added in a mock humble tone, "It is the least I can do." The men chuckled at his generosity. Under his breath to Isabel, who was still only a pace away, he whispered, "And I will not rest until we meet again, my lusty young filly," but said it just loud enough for a few of the men to catch the exchange, which only bolstered the already-elevated excitement in the room and helped foster the rumor that Isabel truly was something special and unique, to which Monsieur du Preix was the first to attest.

François was trying hard not to lunge at Monsieur du Preix. He headed over to where Isabel stood, alone at last, and gently took her hand, raising it up to his mouth in a gentle kiss. *"Ma chérie, comment ça va?* I trust you are well, in spite of your ordeal?" His eyes held genuine concern, mixed with something else. Isabel sensed it was longing, or maybe jealousy, but still, she was touched by his concern. *"Je regrette que ce n'était pas moi.* I did my best to have Monsieur du Preix's place, but it was not meant to be."

"Merci bien, monsieur. But Madame tells me we will be meeting nonetheless."

"And will that be to your liking, Mademoiselle?"

"Bien sûr!" she said a little too eagerly, but it was enough reassurance to convince François that she had more than just monetary feelings toward him, as he suspected from their first meeting, and he would do everything to gain her trust, and in time, perhaps love.

Chapter XI

"*Isabel.* Are you listening to what I have been saying?" Georges turned around abruptly and was staring down at her, hastily untying his cravat.

"*Bien sûr, mon chéri,*" came her innocent reply. He had been droning on about his important meetings and important decisions and something about pensions. She often caught comments when money was being mentioned. "It is such a pleasant surprise that you stopped by unannounced but I am still not feeling that well and wonder if we could meet at our usual time tomorrow, instead. I have a touch of a headache and feel I will be fresher if I am able to spend the rest of the evening in bed." Paulette visibly blanched at her tongue-in-cheek word play, but Isabel's expression remained impassive and le Duc missed the jest. She had been in a dead sleep when he arrived and she was annoyed.

"But of course, my sweet. Tomorrow it is, then. Adieu." He downed his last sip of wine and, cape in hand, strode from the room without a backwards glance.

"Why must he insist on arriving without announcing himself and especially without an appointment? He does *not* own my contract and he has *not*—thankfully—bought it for next term, so what gives him these rights, I ask you? I have had enough of his brutish behavior, do you not agree, Paulette? Am I being unreasonable?" She did not expect an answer but still gave pause to her tirade.

Five years had passed since that November, and she was still seeing le Duc every Friday. Men were such creatures of habit. He had never completely forgiven her for not being her first—not that it was a choice she could have made—but although her original five-year contract with François de Bérgère was ending next month, le Duc had not given any indication that he would try to take it over. She knew Madame would give him preferential treatment because of what had occurred so many years ago, but Isabel hoped his stubborn streak would win out and he would not pursue her contract to make a point. They were all counting on that, in fact. Madame had grown tired of his whiny arrogance and he had been near impossible to please these last few years, as if they *owed* him something after that fated November night. It had all been worth it, though, and Madame didn't complain about the price that continued to be paid to le Duc, a small price, indeed, when the profits realized from her launch were taken into account.

In fact, no one in the *maison* had a single regret. At the time, they couldn't foresee how ideal the results had been. The sizable fee was a mere drop in the sea of what was to come. The reputation of *la Maison de Rouler* elevated overnight, never wavering from top position. Isabel was an instant success and was booked for weeks in advance (which was the longest Madame agreed to book anyone). She set a new fee standard in the city, as Armand had anticipated, and the highbred and low paid dearly—and gladly—for her company. The other girls' fame rose as well, and most of them had learned how to invest their share wisely so they would have money to live comfortably after they tired of their trade, or more likely, their trade had tired of them.

"I will talk to Madame and put an end to this once and for all. Besides, word on the street is there is trouble brewing with our friend Georges, and I would prefer to be outside of shooting distance if what is said is true."

"*Tell me*," Paulette pleaded, as she plopped down on the bed beside her.

"Not now, silly. Armand is about to arrive and he's taking me to play cards at his apartment in the city. We have to get ready. He's due any minute, remember?" He still met with Isabel socially, although their torrid little affair had ended not long after their first night together and he had since become Lisette's regular client and lover. Isabel was still the perfect hostess, though, and at times it proved to be advantageous to have her on his arm. She knew how to have fun and he could relax around her, paying closer attention to the people around him without having a jealous lover on his arm.

"Of course I remember," Paulette snapped back, "but can you not talk while you are dressing? Give me a hint. It is about his lovely wife, is it not?"

"Why, what have *you* heard?"

"No, you first, as I asked first. Now go, before we run out of time." Paulette would not budge, Isabel knew, so she succumbed to her request and repeated what she had heard. These conversations were only ever between the two of them. They respected Madame's rules around privacy but bent them between each other. Nothing ever left this room, but many secrets were exchanged there. Secrets that most people would be appalled to know and even more appalled to know that Isabel, and now her serving girl, were privy to. Some of the most powerful men in the country had unleashed countless secret details while in Isabel's boudoir. State secrets, marital secrets and information that, if leaked, could be the death of some of them. And yet they instinctively knew they were safe with her, and ultimately with Paulette, as their close relationship was almost legendary.

"Okay, but fetch my gray silk gown with the plunging neckline. It still drives him wild to see me in it. And the coin necklace. A nice touch to the evening, *n'est-ce pas*?" She still loved to tease him.

"Yes, yes, of course, but get on with it. What have you heard?"

"Well, you were right about *la Duchesse de Veauville*. Someone sent her an anonymous note with the details of our little bid from all those years ago, divulging the 1,000 francs he had offered. At the time, she seethed but did nothing until another note—same script, no name—arrived this week. Apparently he's been seen down at a gambling house of disrepute on several occasions, and more than once has refused to pay his debts. My guess is that the mysterious note was written by the same person, who is owed a substantial amount of money, but whoever it was is not the point. The point is…" She looked at herself again in the mirror. "My hair is not right, Paulette. It needs something different. Maybe I should do something risqué and wear it down. What do you think?"

"I think your hair is *fine*. Now, the point *is*…?"

"Oh, yes, the point is that she has threatened to boot him out on his finely tailored ass without a single franc if he is seen there even one more time."

"But, could she do that?"

"*Bien sûr*. Where do you think all of their money comes from? *La Duchesse*, of course. She is a Bouchard, an old and wealthy French family, and her tolerance has been admirably high. Just look at his behavior here at the house. Cavorting with us almost night and day. It is one thing to have a mistress or courtesan *and* a wife—everyone knows it is the French way—but use some discretion. He has even had Madame to his home to discuss business. It is disgraceful behavior and I can see *la Duchesse* agrees. Madame does not know this yet but I believe *this* is the main reason he has not picked up my contract and is leading us all to believe he is punishing us. Meanwhile, his wife is keeping a close eye on the family purse strings and he has no way of covering this little expense without it being divulged to her."

"I am sorry for laughing, but he is such a *cochon*. I find it poetic justice, do you not agree?"

"Now, now. Let's be nice. After all, he was instrumental in making me who I am today."

"Oh, please, Isabel. You are who you are today because of who you are. No one could have stopped you becoming who you are. Do not give credit where no credit is due. It is *Armand* more than le Duc who intentionally pushed you to the top. And he did it out of kindness and integrity because he saw in you a rare quality, and that was your purity of spirit. He said those exact words to me, Isabel. 'Purity of spirit,' and he is right. How is *his* wife, by the way?" And both girls fell on the bed in peals of laughter.

Armand had won another major conquest by marrying Juliette, le Duc's only daughter. She turned out to be a force to be reckoned with in many ways, but what he had found the most difficult to deal with was her abhorrence of his visits to *la Maison de Rouler*. It was public knowledge when he outbid her father for Isabel's maidenhead, although only a handful knew the actual winning amount, and it was also clear at the time how worthwhile the evening turned out to be for both parties. Sparks nearly flew when Armand and Isabel entered a room together. How could a wife compete with that? Although she never forbade him to go—one would not dare *forbid* Armand to do anything—she did frown upon it outwardly and made it as uncomfortable as she could when she was aware of his visits. Both girls saw the irony in the fact that the father-in-law had just left—briskly, one might add—and the son-in-law was about to arrive to whisk her off on a clandestine evening with a group of 'unsavories,' according to Juliette, to spend a fun-filled evening together.

There was a lot of love between Isabel and Armand, but they were not in love with each other. She loved the relationship they shared, started that first night together. Their evenings had become quite adventurous and playful, which is why they enjoyed each other's company. It was left unfettered by the normal constraints found between a couple in love. He reserved that for his wife and lover, and Isabel, for François, who had, indeed, won his conquest and become her lover.

More than any man, Armand had impacted her life in unimaginable ways. They shared a kinship that was rare indeed. She shared a kinship with Paulette as well, but with Armand it was different. There was a part of her soul that was only for him. Neither her friends nor her lover saw even a glimmer of it. He would be one of the hardest people to live without, she thought, and she pushed that to the recesses of her mind to be replaced with something a little more wicked. "Paulette, grab me that Persian scent I wore on our first night together. The one in the blown-glass vial. No, not that one. That one is disgusting. It was a gift from Georges—I swear, the man has no taste in scents. Yes, that one there. I want to have a little fun tonight." Paulette passed the intricate vial to her outstretched hand and she dabbed a touch behind her ears and then in the cleft between her breasts.

They continued to talk of the Veauville drama and at one point Paulette was about to share a few tidbits of her own when they suddenly heard a loud knock at the door. It was Armand, annoyingly prompt, as usual. "*Entre*," came Isabel's sultry voice and he stepped into the room, taking it all in at a glance.

"Paulette, you are looking especially gorgeous this evening. Could I tempt you at last to go away with me, never to return to this life of drudgery? Hmm?"

"Paulette was just leaving, weren't you, Paulette?" The sternness in her voice added to the part of her role as jealous lover.

"Oui, Mademoiselle. Anything you say, Mademoiselle," as she backed out of the room toward the door, winked brazenly at the Monsieur and spun on her heel as she exited, leaving the two shaking their heads in merriment.

"Ah, my Isabel. May I say you are looking especially gorgeous this evening?" Armand reached for her hand and kissed it passionately.

"Your cheap words do not work on me, Monsieur, and you know it." The waft of her scent lifted to his senses and he closed his eyes in memory of their sacred evening so many years ago.

"Perhaps not, but I know a few things that will," and he pulled her to him, placing one hand behind her head and the other gently pressing against her nipple through the layers of her dress. "I think you are planning to be naughty tonight, Mademoiselle, *n'est-ce pas*? I would like to remind you that I, too, can play that game."

"I know that very well, Monsieur," and she nipped his bottom lip and then licked it languidly with her moistened tongue, simultaneously pulling him toward her, pressing her hips into his already bulging groin. He let out a muffled groan and slipped his thumb up over the top of her low-cut neckline and under her corset to rest, flesh on flesh, on her now-protruding nipple. Adding a touch of pressure and still looking her straight into her sparkling eyes, he took his other thumb, brushed it across her moist lips and then quickly brought it down to her other unattended nipple, the moisture reducing all friction as he slowly circled around its tip while still maintaining the pressure on the other. She squirmed and quivered but he would not relent. With her right hand firmly on his buttocks, she slid it up and around to the front of his trousers, and in one motion had grabbed his cock firmly in her right hand while still pulling him toward her with her left.

"That's not fair," was his breathy response.

"Who said anything about playing fair, *mon chéri*? You know you can never win this game, so shall we call a truce? Or shall we continue? Me, I have all evening." And she left the words hanging as if she were fully prepared to continue on this track and sabotage the evening's plans.

"You are a devilish tease and you know we cannot stay here. I am the one hosting the evening, remember? What would happen if all of the carriages pulled up outside my apartment to find their host missing? We must get going this instant and I will decide if I will forgive you for taunting me so mercilessly. The Persian scent, no less. What else have you got up your sleeve, you little vixen?" And with one quick motion he gently tweaked her nipples, and was rewarded with a startled, "Oahhhh," then placed both hands on her shoulders and gently but forcefully pushed her away so her left hand fell to her side and her right was drawn up away from what she was holding and returned to safety by her other side.

"Now take a look at yourself in the mirror and see why I should take my wife's advice and stop seeing you. It is reprehensible, Isabel. *Really.*"

She spun around to gaze at her reflection in the full-length cheval mirror and noticed a slightly disheveled appearance, but otherwise found herself quite acceptable. "What? I don't understand."

"Look again," as he pointed to the top of her dress, where two erect nipples were peaking over the lacey edge. "See what I have to put up with? *Mon Dieu*, woman. Get yourself together."

"But *mon chéri*, this is how the dress is meant to be worn. It is the latest fashion here, and all of the women are cutting their necklines to just *below* the nipple. You like, *non*?" She had a serious expression on her face, but then broke out into bursts of laughter. "Oh, Armand, you should see your face. I cannot believe you almost believed me. This is too *drôle*. 'You like, *non*?' I think you like very much, if the front of your trousers is any indication."

"Isabel, *please*. We must get going—now. Okay, if you are not ready in one minute, I, and my recently-fondled ass, will be leaving without you, *comprends?*"

"*Je comprends, Monsieur*. I'll grab my shawl, *tout de suite*." She tugged her dress up slightly, grabbed her shawl and curtsied coyly, slapping him on his derrière as she ran for the door, Armand right on her heels. She continued to run all the way down the corridor and down the stairs, just as Madame was coming out of her *bureau*. Madame gave her a reproving look and Isabel came to a screeching halt, lifted her chin high in the air, bowed elegantly to Madame, and continued to the front door, where the valet opened it for her and Armand, who had caught up and was now by her side, both still laughing.

They ducked into his awaiting carriage and headed up the street to the more fashionable district, where he owned an apartment that he kept strictly for his extramarital pleasures. There was not a lot Juliette could do about it, as it was his before they were married and what a husband did with his other holdings was his business, and his business alone. His wife had never set foot in this property, whereas Isabel had on many occasions. This was where they had their little tryst shortly after their first encounter and she knew the apartment intimately. *I wonder who will be there this evening.* It would be mostly men with their consorts and not a wife in sight. It was the French custom and most men were almost obliged to keep two houses in the city as it wasn't practical or appealing to have to meet at the courtesan's *maison*.

They arrived the back way just in time to greet over 20 guests ready for a night of cards, music, good food and flagrant intimacy. This group met regularly and they all felt comfortable with the arrangement. The only one in the group that caused any discomfort was le Viscount d'Orange, who insisted on bringing two of his conquests at the same time. It was one thing to resort to clandestine behavior but it was quite another to flaunt it publicly in front of your friends and business associates. He insisted that he loved them both and couldn't choose, and it had become almost accepted among the group, but if there was ever a reason for the wives to complain, it would be on a point like this, and no one wanted their boat to be rocked.

Isabel looked around the room at the two dozen or so faces, each with a different story, each with his or her own history. The men were mostly wealthy businessmen with a smattering of royalty thrown in to the mix. But most of Armand's contacts were from the business world, not from the automatically acquired group thrust upon you at the moment of your royal birth. These relationships had been nurtured and created and would likely remain stronger than the other form. There was not a single wife in the group, at least none belonging to anyone in this crowd. The women were either courtesans or mistresses, the latter comprised of a wide variety of different stations. The wives, who were there having affairs with other wives' husbands, took the highest risk at socializing at this type of gathering. Although the same group met regularly, many of the women came and went, which would increase their risk of being a topic of conversation at another gathering when these absent women linked up with other men in other similar groups. The rest of the mistresses were young and old, wealthy and poor and had no ties other than what was to be found in this room. They tended to be the most relaxed and jovial of the group and brought such a cross section of personalities that they were entertainment in and of themselves.

Being a part of the courtesan set was different again. These women tended to be proper and careful, saying and doing the right things, flattering the men—and women—so as not to cause any upset or stress. They were there to entertain the men and they took their role seriously. Except for Isabel. The relationship she had fostered with Armand allowed her a certain latitude and for that reason much resentment shifted toward her from around the room. At times their jealousy was palpable, as Isabel was adored by each man in this room. And because Armand had no formal tie to her, they were all free to associate with her at will, and many of them did. Much bantering went back and forth between Armand and the other men, with Isabel as the pawn in the middle. She could be seen pouting over something Armand had said and sidling over to another man's lap, all in good fun, taunting Armand mercilessly, and the other man as well. The woman on the man's other arm would be furious and the poor man in the middle would react to his escort's jealousy, the situation spiraling downward until animosity took root and her nemesis was born.

Isabel appeared oblivious to the commotion she was stirring, although she was not. She had reached a point in her life where she felt it was time to dig deeper into her soul and stretch her limits. As she looked to each man and woman in turn she thought about their lives and how the outcome of each was mainly due to his or her birth. She found it unfathomable that life hung in the balance of chance, and that if the stars were aligned in a certain way and you plopped down from the sky into a *château*, your life course would be determined solely by family ties and obligations. But if you missed the positive aspects of the skies by one solitary night and you landed in a hovel instead, then drudgery and starvation would be by your side throughout your long and dreary life.

If there was a God then this did not ring true to her. Her God was kind and just. She was determined to prove to herself that birth alone did not make the man, or woman in her case, and that every human on this earth had an opportunity to change his or her lot in life. The struggles varied greatly from class to class but also from body to body. A beautiful woman struggled in ways that were different from those of a homely woman. A crippled man's struggles were different from those of someone who was healthy but poor. But they were all struggles nonetheless. The more she looked around the room at the lives that sat before her, the more she felt that each one had choices as well, and those choices were what determined the outcome of their lives. Much could be hindered by birth, but both sides of the fence struggled equally—albeit differently. Instead of resentment toward them, she felt empathy as she recognized the difficulties they all faced, and she made a conscious decision to appreciate what she had been given and continue to make the most of the evening, despite the animosity all around her.

The sun was just coming up as Isabel arrived at *la Maison*. The party went late into the night and when the final guests had gone, Armand put Isabel in his carriage and sent her home. Their earlier sexual taunts had been just that and neither had the interest nor energy to pursue them. Both would prefer to be with their lovers, and when Isabel finally dropped into her own bed she fell into a deep dream state, holding her lover and her previous meandering thoughts at the forefront of her subconscious.

Part III

Chapter XII

"Wake up! Wake up!"

Someone was shaking her gently but forcefully, and her groggy state was making it difficult to connect with reality. Armand was looking down at her anxiously, and when her focus cleared she looked up and recognized Marc. "Marc, what the hell are you doing here?"

Armand was the man in the book. Marc must have fashioned him after himself. She was still so confused and was trying to shake herself loose from the dream, but it had been so vivid. She must have been swept up in Marc's novel, which she saw lying on the floor, where it must have fallen from the bed. "Oh, I'm sorry about your book. I was reading. I fell asleep. It fell…" She looked at Marc with total confusion.

Marc got the call at eight that morning, already on his computer answering emails generated from last night's soirée. As Sabine lived not too far from him, he decided to call her and then swing by to pick her up on the way. When she didn't answer her phone he headed over there anyway, hoping the doorman would let him in. He had been there several times with Nate and the man didn't even hesitate to let him in. He waited by her apartment door until Marc was inside and heard Sabine's voice, and then headed back to his duties.

"Forget about the book. Sabine, you need to get up. Nathan's in the hospital. His maid found him this morning and called 911. He's unconscious and in the ICU. Get dressed. I'll take you over there as soon as you're ready. What the hell happened last night, anyway? They say he's got a concussion or something. I don't think he meant for this to happen, but God, he's in rough shape." He slowed down long enough to register the shock in Sabine's eyes. "Sabine, I'm so sorry. I'm going on and on like a madman and you haven't had a chance to absorb what's happened. Please, just get dressed and we'll talk on the way. And don't worry. They say he's stable so he'll come through this, I'm sure. Come on, I'll grab your coat. Let's go."

"What the hell happened? How did this happen? I mean, why does he have a concussion? God, I can't believe it. But you said he was okay, right?" She scrambled to pull on some clothes, grabbed two to-go mugs, filling them with the fresh coffee from the timed brew she had each morning, threw on her shoes, grabbed her purse and headed to the door, not even glancing at herself in the mirror as they flew past. "I had to grab the coffee, Marc. I know it's disgusting at the hospital and I don't think I can face this day without it. Here, this one's for you," she said, thrusting the second mug into his hand. His car was parked out front in the loading zone, and, ignoring the dirty looks from the delivery van, they hopped in and sped away. "Marc, I need two minutes to collect my thoughts, okay? I've just been shocked out of an almost other-worldly experience—generated by your book, by the way—and I want to regroup, take five sips of my coffee, and then we'll talk. Fair?"

'Fair.' Marc was visibly upset but chose to also take this time to get his thoughts together. He was still reeling from the shock and now that he had Sabine by his side he could focus on the next dreaded steps.

Not even two minutes had passed since they left her condo but it was enough time for her to set the dream aside and go over the events of last night. "Okay, I'm ready. Tell me what you know and then I'll do the same. Wait. Let me go first. Marc, Nate and I broke up last night."

"Oh, geeeeezus, Bean. What happened? I had no idea things were so off between you two."

"Same ol', same ol'. Let's not get into it now, okay? It was our usual argument and I just decided I'd had enough. He didn't think I was serious but when I walked out I guess it became crystal clear. God, Marc. Is this my fault? Oh, God, I feel terrible."

"Let's not jump to any conclusions," *says the pot calling the kettle black.* "They found an empty bottle of scotch on the table. It looks like he fell as he was getting into bed, and hit his head on the nightstand. They don't think it was intentional, just grossly negligent on his part. Don't take this on, Bean. He's a big boy and he's accountable for his own actions. Anyone who polishes off a bottle of anything after they've been dumped deserves a bit of retribution. It was just pure stupidity. What a fucking idiot."

He banged the steering wheel with the open palm of his hand, swearing and cursing his brother. Sabine knew it was his way of dealing with the situation so decided to cut him some slack, as she would normally not tolerate that type of bashing. When she looked over at him to respond she saw the tears falling unabashedly down his cheeks and her self-control dissolved, opening the channel to her own tears. The two of them cried silently for a few moments until Sabine was able to speak.

"We're just about there. Let's take a minute and get ourselves together and then present a united front when we walk through those doors. He's a well-known and respected figure in this community and the last thing we would want is to give anyone grounds for any juicy gossip. Agreed?"

"Yes, good point. Okay, I think I can do that. Sabine?" His words were filled with pain as he continued. "Are you okay? Is there anything I can do for you?"

"Oh, Marc, no, but thank you. You just worry about you, okay? You're going to need to be the big strong brother here, so don't start taking care of me, too. I'm a big girl and am quite capable of taking care of myself. Please, I don't want to be worrying about you, too, okay?"

"Okay. Thank you. I'm glad you're here with me," he said, and he moved his hand from his grip on the wheel to her hand, and gave it a gentle squeeze.

"I am too. Thanks."

He pulled into a short-term parking stall without caring if he got towed, slammed it into park and jumped out to race to the emergency entrance. They both paused for one more look of assurance before striding over to the automatic doors and headed toward the admittance desk to find out where Nate was. The room held a frantic atmosphere as they witnessed different levels of emergency care required, mostly caused by accidents. One man had a thick rod sticking out of the top of his thigh. Looking at him and imagining what must have happened made Sabine contemplate how precarious life was. If he had been held up at the coffee shop lineup ten seconds longer, he might have missed the accident. What was it about this man that placed him in the precise position in harm's way at the exact moment that rod fell from the sky? All this was running through her mind as they headed toward another victim. By his own careless hand, but victim, nonetheless. How can so many people take life so lightly? She was beginning to realize how precious each day was and being in the hospital today would be another reminder.

They were deep in their own thoughts as they waited silently for the elevator to arrive at Nathan's floor. As the doors slid open they walked into the foyer of the ICU and were handed a plastic bag, each containing a gown, hat, gloves and mask. No one was permitted entry without them

105

because of the risk of contagion among the weakened patients and Marc was personally relieved to be able to wear a mask to protect *himself* from *them*. He'd heard enough horror stories about people going into hospitals with one illness and dying there after contracting another. *It would serve Nate right if that happened to him*. As soon as the thoughts were formed, he banished them, condemning himself, and instantly saying a silent prayer that he would never have to regret them.

The sight that hit them when they walked into his room brought only feelings of sheer sympathy and sadness, for they were not prepared for the sleeping man before them, tubes and wires connected to countless machines, beeping and turning and pulsing liquids into his bloodstream. His face was ghost white and he had never seemed so peaceful and pathetic at the same time. They glanced at each other and then back at Nathan, fighting to keep back the tears. They stood silently for a few minutes until Sabine got Marc's attention and motioned with her head for them to leave, and he agreed. Even though Nate was unconscious they had not uttered a word. They didn't know yet what they wanted to say to him and neither wanted to risk being heard until their words were chosen carefully. They had differing beliefs surrounding unconsciousness. Sabine felt that people in a coma understood everything that was said and done in their presence on some deep level. Marc thought it was a possibility but now that it was his brother lying there, he preferred to err on the side of Sabine's view.

They left his room and took a seat in the small waiting area outside the door. They sat down with heavy sighs and reached out for each other's hands. "So, here's what I think we should do. I'll go in first and give him a piece of my mind and really shake him up. Then you can follow with words of consolation, apologizing for the fight you had and beg him to come back to you. What do you think?" He was joking, of course, but there was a note of pleading in his voice.

"Marc, as much as I care for your brother, what he did has nothing to do with me. I realized that on the way over here this morning. I can't take him back. It would be the worst thing I could do for both of us. And there's this strong voice in my head screaming at me, 'take the oxygen mask first, take the oxygen mask first' and I can't ignore it. Part of what went on between your brother and me was that he has a way of being perfectly comfortable putting himself first, no matter what, and my way is being comfortable putting myself second. It worked for both of us for a while because that is what he's come to expect and that is what I've felt I'm worth.

"But no more. I need to learn to be first in this life. I have a feeling it's one of the most important things I need to learn, and this is one of those tests that would be easier to fail by staying, both here at the hospital, and then later with him. But if I don't start passing these tests they will keep getting harder, you know, and soon I won't be able to dig myself out of the mess I've created. Marc, I need to not be here at all. Assuming he wakes up, he will have to realize that his accident hasn't caused enough sympathy for me to come back to him. He needs to start his life's recovery without me. I'm sorry that you're left holding the bag but I'm certain it's the right choice for me. And for Nate."

At first Marc was stunned. How could she desert them both like that? Then, as her words filtered through to his core he realized his brother had been playing him that way all his life and he was tempted to leave with her, and said as much. "Will you at least stay with me until I'm able to talk to the doctor treating him? You're a lot better with medical jargon and you'll know what questions to ask."

"Of course. If *you* need anything, you just have to ask. This is not between you and me, and whatever happens with your brother, you and I will remain good friends. You've become too important to me to allow your brother to get between us. Now, let's go see what we can find out."

The doctor was non-committal and repeated over and over that time would tell, and nothing else. His body and brain were dealing with a severe trauma, and a head injury of this magnitude was still unpredictable. She suggested they both leave and the hospital would call them if there was any change. Marc left his cell number at the main desk and they left, prepared for a tense wait that could take days, or even longer.

The doctor watched them leave, arms around each other. *Lucky her.* Then she turned around and went back to doing her rounds.

Chapter XIII

"What happens when you die?" Sophie was leaning against Sabine in her canopied bed, interrupting the story once again as she fired question after question about her boyfriend (ex-boyfriend) in the hospital. "Does it hurt after, when you die, I mean?"

"I don't think so, sweetie. I don't think you feel any pain at all after you die. What do you think happens?"

"I think your body gets creamy-ated and then your soul goes up into the sky."

Sabine's brother was downstairs relaxing, sipping on a glass of Chardonnay. He and his wife Beth had invited her over for dinner as soon as they heard about the fiasco with Nathan. She gladly accepted as they both had a non-judgmental approach to their lives and she knew they wouldn't drill her with 'twenty questions'.

Sabine hadn't seen her niece for a couple of weeks and found her to be more precocious than ever. Not having children of her own, she wasn't sure what her brother would want her to say to his five-year old, so she was trying to volley the question back to her court.

"And then?" This could be an enlightening conversation, as kids had more inside information on this topic than anyone on the planet. Sabine continued to listen attentively.

"And then you come back into your new Mommy's tummy and come out through her bagina and be born again."

"Bagina?" Sabine hesitated only briefly until the light came on. "Oh, I think you mean *vagina*, honey."

"Yeah, that's what I said. Bagina. I know those words, Auntie Bean. I have a book that tells me all about my body and if I had a brother, all about his body, too. But I don't have a brother. Do you have a brother?" Her inquisitive mind had just started to warm up.

"Yes I do, Soph. In fact, your *daddy* is my brother. Try to figure that one out."

"That's easy. Your Mommy and Daddy's Mommy is the same Mommy. And do you know who your Mommy is? My *grandma*. Isn't that cool? My daddy 'splained it all to me so now I understand. Do you think Grandma will die some day?"

"What do you think?" she said, desperately trying to stay in control of the conversation but rapidly losing ground.

"Yeah. I think we all die *some* day. But not for a long time, right? When I'm grown up, right?"

"Right."

"Who do you want to come back as next time, Auntie Bean?"

"I don't know. I haven't given it much thought before now. Let me see. Hmm. Who do I want to come back as? Do you know who *you* want to be?" *Keep those questions turned around, Sabine. Surely you can outsmart a five-year-old.*

"I think I'd like to be a princess or a comtesse. It's no fun being poor."

"But Sophie, you're not poor. What gave you that idea?"

"Not *now*, silly. Before. *Next* time I want to be royal—I think it would be a lot more fun. And I want a canopy bed like *yours*. This one is too babyish."

Sabine didn't own a canopy bed, but she didn't want to argue with her, so she just smiled and gave her some platitude, like "that would be nice" or "I agree" so she was able to bring the discussion back to the story where they had left off. When Sophie finally started to nod off, Sabine gave her a giant Beanie snuggle, tucked her in tightly the way she liked, and kissed her gently on the forehead. "Goodnight, my little *chérie*," she said, turning out the light as she quietly left the room. She was feeling slightly disconcerted by their conversation and chalked it up to being concerned about Nate. All this talk about death was depressing and she hoped she hadn't said anything to disturb the little girl's dreams.

She shook off the feeling and tiptoed silently down the hall, and then down the stairs to the kitchen, where her brother was waiting with a tall glass of red wine. "Thanks, bro."

"No. Thank *you* for tucking in Soph. That kid can read the same story forever and she doesn't let you skip a word. It was nice of you to take it on tonight—I wasn't feeling up to it and I know you said it would perk you up. Did it?"

Gavin loved having her as a big part in his daughter's life. Sophie adored Auntie Bean and she seemed to be the one constant in her life.

She had often shared intimate secrets with her favorite aunt and Sabine took her role seriously. She loved Sophie like she was her own, something she had yet to experience, and maybe never would—at least in this lifetime, as Sophie would be sure to say.

"She started asking me all these questions about death and I didn't know what to say, so I just let her tell me what she thought and went with that. Hope that's okay."

"Oh sure. That's one of her favorite topics at the moment. She has all kinds of ideas on death and dying—where she got them, I haven't a clue—but she's quite emphatic about them all and loves to weave fantasies around her ideas. She's quite a little storyteller, isn't she? Did she talk about the royal comtesse? That's her favorite—at the moment, that is."

"Yes, she started in on that and I actually got tingles up my spine. She talked as if it was the present and the past had just happened. It was a bit spooky."

"Kids are spooky creatures. Have you not noticed that before? They have great imaginations, and I often wonder what they would be like as adults if they had never been shot down or laughed at or told, 'no, you can't do that—it's impossible.' Half the time I laugh when Sophie's telling me one of her tall tales but then once in awhile she'll say something incredibly astute and I have to go back on all the other 'silly' conversations only to realize that what she'd been talking about made perfect sense all along. The words she'd been using were childlike and I simply stuck them in their proper box, discounting what she was saying. When that happens I just bow down to her and call her Comtesse Sophie, and tell her, 'Your wish is my command.' She just giggles at how silly I've been and says, *Da-ad* in that tone that only kids can replicate, like I'm the most clueless person on the planet, and how did she get stuck with having to teach me everything? It's quite entertaining and often puts me in my place. Kids are great—you really should go out and get your own, though, Sis."

"Yes, well, in light of what's just happened, that's not going to happen anytime soon, now, is it?"

"Don't be a dweeb, Sis. Nathan wasn't 'the one' and you know it. You've known it from your second date, at least you said as much to me. Maybe you needed to see that more clearly before making room for your prince charming to come along."

"Do you really believe that, Gav? Should I be looking out for a white horse, or what?"

"A more modern white horse. Let's say, a white Ferrari—you know, with the horse insignia on the front? But seriously, I do believe it's available for everyone. Everyone that's willing to believe it, that is."

"I know what you and Beth have is unique but I don't know if I agree that it's available for everyone. And what do you mean, 'if I believe it'? You're starting to sound like that 'Field of Dreams' movie: 'If I build it, he will come.' So what exactly is it that I should be building, O wise one?"

"A better attitude for starters. Seriously, Sabine, the only thing that's preventing it is your lack of faith that it's even possible. That movie wasn't too far off the mark, except for the creepy ghosts and stuff. Don't you ever wonder why some people are always down on their luck and others seem to sail through every adversity? Don't you have a friend who is always whining about everything and has said countless times how lousy the service is in a particular restaurant only to be talking about the same restaurant you frequent, where the service is always excellent? Is it sheer chance that she only goes when the crappy servers are working? No. She gets crappy service because she whines and complains about everything. It's her *attitude* that delivers her abysmal service every time. People can't help but respond to her in a like manner. Negativity begets more negativity and positivity begets…?"

"Positivity. I get it. But what does this have to do with connecting with my prince charming? If I'm all happy and chipper will I attract someone all happy and chipper? Do I even *want* that?"

"Yes, you probably would, but you're missing the bigger picture here. Let's say the world works with energy, and like attracts like, which we both already know. And let's say there's a big guy in the sky, for lack of a better term, or some higher power out there that is orchestrating this whole thing, be it a God, an energy field, whatever—it doesn't matter. So you put out the message, 'I want to meet my prince charming' and that's your mantra for thirty days…"

"Why thirty days?" she interrupted.

"I just made that up. It doesn't matter. Thirty days, thirty minutes, thirty years—you pick. Stay with me, Bean, we're almost there. So, you put out your happy thoughts and just as your shining white Ferrari is about to turn the corner onto your street, you have the thought, 'but I don't believe there's really any such thing,' and whoooosh. He turns left instead of right and meets up with someone who *does* believe in him. When your thoughts are not in alignment with what you want it is impossible to deliver. Remember, like attracts like. No ifs, ands or buts."

111

"Are you also saying that all the good stuff and the bad that happens in my life are because I've attracted them?" She was not buying his line of thinking but it had her interested.

"Yup, it can't be any other way."

"So, Nate's hospital stay?"

"Yup."

"And the guy with the metal rod through his leg? He *attracted* that to himself?"

"Eeeewww, creepy. But, yup."

"And all the crap that has happened in my life has actually been my own doing? No one else to blame? Not even Mother?"

"Yup, yup and yup. It's a much easier way to live than the alternative, I can assure you. If you start to see how you play a part in your own life, can't you see the power in that? The simplicity? The fun you can have? Look at my life. Is there anything in it that isn't enviable in every way? My wife is the most amazing creature on the planet, tied for first place with Sophie, of course. Do you think I was just born into this by sheer chance? No way, José. It all stems from my intention. Do you think for a moment someone as incredible as Sophie would choose to come into a family where she wouldn't be recognized and honored for her talents?"

"Did you say 'choose'? You think we choose where we go? And I chose this family? Oh, that is funny. Of all the families that were available, I chose 'The Simpsons.'" She could barely contain her laughter and Gavin joined in.

"Pretty incredible, isn't it? But it is, when you stop to think of it. I have you, for example, and who else would have looked up to me with such admiration as my baby sister, Sabine? And Mom and Dad? Think of all the hard lessons you learned by their inadvertent parenting and the strengths you gained from their—" and here he mimed 'air quotes' "—mistakes. You are who you are *because* of your family, not in *spite* of them. Good and bad, every member contributed to your whole makeup so you could go through life with the tools you require."

"Gav? Can we take a break from all this mumbo-jumbo for the rest of the evening? Please? I will think about what you said, but for now, let me just drink my wine and try to figure out what I'm going to do about Nate and the aftermath of what's happened. Poor Marc. I feel for that guy. He's stuck with him for life. At least I was able to walk away." Sabine was starting to feel the effects of the day catching up with her and although she had great respect for her brother's alternative views she didn't have the brain space to debate them tonight.

"My lips are sealed. Not to sound trite, but you and I both know this will work itself out and even Nathan will land on his feet. When are you going to start taking care of yourself instead of all of the stragglers like Nathan that you pick up off the street?"

"Funny you should mention that. I was just saying to Marc that exact thing. It's time for me to start putting myself first. It's exhausting work, being a martyr." She smiled and leaned her head on his shoulder. "Thanks, bro. I needed this talk. Even though I listen, kicking and screaming, it all goes in there. You'll see. I'll be back with a witty retort in a day or two."

"That's the spirit. And personally, I'm grateful to Nathan if he was the one to show this to you—finally. Now, let me call you a cab. I'm kicking you out. You need to have a nice, hot bath with those Frenchie scents you love so much, and do some introspectulating."

"Is that a real word?"

"No, but it's suitable, so I can take the liberty of using it as I see fit. And in this situation, it fits perfectly. Enough with the questions. Finish your wine and stop gabbing. Your cab will be here soon. Now, drink up." And they hugged each other tight before Sabine picked up her glass, almost untouched, and polished it off in two gulps.

Chapter XIV

Nathan slowly opened his eyes when a piercing pain jolted through his skull, forcing them closed again. He felt like he had a whopping hangover and was woozy and disoriented. His mouth was vile tasting and furry, like he hadn't brushed his teeth in days. He made another attempt to open his eyes and saw two blurry faces hovering over his bed. He was too groggy to move, but inside, his nerves were frayed. Where was he? Who were these people? Marc, is that you? These questions all turned around inside his head, but he didn't speak any words.

"I think I saw his eyes flutter. There. See? There it is again. He's definitely waking up." Marc was beside himself with relief. He had been in and out of this hospital for a week and a part of him had started to doubt the wait would ever end. The doctor affirmed what he saw and pulled out her penlight to examine him more closely. She leaned over him, tugged gently on one of his eyelids and pointed the light directly into his pupil. It dilated nicely and she was happy with the response. She smiled over at Marc. "Keep talking to him. He'll probably come in and out of consciousness for a few more hours but it would soothe him to hear a voice he recognizes. I'll be back to check on him in an hour or so. You can let me know then if there's been any visible change, all right?" She turned and left him standing there alone, leaving behind only a trace of her perfume. Nice. A bit jasminey.

He closed his eyes, taking in the lingering aroma and then opened them to see Nathan squinting up at him. "Hey big brother. Nice hotel you picked out. Next time ask for one with a better view. All you can see is a giant parking lot." Marc was rambling because he didn't know what he was going to say and everything he wanted to say involved physical actions to go along with the words, like shaking his brother senseless and yelling and cursing, so he decided to put that off until he was fully conscious. "Must be a comfy bed, though, 'cause you've been lying in it for a week. Any plans on checking out soon?" He smiled down at Nate and rested his hand gently on his shoulder. "You're in a hospital, Nate. Apparently, celebrating my success with scotch ended with your head connecting to the corner of your nightstand. *Ouch*. Take your time coming to. I imagine you have one banger of a headache."

Nate gave him an almost imperceptible nod and tried to swallow, feeling only a caked-on dry sensation in his mouth. Marc helped Nate sit up and pulled the pillow up behind him to prop him up. He picked up the glass of water with the bendy straw and brought it in reach of Nate's mouth. "Go slow, Nathan. Your body hasn't been functioning without help for a week and it's probably forgotten what to do. One sip at a time, okay?" Another small nod and he latched onto the straw, sipping slowly at regular intervals.

"That's good. Feel better? Now, don't try to talk. You probably feel disoriented so for now, I'll do all the talking. That voice you hear in the hallway is your doctor. She said she'd be back around now to see you. A bit of poking and prodding, I would imagine. Can't wait to watch." Nathan smiled weakly up at Marc as he turned to watch the doctor walk in.

Dr. Menzies gave him a thorough going over and began with a stream of *yes* and *no* questions about how he was feeling, what he remembered, and the usual "What year is this?" and so on. "I understand your girlfriend left you the night this happened, is that correct?" Small nod. "Does that have anything to do with the quantity of alcohol you consumed that night?" Nod, and sheepish smile.

"Okay, Mr. Bouchard," she said, and turning to Marc, she added, "That's all I need for now. Make sure he has plenty of water," spoken back to Nathan. "Understand?" Nod, nod. "Good. I'll be back in the morning to follow up. You should be doing a lot better by then and your headache will have subsided. I'm sorry, we can't give you anything for it as we need to allow it to heal and it's our best indicator of what's going on in there so I'm afraid you'll have to suffer through this one. I'll see you both tomorrow, then?" Both Nathan and Marc nodded in unison and she shook her head and smiled as she left the room.

Marc stuck around a while longer, filling Nathan in on the details of what he knew but keeping it casual so as not to frighten him unnecessarily. He could tell his big brother was starting to fade, so he said he'd come back tomorrow. Nathan nodded again and then drifted off to sleep, mid-nod. He made a quick call to his parents as promised, but thankfully the machine picked up so he was able to update them without having to go into a full-blown report. His mother had been there every day since the accident but now that Nathan was awake, he wasn't sure if she'd keep up the same routine.

Marc silently slipped out, figuring Nathan would probably sleep till tomorrow. As planned, Sabine was waiting at the end of the hall, and when she saw him leave the room she jumped up and rushed toward him. He was smiling broadly and they went into each other's arms, embracing tightly, tears flowing freely down each of their faces. "He's going to be alright, Bean. We spoke, well I spoke, and he looks good. I'm coming back tomorrow and the doctor was optimistic."

"Oh, thank God. I am so relieved, I can't tell you, Marc."

"Me, too, and thanks for waiting. It means a lot that you're here." They held each other for several moments before heading out, arm in arm. From the other end of the hall, the doctor watched with interest. *No ring – too bad for me, but it's good he has her support. He's going to need it.* With a heavy sigh, she went back to work.

Nathan's mind was starting to turn as sleep began to fade and the grogginess gradually dissipated. He had regained consciousness only yesterday afternoon. That was twenty-four hours ago, and twelve of those hours he had spent sleeping, yet already he'd been able to go over the sequence of events leading up to his ambulance ride. Was there a part of him that regretted he didn't die? He wasn't really sure. He wasn't even sure about his own motives. What he did know was that Sabine had gone from his life forever and he, and only he, was the force that drove her away. And that sickened him. Forty-two years had still not taught him how to keep from pushing people away. He didn't even think there was any marked improvement, as the pattern was so well entrenched in his life that once he got into the groove, there was no stopping him. He had wanted desperately to stop himself with Sabine, but to no avail.

Now here he was, sitting alone in a sterile hospital and she hadn't even come to see him. Marc told him she had been there but had decided it was best not to come in. It doesn't get much clearer than that. She had finished with him for good and he couldn't blame her, as he had been a real bastard. *I am a real bastard, truth be told. Always trying to be the best. Always putting other people down when they're doing better than me. Look at how I treat my little brother.* He continued along this painful route of mental contemplation. Marc, the do-no-wrong thorn in his side. Was it his brother's fault that the standard Marc chose to live by was higher than his own? When was he going to stop trying to keep up and just get on and live his own life? Arghh. The book signing. He'd forgotten all about it and didn't even ask if it had been a success. And Marc had been down here every day while he'd been oblivious to the effects he'd had on his brother's life. He would need to find a way to make amends, for once in his miserable life.

He looked up from his self-reflection to see the doctor peering at him through the small window, inserted at eye level into the door to his room. She entered without knocking—this wasn't a hotel after all, he bemused—and came to stand beside his bed, clipboard in hand, pen at the ready. "How are you feeling this morning? How's the head?" She was poised to make notes but also showed genuine concern.

"Better," came his scratchy reply. "A bit better." He noticed her mark something down and then look back at him with deep brown eyes. She was a beautiful woman and obviously intelligent. No ring, he observed, although that didn't necessarily mean anything these days, unless there had been one. *Wow, Nate, twenty-four conscious hours since Sabine dumped you and already you're checking out someone new. You are a bastard.* His thoughts took him back to the woman standing before him, who caught the slight smile at the corners of his mouth.

"Happy to hear that. We'd like to keep you here until the end of the week, just until all the swelling has gone down in your brain and the surrounding tissue has had a chance to heal. Then we'll be able to ascertain whether anything will need special attention and we'll go from there. Let's set Friday as a release date, unless there are any changes?"

He started to launch into a witty response but thought better of it, and nodded his understanding. He didn't need to impress anyone here. He simply needed to get himself well.

"Your brother and his girlfriend were here earlier but I told them you needed to sleep, so he said he'd be back early this afternoon to check in. He asked if there was anything he could bring in for you so if you'd like I can have one of the nurses call him. Is there anything you'd like from home?"

"No… thank you," he said. It was all he could manage and he closed his eyes to signal he had had enough for one session. She took the hint and left, allowing him to get back to his thoughts.

Girlfriend? He didn't know Marc had a girlfriend. Had he been so self-absorbed that Marc didn't even confide in him about something so important? And how long had they been seeing each other? He felt shame and sadness. Either Marc had told him and he had forgotten, as it was a detail that hadn't registered as important enough for him to keep in his head, or he had decided not to tell him, knowing he didn't give a damn about Marc's life anyway. Either prospect was deflating and as the truth started to filter through, he wondered how many other things he'd been doing, to how many other people, in this way. Sabine. God, no wonder she left. Who else? His associates at work, his family, Marc, of course. This was the way he'd been living his life.

Sabine had once called him her little victim and she was his martyr and he vehemently denied it. On the heels of his denial, she'd also informed him that when you are irritated by a trait in someone else it's a sure indication you have that same trait in spades, and seeing it in someone reminds you it needs some work and you get a chance to see what it looks like in another person. As he listened to the voice in his head, 'poor me' was a common theme and he was appalled at the pattern he saw unfolding. He wasn't a psychologist, but he knew enough about victims—the most irritating attribute a human could display, in his opinion—and how they all needed to blame the world so they wouldn't have to take responsibility for their own shortcomings, as it would be too frightful to contemplate. Sabine's words haunted his thoughts. 'The most irritating traits are ones you, yourself, have.' No. It can't be true. *He* was a pathetic victim? *He* was blaming the world? Oh, God, it was all coming to light now. It was almost glaringly obvious, except he still didn't understand most of it. But he knew he wouldn't be able to let this concept slip back into oblivion without trying to sort through the labyrinth of his emotions.

He started to see how a week in this bed was going to be hell, now that this new discovery would be opening up all kinds of things he'd managed to successfully bury—until now. Let's get it over with, then, he decided, with less enthusiasm than he had hoped to muster.

Denial is a powerful thing and its insidious nature had been wreaking havoc in his life since he was young. He started to wonder if he could hire a psychotherapist to move into his room with him for a week. Then maybe he would be able to get through this by Friday, all in one shot. That was his way of approaching life. The shortest distance between two points is always a straight line. Not always the least *painful* path to take but definitely the fastest. What's the rush, he wondered, and then told himself to turn it off—the self-analysis was taxing his brain and now he wanted to rest.

Sabine and Marc were having lunch a short distance from the hospital. They had discovered a quaint little bistro and were pleased to get some real food for a change. Both of them had spent a lot of time at the hospital this last week, Marc more than Sabine, but she had made an effort to go with him as much as possible while they waited for Nathan to wake up. Now that he was conscious they'd decided that she wouldn't go back, so this lunch was a way for her to be with Marc but not be seen again at the hospital, as neither of them wanted Nathan to get the wrong idea. They talked amiably over mixed green salads and a crisp glass of white wine. The stress of Nathan's unknown recovery had passed and there was a sense of abandon about them and a desire to celebrate life.

"What do you think he will do, now that he's come back from nearly dying? Do you think anything will change?" Sabine had voiced the questions that had been on both their minds, but Marc was hoping she was only curious and not optimistic for a possible reconciliation. As if reading his thoughts she added, "Not that I could ever be with him again. Too much damage has been done. But he truly is a good man, and I wish him well."

"Me, too, although he has been a pain in the ass to both of us, me for much longer, and if *this* doesn't change his self-absorbed behavior I can't imagine anything else will, and we will all be forced to live out our lives with him in his current miserable state." They both groaned at the thought and smiled at each other, knowing it was unlikely. Life had a way of nudging people out of their ruts, and any attempt to go idly along was no guarantee that you wouldn't experience the odd shake-up to get you back on track. Anyone who took the time to look inside at all would usually get more than they bargained for and that was likely what had occurred for Nathan—he had been shaken up. Now they would wait and see what he would to do with it all. Marc paid the check, looked at his watch and said it was time for him to head back. They left together and walked arm in arm to the parking lot, to stand outside Sabine's car for a moment before going their respective ways. "You know I couldn't have gotten through this without you, Sabine. You are a true friend and I can't thank you enough."

"*Shhh.* None of that. It's no more than you would have done for me and we both know it. I'm just glad it had a happy ending. Remember to wish him a belated happy birthday from me, okay? But just that."

"I had completely forgotten about it. I think I'll pick him up a nice journal on my way back. He has some time on his hands at the moment and he might want to put some things down on paper. I know it helps me to get things sorted out when I'm off track. Thanks for the reminder. I'll call you later, okay?"

"Okay, and Marc? You're the best—don't ever forget it…" With those words, Sabine got into her car and headed back home, giving him a wave and a smile before he was out of view. He stood there thinking about her and what she'd said. He wished there was some kind of spark there. Some hint of passion, but there was none. Lots of love, though, for which he was grateful. It would be messy anyway if he were to fall in love with his brother's ex-girlfriend. Having her as a friend was better overall.

Marc rapped lightly on the tiny window and then let himself in to see his brother sitting up, propped against several pillows, reading his novel. "I'll try not to feel insulted that it took a near-death experience for you to finally pick up my book. Maybe I'll take it as an esteemed compliment." He leaned over and kissed his brother affectionately on the cheek. "Here, I brought you something." He laid the unwrapped journal on Nate's lap, sat back on the uncomfortable metal-armed chair, slid off his coat and waited for a response.

He sat there for a few more moments until Nathan finally looked up, as if startled, and said, "Oh. When did you get here, bro? I was so engrossed in this book I didn't realize you'd come in."

"Nice recovery, Nate."

"In all seriousness, it really is quite good. I started it this morning and can't put it down, although it's giving me a blasted headache, but I wouldn't take that personally. Probably more post-scotch related with a mix of eye strain. Thanks for the journal. That's fine calfskin leather, I see. Very thoughtful of you, Marc."

"I knew you'd have some free time this week and thought you might be doing a bit of thinking. Writing has always been cathartic for me so thought it might be for you as well. If not, it's a classy addition to any bookcase so either way I thought it'd be a safe bet."

"Funny you should mention that. I've had a few interesting insights while counting the dots in each ceiling tile. Did you know each one is actually different and they range anywhere from 400 to 650 dots per tile? I'm thinking about doing a little paper on it."

"Amazing. I knew you'd come up with some interesting ideas lying around for weeks on end."

"It's one week, my friend—I had a chat with our lovely young doctor this morning. And seriously, I started analyzing my behavior this morning and came up with a few shocking discoveries. Not quite ready to share but I will say this: some humble pie will be involved and you will surely enjoy the show."

"You've got my attention now. I can't wait to hear the gory details." Marc was half-serious. He thought this experience would change Nate's attitude but hadn't realized it would happen so soon. After years of speculation, maybe, but only one day after waking up? He'd heard of

120

near-death experiences changing people's attitudes forever, but seeing it in the flesh was surprising.

"I knew I could count on you to support me through my transformation. And thanks… for… for getting me through this far." His face had turned serious and his eyes glistened with emotion. "I owe you my life, Marc, and I know someday I'll be more grateful to you than I am in this moment. So thanks, for the future moment, in case we both forget."

"Actually, it's your maid you owe your life to, and I would start by giving her a week off with pay and a spa day, but that's me. You do as you wish, although if you don't at least send flowers and a card I'm firing her on your behalf and she's coming to work for me."

"Point taken. Now enough about me. Tell me about your new girlfriend." Nathan raised his eyebrows up and down in a boyish gesture.

Marc was confused and it showed. "Girlfriend? What girlfriend? I had a date this week—sorry, bro, but you were the one half dead, not me—and she was nothing special. Well, she might be, but we only just met."

"Did she meet you for a drink in the hospital cafeteria? The doctor said 'you and your girlfriend' would be back this afternoon." Now Nathan appeared confused, and seeing Marc's facial expression change to a grimace, his curiosity was piqued even more.

Marc closed his eyes and reached up and touched his fingers to his forehead, gently rubbing it with his thumb and forefingers, a habit Nathan knew well, indicating something serious was coming. "She didn't want you to know so you wouldn't get the wrong impression, but that must have been Sabine. She's been here with me, on and off, for most of the week. I'm sorry, Nate."

"*Sabine's* your *girlfriend?*" Nathan was having difficulty suppressing the rage boiling up through his chest, his eyes taking on that angry glare Marc had been privy to since he was a young child.

"You are such an idiot. No, Nate. That's not what I meant. Sabine is *not* and never will be, my *girl*friend. But she is a good friend and cares about what's happening. The doctor must have seen us holding each other in the hallway when we didn't know yet if you'd come out of it or not. She was pretty shaken up by this whole mess and so was I. God, you have the scariest eyes when you're angry. You still scare the shit out of me, you know?"

Nate thought this was about the funniest thing he'd heard today and laughed easily at himself and his own insecurities. "You're right, Marc. It is so like me to jump to the wrong conclusion and then lash out without cause. Sorry, man. Oh, but the look on your face. Do I really scare you that much? My, my, I *am* a bastard, aren't I?"

"Yes, you're a mean, scary bastard and always have been. But I still love you, although God knows why, the hell you've put me through—just this last week alone, never mind the last thirty-nine years. Better you than me, though. I wouldn't trade places with you for anything." The words were out of his mouth before he had a chance to stop them, or retract them and he sucked in his breath as he looked guiltily at Nathan, wrinkling his face as if preparing to get punched.

"Ouch. That one hurt." Nathan paused for a moment, thinking about what he wanted to say. "But you're right, little brother. The truth hurts sometimes and I think it may be about time for me to swallow a dose of reality. You've said a lot in that mouthful—all words I needed to hear—and I am planning to put that journal to use. There's a lot of buried stuff in here," he said, tapping his chest with his index finger, "and I'm the only one brave enough—or stupid enough, not sure which—to go in there and dig it out. Thanks for handing me the shovel, but I think I can take it from here on my own, without you jumping up and down on it with your steel-toed boots." He gave Marc a wounded sideways smile, and then looked down at his hands in resignation.

"Anytime you need my help, I'll be here. Whether it's to jump on the shovel, twist the knife…" he didn't finish but his attempt at lightening the mood worked. They both felt the pain of the moment. No apology was necessary—that was understood. Marc had spoken a long-held truth and *he* felt better expressing it, which was important to him. If it got Nathan pointed in a healthier direction then all the better.

"And Sabine's been here all week? That is one incredible woman." He saw Marc wanting to jump in to defend her actions but he held up his hand, "Uh-uh-uh, let me finish. She's an incredible woman and I will always regret the day I let her walk… no, the day I *shoved* her out of my life. That's what I wanted to say."

Before either of them could add more to his comment, the door opened and Dr. Menzies walked in, as promised. "Hello gentlemen."

"Hello, Doctor," they responded simultaneously, and then Nathan added, "We were just talking about Sabine and I was reiterating what you'd said about my brother making out with my ex-girlfriend in the hall the other day."

The doctor looked flustered, and replied, "*Your* girlfriend?" Her first thought was horror at betraying this man's secret and the implications it may have already had on her patient. She then quickly glanced over at Marc apologetically, who was rolling his eyes and shaking his head at his brother.

"If it's not too late to pull the plug on his life support, I'd like to reconsider. My brother is attempting a bit of humor at your expense and this may be the only chance I get to legally kill him. What do you say? No other witnesses? Just you and me, Doc, hmm?" and he turned to Nathan with a chiding look.

"My apologies, Dr. Menzies. He's right. We had been having a serious discussion about what a prick I can be and just to nail the point home I added one more piece to the near-complete puzzle, confirming his, and your suspicions forevermore. Sabine is my ex-girlfriend, the one who dumped me on that fated night last Friday. She is also Marc's good friend, and unbeknownst to me, she's been coming to the hospital to give him support and apparently show concern for me as well, although I believe that was secondary. I was confused when you'd made reference to Marc's girlfriend, as I hadn't been aware that he had one, and was pissed at him and myself for not knowing about her. I guess bringing you into the fray was my way of punishing you for what you'd led me to believe. I know, I know—you didn't know, so that's why I am apologizing. More fodder for my journal. Possibly you have the name of a good psychotherapist, now that you know how much damage was done by the scotch." Nathan was suitably abashed and his charm subdued her initial anger at his little prank.

"Don't listen to him, Doc. These issues have been present for as long as I have known him and the scotch was only a catalyst. I think intensive psychotherapy is a fine idea. Let's arrange it before you deem him fit enough to make his own decisions. Where do I sign?"

Nathan jumped in. "I won't fight you on this, Marc. I was actually being serious. I'm one messed up guy and keep getting in my own way."

"I agree," Dr. Menzies was nodding, "about the therapy, that is."

"Me, three," was Marc's contribution, and both men looked at the doctor for a further prognosis.

"Well, then, I can check off one of the things I had wanted to discuss with you both. Next, your release date. I had initially said Friday but now I'm thinking you'll be ready by Thursday, which is only a few days away. Let's plan for that and make sure you have everything organized at home and that you'll have the care you need once you're there. I am also insisting that you don't return to work for three weeks after that. I don't care what you do for a living. They'll have to manage without you and, if you contravene my recommendation I may just have to throw you back in here. So, your choice, capice?"

"I think you might want to look up the word 'choice' in the dictionary, Doc," Nate interjected with a wry smile, "but yes, I understand and will make the arrangements. Anything else?"

She hesitated for a moment before she replied. "Mr. Bouchard, you have had a brush with death. Do not waste it by forgetting too quickly." She smiled warmly at them both, almost embarrassed by her personal words, and left them looking at each other in bewilderment. "She wants me," was Nate's typical reaction.

Marc only laughed out loud and countered, "You wish, brother," and their joined laughter could be heard into the hall.

Madeline Menzies knew they weren't laughing *at* her but she had a strong sense they were laughing at something to do with her, and her curiosity was aroused. It was rare for her to find someone so interesting. Most men she met were so caught up in their own grief— understandably so—that she never saw beyond the extremes of their emotion. She also realized she'd be jeopardizing her practice if she didn't avoid patient/doctor relations, including extended family and friends. If asked, 'How did you two meet?' she never wanted her story to be, 'Oh, you'll never believe it. One of my patients was dying, and his brother came to visit. You know, we just got to know each other, supporting him through it all…

On the flip side, a worse tale would be when the question was, 'Why did you never meet anyone?' and her answer: 'Because I always follow the rules.' She knew 'technically' that it wouldn't be right, but it wasn't like he was her patient. And if she were discreet, who would know? Life wasn't being handed to her on a silver platter. You sometimes had to maneuver your way through it, and she was hoping this might be one of those times, and that Marc Bouchard would prove to be worth it.

She wasn't sure about this Sabine woman, though. They seemed awfully close for just friends. But if the brothers' comments were accurate, hats off to them both. His brother's girlfriend, no less. That takes a lot of certainty on both their parts. All three, really, because Nathan would have to be on board with the friendship as well, which he obviously had been. So, what was she going to do about it, if anything? Come on, Maddie, get off your comfy horse and go for it. She wondered how the hospital board would view the situation. What they don't know… She went home that night, devised a plan and fell asleep with him on her mind.

Thursday arrived quickly for everyone but Nathan. He had spent six grueling days with countless hours on his hands and nothing to do but read (which strained his eyes), write (which triggered unwanted emotional gunk that had been nicely buried for years) and talk to his brother (which was tiring them both, now that he was feeling so much better.)

Dr. Menzies was nervously stalking the main desk of his floor, long since changed from the ICU. When she saw Marc come off the elevator, the butterflies in her stomach lurched and she took a deep breath for courage and headed him off before he reached his brother's room. "Marc, wait up. Can I talk to you about something before you go in there?"

He sensed her unease. *Oh my God, something's happened and he's not being released. They found a tumor or a blood clot, or worse.* He was working himself up to such a frenzy that their nervous energy started bouncing off of each other, escalating the tension in the corridor. Instead of answering, he nodded quickly, up and down, not trusting his voice.

She was unaware of his mannerisms, being so caught up in her own discomfort, so she missed any cues about his impatience and fear. "Marc, I wanted to ask you something—of a *personal* nature—if that's alright." She hoped he'd take the hint and make it easier for her.

His mind was spinning as he tried to guess the relevance of her choice of words but merely nodded again and mouthed, with a small audible sound escaping, "Yes, of course."

She sighed heavily, only increasing his discomfort, and blurted it out, "I was hoping you would consider going to dinner with me, possibly even this evening, if you're free?" She held her breath, waiting for his response, and his hesitation was not a favorable sign.

"To discuss my brother?" still trying to sort out the gravity of their conversation.

"No, Marc. You're making this difficult for me, aren't you? On a *personal* note, like a date. You know, two people going out for some conversation, get to know each other?" She looked at him expectantly, hoping for some indication of his interest. What he did next was so unexpected she was initially deeply offended.

He burst out laughing. "Oh… Dr. Menzies…"

"Madeline."

"Madeline. I'm sorry, this is too funny." The look she gave him was not one of humor and he quickly recovered, reaching out to hold her arm gently in reassurance. "Oh, no, not that. That's not why I'm laughing. Oh, I'm so terribly sorry. I see why you're looking at me like

125

that. No, *truly*, it's not that. I'm laughing in relief. I thought my brother was dying, or dead, or had some incurable disease or something, and you wanted to discuss it in private, friend to friend, so when I finally got it... Oh, please forgive me, Dr... Madeline. Please forgive me, Madeline. I was completely taken aback. But now that I've recovered I would love nothing more than to go for dinner with you—are you allowed to, by the way? No matter. I think tonight would not be soon enough, that is if you're still game after my ungodly behavior."

And the look he gave her was so sincere, so forlorn; she couldn't help but laugh, too. "Well, your initial reaction wasn't the one I was hoping for, but your second made up for it, so I think I can forgive you. How is *Karma* at 8?"

"Perfect. Shall I make the reservations?" Marc had fully recovered and had already started estimating how much time he would have to wait before their date.

"Yes, thanks. I'll be tied up here until shortly before so that would be easier for me. Meet you there?"

Her smile disarmed him and he smiled back before replying, "Yes. I'm looking forward to it." He lightly squeezed her arm and his hand slowly brushed down her forearm to her long, strong fingers. She felt a shock course through her arm and stood gaping at him as he walked away.

He almost skipped into Nathan's room and his brother noticed the change in his mood immediately. "Today's the big day, big brother, and I bet you can't wait to get home and out of this dive." His enthusiasm was a touch over the top and Nathan kept watching him for clues to his exuberance. "I've got the car out front, ready to whisk you back to your place. I also have a service hired to do all your cooking and cleaning for the next three weeks, and they're top notch."

"I thought you and I could have dinner together tonight. You know, 'thanks for everything,' and all that?"

"No can do, mon frère. *I've* got a date, but I thought it'd be nice to call Mom and have her stop over with some of her home cooking. She was here nearly every day, hovering over you like a lioness, and she really wants to see you—you know how she's been. She asked if she could come over tonight and have dinner with us and I said that would be wonderful. That was before I knew I wouldn't be there, though, so it's you and Mama, I'm afraid. Hope you don't mind."

"So what you're saying is some woman you hardly know is more important than me? Is that what you're saying?"

"Absolutely. Always has been. Always will be. No surprise there." This banter was common between them and he knew Nate wouldn't mind, but his brother liked to try to play the guilt card once in a while and Marc wasn't taking the bait.

"Fair enough. Anyone I know?" He raised his eyebrows again in that childish way of his.

"I never kiss and tell. Well, I haven't actually kissed her yet but I tell you what. I'll call you tomorrow and tell you all about it. Or some parts of it, depending how I feel, okay?"

"Wow, that is some generous offer. Thanks *so* much." Then, changing his tone, he added, "I hope you have a nice time tonight. I know it's been a long couple of weeks. You've earned a night off," and then after a pause, he continued. "A bit of brotherly advice? If you need to wind down after, stick with wine and stay away from the scotch."

"Good advice, and I hope you heed it yourself. Now, let's get you out of here before someone changes their mind." Both men headed for the door, Nathan in front, Marc following slowly behind, holding his arm just under Nathan's elbow, ready in case he lost his balance.

"I'm not an invalid, Marc. I can walk unassisted, you know." He flung his arm down, pushing Marc's hand out of the way. Madeline was watching the interaction, visibly enjoying the banter. "Will you tell this idiot behind me to give me some space? He's more likely to trip me with his good intentions and land me right back in this dump if he doesn't back off."

"It's true, Marc. You need to let him stand on his own two feet. He's fine, really." Then to Nathan, "How are you feeling? Are you ready to go?"

"I feel better than I've felt in years, so yes, I'm ready."

"That's good to hear. But don't do too much too quickly. That's an order. And make sure you have people around to help. I don't want you to do much of anything for the next two weeks, and no work for three, as I said."

"Marc's arranged people to come in to cook and all that until I'm 100%."

He's thoughtful, too. She added this data to the notes she'd already started in her head.

"It's so he doesn't have to come over to see me himself but I can respect that. He's got his own life to lead."

"Nathan's pissed because I've got a date tonight that I've chosen over spending another boring evening with him alone in his uptight apartment with our mother, no less."

127

"Ah, I see." Madeline had a flash of guilt herself, but then thought better of it. "Well, that was selfish of you, I agree, but it looks like you two will work it out, hmm?"

The three of them walked leisurely to the elevator, where Madeline had a few more suggestions she wanted to share with Nathan, and then when the doors slid open, both men took her hand in turn, shook it gratefully, and walked on, waving goodbye as the doors slid closed. "She was a great doctor, wasn't she Marc?"

"Yes, I think she is," Marc said, intentionally changing the verb tense and smiling slyly to himself.

Chapter XV

Marc couldn't wait to dump Nathan at his building and get home to prepare for tonight. Okay, maybe that was a bit offensive, but it had been a long time since he'd gone out with a woman that he was actually interested in. There was a niggling feeling in the back of his mind. Something he couldn't put his finger on, but it was strong enough to keep him mildly cautious. Probably just nerves, he thought, and brushed it aside. He picked up the sauntering pace and steered Nathan to the car, stood by the door, careful not to help him, but ready just in case, waited for him to get all appendages in, and then closed the door. Then he ran over to the driver's side, where he hopped in, started the engine, checked briefly behind him and (ignoring the hospital speed zone) accelerated into traffic toward the inner harbor.

Marc made sure Nathan was settled and comfortable in his space before he left, locking the door behind him with his spare key. Nate needed to figure this one out for himself, he thought, and suppressed the feelings of guilt trying to surface. His house was only a few minutes away, nestled in a quiet neighborhood close to the city's center. He would often walk to his brother's house, or follow the ocean on its winding path to the inner harbor, where all kinds of trendy restaurants and shops were springing up. *Karma* was right on the water in the city's core, but he had no intention of walking tonight. Or driving. He would catch a cab in case his nerves increased his alcohol intake, which had been known to happen on occasion.

As soon as he got home, he hopped in the shower and, once dried and freshly shaven, rummaged through his well-organized closet in search of something perfect to wear for this evening. *Karma* was a bit on the glam side, so he opted for a jacket and crisp white shirt with flannel pants and moccasin loafers. His cufflinks were of brushed platinum, an extravagant gift from his parents when they first learned of his novel being picked up by a publisher. They wanted to honor his success and he was touched by the gesture. They had never been overly demonstrative, so a gift like this was rare. Marc savored the feeling as he buttoned up his shirt. No tie, to keep things simple, but not too casual, either. He looked at his reflection in the full-length mirror, propped up against the wall, and was happy with what he saw. He wasn't overly handsome, in his view, but he worked with what he had and accentuated his athletic built and tall stature. He ran his fingers roughly through his wavy hair and tousled it lightly. He was long overdue for a cut but there would be no time tonight, so he shrugged his shoulders in resignation and grabbed his suede coat for an expected cool night later on.

The cab got him there just before eight and he casually headed toward the double doors, where a young girl was standing under the awning, waiting to let people in. Once in the dark foyer, he went straight to the young woman at the front desk and greeted her warmly. "Chantelle, nice to see you're still here. I have a reservation for eight o'clock. Something overlooking the water, I hope?"

"For you, of course. I saw your name on the reservation list, spelled with a 'C' and was wondering if it was you. We haven't seen you in a while. I heard about your book's success, though—imagine that's keeping you busy. Congratulations. Not to sound too much like a groupie, but maybe I could get a signed copy sometime?" Chantelle batted her eyelashes in an exaggerated fashion and winked.

"Depends on the table." He paused for effect. "I'm teasing, of course. You must get tired of the bribes and threats for good seating. I'd love to, any time. Now, what have you got for me this evening?"

She gestured for him to follow as she wound her way to the far left of the large curved dining area and pointed to a quaint booth at the end with magnificent views of the harbor lights. "I was hoping something intimate was what you had in mind?"

"This is perfect. Thank you, my friend," he said, without giving a clear yes or no to her assumption. Just as she was turning to leave, Chloé appeared from his other side, making her way back from the lady's room. She had almost walked by him when he reached out and tapped her shoulder.

She spun around in irritation and then as quickly her eyes lit up in a smile of recognition, "Marc. I didn't see you hovering over in the corner. So nice to see you again." And then discreetly lowering her voice, she added, "I was so sorry to hear about Nathan. Sabine told me that he's recovered nicely—thank God—but it must have been a shock for you. Are you all right?" She now had one of his hands in hers and was looking intently at him to pick up any signs of him trying to hide the truth in his words.

"Thanks, Chloé, I'm fine now. Really. It was a wake-up call for us all." It was in this position, standing facing Chloé, his hand in hers, that he caught a movement out of the corner of his eye and glanced up to see Madeline gliding toward him in a silk dress, with thin straps accentuating her strong shoulders and arms. She had a patterned pashmina draped loosely over her shoulders, and the vision had him stunned. He abruptly pulled his hand free from Chloé's grasp and Chloé turned around to follow his gaze. So obvious from his expression that he knew this person, she merely turned in greeting. What she saw deflated her recent buoyancy, as this woman was drop-dead gorgeous. She couldn't help speculate with a jealous pang that Marc was obviously doing just fine after all.

Madeline also took in the scene with one glance and was quick to feel her territorial instincts flare. Then she remembered how hasty she'd been at the hospital when she assumed Sabine and Marc were lovers and here she was, doing it again. A man like Marc obviously had lots of friends, male and female alike, and she quickly revised her opinion and rose to the challenge of being gracious and sincere. She arrived between them, smiling first at Marc and then at the strange woman with the alluring eyes. Marc leaned in and kissed her lightly on the cheek, whispering "Wow," ever so quietly in her ear. She felt a jolt run through her jaw, all the way down her spine and experienced a sense of déjà vu that momentarily rendered her speechless. The kiss caught her off guard and she blushed profusely, letting all her insecurities melt away. She mouthed "thank you" to him and then turned to the other woman, with her hand extended. "Hi. I'm Madeline."

"Chloé. Nice meeting you," she said, doing her best to sound sincere but her inner dialogue of "I hate this woman" was creating an unavoidable edge to her greeting. "I was just about to head back to my friends, but enjoy your dinner. The crab cakes are the best in the city, if you're so inclined." Head held high, she turned away from them both and walked through the maze of tables to the other end of the room, hips swaying gently, reminding Marc of their first encounter. It felt like years ago, and he had a twinge of regret when he realized he and Chloé had a spark that night that both had intended to pursue at Nathan's birthday dinner. No wonder she was a bit frosty with Madeline. He'd have to talk to her more about it another time.

Looking over at Madeline, his thoughts of Chloé quickly dissipated. He held out his arm, indicating she should sit, and did the same, both sliding around the booth to capture the view and create an excuse to sit closer together instead of directly across the table from each other. "That was Sabine's assistant. We met at a gathering the night of Nathan's scotch debauchery and I think she had hoped we'd connect. I'm sorry if it was awkward."

She was surprised at his direct honesty and thought it boded well for the evening. But she'd have to play her cards right to avoid any mishaps. Chloé didn't appear to be someone to underestimate. To respond in kind, she said, "No, not at all. I would have probably felt the same—a bit like the fish that got away. I'm not the type to play those kinds of games so if it's something you'd still like to pursue I'd rather know at the beginning of the evening, if you don't mind." That was possibly in the white-lie department, as game playing was part of the fun for her, and she felt it was about to begin, but she sensed Marc had more of a distaste for it, so the honesty card was the way to go to keep things on track.

Marc took a long, slow sip of his water, buying time before he responded. There were so many directions he could take this conversation but which way did he want it to go? On its present course it may get too heavy too soon and although these were all topics he wanted to discuss, he wasn't all that sure about starting there. He set his water glass gently down, looked up at her, smiled, and said, "Madeline, life has put us both here at this time. I'm not about to question why or what, if. I live my life from the present moment and play full out with whatever I'm dealt. When I jump right into something with both feet what tends to happen is it runs its course quickly, but I do give 100%. What I mean is that because I'm sitting here with you, this is the direction I know I'm meant to take, until that direction changes. If you stand up, throw your water at me and storm out of here, that would be an example of a change in direction." He hesitated, waiting to see if she had any plans along those lines, and when she smiled back, knowing she enjoyed the example, he continued. "Otherwise, until we are clear— either mutually or individually—that this is not a direction we want to pursue, only at that time would I stop and take a different path. Does that sound fair?"

"More than fair. And if there is a change, I promise not to throw water, or anything, else at you. At least I'll *try* not to." Madeline smiled warmly at Marc, wiggled in her seat to get more comfortable and then settled in for what looked to be a promising date.

They chose a mid-range bottle of red wine (both preferred the more full-bodied variety, so it was an easy choice) and then studied their menus for less than a minute before they closed them and laid them on the table. Neither of them ordered the crab cakes and both inwardly smiled at the intentional pass on Chloé's suggestion but said nothing to each other. Once the details of the appetizers and dinners were decided and ordered they got ready to launch into their first date, both full of questions, both unsure of how much to probe.

Madeline asked her first question and then sat back, surveying this man across the table. His voice was hypnotic and she loved the way he used words and strung them together in unusual phrases and quirky combinations. She thought he would make a great professor of philosophy and felt herself being drawn into his story, his life. He started in on his family roots and his French grandparents and how their culture had been so important but that most of his generation had lost interest. His great-great-great-grandfather had been in Napoleon's army and they had always been proud of that, but he knew little of the history and regretted not pulling those details from family members while they were still alive. There was baroque music playing in the background and as Madeline took a few slips of wine, the lull of his voice and the music lifted the week's tension from her body. Something he said made her grin knowingly and she leaned her head back on the high cushions and closed her eyes for a brief moment of reflection.

In that moment, visions shot through her mind of her standing in a large, elegant dining room and she was flooded with a sense of foreboding and panic. She opened her eyes wide and stared directly at Marc, showing him a look that stopped his speech mid-breath. "Madeline. Are you all right? What's wrong? You look like you're going to pass out." He was hovering over her with concern and waiting anxiously for her to speak.

"I… I… I'm fine… I don't know what happened. I had these strange feelings and you were there, but you weren't there…" Her voice trailed off but she recovered quickly to say, "I think it must be the wine. I realized I didn't have a chance to eat today so it must have gone right to my head. It was so *strange*. Marc, I'm sorry to have startled you. I'm fine, really. I'll just have some of this bread and lay off the wine until after dinner. Please, continue."

She didn't feel completely fine but couldn't pinpoint what had just happened and didn't want to waste any time now trying to figure it out. She would go over it all again later once she got home and was alone. *He really was sweet to show such concern.* "You were telling me about your grandparents' history in France. How far does your family go back, do you know?"

Marc was watching her closely and started back where he left off, one eye on her the entire time he was talking, but he was enjoying relaying parts of his family history and his own part in it all, and she was an avid listener, putting in a question here or a comment there. She even laughed at his occasional attempts at humor and surprisingly got most of his subtle plays on words and concepts. He was enjoying this immensely but was getting ready to wind down. It was her turn to tell her story and he was keen for her to get started. "That's the *Reader's Digest* version of my life so far. What about you, Madeline? Tell me about your family. Your life. Your passions."

"I don't remember you sharing any of *your* passions, Marc. But I'll see what I can come up with on such short notice." She had completely recovered from her earlier lapse and was happy to talk about herself with such an inquisitive listener. The nature of her profession dictated that she listen to people's problems ad nauseam at times, and she didn't discuss her personal life with anyone at work, nor did she share her professional or personal challenges with her friends. They had all known her for varying lengths of time and she had created a habit where she was the strong one. Her friends went to *her* to lean on, not the other way around.

With Marc, she was able to talk about her life from a fresher, more mature perspective. His input and feedback were insightful and appreciated, and she found herself discussing the dilemma of one of the doctors at the hospital whose chauvinistic attitudes were archaic and getting in the way of her advancement. She shared with him the tragic death of one of her patients and the emotions she went through, and was still going through around that. Where did her responsibility lie? Could she have done more? Was there a God, and if so, where was his hand in all of this mess? Questions like these she mulled over on a daily basis. The two of them started picking up one of the topics and hashing out the possibilities. Their food arrived and they ate absently, each engrossed in the other's words and ideas.

They laughed and debated and at one point, Madeline even cried when she spoke of her Mother's recent death, something she hadn't done in over a year. He reached his hand to her face and rubbed his thumb at the edge of her eye, wiping her tear gently onto his skin and then into her hair. He held his hand there for some moments and her heart started to pound as she thought he might lean in to kiss her. She wanted him to. She looked at him expectantly, her tears almost forgotten. Instead, he leaned in and kissed her gently at the crease of her eye, as if to kiss her tear away. His lips rested there for one long-held breath and then he leaned back into his seat, squeezed her hand and said, with great empathy, "I'm sorry." She felt a quick intake of breath as a new batch of tears attempted to come forward in response to his genuine care. For the first time, she realized she might be out of her depth and felt an undercurrent of fear. This was not turning out to be the game she had planned. She looked up and averted her eyes, only to catch Chloé's icy stare as she headed toward the door with her friends. The gauntlet had been thrown down and adrenaline replaced her unvoiced fears.

When they'd poured the last drops of wine and could ingest no more food, Marc gestured to the server for the bill. Madeline insisted on paying, which, for the first time that evening, rattled him. But she reminded him that she had invited *him*, which didn't happen often for either of them, so he needed to enjoy the moment and allow her to do this. He acquiesced graciously and offered to take her home, sharing a cab. When she gave her address to the cabbie, Marc chuckled and said, "I guess I'll be walking home from your place—you live three blocks from me. I'm over on Walnut, two blocks from the ocean. You know where the road curves in Roger's Bay?"

"Of course. It's just up the street. Small world, isn't it?" She almost reiterated a fact she'd read before meeting that a large percentage of couples lived within seven blocks of each other, but she realized just in time that that would be a bold statement. Instead, she instructed the cab driver to pull up just ahead on the right, in front of the tall cedar-hedge fence. Marc knew they were getting out on the ocean side of the street, a prestigious address by anyone's standards, but he had grown up surrounded by wealth and it didn't phase him in the least. He paid the cabbie and held the door open as Madeline shimmied across from her side to his and stretched her long, bare leg, ending with an intricately beaded shoe—unnoticed until this moment—onto the sidewalk outside her house.

Before she opened the wrought-iron gate she asked if he'd like to join her for a brandy. She wasn't ready to let the night end just yet and had a few more enticing tricks up her sleeve. When he graciously declined, not feeling ready to take the next step, that niggling doubt still at play, her outward demeanor shifted and she couldn't stop herself from making a sarcastic jab. "You know, when a girl buys you dinner, there's an expectation..." Inside, she felt chagrined. Marc, on the other hand, was not impressed by the comment. He gave her a tight smile, kissed her lightly on the cheek, thanked her again for dinner and pulled away.

"Good night, Madeline," and he left with the first residue of doubt.

The small apartment across the bridge from the city center had none of the charm or character of a home like Madeline's, but it did possess an uncommon flare born from a strong sense of style and strict budget. Chloé flung her knock-off Coach bag onto her hammerhead chair, hitting the border of tacks with a sharp 'ping.' "Shit. And shit, again. Why do all of the skinny women get the great men?" It wasn't the first time she had been jilted by a more beautiful woman. Men were always telling her how they loved a woman with shape, and big boobs, of course, but somehow when you added up the complete package, it wasn't what they loved at all. Big boobs look ridiculous on a skinny woman, she thought angrily. 'Don't they ever think of that?' She looked down at her bulging cleavage. "Sorry, girls, but I'm not taking you out—again." She glanced over at her reflection in the full-length mirror, propped against the wall in its final resting spot. She pivoted to see her profile, her skirt flaring slightly, her auburn hair bouncing in time with her breasts. Her body was toned and robust with curves in all the right places, plus a few extras. She had always been on the full-figured side—some would describe herself as voluptuous—and she was comfortable with who she was. She had no desire to be waif-like. *Except in moments like this.*

When she saw Marc this evening, she had been so relieved just to know he was okay. Then she hoped to pick up where they had left off the week before. She knew she had piqued his interest at his book signing and was ready to ask him out, when his scrawny date ran interference. Well, if he was one of those 'big boob' guys, Skinny Girl could have him. She grabbed her jacket, phone and some cash, and headed for the door, slamming it as she turned toward the stairs. She needed to get herself back into a positive space. A space she'd been in at the beginning of the evening before facing Marc at *Karma*. Or, more appropriately, facing her *karma* with Marc. *Missed him by that much. Shit.*

As he left Madeline's, the lingering, bitter taste sat stagnant in his mouth. A bit of confusion mixed with a sense that there were a few underlying traits to Madeline that had yet to reveal themselves, and his earlier elation turned to distrust and unease. He decided to take a detour along the water before he went home. It wasn't very late and he needed some time to reflect before settling in for the night. It had been quite the evening. Quite the week, really, and thoughts of the good doctor kept running around his brain.

She had everything he could imagine in a woman. Exceptional beauty, successful career, a great house on the ocean—not that he cared about that, but it still gave him insight into her priorities, and that appealed to him. She was perfect. His mother's unwelcome words flitted through his mind. "If it's too good to be true, it probably is." She was always so cynical, but now he wondered if he should start heeding her advice after all these years. He headed to his favorite rock, grabbing a few skipping stones on the way. The moon was full enough to easily make out the shoreline, and the breeze felt almost warm against his thin jacket. As he got closer, he realized someone was sitting on his rock. He was about to quietly turn away, when the silhouette turned toward him.

"Marc? Is that you? What are you doing here?"

"Chloé? I could ask you the same thing." He took the few steps toward her as she rubbed her sleeve along her cheek. "Chloé, are you alright? It looks like you've been crying."

"I'm fine, thanks. Well, I'm not exactly *fine* but I will be—*eventually*."

"Is there anything I can do?"

"You've done enough, thanks," she responded, more sarcastically than intended.

"Oh God. Is this about my date earlier? I'm sorry you had to see that. I meant to call..."

"Don't bother," she said, cutting him off. "You owe me nothing. I thought we'd connect again after your signing, but it wouldn't be the first time I've been wrong. It was just a case of wishful thinking."

It seemed like lifetimes ago. So much had happened, and yet they *had* made a nice connection, and now he was sorry he had dismissed it so easily. Dismissed her. He could be such an idiot. "We did make a connection, and then things went off the rails when Nate put himself in the hospital. It's been a chaotic couple of weeks."

At those words, Chloé felt remorseful at her attitude and found her compassionate place again. They began talking about their experiences in the past few weeks and the impact it had had. That led to talking about the past few years. He was so different from anyone she'd ever met. He was actually a lot like Sabine, but with a man's demeanor. She felt close to him almost instantly and they shared long-buried secrets, until Marc's practical nature broke the spell.

"Why don't we walk over to my place? I'm only a few blocks from here and I thought we could end the evening with a warm brandy. No funny stuff, I promise, but it would be a lot more comfortable than this rock, and I'm not ready to end our conversation."

They approached his house from the back, and walked up a wide bank of stairs. It was hard to discern much in the evening light, but the house appeared to be the craftsman style so popular on the West Coast at the turn of the century. Chloé loved the simple grandeur of it.

"The sky is still clear tonight so if you're warm enough, we can sit on the front porch and look at the stars." She followed him in to an eclectic back entry surrounded by world art, picked up, no doubt, on many of his travels. It was warm and welcoming without a hint of pretension. They headed toward the open kitchen and he walked right past the island and into the living room heading toward the French doors at the front.

"This must be nice to come home to every day." She turned to him as she spoke and he reached out to hand her a small glass of brandy.

"I never tire of this porch—ever. It has become a part of me and I don't feel I would ever be able to leave this house. It's magical, isn't it?" He reached around her and pulled up the authentic French door slide that bolted down into the floor. Twisting the handle, he pulled it toward them and motioned to Chloé to head outside. The patio was partially covered but he dragged two chairs closer to the edge, where a small antique table already stood. There were blankets slung over the backs of both chairs and he waited for her to sit and then settled into the other, both facing the sky but at 90 degrees, so they could still look at each other while talking, without missing out on the view.

They sat in silence for some time, enjoying the peaceful feeling that had settled in on them. Chloé took a sip of brandy, realizing too late that it was not a narrow-mouthed snifter, and taking a bigger first swallow than she'd intended. She coughed, and Marc realized what had happened. "Sorry about the glasses," he said. "I don't like snifters because they always hit the bridge of my nose and limit how much I can drink with each sip. Then you have to crane your neck back so you're looking at the guy behind you just to drain the last drops. Not very elegant, but I tend to take function over form nine times out of ten."

"I've never thought about it that way before, but you're right. They are awkward, aren't they? I've just become so used to having it served that way that it never dawned on me to change it. How do you feel about champagne glasses?" She was enjoying the lightness of their talk, relieved to learn he wasn't as highbrow as she thought he might be.

"I *love* champagne glasses, and champagne. Wouldn't change those for anything. They're meant to go together."

"Phew. That's a relief," she said as she wiped her forehead in a mock gesture. "I didn't know what I would think of you if you drank champagne from a regular glass. My entire image might have altered beyond repair."

"And then, '*voila.*' Change of direction?"

"Precisely. How did you know? Change of direction."

"A typical response to a typical situation. Wouldn't you agree?"

They were both sheltered by the half wall surrounding the porch, in typical Craftsman style. It created complete privacy from the street when seated but Chloé stood up and leaned against the porch's edge to get a better view of the sky. A sliver of moon was shining high and the stars and planets brightly scattered themselves against the black canvas. "Most definitely. Marc, thank you for this. For inviting me over. For saving me from the cold with this delicious brandy." Chloé was attempting to be gracious without sounding needy.

He stood up to join her, turning his back to the immense sky so he could face her. "I had intended to call you. Before everything came down with Nate, that's what I was planning to do."

"It's okay, Marc—you don't have to explain. I'm fine, really I am."

"I know you're fine, Chloé. I'm telling you because I want you to know, so you don't need to wonder. Seeing Madeline was a mistake. I don't even think she's supposed to be dating patients' brothers, but I can't be sure. It just felt wrong, and I'll clear it up with her in the morning."

"I don't want you to feel pressured to do anything. Or guilty. God, please don't do anything out of guilt."

"I wouldn't. I'm not." Marc lifted both hands to Chloé's face and pulled her toward him, kissing her lightly on her full lips. It was a slow, tentative movement and he hesitated briefly to gauge her response before parting his lips and running his tongue along her top lip, barely touching it, but feeling the moisture and fullness as a shiver coursed down his spine. She showed no signs of pulling away, so he kept his hands on her head and they held each other's gaze, intensifying the moment. She met his tongue with hers and then grabbed his bottom lip between both her lips and sucked gently, releasing it with a tiny pop. She placed her hands on his back and started running them down his shoulders and spine, pulling him instinctively toward her as she did. He continued kissing her, without breaking his stare.

She was getting highly aroused by the intensity of it and the simplicity of his movements. Light kisses, a light brush of his tongue on her mouth, then inside her mouth while looking deeply at her. She was used to closing her eyes and losing herself in her own fantasy, but this was different. She slowed her breathing to match his and slowed her motions simultaneously. She could feel his hardness pressing against her and yet he didn't lose his slow, methodic rhythm. Ever so gradually, he increased the pressure of his lips on hers and searched more deeply into her mouth with his tongue, still maintaining a slow pulse that was starting to drive her wild.

She stopped briefly to ask, her voice deep with longing, "Let me stay with you tonight." It wasn't a question so much as a statement she felt was a natural following of the turn of events.

His response took her off guard, "No, Chloé. I can't." When she started to pull away, her anger and hurt flared, and he increased the pressure he had been maintaining with his hands, keeping her head still close to him. He kissed her again, deeply this time and her head whirled in confusion. Finally, he said, "You and I will only get one 'first kiss,' one 'first time we make love.' I want them both to be memorable." He continued to kiss her gently, whispering as he spoke, while still looking into her eyes. "I want this kiss to leave you wanting more. To leave *us* wanting more of each other, so we both wake tomorrow and can't wait to call the other, not pausing for a moment to wonder if we should, or if this is right, or what the other will think. I want this kiss to leave us both knowing where we stand, without question. And I want us to enjoy the anticipation of our next meeting. Of what it will be like when we finally make love. I want to be madly distracted by imagining the curves of your body and the touch of your skin without knowing from experience. Wondering. Imagining. I want you so badly, Chloé—you are so damn beautiful—but I don't want us to ruin this by rushing."

She remained speechless, not wanting to break the spell he had cast. She was enthralled by his words and had to adjust her tempo and her screaming body so that the moment didn't get lost in her frenzied passion. She returned his kisses and started to give him a little bit more to think about as she teased his mouth with her tongue and pulled back from his lips only to come forward again, nipping his lips playfully. She could feel a slight sway in his hips and his control was starting to strain. "Now, play fair," he said, lustfully.

She slowed her pace as per his request. She had made her point and was now relishing the thought of a slow, almost-painful courtship. They continued in this way for several more minutes, gradually slowing together, not unlike two people having just made love, where there is a natural drawing away. A completion. He slid his hands down to her waist and leaned back into her hands, smiling. Her eyes glistened as she returned his smile. "I think I'm going to have to watch out for you," she said, in a guarded voice that was full of play.

"Oh, you're *definitely* going to have to watch out for me. Be careful, my friend. Be *very* careful." His smile betrayed his sly words. "I think it's time for me to call you a cab before I lose my self-respect and dignity."

When the cab arrived, Chloé grabbed her coat and brushed a light kiss on Marc's cheek. "That was some memorable kiss..." and she left into the star-filled night.

Chapter XVI

Chloé crawled back into bed with her freshly brewed coffee in one hand and Marc's novel in the other. Now that she'd met the man, she wanted to read it again with a different perspective. She'd slept late and was lazily starting her day, with no plans until work on Monday. She was into her third sip when the phone jarred her from her tranquility. "Shit. What is it now?" she mumbled under her breath. She quickly but carefully set her coffee on the nightstand and lunged for the phone. "Yes?" was her abrupt reply, expecting an unwanted intrusion.

"Chloé?" The voice sounded frantic.

"Yes?" she said, again, with more expectancy.

"Chloé, it's Marc. I *have* to see you. When can I come pick you up?"

"Marc, is everything all right? You sound upset."

"No, I'm fine—more than fine, in fact." He heard a deep sigh on the other end of the line. "I don't think I can wait much longer to see you. I've been up for four hours thinking of last night and waited as long as I could to call. So? An answer, please."

"You've caught me off guard. I'm still in bed, Marc. I'm reading and have just started my coffee, but I've just barely woken up."

"What are you wearing?" he asked, with a sexy drawl.

"Marc. It's 9:30 on a Saturday morning. I'm wearing flannel pajamas and wool socks, what do you think?" She never wore flannel and laughed at his audacity as she ran her hand along the smooth silky lines of her négligé.

"I think you probably look hot in flannel. Now, get dressed. I'm coming over in half an hour. We're going out." Click.

But you don't know where I live. Chloé was still holding the phone, mouth open in disbelief. He was pushy, this one. And get dressed? Into what? He didn't tell her where they were going or what they were doing. Exasperated, she hung up the phone, spun her bare feet out of bed and shook her head, laughing to herself. He was definitely going to keep things interesting. She hopped in the shower, keeping her hair dry—no time to wash it—and headed toward her closet, still perplexed about what to wear. She decided to go with her usual Saturday attire—jeans, a dressy T and a simple button-down sweater that she lived in on the weekends, throwing on a long silver and black beaded necklace to top off the look. She would choose her shoes after she saw what he had on. Her Doc Martens were by the front door, along with a dozen other varieties of flats and heels.

She wore little makeup but put on a subtle shade of lipstick and a touch of eyeliner and mascara, and rubbed on a couple of dabs of jasmine aromatherapy oil she liked to wear in lieu of perfume. She couldn't stand most perfumes on the market. They all smelled chemical to her.

She heard the buzzer as she was combing her hair and trying to revive it into life after a night's sleep. Let him wait, she thought, and she took her time finishing her hair. With one last look in the mirror as she passed by her dresser, she grabbed two pairs of socks—one sport and one black—and headed toward the door. It buzzed a second time as she came around the corner, but instead of running to let him in she continued at her unhurried pace and eventually pressed the intercom. "Third floor."

Marc arrived a short time later, barely out of breath. He took one look at her, pushed himself into her apartment, glanced around, grabbed her with both hands and kissed her full on the mouth. He didn't let up until he felt her body relax and melt toward him. "Good morning," he whispered with his lips still resting on her cheek. "Did you sleep well?"

"Very well. You?"

"Yes, but I dreamed of you all night. I had such a wonderful evening and couldn't wait to see you again. So I'm here." He gave her a sheepish grin and she quickly dispelled any of his concerns by smiling broadly and reaching back up to kiss him again.

"I'm glad you did." He was wearing the same buckskin suede jacket from last night, but with jeans and loafers, so she sat down to put on her black socks and grabbed her comfy flats from the closet. "Shall we?"

"Wow—a woman who is ready on time. You continue to amaze me." They descended the stairs and he followed her around to her side of the car, opened the door and waited until she slipped onto the soft tan leather seats. He came around and hopped in, pointing to one of two tall stainless steel mugs. "For you, *chérie*. Strong, dark, and a bit of skim. Hope you like it."

143

"How did you know?" The question was not rhetorical, as she was curious how he picked up this detail when they'd never had coffee together.

"You mentioned it in passing at my house last night."

She remembered now. She had been recounting one of her past relationships and after spending six months together, he didn't even know how she took her coffee—such a basic consideration. "Well done. If you're collecting brownie points, you just scored. Now, if you had anything to go with this, I would have to marry you."

"Be careful what you say, my dear," he said, and reached down behind her seat, pulling out a pink box wrapped in brown ribbon, setting it gingerly on her lap. "Two pains au chocolate—one's for me, so don't get greedy."

She looked at him in mock surprise, and said, "I don't even want to know," confirming he was now two out of two. He responded with his Cheshire cat grin. She untied the package, removing one petit pain, leaving the other in the box and passing it to him so he could use it as a makeshift plate while he was driving. With her other hand, she picked up her coffee and carefully took a sip. Still hot. She smiled to herself. Another small thing, but important.

A feeling of discomfort was sneaking its way into Chloé's abdomen. She wasn't used to this kind of attention. The details. The upfront interest and desire. She thought it was what she'd always wanted, but now that it was staring her in the face, she was scared. Here was a man, sitting right beside her, who met all the qualifications on her long list. He was obviously interested in her—he had already made that abundantly clear—so what was she so afraid of?

As if reading her mind, he turned to her and said, gently, "It's okay, Chloé. We're going to take this slow, I promise. I enjoy your company. Okay, let's be honest. I enjoy you very much. But I'm in no hurry to go anywhere, so let's just go wherever this leads, okay?"

She turned to him, trying to quell her reaction, eyes filling with tears, and said with an honesty that surprised them both, "I'm scared."

He had been heading the car out of town, following the coastal road to who knows where. After she spoke, he waited for a safe place to pull over and then steered the car to a pull-off, turning off the ignition and yanking on the emergency brake. He set her coffee back in its holder, and placed his hand over hers. "Me too," was his simple reply, but there was much more he needed to share. "Chloé, let's not blow this by letting our fears get in the way, okay? We're both scared—of what, I'm not sure, but for a few grand a good therapist would be happy to tell us—

but in spite of our fears we are attracted to each other. I would say 'drawn' to each other, if that's not too bold a word. We know enough about each other's past to know we've both been hurt. That was evident in our conversation last night. But do you want to go on with your life alone, letting fear prevent you from taking a step, albeit a risky one? I can only speak for myself, but I am tired of that road and I want to take the risk. I don't know where it will lead but I feel compelled to find out. And my gut feeling tells me this is the right thing to do. What about yours? What is your gut—your heart—telling you, Chloé?"

"I never knew this would be so hard. My heart and my head don't exactly have the most compatible relationship, my head being the controlling party of the two. I don't want my fears to dictate my life, that's true, but how does one go about conquering one's fears when they're so deeply imbedded? What if I *do* get hurt? What if *you* do? I don't want either of those things to happen, Marc. Not after what I know about you or what I know about my own sorry past."

"So what if we do get hurt? What will happen to us? Will we die? Will we disintegrate off the planet? Will we shrivel up and waste away for the rest of our miserable lives?"

"It's really the last one I'm most worried about." She said it sardonically, but he knew it was rooted in truth.

"I have the same fears, Chloé. But my greater fear is to live a life unfulfilled. Not miserable, but shallow. I want to live, from this point on, with a depth of feeling I have never had the courage to feel before now. And I'm asking you to please take that step with me. No commitment, no pressure. Just both giving 100% to what we have—right now—and then seeing where it takes us. It's true, we might self combust—there are no guarantees, after all."

He recalled using the same words with Madeline at dinner last night and thought how quickly a path can change when you're committed to following your heart. It was scary stuff. He checked to see if his last comment had made her smile and was relieved to see her tears had abated and she was listening. So he continued, "But more and more I know this is the only way to go through life. Full tilt. No holds barred. And I would love nothing more than to work on this together—with you. What do you say? Are you game?" He took a silent breath and held it, waiting for her response. He knew his words were bold. Hell, his actions had been bold since meeting her randomly on the beach last night. Randomly? Ha. But the words had come out before he'd had a chance to think and he knew in his heart he wanted this. And he was sure she did too.

"I need to think about what you said. It's a lot for me to digest."

"Of course, but just for fun, if you didn't *think* about it and went with your gut reaction, what would it be?" Another small inhale, hoping he hadn't gone too far.

"Well, yes, of course. That's the way I would always want to live my life."

"See how easy that was?"

"Sure, that's easy. But the 'living with the consequences' is what makes this so hard."

"Are you sure about that?" Marc wouldn't let up. He had started this and he intended to follow it through. "If your heart tells you to do something does it ever steer you wrong? Your mind might disagree but what would happen if your heart won all the arguments and your head had to follow? I believe s*trongly* that it is the way we're meant to live and our heart is like the voice of our soul. Our head, on the other hand, is the voice of our fears and when we follow *that*, it leads us into all kinds of trouble. That may appear to be easier at first, or safer, but is it the way to live life? Not the one I want. Do you see what I'm saying?"

"I think I do, although it scares the shit—sorry, that's crass—scares the *daylights* out of me. My mind is used to steering this ship. I don't think it's going to be too happy giving up control."

"Who would be? Mine isn't either. But why don't we try it and see what happens?" He was feeling confident with this new strategy and was encouraged by her look of contemplation. "It can be a game we play with each other. I feel safe with you, Chloé, and I know neither of us is the type to deliberately hurt the other, so I don't really see how we could lose here."

"Okay, you've bullied me into it. But I have one request, and it's non-negotiable." She waited for his nod before continuing. "If I ask you for space, you have to give it me. No cajoling, no sulking, no taking it personally. I have to know that I have that available to me at any time, no questions asked—or there's no deal."

"With one proviso?" She wasn't nodding, but waiting to hear it before she granted her consent, so he went on. "Not in anger. You don't get to run away if you're angry. Fair?"

She gave it some thought to make sure it didn't conflict with her needs and answered, "Fair." To which she added, "I eventually come back, you know. It's not a tactic to leave. I just like to be able to contemplate things on my own sometimes and I don't want it to be an issue between us, as it will rarely have anything to do with you, or anyone else for that matter."

"I have the same need, so we'll be able to give that to each other. Now, enough seriousness for one day, okay?"

"Okay." After a pause, she asked, "Where are you taking me, by the way? And how do you know I don't have to be at work soon?"

He started the car and headed back onto the highway, feeling the purr of the powerful engine as he shifted gears. "In answer to the first, it's a surprise, and in answer to the second, you told me last night you were relieved to have the whole weekend off, so I thought it was a safe bet. Plus I checked in with Sabine just to be sure."

They drove along the coast for another thirty minutes before he pulled into a roadway—ocean side—with a sign reading *Resort Côte de Blanc*. "It's a little early for lunch, isn't it?" she prodded, hoping to get a hint into the mystery, while knowing it would soon be revealed to her.

"Much too early." Nothing from him. He was guarding his words and expressions, enjoying the suspense. He parked the car under a massive chestnut for full shade, walked around to open her door and glanced casually at his watch. We have about thirty minutes. Shall we go for a walk along the beach?"

"A walk would be perfect. It's a gorgeous morning. But, thirty minutes for what?" Chloé was intrigued. He had obviously planned this out well, with little room for error in the timing. But *what* had he planned out?

"You will just have to wait. Lucky for you, my impatient little minx, thirty minutes is not a long time. Let's go." He reached over to grab her hand, leading her to an obscure winding path, one he had obviously followed before, and pulled her toward the sound of the waves.

Neither of them spoke, both enthralled by the beauty surrounding them. A bald eagle was perched high on an abandoned pole that once belonged to a dock. The clouds were softly scattered across the expansive sky and the tide was out, reflecting thousands of tiny pools teeming with small fish and other sea creatures. The miniatures eels darted around frantically, sand crabs becoming their obstacles. Chloé crouched down to pick up a sand dollar, admiring the pie-top cutouts symmetrically formed on the top. Noticing it was still alive by its dark gray-brown color, she placed it back in the wet sand, stood up and continued on, happy with her choice of rubber-soled flats. Marc eventually steered them back to the resort. They were nearing the back deck that overlooked the water when Chloé lifted her wrist and gazed down at her Tank watch with relish. "Twenty-five minutes. I think you can tell me now."

Marc pulled her toward him, grabbing her other hand and answered her impatient request. "You're right. We have to get going. Remember you were saying you'd had a stressful week and needed some time to unwind? Remember whining about that kink in your neck?" He was playing with her, she knew, and didn't mind his crack about whining, especially since it had a ring of truth to it.

"Yes…" she answered, with some hesitation, curiosity getting the better of her.

"I've booked us both into the spa here, Spa Paisible—thought we could both do with a little peace. Massages for both and then, if you're not too squeamish, pedicures. I've never had one but they insisted men have them done all the time so I thought it'd be fun." His eyebrows were raised, like a young boy waiting for approval from his mom. He didn't have to wait long.

She jumped up and threw her arms around him and covered his face with little kisses. "I *love* it. Thank you, thank you, thank you. I have heard of this spa, but I've never been. Ooooh—a massage. Do I *ever* need a massage," and she continued kissing every inch of his face.

Even though she was being silly, he could feel himself getting aroused and gently pushed her away, smiling. "Come on, then. We mustn't be late." And he guided her to the back entryway, following a path under the large patio that wound its way down to the spa.

They entered a dimly lit room, elegantly decked out in sumptuous fabrics and furniture. Glass apothecary jars lined the shelves, filled with glowing liquids and shell-shaped soaps. Its tranquil setting had Chloé instantly relaxed.

"Marc, how good to see you again. I hear you've made quite a name for yourself since you were last here." A willowy young woman leaned in to kiss one of Marc's cheeks and then the other, in traditional French fashion.

"Annette, it has been too long, *n'est-ce pas*? You look ravishing, as always." He caught a look from Chloé that was mildly hostile, but ignored it.

"Don't let my husband hear you say that, you rogue, or he'll string us both up." The lovely Annette had gone back behind the counter to look at the reservations, pointing at the book with her elongated and well-polished index finger.

"Speak of the devil, there's the man himself. Henri, how are you, my friend?"

A large, burly man came out from the back room and rushed up to Marc, encircling him in a bear hug, nearly lifting his feet from the ground. "Marc, my boy. Are you flirting with my wife again? You know I don't tolerate that from anyone, especially my friends." He twisted his back and winked playfully at his wife, who stuck her tongue out at him. "But who have we here? Maybe some arrangement could be made, *non*? One woman for the other, perhaps?"

Annette swatted the back of her husband's head, mumbling, "you wish" under her breath, and Marc said an emphatic, "No way. This one's not for trade," making Chloé wonder if perhaps others before her were? She was caught up in a flurry of banter, not knowing what to expect.

"My friends, I present to you: Chloé. I am entrusting her into your care, so do not disappoint me, *comprenez*?"

Chloé reached out her hand, first to Annette, and then to Henri, sharing pleased-to-meet-yous all around. She was starting to wonder how many other tense and stressed woman he had brought here before her when Annette cleared up the mystery, which both humbled and embarrassed Chloé. "How is your mother, Marc? We haven't seen her in ages?"

"She's as well as can be expected, considering her age and stubborn personality."

Annette turned to Chloé and confided, "Marc used to come up here with his mom when he was just a little boy. I was young then, too—much younger than him, in fact," generating two groans from the men. "He used to sit in that chair over by the window, and wait while his mama had her nails done. He was so cute and quiet. Between you and me I had a little crush on him," she said, deliberately loud enough to reach Henri's ears, "but alas, he didn't even notice me, so when Henri arrived with his parents to run the resort, I hooked up with him to make little Marc jealous. But life has a way of throwing curve balls, so…"

"So—what? What happened?" Chloé couldn't resist asking.

"I didn't plan it, but I fell in love—with Henri. Marc's loss, in my opinion." Her eyes twinkled as she looked over at her friend, who was nodding in agreement.

Henri piped in, "And ever since then he hasn't been able to keep his eyes off my wife, isn't that so, my friend?"

"He exaggerates, Chloé. Don't listen to these two. They've been ganging up on me since I was ten years old and it doesn't get any easier. I brought you along for protection and to witness the abuse. And for a little pampering, which, by my watch, is late in being delivered." Marc tapped his watch with mock impatience, and Annette began rushing around, bowing to them both, and ushered them in to the back room that was adjacent to the main entry.

In a professional tone, she pointed to the *Madame* dressing room and explained, "There's a robe in there for you, Mademoiselle—leave nothing on underneath, *d'accord?* When you are ready, go through that door, there," pointing ahead to a door opposite the one they had just come through, "and everything will be ready for you."

Annette and Henri left them alone in the cozy corridor. Marc whispered to her, seductively, "Would you like my help?"

In response, she opened the door to *Monsieur* with one hand and waved him inside with the other. "No, thank you." And before she'd closed her door, she added, "but perhaps another time."

He heard the door click shut and a muffled giggle from the other side. She handled that well, he thought. Those two could be quite unnerving in their flirtatious comments. He was curious to see how Chloé would react and was impressed as he watched the uncertainties flit behind her eyes, and then the dawning of understanding and her obvious appreciation for the camaraderie.

Marc was the first into his robe and went directly to the room he knew so well, where everything had been carefully arranged. There hadn't been much time, but when he called this morning, Annette had been more than happy to oblige him. She'd called and rescheduled the other appointments and when she explained the details of the dilemma (not disclosing the particulars, of course) they had all been understanding and enjoyed being in on the little secret. Marc didn't know exactly what to expect when Annette said, "Leave it to us," but he had.

When he entered the massage room, he was not disappointed. He sat in one of the plush Bérgère chairs, covered in some luxurious fabric, with mohair blankets hanging from the backs. He looked up when he heard the door open, to see Chloé tentatively walk in.

She was relieved to see him there, alone by the window, and was momentarily taken aback by the unobstructed view. There were a few beach dwellers, mostly reading or making sandcastles with their children, but other than that, the floor-to-ceiling windows took in the expansive view of the bay scattered with birds and the odd boat out on the water. She felt like she was in a fishbowl and when one young boy wandered close to the windows, she smiled and waved. He didn't respond but continued to dig and examine a newly-discovered shell. Marc stood and walked to the window, his back now to Chloé, and opened his robe and flashed the little boy. She was horrified, and shrieked her disgust.

He laughed and she noticed the little boy hadn't batted an eye. "It's one-way glass. The film on the outside prevents anyone from seeing in. We're in complete privacy in this room. That was a poor attempt at humor, wasn't it? But your expression is priceless." He was still laughing and she couldn't help joining him.

"I couldn't believe it when you did that. Not much shocks me but *that?* That shocked me. You really are deranged, aren't you? Will I even be safe from you with my innocence and naïveté?" She batted her eyelashes at him.

"Innocence and naïveté, my ass-*scot*. You'll manage just fine, I'm sure. Now come back over here and sit down. It looks like our friends have left us some refreshments." He pulled the carafe out of the ice bucket and poured the orange juice mixture into the two champagne glasses on the table between them. "Care for a Mimosa?" and without waiting for her response he filled both of their glasses.

"Champagne and orange juice? Breakfast of champions, no doubt." She tipped her glass to her mouth for a sumptuous sip.

"Yum," was her response, licking her lips with pleasure. She was already starting to relax, feeling the bubbles go into her head, calming her nerves. She took her first close look around the room and saw the two massage tables facing the water, in the center. "I've never had a massage before, let alone with someone else in the room to hear me groan. I'll have to bite my lip." She wasn't sure what this would be like, side by side, sharing this experience. It seemed so *intimate*. But she was looking forward to trying it and knew a massage would do her good.

"No holding back, remember? After a few minutes, I won't even notice you're here, I'll be so caught up in my own pleasure. Just enjoy yourself and take it all in. It will be like nothing you've ever experienced, I assure you."

Chloé wasn't sure if she should be more nervous now, after a comment like that, but she decided to trust him completely and go with whatever was planned. They both glanced up when they heard the door, and Henri and Annette came in carrying blankets under one arm and what looked like massage oil in their other free hand. They stood with their backs to each other, each facing a table with ample room between them to move around, and motioned for the two guests to come forward.

Chloé assumed Henri would be working on her and was a little uncomfortable with both that prospect and the other—having Annette work on Marc—but Marc headed to Henri's table and although surprised, she was pleased. She was standing in front of Annette and

Marc in front of Henri when they both said, "Drop the robes and lay down on your stomach." Before she could resist, Annette opened the blanket and held it over her head, creating a wall between her and the two men. Chloé quickly dropped her robe and leapt onto the bed, face first, exposing only her backside for all the world to see, and then felt the blanket come down over her body, just below her head, covering her entirely. She looked over to Marc, seeing the same result, and appreciated the simplicity in the act and the discretion in their movements. Now that her initial self-consciousness was quelled by their professionalism, she felt safe and began to relax. In the background she heard faint music. Not the new-agey stuff that one normally heard in spas around the world. This was quiet and subtle, with strings and harpsichord tones and a slow hypnotic beat.

Annette pulled the blanket down to rest just above her backside. She felt a little bit exposed but was beyond caring. The first squirt of oil was warm and smelled of exotic flowers. The hands touching her back moved in slow monotonous circles, starting at the base of her spine and working their way up to her shoulders, where they split apart and slid to each shoulder blade, working out the long-held knots on each side. Then back together, circling, slowly moving downward, pressuring the base of her spine. The motion was soothing and put her into a trance-like state. With one hand moving gently down her spine, Annette reached under the table, pulling out something that she couldn't see but that made a harsh rubbing sound in her hand. Still touching her back (although she couldn't figure out how she did it) she now placed both hands back on her shoulder blades now holding something warm and slippery in each hand. What was it? Oh, God, it felt sooo good. The rubbing and the heat and the smooth texture. A low groan escaped her lips as she released some pent-up tension, feeling immense pleasure in the sensation.

She looked over at Marc, who had his eyes closed, a sensual smile on his lips, and could see that Henri was holding two slick black stones, running them up and down his spine. *Ahhh, stones. What a sensation,* she thought lazily, barely remembering what she had been trying to determine. Annette started to work deeply into her muscles, pressure, then release, pressure, then release. It was quite painful yet pleasurable and she felt her mind gradually empty into blackness.

She lay there on her stomach, a hand continuously rubbing her gently up and down her spine. She was completely naked, the sheets now kicked onto the floor, and the hand started dipping lower on each side of her back touching lightly on the sides of her breasts as if brushing them accidentally, not realizing how close they were. A hand traveled down her spine, making tiny circles at its base, traveling lower, lower, and then turning back up to follow the same route as before. She could feel herself getting aroused and yet she didn't want it to stop so she played indifference. She was so relaxed, felt so much bliss, languidly lying there with her lover attending to her body so intimately. She turned her head to smile at him and looked up to see Armand looking down on her with his teasing devilish smile. "Armand?" She didn't mean to speak out loud, but heard her own voice, which shook her back to the present.

"*Pardon?*" Annette leaned forward to catch Chloé's words. Chloé had obviously been sleeping and was dreaming about faraway places. She blushed at her fantasy. Marc was there, rubbing her back, oh-so sensually—and another groan escaped her at the memory—but she had called him 'Armand.' And the bed was so luxurious, and the room—like one of those old hotels she'd seen in movies set in Paris. What a strange dream. Her mind stayed focused on Annette's fingers, leery of drifting off again.

The stones continued their slow travels, now working their way up and down her legs. Finally setting the rocks down, Annette slid the blanket up to Chloé's shoulders and had her roll onto her back so she could take one foot at a time in her hands to start working deeply into the painful spots that Annette had explained reflected other parts of her body. She almost yelled out in agony when Annette zeroed in on a spot on her left foot along the outside of her arch. "Ah, your stomach. You hold all of your tension there, *non?*"

"No," she answered groggily. "I mean yes, that's right, I do."

"We will work on that, then." And she continued to work deeply in that area, gradually lessening the pain. She was oblivious to Marc, as he said she would be, and allowed herself to take in the pleasure she was receiving from this experience. She made a mental note to do this on a regular basis and couldn't believe she'd lived her life thus far without experiencing it. What a shame. And what a wonderful, thoughtful man, she mused, drifting away again into the unknown.

She heard Annette say she was finishing up, and Chloé was to lie there for as long as she liked. She barely heard her leave and was in her own blissful world when she felt a brush of lips on the edge of her mouth. Thinking she was dreaming again she opened her eyes to see Marc hovering over her, rubbing her cheek with the back of his hand. "You look relaxed, *chérie*. Do you feel better?" He was leaning over her as he spoke and she started to sit up but she felt his hand press gently on her shoulder. "No, stay there for a few minutes and just relax. When you're ready, come join me at the window. No rush, okay? We have all morning." He straightened up, seeing her smile weakly, and close her eyes, heeding his request.

When she finally forced herself up she pulled the blanket around her and walked over to her place by the window, falling into her chair with an ungraceful thud. Every muscle was like rubber and she stuck her legs out in front of her, arms flopping at her side, her head lolling back to rest on the edge of the chair's wooden frame. "That was incredible," she said, her breathy words coming out with minimal effort or strain. "I feel so good. Thank you. This was really special."

"I thought you would enjoy it and knew you did by all the groaning," he said, laughing. She knew it was true. "You were mumbling a lot, too, but I couldn't catch the words. Sounded quite erotic, though."

"Oh, yeah. I was having this bizarre dream and you were there, but it wasn't you, and you were giving me a back rub, but it wasn't really a back rub, and…" she stopped and felt the blush come into her cheeks, "that's all I remember."

"Too bad. It sounded enticing. Maybe you'll remember another time. They say by replicating the same conditions…" He left the thought unsaid but she caught the message, loud and clear.

"We'll see," she said, not giving an indication one way or the other but grinning wickedly, which helped assure him that her dreams would be revealed, fulfilling some of his at the same time, no doubt.

Annette and Henri came back into the room, pushing two tables on wheels and another assortment of tools. Without having to move, everything was set up for their pedicures, and after pulling up two salon chairs the four of them settled in for round two. There was a relaxed atmosphere now, all of them talking to each other. This time Henri was working on Chloé and 'tsk-tsk-ing' at the state of her feet. It was fun to hear about some of the escapades of Marc's youth and she found her stride in the conversation. They were so intimate with each other and the questions flying back and forth were often so personal, but none of them flinched when responding and she began to appreciate how they had learned to keep things real between them. At one point, Henri shared about his father's sudden death and Marc stood up and leaned over to hug him, patting his back with affection as his tears flowed unabashedly down his cheeks. Then, after a few moments he sat back down and everything resumed.

When the pampering finally came to an end and they were both dressed again, Chloé and Marc both thanked Annette and Henri, promising to return soon and also inviting them down to the city for dinner in the next week or two. No money changed hands and the two guests walked out and back to the beach. Chloé assumed he must have taken care of the bill before they left the city or they had some standing arrangement. Whatever it was, she appreciated the class in the gesture and was once more impressed by his character.

"I'm starved," he reported, as they neared the top of the path. "Shall we eat?"

She had forgotten about food and heard a loud growl coming from her abdomen at the sound of the word 'food'. "I'm famished, too. Where would you like to go?"

He pointed to the bank of stairs that led to the restaurant patio she had spied earlier. She headed to the top first, taking in the ocean scene once more, now from one storey up, and he took her hand and led her toward a table set for two at the edge of the Plexiglas rail, giving an unobstructed view. When they got closer, Chloé noticed there was a 'reserved' sign on the table and she raised her hands as if to say, "Oh well, too bad," but he just smiled and pulled out one of the chairs as it dawned on her that this was part of the arrangement. "You are full of surprises, aren't you?" was all she could think of to say, having been inundated all morning with one after the other.

"I warned you," he said, and then motioned to the server. Thinking again of his stomach, he said, "No more wine for me. I was thinking of having another coffee, but go ahead if you'd like, as you're not driving. And the food here is magnificent, so we're in for a real treat." There were more greetings to the staff, discussions about the specials, two coffees ordered and then two light lunches, all executed within a minute of arriving, the decisions made with little input from her. "I hope you don't mind, but you seem a bit out of it so I thought I'd order for us."

"You're right, again. I could care less what we eat at this point. I'm so relaxed and at peace. I can't even remember what you ordered. I can barely remember my name." She put her sunglasses on and sat back, sipping her lemon water and watching the waves lap against the shore.

"I was hoping that would happen. You need to do this for yourself at least once a month. You have an extremely stressful job working for that slave driver and you're no good to anyone if you don't take care of yourself. I want you to promise me you'll keep this up. Once a month. Promise?" He was being pushy and she knew he meant it but it was easy for her to acquiesce.

"You'll get no resistance from me. In fact, you could ask me just about anything right now and you'll get no resistance." Her voice still had a lazy quality to it and she was only half present.

"I could have a lot of fun with that if I were a bad boy—which I am not—so I will not take advantage of your vulnerable state, I promise."

He looked disappointed by his own decision but meant what he said and she relaxed again, not contributing much to the conversation, still off in her own reverie, not wanting to rush back to her busy world, her hectic life.

Their meals came and they ate with relish, her energy starting to pick back up again, and his, still light and easygoing. They headed back to the car, which was now in full sun. As they got in, windows opened wide, sunroof back, the heat contributing to the laziness of the day, Chloé sighed deeply as she settled in, locking her seatbelt firmly in place, seat tilted back. "Marc?" she began.

"Mm-hmm?"

"Thank you for today. I really mean that. What you gave me was an incredibly thoughtful gift. I don't know what else to say, except thank you."

"It's been my pleasure. You know that, I'm sure. But you're most welcome all the same." They rode back with the only sound the quiet hum of the car on the road, windows still open for the fresh breeze, deep in their own trains of thought, not too dissimilar. They both went over the day, recalling the pleasant details. Each of them analyzed the other's character and what showed up throughout the day, adding it to their insights from the night before. They were both pleased with what they saw.

Chloé was getting nervous as they approached their neighborhood. She wasn't ready to let him go and said as much. "Do you know what would make this day even more perfect than it was? Come in with me, take me upstairs and make love to me until the morning." The look she gave him was almost pleading and she waited for his affirmative answer with hope in her eyes.

"I would love nothing more than to do exactly that but it's not time yet. Truly, we're not ready. Our physical bodies have been ready for, oh, about 18 ½ hours but that's the easy part. We've only known each other for one day and we're on a path where I want to tread lightly. Conscientiously. I want you to agree with me on this, Chloé. Come over to my side. Let's be patient a bit longer." And now it was Marc who was pleading.

"I can't see the harm in waiting, except that it's killing me. I will respect your wishes and wisdom—or stupidity—whatever the case may be." And she threw him a defeated smile. When they pulled up to the house, she said, "Don't come in—I don't have the reserves to stop myself, so I'll say goodbye here."

The longing in her voice and her kiss almost broke his resolve. She thanked him again, kissed him several more times and then got out of the car, waved, and disappeared inside the front door of her building. He sat in the car for a few more moments, pulling his pant legs away from his uncomfortable groin, and asked himself, 'What the hell am I thinking?' before he drove the short distance to his house.

Chloé wasn't in the mood for eating and she didn't feel like doing the laundry she had planned to do this morning, but she did like the idea of picking up where she left off this morning with her book. She poured herself a glass of dry white wine and headed upstairs, where things were exactly as she left them several hours ago, although she now felt completely different. She slipped her négligé down over her head, crawled under the crisp sheets, kicking the covers to the end and other side of the bed where they wouldn't weigh her down, and picked up the book.

It was well written and the characters especially drew her in. Not your typical romance—lots of resistance but still some heat. She started reading one of the passages where one of the couples was alone in a boudoir and she knew where it was heading. When the man grabbed the woman by both wrists and kissed her neck, Chloé knew she wouldn't be able to handle it and dropped the book beside her bed and started rubbing her thighs, still oily from the massage. Pleasuring herself was going to be the only pleasure she'd be getting tonight and possibly for many nights. She had so much pent up sexual energy and she knew she had to release it.

Men always thought they cornered the market on masturbation but they were just more vocal about it. Woman did it in the privacy of their bedrooms more often than not and she smiled at the misconception. She knew exactly what her body needed, what it wanted, and she continued caressing herself, slowly at first, all the while imagining it was Marc touching her breasts, her thighs, her entire body, which brought her quickly and furiously to an orgasm. She cried out with pleasant anguish, and then laughed at the possibility that Marc was still parked outside, listening to her moans of release. Her next thought was that, unless he wasn't human, he was most likely going through the same exercise at this exact moment. Damn him. They could have been having sex together instead of this half-satisfied feeling that left her wanting. He knew what he was doing, though; that was for sure. She hadn't thought this much about making love to a man in... well, forever. He was certainly keeping her interest in him piqued. Damn him.

Part IV

Chapter XVII

She woke with her hand resting against her pubic hair, still sticky from the night before. She rested her hand there for a few moments, remembering last night. After the sex, she hadn't slept well, disturbed by dreams that even still had her puzzled. *The mind is a complex beast*, she thought, as she tugged gently on the curly hairs beneath her hand. Another hand pushed hers away and she woke with a start. "What are you doing, playing with yourself? Am I not enough to satisfy you, *chérie?*" Armand had a hurt expression on his face, and started tickling her erotically to prove the myth wrong.

"Please, Armand. Stop. I was dreaming, of you, of course, and I reflexively started remembering our lovemaking. I was sleeping but the dreams were so strange. I couldn't make out your face. It was you, but you were different. Your hair was shorter, like a monk's, and you had on tight clothes. Your eyes were the same though. Your enthralling eyes."

"What else do you remember? Do you remember this?" and he leaned over and kissed her soft belly. "Or this?" Now moving upwards, heading dangerously to her nipple.

"Armand, *please*. Stop, silly. You have to get out of here, back to your wife before she fin0ds out you've been gone from your precious little *château.*" Lisette giggled as she pushed him toward the edge of the bed, and then leapt off herself.

He was madly in love with this woman. Had been since their meeting, five years ago. After winning the début with Isabel, he had no interest in pursuing that one any further. After their first night, they continued to enjoy each other and he would always remain like a mentor to Isabel and a dear friend, but once he met Lisette he rarely spent time with Isabel, and when he did it was mostly for social gatherings, where she was more suited than Lisette might be.

Shortly after he married le Duc's daughter, he returned several times to reacquaint himself with the lovely Isabel. They would get together for mere distraction more than anything and although they were occasional lovers, they remained as friends alone. But Armand didn't like to share and he felt it was time to visit *la Maison de Rouler*, to discuss a more suitable arrangement. He and Isabel had run their sensual course and it was time to put that chapter behind him.

Madame, whose judgment, he had learned from first-hand experience, was impeccable, suggested Lisette without hesitation. "She is the only girl who will satisfy your good taste and sharp wit, Monsieur. You will find her to be your equal on many fronts and you are a secure enough man not to be offended by the aspects where she surpasses even you. Get to know each other and I think you will both be pleased by the match." When he hesitated, her final words clinched the deal. "Monsieur, she is a younger version of me but with a much finer body," and she smiled cunningly at him, knowing he would take the bait. The two had maintained a flirtatious chemistry ever since that first night they met, negotiating Isabel's début. Although they both knew their joining would never come to pass, neither of them was the type to live with regrets and instead valued the friendship they had fostered.

Lisette's character shone through, after and during Isabel's launch into their mutual worlds. Isabel took Paris by storm and had Lisette been a lesser friend, or person, for that matter, she might have developed a resentment that she could have easily justified. Lisette was virtually dropped from the top of the heap down to the bottom, and even though she saw it coming, it was hard to accept and deal with on a day-to-day basis. All the men who had previously been Lisette's regulars stood in the long queue to meet Isabel, the youngest, most beautiful, loveliest, sweetest—it went on and on. They had forgotten that at one point in history, not too long ago, these same men had used those same words to describe Lisette. But memories are short in the business of pleasure, and anticipating Isabel's launch gave Lisette a chance to prepare for the inevitable. Instead of begrudging her friend, as they had become that first year, she chose to appreciate her each day for the time off that had been bestowed upon her. Never in her life had she had so much free time.

There was an abundance of money pouring into the house so she didn't have to worry about that, either. Her role as Isabel's support earned her almost as much as lying flat on her back. She always loved the play on words, 'to lie flat on her back'. She certainly did her share of 'lying' on her back, and upright, for that matter. "Oh, yes, fine sir, I have never had such a wonderful lover as yourself," or "Oh, how handsome you are. The scars hardly show in this light." They all wanted her lies and paid handsomely for them.

When Madame told her Monsieur du Preix had requested to meet with her, she was slightly miffed (being second choice to anyone was an insult) but she recovered quickly and decided to give him a run for his money. Lisette was acting from an inexplicable hurt and wanted to punish Armand for the innocent part he had played. Madame asked her to be on her best behavior, as he was keenly interested in forming an alliance with her, which only enraged her further. "*Oui, Madame. Oui, Monsieur.* Anything you say, *Madame, Monsieur.*" She was tired of bowing to everyone's wishes. No, their *demands*, as these were not requests they made of her, but merely disguised as such.

Not knowing her true feelings, Armand entered her boudoir ill-prepared for what she had in store. He held his hands out to her and she curtsied deeply, giggling under her breath. He directed his arm toward the table by the window and she scurried over, held the carafe and looked dumbly at him, asking with her body language, "Would you like some?" and not saying a word. He nodded, wondering how such an obvious gesture could escape her allegedly intelligent head. She curtsied again and then poured for herself, exceeding what she'd given him by more than a third. She sat down, poised and ready to talk.

He started out slowly, attempting to draw her into the conversation. The topics were of a general nature and he had always prided himself in his ability to make anyone comfortable, no matter what the circumstances. He gently probed her with questions, but got little response. He changed tactics and started outlining some of his basic business strategies and current concerns in order to gain her trust. She fawned over his every word, batting her eyelashes like a dumb schoolgirl.

At first he was dumbfounded, but as the evening painfully dragged on, he began to understand her cunning mind and decided he would set out to destroy her little scheme. It was simple to see how this lovely woman would see him as a man taking second best, and how any self-respecting woman would resent that. He never looked at a courtesan as any less of a woman than the rest. This was their lot in life, simple as that. He had been with enough of them to know they could be as ruthless, cunning, intelligent or loving as any other woman. And why not? They were women, after all. And many of them were forced into finding out the hard way what that really meant, becoming truer to their sex than most. If Madame had given high praise to Lisette, then he would take her words over this girl's annoying behavior and turn the tables on the situation. It sounded like fun to him, something he had in short supply at the moment.

Lisette was watching him intently, hoping for an impatient gesture that would end their meeting so she could run to Madame, saying, "I don't know what happened. I tried to be a good girl. He just didn't like me" or other such nonsense that she would make up as the occasion required. That was what she excelled at. That was her trade. It was harder with Madame but she could do it when required.

She watched as he lifted his glass, peering at her from over the rim. She picked hers up and slurped—only once—and then clumsily put it down, apologizing under her breath. He continued to look at her and smile, as if devouring her in his mind. He didn't say a word but kept sipping his wine. At a loss for what to do next, she swept her arm across the table as if to say something witty, caught the carafe with the back of her hand and sent it flying into Armand's lap. She mumbled an apology while his quick reflexes grabbed the carafe and set it upright on the table. He then calmly took another sip of wine, set his glass down slowly, kicked off his boots and unlaced his wine-soaked pants, dropping them to the floor so he could kick them freely from his legs. He sat back in his chair, now naked from the waist down, picked up his glass and took another sip, all the while looking directly into her eyes.

After only a minute he leaned forward, casually swinging his arm across the table as if to listen more closely to her words, careening her glass directly at her bosom, dousing her breasts and front with the rich color of wine. Apologizing profusely while fighting the smile that entered his lips, he watched as her eyes opened in shock, and then slit like a cat's in steely determination. She stood up, facing him, and started to undo the outer fastenings of her gown, moving two steps from the table before letting it drop and then kicking it off to the side like a discarded rag. She then proceeded to sit, crossing her legs, boots still laced up, undergarments in full reveal. She picked up the half-empty carafe and tipped it to her mouth, letting the excess drip down her chin, her breasts and then her lap, where a blood-red pool was collecting. She set the carafe down with a loud bang, raised her bare arm to her mouth and wiped, catching any remnants of wine on a long path across her forearm.

He stood up and grabbed her from her seat, roughly but not enough to hurt her. With both hands, he wrenched the front of her thin chemise, tearing it from neck to waist and pulling it from her shoulders so it, too, dropped to the floor. With his bare foot, he picked it up and flung it to the heap where the dress lay. Unwilling to let this man outdo her, she reached down into the back of her boot and pulled out a knife that glinted in the candlelight, rotating it slowly in front of his face. Not a flicker of fear showed there. She smiled slyly and, with her other hand, grabbed his tunic tightly from its waist and then slit the knife up toward his neck, forcing Armand to lean back as it neared his chin but otherwise, standing firm, still gazing directly into her eyes. She slammed the knife on the table and ripped the remains of his shirt from his shoulders and flung it onto the heap of already discarded clothing.

She stood before him in her stockings and boots and stared downward to see him standing erect, aroused by the ordeal and out of items of clothing to shred. He leaned over to grab his shirt and trousers with one hand and her with the other and led her to the bed. She was not intimidated by him—she knew she had no need to be—but she was nervous about his next move. He caught the fear in her eye and played it to his full advantage. Pushing her forcefully onto the bed but in no way harshly, he grabbed her right arm and with his torn shirt, wrapped it around the bedpost – thank God for those – and then around her arm, securing it for the time being. Before she had time to react, he had whipped his belt from his pants and had her left wrist secured to the other bedpost, rendering her helpless.

"Now we are going to play this my way, since your way is so much more tedious, *non*?" He saw her fight the smile between her struggles. She was feisty, he would say that for her, and had guts to pull a knife on him with enough confidence to know he wouldn't turn it back onto her. He unlaced each boot, knowing they would be weapons to her if required, and unwound her garters before pulling off her stockings one by one. When she started to kick, he pointed to her wrists, raising his eyebrows in a questioning gesture, checking to see if she wanted them to be next he'd be happy to oblige her on that account. He tried pulling off her slip but realized it was tied, so in one swift motion headed back to the table, grabbed her discarded knife and, without hesitating, slipped one hand between her waist and the fabric and slit it down the front with the other, revealing a taut, ivory belly and a glistening soft mound of hair. His short intake of breath assured her he was pleased with what he saw.

Once he was sure she couldn't free herself, he set out to dismantle her in a way he was sure had never been done. She had always been the one offering every imaginable pleasure and he sensed she had hit her limit. Instead of being angered by her insolence he thought the only way to save her from herself, and himself in the crossfire, was to be her courtier for the night.

Slowly, he roamed her body with his hands, caressing it at times slowly, at times brusquely, depending on her reaction. It was a long process as her resilience was ingrained and she refused to relent, but he persistently plodded along, taking no pleasure offered and lavishing her with all he could muster. Not once did he enter her for he felt she would feel that was his way of satisfying his own needs after all, so he continued to tease, taunt, and kiss parts of her body that rarely saw this kind of attention. She started to raise her hips to him, a sure sign she was weakening, and a sweat appeared on her forehead and then breasts, which he leaned over and licked hungrily, nipping her nipples gently as he did.

She begged him to untie her. "Monsieur, please. This is not right. It is *I* who must satisfy *you*, not the other way around. Untie me, please, Monsieur."

But he adamantly refused, shaking his head, and then went back to his task. She had started to shake and he untied her one arm as he went down on her, licking her moist sex and forcing his tongue up into her, joined by his two fingers for added pressure. With her free hand, instead of pushing him away, she pushed his head into her while thrusting her hips to join him, thrashing on the bed, fighting a losing battle. Her blood-curdling scream brought Josef but he saw the *monsieur* raise his hand, saw Lisette writhing freely, and so closed it quietly behind him.

Her body was wracked with spasms and he continued to burrow into her, sucking forcefully on her budding clitoris, bringing another rush of spasms, and then whimpering. At that moment he entered her, releasing her other arm, and thrust deep inside her while she climaxed again, pulling his buttocks to her with the last strains of her strength. He came quickly, riding on the wave of her reckless abandon. Nothing would get his blood heated more than seeing a woman lose control. She was covered in sweat from head to toe, panting breathlessly. She held him to her but was unable to speak from exhaustion.

"Now, *ma chérie*. Shall we start again? I think, perhaps, we may have gotten off on the wrong foot."

And it was in this way that he won her heart. She was no match for him physically and she knew he could take her at his will, but now she saw how she couldn't manipulate him and she was slightly embarrassed but more secretly pleased at his reaction.

Untying her other arm, he pulled her up from the bed, wrapped a sheet around her shoulder and sent her in search of more wine. "Josef is worried for you. Go reassure him and get him to refill the carafe. Ask him to fetch some bread and cheese as well. I'm famished." And he sent her to the door. Wrapping another sheet around his waist, he headed over to the chair and sat slouched and relaxed. When Lisette returned with a tray, she poured them each a glass—making sure they were of equal measure—and sat down to nibble on some bread, dipping it in her wine and sensually sucking the juice from it.

"Don't even think about it. You had your chance—and you will get another, I promise—but not tonight. Tonight, we talk, we listen, we lay some ground rules. No more wild antics. I'm an old man and can only handle so much." He smiled warmly at her and she laughed at his candor. "Firstly, how do you feel?"

She was still playing with him but now he could enjoy her antics. "I feel a touch sore, right here," and she pointed to the slit between her legs, "and right here," pointing to each breast in turn, "but otherwise I feel very, very good."

Her grin was wicked but he called her bluff when he rose to his feet, dropped his sheet and fell on his knees. "Let me remedy that for you, my sweet." But she had no play left and pushed him away, in mock agony. "No, please. No more. I can't. You must stop."

"All right, but be careful what you ask for, *chérie*, as you will surely get it." He was not a man to trifle with and she knew now to heed his words.

Chapter XVIII

Lisette had never met a man like Armand. What he had given her that first night was more than she had ever been given by all of her clients combined. He had enough self-assurance that he didn't need constant attention, and he expected the same from her. This was a man of few words, and when he spoke, he required you to contemplate what he'd said. He never said anything lightly nor spoke on topics of the mundane. He abhorred gossip and chastised people regularly for their indulgence in it. Rather, he spoke of people so that he could learn more of them and what made them tick. He wasn't interested in what they did, particularly, but why they did it. Lisette was continuously amazed by his intuitive insights into human nature and began to rely on his opinions to complement her own. She, too, was an amateur study of man, which is why she enjoyed her profession. She hadn't wanted to be a courtesan, but it had been thrust upon her at a young age by a father who cared little of anyone else and of nothing besides his drink.

It started when he began selling her to his friends, mostly in recompense for his debts. Due to a turn in fortune, one of them was also a client of *la Maison de Rouler*, where he approached Madame about this young girl, who was being abused and used by her father, and felt certain of her demise. Would Madame consider taking her in? Dressed as an old beggar woman, she set out to find their hovel and spy on the enchantress that so caught the Monsieur's eye. She did not have to wait long before a young woman with wild, dark hair stepped out into the street, pulled by what must have been her father, made obvious by his drunken appearance. He was causing a ruckus with his slurred speech and stumbling walk, but this young girl gave the impression she was on the arm of a prince and showed no sign of embarrassment or shame, nor did she easily bend to his abusive will. He was trying to lead her and, without seeming to do so, she created much resistance: a false trip on

168

her part sending him careening off balance; a slow step forcing him to attempt to drag her along, all the while speaking platitudes to him, tricking him into believing it was due to his own drunkenness and not the wily ways of his only daughter.

Madame spent most of the afternoon there, hoping to see her alone, which occurred near the end of the afternoon. With hood pulled tightly over her head, the young girl left the house with a bucket to replenish their water supply. The fountain was not far and Madame followed her there. She approached her from behind, tapping lightly on her shoulder under the guise of begging for food, or some coins. The young girl turned and smiled brightly but was holding a knife at her belly and through her smile, spoke under her breath, "I have seen you watching our house today. If you try anything, I will slit you from head to toe."

Madame laughed lightly and said, "Bravo, my child. You have done well to defend yourself and your honor. I have only come to have a word, if I may, that involves you and a choice you can make whether to remain in your life here or come with me and trust I will not lead you to a worse fate." She waited to make sure she had the girl's attention. Lisette had turned to the fountain and was filling her bucket. "My name is Madame de Rouler and I have a *maison* for girls who provide services to men, but for money to line their own pockets, not their fathers'. I will be here again tomorrow at this time and if you are interested, we will leave together. If you are not here I will have your answer and I shall never bother you again." Madame turned in her hunched manner, shuffling alongside her cane until she rounded the corner, where she stood tall to walk briskly back to *la Maison*.

Dressed in the same beggar's attire, she set out the next afternoon, waiting to see if the girl would show. She was starting to have her doubts when she caught a glimpse of her rushing toward the fountain, no bucket in hand. She looked from side to side in search of Madame and when she spotted her she started to walk toward the corner where she stood.

Madame signaled for her to follow, and started walking down the crowded street with the girl in pursuit. She was walking briskly and the girl noticed her slump and limp had only been part of her act. She wondered what else was an act but continued on her path until they came to a small alleyway where a door stood open a crack. Madame pushed it in, turning to wave her to follow and then Lisette heard a loud slam as the heavy door clattered shut behind them. She shuddered, a spark of fear igniting in her gut. The room was dark but dry and it took her a few moments to adjust to the dim light cast from a single candle.

169

Madame headed toward another door, opened it with Lisette apprehensively on her heels, and entered an antechamber that had no windows but was more comfortable and lighter than any room she'd been in before. She motioned for Lisette to sit on a small chair with a wool blanket thrown over the top. Only later would she learn the blanket would be boiled and washed to kill any possible mites and germs the waif would most certainly be carrying.

Madame slipped off her cape to reveal a simple but tasteful gown in rich hues of green and brown. She sat on a chair opposite Lisette and poured them each a mulled wine. She offered the girl a mug, which she accepted with only a slight hesitation, and began to speak. "It was courageous of you to leave with me today, knowing you would be leaving your life there forever."

"That was no life," she spoke with vehemence.

"Nonetheless, you did not know me nor did you know my intentions. In the future, if you want to survive in this world, some precautions must always be taken. Fortunately for you, I have your best interests at heart and I know you will be relieved by your choice." She hesitated for a moment, waiting to see if there would be any further outbursts, and then continued.

"I run a small, exclusive house here that is based solidly on the impeccable reputation of myself and my girls. This is not a random meeting, you must understand. One of your father's, shall we say 'acquaintances' had the privilege of meeting you and you left quite an impression. He was appalled at your father's method of payment, but despite his unease he accepted, knowing there would be nothing else forthcoming. He found you to be witty and intelligent with no indelible signs of cynicism from the life that had been forced upon you. Let's hope he was right, hmm? He recently approached me to suggest you might be better suited to a place like this. Do you have any questions thus far, my child?"

"Yes, Madame. May I ask, who is this man, my benefactor? I should like to thank him for his kindness."

"On our next meeting I shall ask him if I may reveal that to you and then relay the information at that time, or not, as he requests. But I will pass along your words of thanks either way. Anything else?"

Uncertain of what she had just done, but knowing there was no turning back, she resigned herself to her new circumstances and chose to make the best of them, whatever they might bring. "Madame, I have many questions but none seem important at the moment. Shall I start to work right away? Would you like me to begin by helping with the cleaning or cooking? I am quite good at both, although not according to my father." Her guts wrenched when she thought of him and the atrocities he had committed in that role.

"First, what is your name, or what would you like me to call you?"

"My name is Lisette, and that would be my choice—Lisette. I am not prepared to change it so late in my life."

Madame smiled at the young girl's perspective, but didn't give her the feeling she was mocking her in the least. "*Alors*, today is Saturday, *n'est-ce-pas*? Today it will be you who will be cleaned, not the *maison*, and tomorrow, being Sunday, it will be a day of rest for you. I am guessing that is not something you would be familiar with but here we all take Sundays as our day of rest."

"Every Sunday?"

"Yes, every Sunday. Sometimes the girls choose to meet with their clients, but it is at their whim, not mine. You will see. You will work hard and will come to rely on a day off. It is necessary for the body and soul to rejuvenate itself. Now, I will introduce you to some of the girls—they are half-expecting you, you know—but first I will take you to the kitchen. Cook will be preparing dinner but there is always a lot to eat—something else that will be a welcome change for you, *non*? Your meals are all prepared and there are plenty of things to have in between, if you so desire.

"I advise you to start slowly, though, Lisette. You must not hoard the food. You will need to free yourself from the starvation mentality you are surely caught in. It could be your demise otherwise. You will never need to beg for food again. Remember that when you are about to take your third helping, which will surely come back up later if you overindulge yourself now. You have been brought into a world of temptation and you would be wise to learn to resist, starting with food."

Her little speech ended and they walked out into a corridor where wafts of food were drifting, leading Lisette by her nose to the kitchen. She was salivating uncontrollably and her eyes opened wide as she entered a room ten times larger than her home, pots hanging from the ceiling, large tables and counters with an array of food in different states of completion. A floured surface was covered with massive rounds of dough like she'd never seen, that would surely be baked in one of the large ovens surrounding her. The table she was motioned to had a thick rough top with worn marks and multiple burn marks, indentations and stains. Two long benches ran along each side and there was a large basket of fresh apples in the center.

Cook came over and gave Lisette a small curtsy, then ladled a thick stew into a bowl that she placed in front of her. A basket of bread appeared on her other side and Lisette used all of her reserves not to tip the bowl up to her lips and gulp it down in one motion. She smiled up at the plump, kind-looking woman, both saying *enchanté* to each other. Madame looked at Lisette and gave her a slight nod, watching her movements with a keen eye. Lisette gracefully picked up the spoon, dipped it into her bowl and blew on the stew before slurping it hungrily. As expected, it was delicious and she thanked the cook again. Tearing a chunk from the bread, she dunked it in the thick broth, stuffing it in her mouth all the while smiling at Madame and the cook.

Madame knew it took immense restraint for her to eat as slowly as she did, but she also knew there was a lot of work ahead. She excused herself and said she would return shortly, leaving Lisette to finish eating. When she had all but licked her bowl clean, Cook came over, ladle brimming, to offer more. Lisette graciously declined, fighting the survival urge to give in. Madame was impressed when Cook later gave her report, as Lisette suspected she would. Cook acted simple enough, but Lisette sensed she was much more aware of the goings-on in this house than she let on.

Not much time went by before she heard voices, and Madame returned with two other girls, one of similar age to Lisette and one a bit older. Their frocks were simple cotton but beautifully sewn, and the detail was evident to even an inexperienced eye like Lisette's. "Lisette, may I present Marie and Jeannette. Marie, Jeannette, this is Lisette of whom I spoke earlier." Then directly to Lisette, she said, "They will help you in the bath and then take you to your room so you can get settled and changed before dinner. After dinner they'll give you a tour of the house, *d'accord?*"

"*Oui, Madame. D'accord.*" The three left, leaving Madame to talk to Cook. The bath routine upon arrival was legendary in the house and Lisette did not escape it. She had never had a bath and was petrified of being submerged in so much water, but the two other girls put her at ease, splashing and laughing and blowing bubbles, a phenomenon also new to her young and inexperienced eyes.

Both girls were shocked to see the fresh bruises covering Lisette's delicate skin and were careful not to rub them with the abrasive cloth they each had. They didn't give any hint to Lisette of their surprise, but, like Cook, made a note to report back to Madame. She always wanted to know these details so she could best prepare the girls based on their individual backgrounds. When Madame learned of the extent of damage, she was tempted to send someone out to pay a visit to Lisette's father, but realized that without his prized possession many others would be there before her, demanding payment he could no longer provide, and she smiled wickedly, knowing justice would be served on its own accord, as always.

After the bath, Lisette was escorted to her room, which she shared with three other girls. They showed her to her bed, piled high with blankets and covers and a mattress stuffed with fresh straw. It was simply heavenly. Her clothes were hung in a separate closet and there were three dresses and several underclothes, most of which Lisette did not recognize or have any idea how to put on, but she was excited by the selection, three times the size of her current number of dresses. "Madame Sévigné will be by on Monday to measure you for your dresses and undergarments. These were left over from another girl, so we hope they fit, as they will have to do for now. But you will need dresses for the evening and it is so much fun—you will *love* it."

Both Marie and Jeannette chatted in unison and over each other to tell Lisette about her clothes, then about the house and some light gossip about the other girls, but not ill-intended. Lisette sat on her bed and listened in rapture, pinching herself at her good fortune. Her mentors left her to get settled and she promptly fell asleep on top of the covers in her new slip.

She was startled awake a couple of hours later when Marie returned to gather her for dinner. "You must get dressed, Lisette. Here, let us try this cream one on. It looks to be the right length and, although a touch too big, perhaps, it will feel comfortable for you." Lisette started to step into the dress but Marie snatched it away and tossed it on the bed. "No, no, no, silly. First, you must put on these," and she started pulling several items from the closet. She handed each item to Lisette in order, instructing her on how it needed to be fastened and which side faced front (sometimes surprising her) and when all of the layers were secured, they lifted the dress over her head to fall loosely into place. Marie tugged on the laces in the back to the last possible position, and even though it gaped a little bit at the front, the transformation was miraculous. She fussed with Lisette's hair, pinning some back from her face, allowing most of it to fall loosely down her back. She then glanced at her feet and chose a pair of cream slippers to finish her outfit. "Are you ready to see yourself?"

Lisette was not sure what she meant. She looked down and saw the dress and slippers, but Marie had something else in mind. "*Viens*. Over here," she said, opening a closet door to reveal a shimmering mirror, something Lisette had never seen. She'd caught her reflection in shop windows and even in water at times, but she was not prepared for what she saw and gasped, thinking an apparition had appeared, not even knowing it was her standing there.

"It is you, Lisette," Marie piped up, having seen this reaction before. Mirrors of this size were relatively new to Paris and the quality of this one was superb. Lisette began to cry and Marie consoled her with assurances that she would become adjusted to her new form, her new life. Lisette stood tall, sniffed one last time and nodded to say she was ready. Ready to face whatever it was she was facing. Marie squeezed her hand and the two of them left the room, scurrying down the hall to the back stairs, arriving in the kitchen to a cacophony of noise.

All the girls were gathered around the large tables, chatting noisily, waiting for the evening meal to be served. Casual introductions were made and the girls gave their names and smiled warmly, welcoming Lisette to their family and offering to help with anything she might need. Lisette had never had friends, or a family for that matter. She and her father had been alone for many years and she didn't have time for the luxury of such frivolities as friendship. She sat back and watched the scene unfold before her, unsure of what she should or should not say. They were all so free with their words, joking and laughing and mocking each other. They attempted to bring Lisette into the conversation, asking general questions about her life, her age, her home, but knew better than to probe her for details. Madame's instructions were always the same: "If they are here, the life they are leaving behind is not worth remembering, so let it remain in their past."

A few of the girls brought in trays of food and Lisette sat gaping, still feeling the warmth of the stew in her belly. She had never seen so much food in one place at one time and had to remind herself constantly of Madame's warning. She would try everything tonight, but take small helpings.

Madame appeared at the head of Lisette's table as if she had somehow materialized out of her own thoughts. An imposing figure, she stood silently, waiting for the girls to settle down. When they did, she waved her hands over the plentiful table, saying, "Let us feel gratitude for the bounty of food before us. *Alors, mangez,*" and she sat down to join them.

Lisette watched in awe as the girls manipulated their knives and forks with grace—tools she had never held in her hands—and tried to imitate their motions, often stumbling in frustration. Madame watched her from the corner of her eye. She noticed Madame watched all of the girls that way, pointing out a certain posture or an action simply by looking at them individually and hinting toward the action she wanted them to change. Their response was immediate and unapologetic, and then Madame would move on to say something else or comment on something another girl was doing. It was all subtle, not bringing attention to any individual but always guiding them and showing, by her own actions, how to eat and converse like ladies. Lisette knew she was making a fool of herself and yet Madame didn't once point out any flaw. She allowed her to watch the others and practice, which was a relief, as she was trying so hard to please everyone at once and feeling overwhelmed by all there was to learn.

When the meal was finally over and the last morsels on Lisette's plate had been savored (she felt proud to have declined seconds of anything), one of the girls stood up after asking to be excused and started gathering the empty plates to the kitchen. Lisette jumped up automatically to help, feeling embarrassed that someone was cleaning up after her, but the girl gently pushed her back down. "Do not worry, Lisette, you will get your turn, but not tonight. You will soon learn which meals are your responsibility and Marie will explain what you need to do, but tonight is my night, so please sit. Thank you for the offer to help, though. It is much appreciated." And smiling graciously, she continued on with her duties.

They were all so kind, so polite, and Lisette felt tears prick at her eyes. She could never imagine a life this fine. She knew there were expectations that she would have to fill, expectations she dreaded, if the men in her past were any indication of how beastly men were in general. But even so, she had never experienced such abundance in life. Not ever, and she felt such relief and joy that she was having a hard time containing these unknown emotions.

Marie had been watching her closely and saw the tears and her strained effort to maintain her composure. *She will do well here.* Marie gave her a smile, letting her know she understood and that it was okay. She would need to talk to Lisette about that later. Tears and food were meant to flow abundantly here at *la Maison* and although everyone was quite subdued this evening, giving the new girl a chance to adjust, Lisette would soon witness the full gamut of emotions at this table. It was their way of releasing everything, surrounded by support from others who may have experienced similar pain or distress.

Lisette was finally given a tour of the house, showing her all of the boudoirs and the grand salon along with the back stairways and corridors. It was like a maze and she had a hard time believing all of these rooms could actually exist in one house. *Her* home, no less. She was finally led back to her room and introduced to another girl, Sylvie, who would also be sharing the *chambre*, making it a cozy foursome.

They all sat cross-legged on their beds, talking about themselves, each other and their lives here with Madame de Rouler. Their stories were varied but all had a common theme: a tragic beginning that led them all here to a life of serving and satisfying men. What a strange life, Lisette thought. Wouldn't it be glorious to be born in an age where men lived solely for the purpose of serving women? She smiled to herself and Lisette saw the look, pressing her to share what she had found so funny. When Lisette shyly told them her wish they started laughing hysterically, acting out their new roles perfectly. "Monsieur, come here this instant and lick my boots." Or "Monsieur, pour me some wine and scratch my back. No, higher. No, lower. No, left. Yes, there." They were now prancing around the room, imitating their own experiences but reversing the roles and laughing and joking, mimicking the men they had served. Lisette started to enjoy the irony and humor of the images and joined the game.

"Oh, Lisette," Sylvie said, "you are too funny. Such an imagination. I will recall this the next time one of them asks me to scratch his back," and they all hopped back on their beds, enjoying the joke and praising her wicked sense of humor. Lisette followed the others and lay down under the covers on her heaven-sent bed. She listened for a few minutes as the girls' voices got sleepier and quieter and fell asleep to the background sounds in the room.

As time moved on, she quickly learned the ways of the house, the expectations. And after a short while, when she started meeting with the men, she found the experience surprisingly enjoyable. What she had to compare was brutish and abusive behavior by often drunk and angry men, trying to extract payment from her and revenge at the same time. This was so different. These men—some whom she had known before—came to her to receive pleasure and obtain something that was missing from their lives. Often their wives were cold or fearful of sex, or had simply grown bored with them. Their youth had passed and their handsome looks had faded, leaving them feeling inadequate. These were not their words, but Lisette's deductions and she learned to see how vulnerable these strong men were once their armor had been removed. Many cried. Often, they would spend the time talking, and then realize too late their physical purpose would have to wait for another meeting.

She became popular with the men. Accustomed to aloof and more professional woman, they found her refreshing. Her sincerity was what the men longed for and the way she listened to them made them feel heard and understood in a way they had never experienced. Lisette was genuinely interested in them and she remembered their stories, their children, their struggles, asking them questions at their next meeting; "Did you find your ring?" or "Is your son's cough improved?" Without any experience with friendship, Lisette didn't know any differently than to treat them like friends, developing close relationships with them. She was set apart from the others and although she enjoyed the girls' company, she preferred that of the men. Paulette was the exception. She was like a little sister to Lisette and she loved her like no other. When Isabel arrived years later, she adored her, too, but Paulette was the only one who secured such a large piece of her heart.

When Armand came into her life she was twenty-three, and had been with Madame for seven years. She felt she had seen and done everything there was to do in her world and yearned for something new. After her first night with Armand she found herself looking forward to their meetings as she had never done with anyone before and taking extra care with her toilette and dress. She also contrived little games and ploys to keep him interested. There was no more tearing of clothing or wielding of knives, but the teasing and taunting took on a life of its own, torturing them both into ecstasy and joy.

After only two months, Armand came to the excruciating realization that he loved Lisette. More accurately, he was in love with her, which could only lead to great pain and heartbreak for them both. He did not share his feelings with her, as he wanted to protect her from the distress that would surely be caused if anyone else knew. After each visit he would leave her with a longing in his heart, not his groin, which caused him countless hours of anguish when they were apart. His wife was abysmal, which he half expected when they married, and the price he had been willing to pay for her name and title had long ago surpassed its value. He detested her petty attitude. She was still merely a spoiled child who cajoled and manipulated everyone to get her way. But her games had advanced to adulthood and involved real pain and suffering. He knew if she got wind of his amorous feelings, both he and Lisette would suffer and their lives would be tortured, or potentially be in real danger.

More than that, he couldn't imagine his life without Lisette. He wanted to run away with her to some remote cottage and spend languorous days and nights together. He had lived only forty-five years so far and dreaded the possibility of continuing in the same monotonous manner. He had enough money to live like a prince for another forty-five, most of it stashed away out of the clutches of his greedy wife. He was astounded at how much money she went through, and how she paid no attention at all to its extravagant release. Most of Paris was getting rich by him, from the man who made exquisite bonbons that his wife couldn't live without, to the luxurious couturier delivering countless dresses almost daily. He, too, loved the finer things in life but didn't understand the excess of her needs and hoped to never follow in her well-shod footsteps.

Just this morning she had come downstairs complaining about the staff and their incompetence. She was particularly abusive to his valet, Claude, who had been by his side long before Juliette arrived in his life. He winced as he watched her swipe him with her fan, yelling at his insolence and stupidity. At one point Armand grabbed her arm and tore her away, careful not to chide her, as he knew Claude would be the one to suffer in the end, but needing to halt the abuse nonetheless.

It was after one of those instances that Armand came to a chilling realization. There was only one solution to his problem. He was shocked that he was even considering such a thing but he knew, unless he was willing to live a life with her constant tyrannical behavior, he was left with no other choice.

He would have to kill her.

There was no other way out of his lifelong dilemma; albeit one he had created himself. Except for le Duc, there would be little loss felt for his wife's demise. She was despised by his staff and even more so by her friends and obliged acquaintances. He could feel his mind justifying what he was contemplating and attempted to shrug it off as necessary under the dire circumstances in which he found himself.

At his meeting with Lisette later that day, she found him in a jovial mood with almost a bounce in his step, something new for both of them. "What have you been scheming, *mon chéri?*" she prodded, trying to weasel his secret from him. He was surprised how good he felt and began questioning his plan in his mind, thinking maybe his attitude alone would be enough to shift his life's happiness. That lasted a brief moment until reality came crashing down, his bounce deflating with the realization.

"It is nothing, mon amour," he said, and became his usual distracted self again.

He had never referred to her as 'his love' before and she was about to question him when she caught herself, realizing it would be impertinent. But she tucked the words away, deep in her mind, to recall later when alone with her thoughts. "How is Juliette?" she queried.

"She's the same as always. Bored with her life and punishing those around her for it." He had better be more guarded with his thoughts. Lisette knew him well, now, and at times he felt she was reading his mind. This was one thing he must keep to himself at all costs, as he knew it would endanger them both and, worse, Lisette would surely try to talk him out of it.

When he went home that evening he took a brandy to his *bureau*, sat in his favorite leather chair and gazed out his windows at the stars in the cloudless sky. He would need to devise a plan that would not implicate anyone and would ensure a quick death to reduce her suffering, although why, he thought wryly, when he looked around at the carnage of suffering she caused on a daily basis. The most important part of his plan must relate to what followed her death. When enquiries were made—and they would be with le Duc as her father—everyone would need to come off blamelessly. He had never contemplated a murder before and was inwardly horrified at the idea on one level and eerily serene on another, which surprised him, as well as helped convince him it was the right thing to do for everyone's sake.

After three brandies, he went up to his *chambre* where his wife was snoring loudly, lay down beside her, facing her back, and began to caress her in a way he knew she was unable to resist. Deep in sleep she gradually started to squirm under his touch and when she was fully present he slipped inside her from behind, allowing her to stay half asleep, enjoying his affection without having to do much in return. She came quickly, as he knew she would, and he continued with a slow undulating motion to match his touch on her thighs and arms. She was relaxing now and starting to fall asleep again.

In the morning she awoke, unsure if it had been a dream or had actually happened until she felt for the moist residue left between her legs and then sighed with contentment, loving what her husband did for her, asking little in return. She knew her husband adored her—who wouldn't with her title and beauty. It made her smile to think of his lowly birth and how high he had risen. With those thoughts she got up and began her day anew.

Juliette was the master of manipulation and he had learned well by her. In this way he had her as an ally and led her to believe he adored

179

her, a feeling he had never felt for this cold woman, not even from the beginning of their acquaintance. His plan was simple and a method used throughout the ages. Also, the most likely to succeed. He would poison her. Not the most pleasant way to die but the most effective and least likely to evoke suspicion.

His biggest obstacle was that he needed help and would have to engage someone whom he could trust implicitly. He knew he would be asking a great deal from that person, knowing his or her life would be in grave danger if the plan failed. Not danger, but certain death, truth be told, and he despised the idea of enlisting anyone on such a risky undertaking. He knew who it would have to be and planned their encounter meticulously, realizing that from this moment on, witnesses would recall all his actions leading to this event. "Yes, I saw Monsieur du Preix talking to so-and-so. It was unusual, yes" or something to that effect, whereby the entire household would be put under observation and questioned rigorously.

He knew there were poisonous mushrooms on their country estate and he knew where they were located. That part was relatively simple, and he would be able to go out on his horse the day before leaving for the city, which he often did. Once back in Paris, he would need to get them into the kitchen and swap them for the others. For this he would need someone in his household and he planned to approach his valet, Claude, before they left for the country later in the week. Even asking would put them both at risk, as he intended to give Claude full right of refusal, doubting the poor man could ever dare make that choice to his master. What a pompous ass he was, endangering his servant, his friend, in this way. But he'd made the decision and longed for its cruel success.

An opportunity presented itself that evening, giving Armand the weak impression that fate was on his side. One of his wigs had gone missing and he suspected he knew who had taken it. He would need to punish the little rascal (a young street urchin named Eugène who he had taken in as a serving boy but who hadn't completely rid himself of his sticky fingers) and as Claude was responsible for all of the staff under him, he would need to be questioned and reprimanded if necessary. The entire household was talking about it, as someone had found the wig in the stables, tied to the back of a saddle form being used as a horse's tail. The effect was quite a good likeness, but Armand was not amused, at least outwardly—inwardly, he thought the gag rather clever—and the entire household anticipated the meeting that was sure to ensue.

When those details were brought to Armand's ears, he summoned Claude, asking the household where he was, and yelling his name so that it was well known that his valet would feel the wrath of his master's anger. A rare occurrence indeed, but one no one wished to experience. Everyone agreed that rare anger when expressed was far more fierce than anger expressed on a daily basis. Many other things, long held, could be unleashed on the poor soul that bore the brunt of the moment of its release, and tonight it would surely be Claude.

The young boy heard Claude's name being called and ran to intercept him, apologizing and admitting his wrong, and begging him not to tell Monsieur, who would surely throw him back on the street. Claude had always been kind to the boy and his short-sighted prank could end his happy, yet short stint at his whim, leaving the boy with one of his first ever feelings of regret. He turned to him and said, brusquely, "I will deal with you later. Now, I must face the wrath of our master." But he saw the look of fear on Eugène's face and winked as he turned to rush off in pursuit of Monsieur du Preix. He had been with Monsieur since he was a boy the age of the rapscallion he had just left, who was not too unlike the Monsieur in his devious pranks. He hoped he could remind him of his own similar stunts, reducing the punishment on the poor lad, now waiting for his fate to be determined.

Armand was standing on the landing outside his *bureau* overlooking the lower foyer. His eyes were angry slits as he watched Claude almost run up the stairs. "You called, Monsieur," he said, staying composed but inside, feeling the concern creep in after seeing into his master's eyes.

Without a word, Armand swung open the massive wooden door, waited for Claude to enter, followed him in and then slammed it with all his might, causing the reverberation to be heard throughout the floors above and below. Both men were surprised at the sound. Claude cringed but Armand was able to hide his surprise, launching directly into his well-prepared rebuke. "What the *hell* is going on this house? *You* are responsible for this…this… bite-sized horror, and I would expect more from you, Claude. Much more." His voice was loud and although it carried to the hall, it was muffled by thick walls and doors. Armand had had the sound from this room tested many times to know exactly how much traveled to the rest of the household. Tone and feeling did, but words were safe in his haven. The poor man started to stammer an apology and explanation and unexpectedly, Armand stepped right up to him, grabbed his arm and leaned into his ear, scaring him half to death.

"Claude, I need to speak to you urgently, and you must listen carefully." His tone was hushed and Claude was confused, trying to connect his words to the wig incident.

181

He continued, "Don't worry about the wig. I know all about it—thought it was quite, well, funny, really—and trust you to handle it effectively. Now, I'm going to have to start yelling at you in a moment, so be prepared," as he launched into, "I don't *care* how young he is. He should know better and so should you. Now then, what are you two going to do about it, heh?" and he returned to his conspiratorial tone. Claude was just catching on and now gave his master his full attention, realizing he had beads of sweat on his brow that had no bearing on the original summoning to this meeting.

"Claude," he began, great hesitancy in his manner, "before I ask this of you, you must *promise* me that you will decline if you cannot do it. Do you promise me that?"

Armand's look was sheer pleading and now Claude's stomach lurched with fear, knowing that whatever would be asked of him, he would have to comply. Not because it was his master's wish but because of his duty to him, knowing that if he was asking something of him, it was his only solution and he must honor his request. "Of course, Monsieur," he answered, lying slickly through his teeth.

He paused again, the energy in the room now palpable with anticipation and fear. "I need you to help me kill my wife." He hadn't intended to blurt it out like that but there was so little time and there really was no easy way to broach the subject. He could tell that Claude was waiting to see if he had turned the tables to play a trick on him in turn, but the man could readily see by his expression that he was serious—deadly serious, was the dry thought that ran through his head. Armand backed away to yell random thoughts in the air, giving him a chance to absorb what he had said and to keep up the ruse of their meeting.

Armand paused again, leaning in to whisper in his ear and outline his plan, giving details of what Claude's role would be. When he had finished, he reached for Claude's hands, looked him in the eye and said, "You have been my most loyal servant, my friend. I will give you tonight to think about this request—one I sincerely regret having to make, as I know as well as you the implications of what I am asking—and tomorrow evening you will come looking for me, with the boy in tow to discuss his punishment. You will stay after and give me your answer. Do not say anything more. I beg you to think long and hard before tomorrow night."

Claude left, face ashen, sending the maid *de chambre*, who had been lurking close by, scurrying off in search of the boy so he could fetch a pitcher of water and some strong ale to take to Claude's room. He headed there directly, refusing to look up or reply to the many who awaited news of his meeting. None was forthcoming, putting fear in the lot of them, especially the young Eugène. Claude locked his door and refused entry to anyone, except when he needed his ale replenished, which was twice more that night. The young boy stationed himself outside his door for the night, finally curling up on the cold stone floor with a coat as a blanket. Claude knew this was more than the punishment he deserved and hadn't intended to make it so harsh for him but he put his own needs above the boy's, as it was critical he keep his composure to sort through this disastrous request. Besides, the boy's duress was brought on by his own behavior so maybe this lesson would prevent others like it from following. He didn't know, and at this moment didn't care, knowing what he had to deal with was far graver than a missing wig and the hurt feelings of a young lad.

At dawn, he found him curled up outside his door and before anyone else discovered him, brought him in to sit down and give him the half-hearted lecture that would be required. By this time the boy was chastised considerably and few words were necessary to bring the point home. The two sat for some for a few minutes before Claude sent him off to get on with his chores and reminded him of their meeting with the Monsieur later that evening. He couldn't handle the pain in the young lad's eyes and stopped him as he was halfway out the door. "Eugène, just a minute. You know what you did was wrong, *non*?"

The boy nodded rapidly, eyes wide in anticipation of what was next, so he continued, "There are many things in this household that go on that are of no concern to you, do you understand?" More rapid nodding. "Good. Now, last night Monsieur had some of those other things on his mind when he met me in his office. What you did was wrong but it was only one of many things that had gone wrong for Monsieur. He was mostly angry with me for allowing the household to degenerate in this way. Your prank was the catalyst, no doubt about it, but his anger was directed at me. Do not overly concern yourself about tonight. Your master is fair and just and a sincere apology will go a long way, hmm?" The nodding continued, bright tears added at the end, convincing Claude that he was indeed a fine boy and had learned a hard lesson. His timing couldn't have been worse, which was no fault of his own. With no more thought of the boy, he dismissed him with a wave and a gentle smile, and he the boy left after breathing an audible sigh of relief.

When Claude knocked at his master's door the next evening, the solemnity in the room was palpable and his heart went out again to the boy, who, as a child, would believe he was the sole cause of the mood. The meeting between the three was short, giving Eugène enough time to offer a well thought-out apology, Armand to reprimand him—but not too harshly—and then the two men to send Eugène away so they could 'discuss other issues at hand'.

Armand held his breath even though he already knew what Claude's answer would be. He patiently waited for him to speak, trying to ease the pressure of the moment.

"Monsieur, I have given much thought to your request and I am willing to play my part. I am honored by your trust in me and will not fail you. You have my assurance." Armand took a breath, sounding almost as if he were stifling a sob, and embraced the other man warmly, the first time ever in the long history of their relationship.

"Until the night of our return, then. I will ensure the *champignons* are on the menu for an intimate dinner for Madame and myself, as we often do after the country. I will wait for your nod that it has been done before we sit down to eat. Then we shall wait." He wanted to apologize again but felt it would be a paltry attempt to make right this wrong situation, so he said nothing and returned to his desk where he had been half-heartedly catching up on some of his missives. Claude left the room, leaving his master alone to his work, and himself to his own reflections.

Chapter XIX

Four days in the country was the last thing Armand wanted, but he had to keep up all appearances and was careful not to change his attitudes and habits toward Juliette. He continued to answer her brusquely, not interested in her incessant prattle. As she fussed over the preparations for the evening's dinner party, he gave her his usual bored expression and she rolled her eyes in frustration, making a crack about the bill becoming larger than he anticipated if he wasn't willing to get involved. "Fine," was his standard reply, both knowing his time was worth far more to him than the massive quantities of money he was shelling out. At dinner he was attentive to her but not overly and spent most of the evening discussing business and politics with the influential men around his table. At one time he leaned over and whispered something lewd in Juliette's ear, making her giggle and blush and she turned around, swatting him affectionately on his shoulder. It didn't go unnoticed among their guests, and a few of the wives secretly wished their husbands were more like Armand.

The only break in pattern happened after the guests had all retired to their own *chambres* and Armand decided to be more generous with Juliette and give her something a little more, on what could prove to be their last night together. He feigned fatigue when she made her expected advances and he relented, giving her the mistaken impression that it was she initiating their lovemaking (after all these years she was so easy to play) and he who was giving in to her wishes again. She lay there waiting for him to enter her but instead he took his time, caressing her gently, watching the rise and fall of her small breasts from her breathing. She looked nervous and was unaccustomed to her husband doing much other than grunting and pushing and then shaking upon his orgasm, and if she'd had enough time to prepare herself on a rare occasion she could climax with him. Otherwise, it would be too late and she would have to wait until he was sleeping or forget it altogether.

But tonight he was slowly moving in and out, now kissing her neck, her breasts. She could feel her pulse racing and she started to groan with pleasure. He all but stopped, letting the feeling grow inside her and then started again, more quickly now but still rhythmically. She was starting to pant and pulled him closer to her, urging him to go faster, deeper. Anything to satisfy the longing that surged up from her core. Never before had she felt such intensity. A sensation of being ready to explode. He felt her response and all but stopped, her eyes opening wide in tortured pleasure. After a few moments he began pushing into her more deeply and more quickly, faster and faster until she started to scream out in the throes of passion. He picked up his pace, creating pandemonium in her body until she was writhing uncontrollably, wracked in spasms, her throat hoarse from her screams. He came with a long, deep groan and fell on her in a heap before rolling over on his back, covered in sweat and his own juices intermingled with hers. She lay like a starfish, spread-eagle, unable to move a muscle, staring up at the ceiling in a blissful daze. They both lay like that, wordless, until he heard her breathing change and knew she had fallen asleep, exhausted and satisfied, probably the first (and last) time in her life, he realized with pity. He rolled over to join her slumber, quite sure that their friends on both sides of the wall (along with most everyone else in the house) had heard their lovemaking, and fell asleep knowing he had taken another successful step toward his ruthless plan.

She awoke to an empty bed, knowing full well he needed to avoid her amorous feelings the morning after their lovemaking. He went for a ride with one of the guests, who couldn't resist ribbing him about his comfortable sleep last night, winking in a gentlemanly conspiracy.

"I slept very well, thank you," was his noncommittal reply, a devilish smile playing on his lips. The two rode out to the edge of the property and then traveled back along the fence line, giving Armand a chance to inspect any obvious damage and report it to his staff.

Breakfast was being served in the large dining room, now floodlit with sun coming in through the unencumbered windows and reflecting against the mirror-paneled doors throughout the immense room. Several of the guests were there, Juliette acting the perfect hostess, but noticeably more amenable than usual. When he saw her, he strode purposefully up to her and kissed her on her cheek, lingering for a brief moment before standing and walking over to a gentleman he had wanted to speak with last night but hadn't the time to approach. The woman beside Juliette watched his strong figure walk away and then looked at their host, who was grinning slyly. Her thoughts were on last night and she wished they weren't going home today for she would like to attempt to convince Armand of a repeat of last night's performance.

He caught her looking at him and smiled in his condescending way, turning back to his guest with interest. She shrugged, realizing it might not be as easy as that, but she would enjoy trying, and she turned her attention to the woman nattering beside her. *When will these women shut their mouths?* Their talking was annoying and never stopped. She stifled a yawn and put on her expression that perfectly stated, "Although I'm interested, I've heard this before, so it's time to move on," which invariably made a quick end to the story, allowing her to talk to someone else. Her high breeding gave her the finely-honed skill of communicating what she wanted without saying a word. It was a skill that most royalty possessed and none of them enjoyed when it was inflicted upon them. Juliette always liked to add her own twist, confusing the party she was speaking to so that they left feeling darker somehow, but couldn't pin it directly on anything she had said.

The group started to disassemble in preparation for their departure back to Paris, and in some cases their own country estates in other directions. Armand slipped away on his horse 'to check on the fences one more time' and discreetly gathered the few mushrooms he required for their final dinner that evening. He was careful to leave the area undisturbed, leaving his horse tethered by the damaged fence and then covering up his tracks underneath the large oak where he had discovered the mushrooms on their last trip to the country. Not knowing why at the time, he mentioned his discovery to no one. Now he was relieved by his prudent foresight and returned to the *château* with instructions to the farm hand to fix the fence where most of the damage had been discovered.

Armand and Juliette's carriage was the last to leave and they sat quietly, side-by-side for the long and arduous journey back to the city. It was still light when they arrived and amidst the unpacking and rearranging of their luggage, Armand slipped away with his stash of mushrooms, passing them discreetly to Claude so he could clean them and brush away the obvious markings that set them apart from the harmless variety. He had already secured a small dose of belladonna root and had left an indistinct pouch for Claude in the wine cellar. This would be the trickiest part as he would need to sprinkle it on the mushrooms without detection, and the risk to Armand was extreme, as Cook would be delving out the portions, not Claude. But he needed to be sure, and the belladonna would give the mushrooms the surety he needed without undue suspicion.

Juliette headed to the kitchen in search of Cook, to discuss the evening's menu, and suggested some fresh mushrooms would be a nice touch. She gave a slight smirk as she said it, thinking of last night's encounter with her husband and still wanting to please him. Cook found the look odd, but sent one of the scullery maids to the cellar in search of her request. Armand and Juliette had discussed the evening meal on the ride back, and Armand dropped the idea into the conversation as a casual suggestion. The driver wouldn't have heard, and Juliette, true to form, started believing it was her idea, and what a good one, she might add, so that by the time she made the request it came out as something she thought as a nice gesture to do for Monsieur. Cook wasn't used to doing nice gestures for Monsieur—not on Madame's instruction—but was good at doing what she was told so went on to her duties, putting Madame's strange behavior out of her mind.

When they first arrived, Claude managed to sneak away to the cellar unseen, grabbing two bottles of wine while he was there, before heading to the food storage area near the bottom of the stairs. If he were found down below, the wine would be a perfect alibi as it was his responsibility to ensure a supply of wine was always on hand. He found the fresh mushrooms exactly where he had left them when he had been down here rummaging around before leaving for the country, and was relieved to see there were still only a few left on the shelves. He added the small bundle Armand had slipped into his pocket making up just enough for two servings. His breath was heavy and erratic, there was sweat on his brow, and his ears were alert for any signs of the maid, who could arrive at any moment. Leaving the rag on the floor among others rags in a random heap by the stairs, he took one last look at the grouping to see if they blended together and then soundlessly headed back to the dining room, wine in hand. As he was about to place the wine on the buffet, he noticed the maid heading toward the cellar and quickly set the wine down, his hands shaking.

Dinner was served three long hours later. Juliette had taken extra care, choosing one of her low-cut dresses, now all the rage in the Paris fashion circles. Armand looked handsome in his velvet pants and ruffled blouse, tied loosely at the neck, his velvet jacket unbuttoned over top. The wine had been opened previously, so he strode over to the buffet and poured a glass for both Juliette and himself. He downed it quickly and discreetly, topping his up as he turned to head toward the table, which had been set intimately for two, at his wife's request.

"This is lovely, Juliette. I haven't seen fresh flowers on the table for some time. What else have you got planned for this evening?" He was acting his part, despite the terror he felt welling in his gut. She really was lovely, physically, and he had a momentary lapse of confidence where he questioned his actions and motives.

She smiled sweetly at him and then turned toward the doors leading to the kitchen. "Where *is* everyone?" she demanded, the grating whine back in her voice. "We've been sitting here for five minutes and not a soul to attend to us. Cook. Antoine. What is taking everyone so long?"

His courage quickly returned. This woman's bitterness could not heal. Not in this lifetime. Perhaps never. He steeled his reserve and put his focus back on the night's proceedings. Three members of the staff rushed in, clacking and clucking around Juliette in a flurry of profuse apologies and regrets. Claude followed shortly after, calm and reserved, despite the gruesome knowledge of what was about to take place. Armand took strength from him and thanked God again for this incredible man, who had been by his side for as long as he could remember. He caught the man's subtle nod and both men averted their eyes, making mental preparations for what was now sure to come.

Armand had always been a creature of habit. His clothes were organized by color. His jewelry as well. Everything in his personal life had its place and his habits had been engrained in him since he was a young child. He ate in the same way. Meat first, the most important sustenance. Potatoes second, satisfying his hunger quickly, and vegetables and jellies last, depending on how much room or interest he had at the time. Juliette lived haphazardly, relying heavily on others to pick up after her, to find what she had misplaced. She ate in this same haphazard way, poking her fork into a piece of meat, jabbing a mushroom on the end of it. Then having her potatoes, more mushrooms, more meat.

He watched her closely, keeping pace with her bites, but still working through his potatoes by the time she had already eaten several pieces of the deadly fungus. She was flushed and sweating lightly, but it was a warm evening and she was on her second glass of wine. No sure telltale sign yet. She continued to eat, near finishing what was on her plate, he, just finishing his potatoes, when he noticed her breathing starting to become shallow. He looked away, spearing a large mushroom—praying it was one of the non-toxic varieties that he'd noticed tended to be larger—and popped it in his mouth. He chewed slowly, making sure someone other than Claude had seen him and was happy to see Cook, always seeking praise, watching him expectantly. He smiled and nodded and speared another before looking back at his wife.

She was starting to show signs of struggle and reached for her wine, gulping frantically. Armand was out of his chair and over to her instantly, the mushroom still stuck on the tines of his fork. He got to her just as she collapsed from her chair, falling into his arms, where he lay her down clumsily, quickly resting her head on his lap. He screamed at the staff to get help and for someone to fetch a doctor just as she started convulsing and gripping her stomach in agony. Claude was standing ready for any instructions when Armand grabbed him to come down and take Juliette as he pulled himself away and began retching uncontrollably onto the carpet, pain stabbing his insides. He heard Juliette's agonizing screams but was helpless to do anything, immobilized as he was by his own pain and retching. The pain was intolerable and he quickly passed out, leaving chaos in his wake, and Claude to clean up the mess.

Chapter XX

Armand awoke to a pounding headache and a dryness in his mouth and throat, desperately in need of water. He saw Claude hovering over him and as his eyes came back into focus the doctor came into hazy view, standing on the other side of the vast *chambre*. There were several other people in the room besides the staff who had witnessed the dinner and its demise. Le Duc was there, which Armand found odd until the memories flooded back, gushing into his head instantly. He pushed himself onto his elbows and looked into Claude's eyes before he had the courage to speak.

"Juliette?" he asked. His voice was raspy and barely audible but everyone in the room caught what he had asked. He heard sniffling over by the door and waited for him to respond, receiving only a shake of his head and the words, "I'm so sorry, Monsieur. Juliette did not survive. She died quickly, which I know you would want to know and..." he tried to continue but seeing the tears in his master's eyes, caught his words, and then the anticipated but never prepared for wail, *"Nooooooooooo."* Armand broke down to cry in uncontrolled sobs. He saw now that his father-in-law's eyes were red and swollen, and wondered how long she'd been dead. No feelings of relief or gladness filled his heart. Only the piercing sound of her final screams before his own pain took over his consciousness.

Claude stepped back as the doctor came to his side, asking the usual questions: how was he feeling, how was his headache, his stomach. But Armand interrupted him to ask the question on everyone's mind, "What happened? I don't remember much after seeing Juliette—*Oh God, Juliette"*— and a few more sobs, before he continued, "before I saw she looked ill and I grabbed her just before she collapsed. Then I felt ill and started heaving, and then she screamed—*Oh God, that scream*—that's all I remember."

The doctor spoke softly to Armand, not wanting everyone to hear his words. "We believe you were both poisoned."

"Poisoned." Armand interrupted, "By whom? Why?"

"These are all questions we're trying to answer and we have started questioning the staff. We have no answers yet, but we're quite sure it was the mushrooms. It may have been accidental. Gross negligence, if you ask me. How any person could make this kind of stupid mistake is beyond me." The doctor's anger covered his obvious relief at his patient and friend's recovery, and he searched for someone at whom he could lash out. "We are tracking down the market vendor where they were purchased, in hopes of gleaning some answers, but at this time we know little. You must rest. You, too, almost died, my friend." He shuddered. *If Armand had taken only a few more bites...* "I will be up later to check on you. Now, everyone *out.* Except you, Claude. I would like you to stay by his side in case he requires any further attention. Do not sleep or leave his side unless you replace yourself, understand? The worst may not be over."

He patted Armand affectionately on the shoulder, gathered his bloodletting tools and scalpels and bowed to le Duc before leaving the room, pushing the others out ahead of him. Le Duc came over to offer his sympathies and thank him for making his daughter as happy as was possible, considering her high demands. Fresh tears sprung to his eyes as Armand remembered his kindness over the years and returned his condolences to his now-deceased wife's grieving father.

When everyone had left, leaving Claude alone with his master, he came back to Armand's side and asked if there was anything he could do. Both men looked at each other, tears flowing more readily, now that they were out of the peering glances of the others. He leaned over and Armand reached his arms around him, hugging him close as both men sobbed in each other's arms. If anyone witnessed their behavior they would see it as the natural grieving of husband and friend for the woman lost. But the two men knew their sorrow stemmed from remorse and regret at the crime they had knowingly committed together. Claude finally stood and Armand spoke for the first time since the dinner. "Nothing would ever happen in this world if man knew ahead of time the true implications of his actions, my friend. Nothing would ever occur." He continued to sob, and Claude felt the truth in his words to the core of his being.

Part V

Chapter XXI

Nathan bolted up in bed, drenched in sweat from head to toe, his head pounding and his body shaking with fear. A nightmare. God, it was horrible. Such pain and death all around him. The images were hazy but he saw this beautiful woman. A sad, beautiful woman, and a man, both dying. They looked vaguely familiar, but he couldn't place them. Was he the man in the dream? He couldn't be sure. He lay back down and then quickly changed his mind when his bare skin touched the clammy sheets. He padded to the shower holding his head in his hands, wanting to shake the nausea rising in his throat.

He ran the cold water and stepped in, jolted suddenly awake and feeling the shock subdue his bodily pains. After one minute he switched to hot. Not scalding, but after the cold it felt like it was burning his skin. One minute and then he switched again. Then cold, then hot and finally ending with cold. It was a routine he followed whenever he felt he was catching something and was about to fall sick. It seemed to force his body to pay attention and knock out whatever was trying to take root. He toweled himself dry before stepping out to examine his reflection in the wall-to-wall mirror above the granite vanity. "They don't call this one 'vanity' for nothing," he said, and looked up, chuckling at his own attempt at humor.

He reached back to close the shower door, keeping the steam from hazing his reflection. It had already blurred along the edges and before he knew what had happened he saw the woman's face—the one from his dream—staring back at him where his own reflection should have been. He stood stunned momentarily, before pulling his towel from around his waist to wipe the mirror in broad, fast strokes clearing his own image that now thankfully reflected back at him. The doctor had told him it would take a few weeks to recover completely and that he may experience some intense emotional outbursts, but he didn't think this was exactly what she'd meant. This was all too real. Too ghostlike. He would remember to ask her about this when he went back in on Friday for a 'once over' as she'd called it. He was extremely unsettled by what he thought he'd just seen, so in his usual manner, he deflected his thoughts elsewhere. They settled on Dr. Menzies. Nice woman, the good doctor. A real looker, too. Maybe he would ask her out after their appointment. Naaa, she really wasn't his type. Too smart, for one thing. He didn't appreciate a woman who was smarter than him. Too independent, too.

He pulled his robe down from behind the bathroom door, slipped it on and headed to the kitchen in search of something to drink. He was pretty sure a nurse would be there, ready to prepare food and check his vitals. He would mention the dreams and the sheets so she could get the woman on shift two – more like a maid than a nurse – to take care of it. He was grateful to Marc for arranging the help, even though he thought at the time he was being overprotective. But now he valued the round-the-clock staff. Round half the clock, that is, as they were only there now from eight in the morning until eight at night, but that was more than enough to cover the essentials. He had been sleeping through the night since the third or fourth night home so those shifts had been dropped. What do people do when they don't have any money, he wondered, but only allowed the thought to skim through his mind before it flitted on to something else.

Today he was going to get up the courage to call the therapist, something he'd been putting off, but knowing it was inevitable. Especially in light of the incident with the mirror. There had been too much brought to the surface. Too many unresolved pains that demanded his attention. He found himself curious and mildly interested, even though the case study was his own personal life. Being a banker like his father, there hadn't been a lot of personal digging in a long line of conservative banker types. Marc strayed far from the pack by becoming a writer, so he was exempt, as the black sheep, making his behavior understandable and always excusable.

Nathan, on the other hand, had lived under the microscopic glare of his father, who made his expectations known from a young age. His week in the hospital reminded him of that, and gave him a chance to look at what it was like for him growing up, wanting to play, to have fun, without a care in the world. He could feel his anger welling up to the surface and made a mental note about his reaction. All very interesting, he pondered. With his self-analysis fresh on his mind, he went to the counter to pick up the business card of the guy Dr. Menzies had suggested. 'Dr. J. Cameron, PhD, ND.' He didn't know half the time what the acronyms were at the end of anyone's name, so he was not surprised to be stumped by 'ND'. He reached for his cell and dialed the number, then picked up the freshly brewed coffee, à la nurse what's-her-name, and headed to the patio, closing the sliding door behind him. The privacy would be optimal out here.

He waited for someone to pick up. "Doctors-Olson-Cameron-and-Davies. How may I help you?"

He was tempted to ask the chipper voice was at the other end whether she had any idea how she sounded when she answered the phone, but thought the question would end up in his file, so he changed his mind and asked to make an appointment with Dr. Cameron. "Just one moment, please." And then after a few seconds, she asked, "Is this a referral from another doctor?"

"Yes, from Dr. Menzies." Short and sweet reply, still holding the thought that his comments were being recorded and could be held against him at a later date.

A slight pause and then, "He's had a cancellation and can see you this afternoon at two. What is your name, please?" After he gave her his details, she asked, "Do you have our address?"

"Yes, I have his card."

"Good, we'll see you at two, then." Click.

Whatever his intentions, they had nothing to do with seeing a therapist today. He was tempted to call and back out, but it would always be difficult to take this step and he had implied to Dr. Menzies that he would try to see him before Friday. No time like the present, he thought, and set his phone down, looking out on the spectacular view below.

He spent the rest of the morning relaxing, reading a book and eating an unusual but delicious pita sandwich his East Indian home-care nurse had whipped up for lunch. He asked her if she would marry him and she said she'd wait to see if he had anything to offer before she agreed—touché. He was sure she heard proposals all the time and was quite tired of fending them off. Then he felt stupid for his words and wanted to take them back. Instead, he gave her a feeble apology, but she didn't seem phased by him in the least. It was part of her job, he imagined, and what she had signed up for. Still, dealing with sick, lecherous men all day long. There wasn't enough money in the world...

At one thirty he called a cab, waited fifteen minutes for it to arrive—not unusual for this time of day—and then calculated that, if the traffic was perfect, he would arrive on time. If not—more likely—he would be five to ten minutes late. He wondered what ol' Doc C would have to say about that.

He took the stairs two at a time and entered the offices of Dr. James Cameron, Naturopathic Doctor. So that's what ND stood for. He didn't have long to wait to find out. After Nate took a few minutes to answer the usual barrage of extremely personal questions, a man in a crisp white shirt and jeans appeared from the door adjacent to the waiting room and called his name. Nathan stood up and reached out his hand in greeting, like he was meeting a fellow business associate. The doctor seemed to take it in stride. Old habit, he thought, and followed him in to join him near the edge of the room, where two chairs were positioned facing each other. No windows on three of the sides and a large modern painting covering most of one of them. The chair he'd sat in faced a large plant and across, the doctor.

"It's nice to meet you, Mr. Bouchard. Dr. Menzies filled me in on what happened last week to bring me up to speed, but I'd like to hear your version a little later, if you don't mind." Without waiting for a response, he continued. "I don't know if Dr. Menzies mentioned my policy regarding fees, and sometimes the receptionists forget to go over it on the phone, so I'll tell you up front and get that out of the way. If you're late—one minute, five minutes, twenty, it makes no difference—your appointment will still end at the allotted time and of course, you will still be billed the full fee. Because of this, I find most of my patients are never late more than once, so I guess this will likely be your last time? Funny how our minds work, isn't it?" He took a breath and kept on going. "Which brings us to why we're here today, doesn't it?"

Another rhetorical question. At least Nathan was keeping up. "Why do you think you need to be here today, besides the obvious, being what other people might want for you?" Then he stopped as abruptly as he began and sat perfectly still while he waited for Nathan's response.

The question everyone always knows is coming. Probably the first question out of every shrink's mouth at every first meeting they ever have. Yet Nathan was unprepared. He hadn't thought it through. He'd made the appointment so quickly and then, *Bam.* He was here. The silence was starting to feel awkward but the doctor looked unruffled. "I think I'm fucked up, Dr. Cameron. That pretty much sums it up."

The doctor wrote something down and then looked up, "May I quote you? That was good—I liked it. Refreshing to hear a bit of honesty. I don't see that too often from this side of the desk, so to speak." His smile was genuine and he didn't appear to be mocking him at all.

I'm sure he sees all kinds. It made Nathan feel something like pride after he'd done something unique. Then he realized what just passed through his head. *God, you're pathetic, man.*

"What was that all about? Your face changed about five different times in five seconds. What went on there?"

This guy would be tricky. Perceptive. Extremely blunt. He wasn't sure if his usual charm would weasel out of this one. Then he realized he needed the opposite tactic and jumped right in. "My train of thought went something like this: 'Wow, the doctor thinks I'm special. That feels so good and nice to hear. Rare, but nice.' Then 'You're pathetic. Get a life.' That's most of it, I think. I was also trying to psychoanalyze myself while I was doing it and then stopped, realizing there was stiff competition in the room and thought I'd turn the floor over to you." Nathan was starting to warm up to this guy and felt surprisingly good about saying what he'd said, not because it was eloquent—it sounded ridiculous when he repeated it back to himself in his head—but because he wasn't used to expressing himself in this way and he knew he needed to start somewhere, and this guy seemed to be a good place to start.

"Impressive." Then smiling, "Did it feel good when I said that, too?" He paused for a moment, and then went on to explain, "It sounds like I'm joking but that's a common reaction, and telling for what we want to discover about what's buried deep down inside. Are your parents still living?"

Try to keep up, Nate—this guy's jumping all over. "Yes, they both are."

"Describe your relationship with your father. How it is now and how it was when you were, say, three. It will help you if you put it into words. So, bear with me while we start with the basics. Okay, go…"

"You know you're charging by the hour, don't you? It would benefit you financially to slow it down a bit, don't you think?" Nathan's attempt at humor wasn't lost on the doctor and he laughed lightly, and then waited for the rest. "My father is a banker. I'm a banker. His father was a banker. Textbook case so far, I'm sure. Our relationship now is all business. We meet to discuss stock options and market trends. He, asking pointed questions, as *he* says, 'to see where my horizons are at' and me, hearing disappointment in every word he mutters. I have never been good enough for his high standards and the word 'failure' has crossed his lips on many occasions. Quite recently, in fact. Don't remember now what it was about. Doesn't really matter, does it?" Now it was his turn for rhetorical questions.

Nathan was on a roll and continued with his next breath, "My father is an incredible man but he was not, and *is* not a good father—in his son's opinion, that is. Or more accurately, in *this* son's opinion. I think my brother feels the same but I'll let him spend his own $200 to tell you about that if he wants. If you asked my father directly, he would claim his skills as a father (although lacking in some unimportant areas) are excellent. But for me, I always think of that British poet, what's-his-name? The one who wrote, *Our Parents Fuck Us Up* or something close to that, and it goes on to say how they don't mean to but it always happens nonetheless. Do you know the poem?"

"Philip Larkin. I have it framed in my office at home. An eloquent description. Go on."

"Well, that's my take on our relationship. Even though he didn't *intend* to mess me up, toning down the poet's language a notch,"—to which the doctor muttered a "thank you"—"he's still culpable in my opinion because, intentions or not, his actions created my reactions. Simple Law of Relativity. 'Officer, I didn't *mean* to run him over but I was drunk and didn't see him' doesn't give the guy a get-out-of-jail-free card, does it?"

"No, I agree. It does not. What about your mother?"

"Oh, my mother was a player in my game of life, too, although he was the main villain. There's still a bit of anger there, I know. I'm working on that part as we speak. Shall I continue on with my childhood?" The doctor nodded without interjecting his comments, and continued to sit back, one leg crossed, one arm under his elbow, the other with his index finger resting on his chin, a bit like Rodin's, *The Thinker.*

"When I was two, my father adored me. That lasted until I was three, when the evil baby brother arrived, attention stealer extraordinaire. People say kids don't remember that far back but I remember Marc's arrival vividly. My father was a busy man, as I'm sure you surmised, but he was around a lot more when he was just starting out, newly married, his first son at home to carry on the family name, the family traditions. I remember he used to hold me for hours in the evening. Me, sitting on his lap, him, reading the newspaper or a financial journal or some other relevant rag he was interested in at the time. I would lie against his chest and eventually fall asleep and then Mom usually took me up to bed.

"When my brother arrived, Dad dropped me like a hot potato. Son number two was cute and son number one was well on his way in the world already so he didn't really need a father any more. I hated my baby brother with a passion. I tried to suffocate him once, when he was about six months old. Is there a statute of limitations on attempted murder, by the way? It's a good thing mothers have a sixth sense. She came running down the hall—I was as quiet as a mouse, so not sure what triggered it, but it wasn't sound, that's for sure—and she flung open the door, shoving me aside and checking little Marc's breathing. He was fine. I'd just come up with the idea and had only started, not knowing then what to do. I just knew I wanted him to shut up forever and thought it was a good plan. My Mom hauled me off to Dad, who was stoking his pipe in the living room, trying to relax after a hard day.

"I don't think he ever forgave me for that and I don't think I ever recovered from his rejection. He still likes to say, at a large family gathering or an office party, 'Nate, tell everyone about the time you tried to kill your brother, ha, ha, ha,' but it stopped being funny when I was three and a half." He hesitated for a moment and then asked if he should continue or if that was enough information to get him started.

"Based on what you've just told me I think I have a pretty good idea how difficult it has been for you to tell me all of this. The classic symptoms from this type of father are passive/aggressive, keeping your feelings stuffed down, anger usually expressed as a victim mentality. All characteristics that make it challenging to share your feelings with your therapist. Well done. I know it couldn't have been easy, but I think you're starting to see the alternative is worse, don't you agree?"

"Agreed."

"Good. Now it's my turn. I'm going to give you an idea of what I see happening here and some possible approaches on how best to work through it. Notice I don't say 'solve.' This is not a problem that we need to make go away. This is a part of who you are and we're going to get you to make peace with it." Another small pause gave Nathan a chance to digest his words, and then the next piece: "I use several different kinds of therapy, depending on the patient's needs and personal tolerances. I've been doing this work for twenty-five years and have found many of the alternative techniques to be an excellent complement to the traditional training that I base everything on. Now, here's some good news for a banker like yourself. My first session is free. I don't charge because, frankly, you might not like me and it seems wrong to charge you $200 just so you can come to that conclusion."

"There's bad news, isn't there?"

"Yup. The bad news is that if you sign on it will likely cost you a lot of money. I would want to see you three times per week for the next four weeks while you're off work, and then one or two times per week after that. But there *is* a guarantee."

201

He'd definitely caught Nathan's attention. "You'll refund my money if I'm not totally satisfied?"

"Better. I guarantee your life will be *much* better after the next two months and your life will be permanently changed for it. I don't take on everyone who walks through that door, by the way, but I think you'll be a snap to get back on track. You're open at the moment, against your natural grain I'm guessing, but open all the same. I don't see you meeting with me much beyond these first four weeks. They could be extremely intense, I must forewarn you, but 'no pain, no gain' as my Pilates instructor loves to say."

Nathan wasn't about to ask what 'Pilates' was and he'd forgotten to ask what a Naturopathic Doctor was, but he could do his own research online at home. Doctor Menzies said he could go onto his computer as long as it wasn't work related—at all. Surprisingly, his father had given his full support for his leave, but not without mentioning the scrambling that would have to occur, and whatnot. He had to mention the 'whatnots' involved. He could never just make it okay for Nathan to be sick, or tired, or sick and tired, which is what he was now.

"Think about it and let me know. You can call the front and they'll put you through to my voice mail."

Nathan was brought back to the present and only half caught his last words, but then realized what he had been saying and simplified it for them both. "Sign me up, Doc. I'm a banker, trained to make decisions on the fly. I know a good deal when I see one." And he stood to reach out and once again shake the other man's hand, liking him very much by now. "You're not what I expected. That's a good thing."

"Glad to hear it, although I've worked through most of my suppressed emotions so whether you like me or not has no effect on me whatsoever."

He smiled at Nathan, shaking his hand, but his words spoke of the truth and the comment fascinated him so much he had to ask, "Will I ever get to that point? Not caring what other people think of me?"

The doctor scrunched his eyebrows together as if contemplating a difficult question and wasn't sure how to respond, but then smiled and said, "Of course. I was just playing with you. After a month with me, that joke won't even affect you."

Nathan finally got it and laughed, mostly at himself and his own vulnerability. He felt something close to relief tinged with fear by the time he collected himself to leave.

"Today's Monday, right? When you go out, see if you can book Monday, Wednesday and Friday for the next four weeks. Those are the best times. Mondays are hell, but you'll learn to appreciate them. And Fridays are the best. You'll love going into a weekend after a session."

He was so positive. So confident. He spoke his words from a place of fact, not fanfare. *I want to be like him when I grow up.*

"Starting this Wednesday—eight thirty sharp—and then Friday this week, Monday, Wednesday and Friday, the next for a total twelve sessions, for now. Got it? See you in a couple of days."

What had he done? But he knew the question to be asked was, 'What had he done before coming here?' and that is what he was going to find out. Without a doubt, he'd spent $2,400 on more frivolous things.

Chapter XXII

A few hours later, Chloé was sitting in the same doctor's office, flipping through *Vogue*, not caring if anyone saw her, admiring the designer clothes and designer bodies, letting her thoughts drift back to Marc. He was so perfect for her. An up-and-coming success, thoughtful, kind, funny. That was paramount.

"Chloé?"

"Hello, Dr. Cameron. Come stai?" She'd started greeting him in a different language before each session (studying them before she arrived) to see how many languages he spoke. This was the third, preceded by French and Spanish. She decided to start with the basics, going with German and then Latin next.

"Bene, bene." It wasn't until many months later, after her final session, that she learned he had memorized twenty greetings and responses purely for her benefit, greatly amusing himself at her expense.

"Alora," he began, "how is our bella donna today?"

"Well, except for the fact that I've started dating this amazing man, I'm great."

"But why is this an exception?"

"Because I still don't feel good enough about myself to attract someone like Marc."

"Brava. What else?"

"That I need to trust that when life throws an*other* curve ball my way, it's only reminding me of what I need to see, and to trust the process and that everything's going to work out better than I expected."

"Excellent. Now, you don't believe a word you said, do you?"

"No, not really."

"Excellent. And what if I told you it doesn't matter what you do or don't do. Have or don't have. Be or not be. Would that make a difference? If I knew this for *fact*?"

204

"I'm not sure. If no one out there gives a shit, what am I doing here then?"

"Ah, but that's not what I said. If something doesn't matter, or makes no difference, it doesn't mean that no one cares. Think of a young child. Ten months old, adoring his Auntie Chloé. Reaching up to get picked up. You're five feet away. What would your thoughts be? 'Get up and walk, damn it?' No, you would think that it doesn't matter that this beautiful child can neither walk nor talk. But does that, in any way, imply you don't care? You can see how the two points have no relation to each other, si?"

"Do you really speak Italian?"

"Si." Besides a bit of French, Italian was the only other language he actually spoke.

She mulled over his words, trying to relate them to what she had just gone through. She liked the baby analogy—she loved babies, which didn't hurt—and wondered if she'd let that slip at an earlier session. This was one slippery cat and it was hard to get the upper hand. "So, it doesn't matter what I do or don't do?"

"Nope."

"Be or not be?"

"Still, nope."

"What's the point here? I'm missing something."

"Chloé, how would you feel if you could do *anything* you wanted, knowing it wouldn't matter one way or the other? Whatever you wanted to do was exactly perfect. No pressure, no expectations, no failure. You were surrounded by nothing but support."

Chloé started to cry. She didn't know why she was crying exactly, but could guess the good doctor would be able to tell her—that was his job, not hers. She contemplated a life where she could do no wrong. Where her choices were unrestricted by status, class, race, religion. She could date any man she wanted and be happy as a clam. Her parents would be thrilled. She would be thrilled. He would be thrilled. How liberating, but oh-so-far-removed from her world. More and more she realized how intrinsically woven her world was through her obligations of what was 'right and wrong'. What Dr. Cameron was speaking of would alter her perceptions completely, freeing her from the binds her parents had imposed on the past. But what else? Her mind was reeling with possibilities.

"Stay with me on this, Chloé. I want you to continue thinking along these lines. I can tell from your reaction you know exactly what I mean. This is affecting you because you know how unnatural it all is. You yearn to get back to a place of acceptance and away from the letdown of unfulfilled wishes and dreams. Everything you're experiencing is a result of past thinking. Everything. Where you are is *exactly* where you wanted to be, consciously or unconsciously—it doesn't matter. Both are controlled by your thoughts. So, I ask you. Where do you want to be? Think about it. It's a bold question." He sat, not expecting an answer, but expecting her to take his words and work with them, integrating them into her own frame of reference.

"Are you fucking kidding me? *I* am behind all of this mess? *I* created the mess-ups in my life? The failures? The lousy relationships? It's been me the entire time?"

"Yes, but think of how empowering that is. *You* are the only one behind your life. *You* are the driver. True, it's no one else's 'fault'—oh, that word is the bane of my existence—but blame is the most disempowering action on the planet, and believe me, it *is* an action, and it speaks louder than any words known to man." Then taking a moment to let things settle in and to also collect his own thoughts, he waited a few more moments before continuing.

"Chloé, I want you to think about what we talked about today. I also want you to write out what your life would look like if you had no one judging you. If you knew everything you did was perfect. Write it down. And then next session we're going to talk about it. And don't worry about not being good enough. I'm sure this new guy is smart enough to see you for who you are: a strong, beautiful woman about to take hold of her life. You might try asking yourself if he's good enough for you, not the other way around. Give it some honest thought, and see how it feels."

Chapter XXIII

Nathan slept poorly both Monday and Tuesday nights. His second session with Dr. Cameron was this morning and he was already running a bit late. What was it with him and always being late? Sabine always said it was defiance but that sounded a bit juvenile to him. He'd ask the doctor, if he remembered. He was dreading this meeting. After he left Monday, a lot of emotions started coming up. A lot of memories. Nothing horrific, but attached to the accompanying sadness they made him feel lonely. He assumed today would bring more of the same.

He had decided to approach this four-week stretch as a blip in his life that he would simply ignore. He would go through the motions but detach himself from it so he could get through to the other side with minimal damage. This was a coping strategy he had picked up when he was a young boy. He was petrified of going to see a dentist and created a 'pause' button for his life during his visits. He still used this pause button whenever he got into a life situation that he knew would make him uncomfortable, either physically or emotionally.

He skipped the idea of catching a cab—he had left it too late—and pulled his car out of the underground parking, speeding as he headed off to the appointment. The traffic was bad and he found himself panicking that he wouldn't make the eight thirty deadline and realized he didn't care so much about the wasted $200 but more about not wanting to disappoint Dr. C. Interesting. He might have to mention that little tidbit as well. The clock read 8.25 a.m., and there was a parking spot just out front. *There is a God*, he decided. Now he had just enough time to run up the wide steps of the Victorian mansion and get to reception, bringing a wash of fresh air into the cozy lobby as he entered. There must be a secret communication between the front desk and the doctor, because no sooner had Nathan hung his coat on the rack by the front door than Dr. Cameron's door opened, revealing the man himself, accompanied by a warm smile. Nathan got the sense he was standing on the other side of the door, waiting to pounce on his next patient, and chuckled to himself at the image.

"You look in fine humor this morning, Nathan. Having a good week so far?"

"It's been interesting. You?" he asked, automatically deflecting the man's question.

"Excellent. I'm having a great week. Come on in. Have a seat. Would you like a coffee, or tea?" Nathan noticed he had a large mug already started by his chair.

"A coffee would be great, thanks. Just black."

He headed toward his credenza, where a high-tech espresso machine sat, dominating the space. Pushing one button, he waited less than fifteen seconds before the hissing and sputtering stopped and then removed the mug with freshly ground, freshly brewed coffee, and passed it to Nathan, who looked awestruck. "I need to get one of those. Remind me to get the details after our session." He accepted the coffee, saying "thanks," and then both men took their places.

"Could you recap the last two days for me, Nathan? It's where I like to begin each session."

The man did not waste time. Nathan appreciated that about him, and followed in kind. "A lot of different emotions have been coming up for me since Monday. When I try to look at them I mostly feel sad, if that makes sense. And angry. I didn't realize how angry I've been, mostly directed at my father, as I'm sure you've already surmised. I haven't been sleeping well but I think it's been nerves around this meeting—no surprise there—and the night before I came to see you, I didn't tell you because we ran out of time, or I didn't know if it was important, but I woke up drenched in sweat from a horrific nightmare."

"Are you able to recall any details?"

"Not much anymore. I've put it out of mind, mostly. But I remember a beautiful woman and a man, who could have been me—I wasn't sure—and there was an agonizing death. The woman—the man's wife—died. The scariest part was, after I'd had a shower that morning, I was standing in front of the fogged-up mirror and I looked at my reflection and saw what looked to be the woman from my dream. It really freaked me out. I wiped the mirror down immediately and the image was gone." Nathan had lost some color in his face at the recollection. He hadn't realized until recalling the memory how scared he'd been. To recover, he added, "I think I was still shaken up from the nightmare and the fogginess blurred my own image. I don't know what else it would have been, and don't like to think about it, truth be told." He added a feeble laugh and waited for some feedback.

"The dream intrigues me. Sounds like a bleeding through to another time. Where do you stand on the concept of past lives? And while we're on that subject, where do your beliefs lie regarding God, or a higher being, or however you might refer to the super-almighty? Think about it for a moment and then give me your thoughts."

Reincarnation? He'd barely even known the word until Sabine made a few references to it. God? He thanked God a lot, but wasn't sure if that really counted. He hadn't given death and dying much thought, and although he didn't think 'this was it,' and when you died you simply rotted in the ground, he never bought the whole 'heaven and hell' fairy tale. He said as much to the doctor, explaining how he didn't know much about either subject, so obviously had no strong beliefs either way. He was compelled to ask, though, "How does it work—reincarnation, that is?"

"The beliefs around reincarnation are as varied as the beliefs within Christianity. But the basics in each are pretty constant. Reincarnation is based on the premise that when your physical body dies your soul goes to another plane—much variation as to the details there—and then it comes back at a different time in a different physical body with the whole intention of growing spiritually closer to—for pure simplification of the word—God, but you can call him or her whatever you like. Each lifetime offers different challenges and you keep coming back until you figure out what they're about, with the hope that each time you get *closer*, not *further* from the source."

"And people really believe that?" Nathan was having a hard time grappling with the concept. It seemed too otherworldly for a man who placed both feet firmly on the ground.

"The majority of the world's population, actually, which in itself is not enough reason to jump into something and make it your own, but it does make it worth looking into."

"So, when you were talking about 'bleeding through' before is that what you meant?"

"I work with a technique called 'regression therapy'—you've likely heard of it, as it's become 'in vogue' lately—and, usually under deep hypnosis, it's designed to take the patient back to the first incident or trauma to release the emotions that were locked in at that time. Although many doctors don't appreciate this particular approach, I've found it highly effective, which is why I work with it in certain situations. Without any prompting from me, many of my clients start talking about

209

their surroundings and people that could only be from the past, sometimes very distant. Other eras. Whether these are memories or stories they've made up to deal with their deep-seated pain, only you can decide, but most don't remember anything about them on waking, and when probed about their knowledge on, say, the Crusades, where their trauma occurred, they don't even know what they are. It's uncanny to witness but for me, I don't try to make it one thing or the other, as it's irrelevant to their healing to label it 'true' or 'not true.' If they're open or in line with that belief structure, we talk about it in depth. If they're not, I don't bring it into the conversation. That's why I'm trying to determine from you whether or not to use any of that genre of information that might come up. It's your call, really."

"Let me do a little research before I answer that one. At this moment I'm inclined to go running from your office waving my hands above my head. It's a lot to absorb, as you can imagine. The possibility that I knew the woman in the mirror and in my dream, in another time, alarms me and I'm not sure how to process the information. Is this all related to what's going on inside?"

"It's hard to answer that without giving you my personal opinion."

"Go ahead. I'd like to hear it."

"Then, yes, I believe it's related and whether you believe it or not, images and dreams will continue to haunt you until you face them, just like your past in this lifetime. Until you face all the buried gunk, it will keep coming up. There's no avoiding ourselves, is there, my boy?"

"I guess not, although I've been doing a pretty good job of it up until this point."

"Have you? I think that depends on your definition of 'good job.' I would venture a guess that the satisfaction level of your life is extremely low. And I would also hazard a guess that you are either divorced or have never been married and haven't quite got the whole 'love' thing figured out, either."

"Right on all accounts."

"It is possible to work through some of your major life challenges once and for all. We have enough fodder from this lifetime to work with if you want to keep it within this timeline. You are living from such a tiny fraction of your potential at the moment. I'm not talking about your physical potential—lucky for you, you've managed to sort that one out—but your emotional potential is what limits your life. To never feel deep, passionate love is a tragedy. Thankfully, you don't know what you're missing so, like most people, you learn to manage without it. But once felt—man, Nathan, you can't imagine. It's magic. And it will transform every fiber of your life."

"This is not at all what I was expecting today and I'm not sure how I feel about it yet."

"Good. That means it's churning up the gunk. Don't be surprised if you feel physically nauseous this week, too. The physical body is hard wired to the emotional body and considering what you've already told me, to be blunt, I'm surprised you're as healthy as you are. The two do not usually go together, so pay attention to your health as well."

"Now you're just scaring me." Nathan meant what he said. He was starting to feel like there was a conspiracy building, forcing his hand to go down this road. He didn't like being pushed or cajoled into anything and he was tempted to follow his early idea and run, bypassing the 'hands over the head, screaming' part.

"Nathan, let's be real. This is scary. You've had a serious wake-up call. What you've just put yourself through is scary. Have you ever heard the expression, 'there's no way out but through'? You're at a crossroads and a wrong turn could be fatal. It is not my intention to scare you into anything, but I am not one to downplay something to make it more comfortable. This is uncomfortable work. *Life* is uncomfortable work. I know this work will help you—I'm good at what I do, by the way—but to go ahead or not is entirely your choice, and I fully respect and honor whatever choice you make."

"So, you wouldn't care one way or the other?" Nathan was getting irritated at the direction this was going.

The doctor was used to this rampant theme. "I didn't say I wouldn't care. I said I would honor your choice, knowing that whatever way you go, it's the right one for you at this time."

"Even if that choice is to drink myself into oblivion and die?"

"Yes, even then. If you're not ready, you're not ready. Only you know what's best for you."

"I hate that 'you're not ready' crap. Sabine used to use that on me, and it's so condescending, like I'm not *evolved* enough or *spiritual* enough. That's just bullshit and another way for people to place themselves higher than others." He could feel his blood starting to boil and he was starting to plan his exit.

"You're right, it does sound condescending. Let me put it in another context for you." James prepared himself for the usual lecture. Anyone who confused 'it doesn't matter' with 'you don't care' needed to get back to the fundamentals of his or her ideals. He recapped the toddler analogy, which seemed to strike a chord in most everyone. He

211

finished by asking, "Would it be a judgment of this child's incompetence in any way that he wasn't able to walk, or would you trust that eventually he would be able to figure it out even though you knew he would continue landing on his butt in the process? Sometimes people can come across as condescending, but that doesn't automatically mean what they say is an untruth. Here's the litmus test to see if you're ready for something: if you do it, you're ready; if you don't, you're not. Simple. I'll leave you with that for now and remember to give me 24 hours if you decide not to keep our appointment on Friday, okay?"

'Okay.' He was getting the brush-off. Nathan was used to being sold on something. This was the complete opposite. Either this guy was really lame or exceptionally intelligent, and already had Nathan's number. He wasn't sure which, but he was leaning heavily toward the latter, a scary proposition in itself. He had never encountered anyone who could look deeply into his character and figure anything out, and he wasn't sure if he was 'ready' to try. This whole conversation was pissing him off, which was a common result when things didn't go the way he'd planned. He stood up to leave, knowing the session was over, and shook the doctor's hand, which was warm and soft to the touch. His smile took Nate off guard and he felt a bit like the toddler, and the doctor was patting him on the head saying, "It's okay, little man." He was surprised to realize he wasn't insulted and that the guy actually came across as sincere.

No goodbyes were exchanged. No inquiries about the espresso machine. No 'See you Friday'. Nathan walked right out the door without a word. As he looked up to locate his coat among the others on the rack, he noticed a woman sitting in one of the large comfy chairs in the lobby. She looked familiar, and then he remembered she was Sabine's assistant and they had met at Marc's book signing. He wondered if she was Marc's date last Friday. He didn't want to be seen here and, following that train of thought, he couldn't help wondering what she was doing here. Too late to escape without being rude, he walked up to her. "Hi, I'm Nathan. We met last week at my brother's book signing. I'm sorry, I don't remember your name."

You wouldn't remember. But she remembered him well, and what a self-centered jerk he was, otherwise referred to as Sabine's ex. And Marc's brother. Shit. She needed to make an effort. "Yes, I remember. I'm Chloé. Nice seeing you again." And then forgetting all protocol regarding her surroundings, she asked, "Did you just see Dr. C? He's amazing, isn't he? This is my fourth session and I've already noticed results. I love his guarantee, don't you? I didn't mean to be personal, but

212

you are standing in his office, so I just assumed..." They both recalled the events following last Friday night, he, realizing she must know, and she, realizing he must know she knows. An awkward moment she was determined to push through. "Sabine told me about what happened, as I'm sure you know. I'm sorry to hear about it. You look well, though, thank God."

"A close call for sure, and I'll be fine in time, thanks. Anyway, must run. Nice seeing you again." He grabbed his coat and almost ran down the steps to his car.

He drove straight home, booted up his computer and Googled 'reincarnation'. Over five million hits. A little too broad. So he tried more detailed combinations and started clicking through different related sites. A lot of them needed the theme song from *The Twilight Zone* playing in the background, but there were a few on Buddhism and others with definitions very close to what Dr. C had described. It was not unlike reading a fairy tale, and he found the idea interesting, like you'd find *Star Wars* interesting. The jury was still out on it, though, and so far there was nothing conclusive in his research.

He read a few 'real-life stories' about people who had recalled their past-life experiences with chilling detail, and 'real-life doctors' had documented the stories, too. He knew you could put anything on the Internet but they were interesting all the same. One in particular was about a woman who remembered dying of the White Plague, leaving a young child behind, and she came back this time still looking for her. Very hard to comprehend or believe. The underlying message for her was about loving someone, soul to soul, and how it never changes. She was on a continuous cycle with her child and they made agreements to come back here together, supporting each other's experiences along the way.

As strange as it sounded, he started to think of people he felt really connected to. Marc was one, and he did feel they still had stuff to work out. His grandmother had been another, but she was dead now so he couldn't talk to her about it or work any more out with her now, in *this* lifetime, as the sites were all so fond of saying. His father was a player for sure, but he wouldn't dream of bringing this up to the esteemed banker. There was no one else he could think of who was tied to him in that way. No girlfriends or friends. He wondered how Marc felt on the subject. He would ask him. Explore it a bit more for fun. But how could he see a woman's face in his mirror if she had been dead for hundreds of years? That part didn't make sense to him and he couldn't imagine anyone, including Dr. Cameron, explaining it away.

Later that night, as he fell deep into sleep, the nightmare returned. More detail and images. An old clock ticking on the mantel. The man leaning over his wife, then the man collapsing beside her. Such pain. The cries, the convulsing. He woke in the middle of the night, drenched again but too afraid to get out of bed to splash cold water on his face and body. He couldn't bear the thought of seeing that face in the mirror again. Not after just witnessing her death in his dream. What the hell was going on with him? He wanted it to stop and felt instead as though he'd opened Pandora's Box. What if there was some truth to a past life? He could barely deal with *this* life and now he was expected to deal with another, or dozens, hundreds, maybe thousands of others? It was too daunting a task and he lay back on his bed and wept. He finally drifted off and slept soundly through the night, although on waking, he felt chilled from sleeping on damp sheets. He got up quickly, turned on all the lights, headed for the shower and refused to look into the mirror until he had dressed and was brushing his teeth, the last step in his morning bathroom ritual.

He knew what he had to do. He did not want to face it, but he felt instinctively that he had no choice. It was do or die, which was no choice at all, so he was going to 'do'. His next appointment with Dr. C was tomorrow, and today he was going to take what might be his last day off before diving into the abyss.

His palms were sweating as he shook Dr. C's hand. You can't get away with sweating palms in his world and he was surprised at the physical reaction this meeting was already causing before it had even begun. Dr. Cameron took one look at Nathan and knew something was up. He was in rough shape, possibly signs of a hangover, and he hoped a repeat performance of his hospital stay wasn't in his near future, or ever, for that matter. Nathan's seat was already familiar and he had no uncertainty about who sat where. Once they were both settled, Dr. Cameron waited in suspense as Nathan gathered his courage for what he was about to say. He watched him struggle with the words but didn't make a move to step in. After mere moments that dragged on like minutes, Nathan got to the point. "I want you to regress me. To use that therapy technique you talked about." That was all he had to say and now he waited, hoping to get started before he lost his nerve.

"You mean regression therapy? I take it you've been doing some research on the subject. Are you clear on what's involved?"

"I only looked into past lives and saw enough to show me it's in the realm of possibility. I'm not convinced, but then who is, really? I don't know anything about the regressions. Only that my dreams and the mirror incident are causing me some concern and if that's what's creating havoc in this life then let's just get to the bottom of it, shall we?"

"Fortunately for you, Nathan, you have a built-in guidance system that will only reveal what it wants to reveal, so if we decide to follow this course of treatment, as I mentioned earlier, you don't need to be convinced of anything, or believe in anything either. Whatever *you*—the innermost part of you—want to happen, will happen. It's really quite simple and truly remarkable. Would you like to hear more about the process?" Dr. Cameron was surprised and weighed in his own mind whether this course of action was wise. He would see how this session played out before he committed to going ahead, but he was intrigued by his patient's decision. Perhaps not the open and shut case he first predicted.

"Tell me what to expect, but not too much detail, please. If I overanalyze it I'll never go through with it." He was already second-guessing his decision, which he anticipated he would do. Because he trusted the doctor implicitly, he would not let his fears cloud his initial reaction, which consistently turned out to be the best one.

"Basic information. Got it. Have you ever been hypnotized?" Nathan's look said, 'you've got to be kidding,' so he safely assumed this was new and went on. "I'll take you deep into a hypnotic state, freeing your thinking mind from your subconscious mind. The ego likes to be in control at all times, so we're going to distract him and keep him busy over there," motioning to his left, "while bringing the rest of your mind present to my voice and instruction. It will feel like I've done nothing at all as your ego will be aware of everything I'm saying but aware of nothing you're doing. I videotape every session and give only the patient a copy, which I would suggest you watch when you're alone and then put in a safety deposit box or destroy. Watching it will be far more disturbing than the process itself.

"From that state, I start digging for the first cause or root of a trauma, giving character displays as hints. Most insecurities, for example, usually stem from abandonment by one or both parents. If you showed signs of extreme insecurities it would be a good place to start. I ask the questions and you find the answer in the recesses of your body, soul, mind—whatever you want to name it. Often, it's something that your conscious mind has blocked, and it occurred when you were young. You may have memories from an early age, but this is unlikely. Many people have only vague recollections of their childhood from before six or seven—even older—which is a likely indicator of abuse of some kind." He stopped to collect his thoughts. "Sorry, I may be giving you too much information. Is that alright so far?"

"Yes, it's good. I find it fascinating. Please continue."

"There's no predicting where you will go with it, so I just allow you to talk and then when images start coming to you, I'll probe deeper, watching your facial expression and mannerisms, and you'll get vividly clear on the events *particular to this trauma*. Keep in mind we are only touching on a nick in your armor. It points us in a direction and then where it goes from there is always a bit of a surprise to both of us. If you go in with an open mind I promise you it will be easier. And more importantly, you'll need to come out of it with an open mind. You may not believe a single thing I tell you at first, until you watch the tape. It will potentially be that extreme. Any questions so far?"

"None. When can we get started? I'd like to do this before I lose my nerve."

"I agree, and unfortunately this morning is out. It needs to be in the evening as they sometimes run long and it's better at night, when you can go home, have a glass of wine and then go right to bed. Your body will be spent. I don't usually book Wednesdays but I think tonight would be the best. Could you come back at, say, six thirty? And eat something light before you come, but *no* alcohol, or other drugs, if that's your thing. That could really mess you up. And wear comfortable clothes: jogging pants, sweatshirt, whatever you like. Does that work for you?"

"Yes, it does. I can't say I'm looking forward to it but I'll see you then. And, thank you, Doc—I think." Nathan's charming smile gave Dr. Cameron enough reassurance that he would be fine. He was really looking forward to this one.

Chapter XXIV

Chloé called Marc in the morning and asked how he had slept. She made hints to her big, lonely bed and what a long night it had been, but he wasn't taking the bait. They both had things to do that day and agreed to have dinner at his place that night. He would prepare his specialty— a nice light Roquefort cream pasta with an arugula salad with maple syrup and balsamic dressing. He loved cooking and when there was time, was quite accomplished at it. Tonight he would make time, as he wanted to give her a good first impression of his culinary skills.

The evening was a success on all fronts. She loved his house and was obviously surprised at his talents in the kitchen. By ten, Chloé said she had to go to bed, and if he wasn't offering, she'd start walking home. She didn't like the position she was in at all and had never been on this side of this situation before. It gave her great sympathy for all of the young boys in university that she put off, mostly permanently. Marc wasn't enjoying it either and knew he would soon break from the pressure. He walked her back to her apartment, and by the time they'd finished kissing goodnight and had finally pulled themselves apart, it was eleven thirty. Knowing she had an early start the next day, he regretted his part in keeping her up so late.

He also knew he was in trouble. Big trouble. He hadn't meant for it to happen, but he was falling in love with this woman and it scared him in an almost unreasonable way. It was too soon, for one. They hadn't even had sex yet. What if she was lousy in bed (highly unlikely if her kisses were any indication)? And being *in love*. Oh, God. This could really hurt. He felt a sense of panic constricting his heart and, once back at the house, he took a glass of wine out to the verandah to sort it all out. Where was the euphoria? The blissful feeling of peace? What was he going to do? He had to tell her *before* they made love. *Shit. I wish I hadn't realized it until after. Now it's going to ruin everything.* His thoughts were

217

in a turmoil and he was tempted to text her or leave a message on her voice mail. Maybe email? What a coward he was being, he realized. But when he thought of her he could see them spending their lives together. He couldn't imagine his life without her now, which is what confirmed for him that he was in trouble.

The next day, he didn't call. He had intended to but he didn't know what to say and he'd put it off too long. The following morning he sent the biggest bouquet of freesias to her apartment, with a card that said, *'Can't stop thinking of you. Dinner? Thursday? Marc.'*

He spent the days giving some serious thought to what he was doing and no matter which way he looked at it, Chloé had to be a part of his life. They were meant to be together; he just knew it in his bones. By Wednesday he was frantic, so he called Sabine. "What are your plans this evening? I'm whipping up a little salmon on the bar-b—care to join me?" His tone was light but she sensed he had something specific he wanted to talk about and she replied, "I'd love to—what time?" and then hung up to politely cancel drinks with Chloé, insisting it was important and could they meet on Friday instead? Chloé seemed a bit strained but agreed, and Sabine headed out to pick up a nice bottle of something French and red, and some fresh flowers from the local corner store.

When she arrived he said he loved the flowers and blurted out he had just sent some to a woman he had met and wanted some advice. She helped finalize things in the kitchen and then they grabbed their half-empty glasses and headed to the verandah where he had laid a quaint table of Provençal linens and hurricane candles. "Oh, Marc, I've missed this. Remember all the great times we've had here? You, Nate and me? How is he, by the way? I haven't been calling to bug you but please tell me he's doing alright."

"He's doing quite well, in light of what happened, and he's seeing a therapist. I don't think he'd mind me telling you as you were always pushing him to do that. Sorry, I didn't mean to say 'pushing.' Encouraging is better, hmm?" They both laughed, knowing 'pushing' had been the right word. "And how have you been, Bean? I always love saying that. It's just so… you."

They clinked their glasses in mutual understanding and leaned back, nibbling at their dinner, catching each other up on what had been going on. When Marc confessed that the woman he sent flowers to was her assistant, Sabine feigned surprise, but then confessed that she'd already talked to Chloé twenty-seven times since the evening at *Karma*, and had heard most of the sordid details. She was beside herself with happiness for both of them.

"Sabine, don't toy with me here. I'm in deep and don't see a way out except to go deeper. Sabine, I'm in love with her."

There was silence between them and then a shriek while she jumped from her seat—almost tipping her wine—threw her arms around him and kissed his cheek affectionately. "Oh, *Marc*. That is *so* incredibly wonderful, I can hardly speak. What did she say, tell me?" She waited and then stopped. "No. You haven't told her? You're kidding me. Are you crazy? Tell her, you idiot, or I'll have to do it for you. Don't you see you can't waste a minute—a second? Grab hold of her and never let her go. You love her—wow, that is so special, I think I might cry."

They both smiled at each other, fighting the tears, and Marc started to feel the bliss that he always knew in his heart of hearts would follow with loving someone. They spent the rest of the evening talking about what might come, what Sabine's desires were, mainly for her to have 'someone exactly like you, Marc, but with the spark'. They were deep in their conversation, drinking their wine, laughing, enjoying their friendship. Neither of them saw the shadow of a figure approaching the house, seeing the two of them there together—laughing, candles, wine—and then turn to walk back in the same direction.

Chapter XXV

The doctor's office looked different at night and for a moment Nathan had to double-check that he was walking up the right steps, so many like them lined the street. He stepped into the empty reception area but saw the light on and the door open in Dr. Cameron's office and he strolled right in. James Cameron had done this type of session hundreds of times but each time he felt a giddy anticipation accompanied by a nervousness in the pit of his stomach. He couldn't help it. No foreshadowing was necessary to know what potentially lay ahead.

He left the room to lock the front door and then returned, motioning Nathan to a quasi-chaise lounge. It was an Italian leather chair with a curved back, giving the sensation of lying down but still maintaining a sitting position. Nathan had one in cream in his office and it was where he went to escape when things got chaotic. He thought it was funny that it appeared here in chocolate brown and he explained the coincidence to the doctor, who smiled in a way that said he didn't really believe in coincidences. There was a soft mohair blanket that he could pull over himself, and a plastic pitcher of water and plastic glass perched on a table within reach of the chair. Nathan thought a doctor of this caliber could spring for something a little nicer when his thoughts were broken with, "Plastic is safer. Things tend to get flung around here sometimes." Nathan smiled at the mind reader and settled into his chair, pulling the blanket loosely over his legs.

James dimmed the lights, lit a couple of candles behind him on his desk, and then asked Nathan if he was comfortable, so they could start.

"Ready when you are, Doc." Nathan tried to keep things light but inside, his stomach was churning and he was really scared. Scared in a way that was unfamiliar to him. He hoped it wasn't some prescience of what was to come. His arms rested comfortably, folded across each other on his lap, but he was clenching and unclenching his fingers, the only 'tell' that he was nervous. *Impressive*, thought James as he began slowing his own breathing and relaxing his body, starting with his toes and working up to his scalp.

When he began speaking, his voice was sonorous and monotone, setting a mood that was almost somber, just like in the old movies where the hypnotist held a watch and recited, "You are getting sleepy, sleepy." Nathan found it amusing but wasn't sure why. "Follow my breathing, Nathan. Breath in," and then pausing, "and out" pausing again. "In. And out. Good. Keep following my breathing and listening to my voice." James was watching Nathan's eyes and could see them relaxing with each breath. He was responding well and he continued on with the process he'd used for many years. In less than ten minutes Nathan was under completely. The video camera was inconspicuous on the bookshelf behind him and he turned to it to give a 'one thumb up', indicating so that Nathan, while viewing it later, would know that he was now ready to begin.

"You are completely safe and secure. Now, let's first talk about your brother. What do you see when you remember him?" It was a long shot but after he'd heard the story of him trying to suffocate Marc with a pillow, he sensed there was something there, deeply hidden. More so than even his father.

"We're playing. He scrapes his knee on the truck and starts crying. I get mad and grab the truck. Mama sees him crying and spanks me." His voice had a slurred quality to it, as if he were drunk. Monotone as well, mimicking James', but in actuality, James was choosing the tone that he knew was coming. "Mama's really mad. Dad's mad. Baby Marc is crying but now it's because he feels bad. He didn't mean to get me in trouble, but I don't care. I'm mad at baby Marc and when Mama goes away I poke his knee and then leave him to cry. I hate my brother." His dialect was juvenile. Simple words and phrases, but his voice remained steady.

"What else, Nathan? There's something else you're not telling me. What is it?" This was a classic line he used in each session and it invariably turned up a hidden secret. The patient cannot lie but would often attempt to skirt the issue.

"Nothing. Really."

"Are you sure? Look back, further. What do you see? Tell me about your brother Marc. Describe what you see."

There was a shift in the energy of the room and Nathan gave one twitch with his entire body. James had the sense that he was going back to the place of his dreams and guided him along. "Tell me what you see.

Tell me about the room. The people. Where is Marc?" and he sat on the edge of his chair and waited.

"It's in the dining room. The table is large but only two of us are eating."

"What else?"

"Daddy? Oh, Daddy. I love you too, Daddy."

"Where's Daddy? Tell me about him."

"He's not here. Daddy loves me. No one else does, but Daddy loves me." His voice was strained and high pitched, no longer that of a child's. He was flitting from one place to another, but James knew to expect that and allowed the memories to flow without trying to box them into anything too specific. He was looking for an incident and sometimes he had to be led through a maze of seemingly unrelated events. "Your Daddy loves you. Now, who doesn't love you? Who do you mean?"

"My husband. He pretends to love me but he doesn't love me." Nathan would be surprised when he saw this. It was always a bit of a shock when a female showed herself during a male's regression, and vice versa.

"Tell me about your husband. Who do you see?"

He started to cry, sobbing deeply, tears streaming down his face. He tried to speak, but the words caught in his throat.

"It's okay. Tell me who you see."

"It's—" and another sob wracked his body. "It's—" hesitating, not wanting to reveal the identity but unable to prevent the healing from taking place. "It's Armand." His sobs turned to short intakes of breath, tears still flowing freely.

"That's good. Now, tell me why Armand doesn't love you. Tell me what happened."

"No, I can't say. Please, don't make me say." His voice was frantic, like a frightened child's.

"It's okay. You can say it. Nothing's going to hurt you. Tell me what happened with your husband." James knew whatever was next would be a shock to both of them, so he waited, alert and ready to bring him back if necessary.

"We're having dinner. Just the two of us. Last night he made love to me."

"Tell me about the dinner," he said, keeping Nate's thoughts on track.

"We were having a nice dinner. But the cramps. Oh, God, I feel sick. I think I'm going to be sick." He leaned over the chair and started dry retching, gripping his abdomen with both hands.

"It's okay, you're not feeling well, but you're okay. What's happening at dinner?"

"I can't. Oh, god, the pain. My stomach. Oh no, I'm going to die. I know I'm going to die." James was soothing him now and sitting by his side. This was always the worst part but he knew it was necessary for his recovery. "It's okay. Tell me about the pain. Tell me about Armand."

"Oh, *Armaaaaaaaaand. Noooooo.* It's him. It's my husband. He did this to me. Why, Armand? *Whyyyyyy?* Please let me die. Please, I can't handle the pain. Why did you do it? I thought you loved me? Oh God, *noooooooo…*" He was writhing in apparent agony, still holding his stomach, sweat on his brow, mumbling "Armand, Armand, Armand," over and over until he gradually stilled, his breathing heavy but still steady.

"It's okay. It's over now. You made it through. You're okay. Keep breathing slowly, slowly. That's it. Keep breathing." James waited until his breathing had returned to normal and then allowed him to remain in a near-sleeping state before he felt ready to bring him back to reality. It would be a shock to the system, even if he didn't remember anything. Being murdered always left its indelible mark. Hopefully, he would start the long slow process of healing the wounds now.

"…and when I say your name, you will slowly open your eyes, and be fully present. One, breathe in. Two, and release. Three, breathe again. Nathan? When you're ready, you can open your eyes." James had pulled up his chair so that he was closer to him, ready to lean in if necessary but far enough away to give him the space he would likely require.

Nathan opened his heavy lids to a blur. The room started to slowly come into focus and he turned his head to see James looking at him intently. "The doctor. Dr. C. We were talking. Talking about breathing." His thoughts remained jumbled and he closed his eyes once more, willing the images to go away. Willing this room, this life, to take hold more strongly. He felt nauseous and thought he tasted bile in his mouth. He opened his eyes again and settled them on the water on the table beside him. James leaned over and poured a glass, half full, handing it to him, guiding it to his hands and then his mouth. Nathan just nodded his thanks and drank deeply, finishing the glass in one long gulp. He set the glass down and sat back, exhausted, eyes closed again.

"When you're ready, tell me what you saw. What you remember." James knew this was the most critical stage of the process. The images may have already faded and nothing would be recalled, making it more difficult to discern the message. If the images remained clear, the patient could react with mild shock and disorientation. He waited, knowing the experience had been profound and would alter this man's perspective for the remainder of his life.

Nathan cleared his throat, coughing slightly before attempting to speak. "I remember it all." He took a slow deep breath, pain revealing itself on his face. "The room, the table, the clock on the mantel, ticking loudly. Cook was there. And Armand. He killed me. He hated me. I didn't know he hated me, until I looked into his eyes and I knew. No one could love me. I was a selfish cruel woman. I was horrendous. But I thought he loved me like I loved him." He looked up at James, confusion spreading itself across his features, but still bravely continuing. "It's all a bit confusing, Doc. I was there. I saw everything. It was me but it was not me. I was in her eyes. I saw myself in her eyes. It's all so strange, I'm not sure if I can process it all. I remember dying and seeing my pathetic life unveil its shallow scenes. My father was the only one. He loved me and I thought him weak for it." Pausing again, he poured more water and drank. "This is so hard. I want to forget but I know I need to remember. Something is pushing me to remember."

Not wanting to interrupt but intuitively guiding the process, James asked, "What did you see at the end of your life when you looked at all of your experiences? What did you decide?" James's heart went out to this man, whom he'd met only days before, but he needed to push him through this or the jewel of the experience could be lost, stuffed far away to reside alongside his other painful memories.

Tears were falling unchecked down Nathan's cheeks, pooling on the shoulders of his shirt. "I'm unlovable. And, love is dangerous. Fatal." He closed his eyes again as realizations started flowing through his mind, connecting what he saw with his current life and how he'd been leading it. Another clear image burst through and he wailed, "Oh, God. Marc. It was Marc. Armand is Marc. My brother. I have been hating him all of my life. I even tried to kill him when he was little. He killed me. Oh, God—what do I do with that? How do I integrate this into my life? Dr. C, I had no idea it would be like this. I have truly opened Pandora's Box, haven't I?"

"No, Nathan. Not Pandora's Box. Merely the steel vault you have built around your heart. You have unlocked the safe and you're about to step through the door to see what's inside. There is nothing there that can harm you but many of the things have lain dormant for a long, long time, so take your time in going through it. You have the rest of this life, and more if you need." James was giving Nathan a reassuring smile, his eyes twinkling with excitement. "What you have done here today took great courage, my friend. You solved one of the biggest mysteries of your life. Understanding will come in time, but for now, go home and write. Write every memory and feeling you can. The memories will slowly begin to fade as each day passes. So, unless you want to go through this again…" His first attempt at humor and he was pleased to see Nathan's grin. "I would suggest you unplug your phone, lock your door and write. One more thing. I'm going to give you some Epsom salts to take home with you. Before you go to bed, take a long hot bath and put the salts in the water. They will help you relax and draw out some of the body's lingering pain. We're still scheduled for Friday, so take it easy tomorrow and try not to interact with too many people. You need a day of introspection. Give it to yourself. I can't stress strongly enough the importance of that."

"What about Marc? I need to talk to Marc."

"If you feel drawn to talk to him, then do. He may even be willing to go through the same process so the two of you can work through this together. Have him call me if he does. It's a great gift you could give each other. You've done some powerful healing here tonight. Call me if you need to. I'll jot down my cell when I grab the salts." It was only eight, but both men were exhausted. Nathan got up slowly, still feeling disoriented, but the nausea had finally dissipated. He called a cab, relieved he had decided not to drive, and gathered up his coat and bag of salts as he headed for the door. "Thank you, Doc." His eyes showed his gratitude but no more words were spoken, the effort too great.

James shook his hand, placing his other on Nathan's shoulder. "My pleasure. You will feel much better soon, I promise you. Better than ever."

"Just like the guarantee says." Nathan smiled as he remembered the cryptic words.

James was glad to see the humor return. "Yes, just like the guarantee." They looked at each other, deep understanding passing between them, and Nathan walked out into the warm fall evening.

When Nathan entered his condo, the first thing he did was pick up the phone and call Marc. His hand was shaking as he misdialed, and then dialed again. Marc picked up after several rings and he sounded out of breath. "Marc, it's Nate. Is this a bad time?"

Marc held his hand over the phone and mouthed, "It's Nathan," to Sabine, giving her the signal that he needed to take the call and wanted privacy. She headed back out onto the verandah and he sat back on the couch, propping his feet on the leather ottoman. "It's fine. What's up?"

"It sounds like I've interrupted. Do you have someone there?"

He hesitated only slightly before confessing, "Sabine's here," and held his breath waiting for his reaction. What he got was not what he expected.

"Good. I want to talk to her, too. Can you guys meet me tomorrow? At my condo, for lunch? There's something important I want to talk about and I think it would be good if Sabine were there. She'll understand the situation better than me." He could feel Marc hesitate, so he added, "Marc, I'm okay. Something quite incredible happened today. Tell Sabine not to worry. This isn't about me wanting her back, which I don't. This is about closure. Tell her I had a session with Dr. Cameron today. That will pique her interest. Can you make it? Say, twelve thirty?"

"Sure, Nate. You've got me curious but I'll wait until tomorrow. I'll ask Sabine and call you right back if she can't, but I'm sure she'll be there, too. See you then, big brother."

It felt strange talking to Marc with all of this new information. He thought he might feel angry and lash out at him, but unexpectedly, he felt serene. He headed for the bedroom, knowing he'd left his journal—the one from Marc, that synchronicity not escaping him—on his bedside table, and came back to the living room, turning on his reading light and settling into the only comfortable chair in the room. He swiveled to face the water and rested his feet on the matching ottoman. Pausing briefly, he picked up his pen and wrote.

Part VI

Chapter XXVI

Madame's circle of contacts was wide and she had untold resources for having important information relayed back to her at all times of the day and night. Because of this, Lisette was one of the first in the city to hear about Armand's wife's death. She wanted to run to him and console him but was warned to stay away. Madame was arranging for her to leave the city this very day, as she wanted nothing to connect the two or stain Monsieur's reputation at this time of certain inquest. Madame had her own suspicions but said not a word to anyone, nor would she. Lisette thought only of Armand and how shaken he must be. She knew he had detested his wife but their arrangement seemed to suit them both and the implications of her death would still impact him. Lisette and two other girls headed for the country estate, which Madame had purchased with some of the proceeds from Isabel's début. Lisette liked to play a little game in her mind that Armand had bought the estate just for her, which, indirectly he had. It always amused her that it was his money that supplied this desirous haven.

It was small by the standards of the day, but had ample rooms, all luxuriously appointed, and Lisette loved going there to get away from the noisy, dirty city she called home. There would be little work done on this trip as Madame did not want many to know where they had gone or when they arrived, knowing the house may be visited as part of the investigation. The impression would be that they had been in the country for a few days and would not be coming back for a week or two. Neither of the three girls had had appointments during the few days prior to leaving, so there was no one outside of the *maison* who could dispute her claim. The three girls left in an unmarked carriage, their unadorned entourage following behind at a measurable distance. They arrived a full three hours after the girls, which caused some commotion as all three were hungry and began raiding the pantry. By the time the others arrived, there was food strewn across the counters, exposed to the grateful flies and mice, and crumbs were scattered on the floor, surrounded everywhere by droplets of wine.

They were shooed up to their rooms where they giggled and talked for the rest of the evening. It had been a tiring journey and they had smuggled a stash of wine and bread under one girl's cape, so there was no need for any of them to be involved with the rest of the goings-on of the household.

This would be a short holiday and the best part was that it would be free of men. They did not have to primp and polish or worry about what clothes to wear. Their hair could fall freely and blow in the wind if they so wanted, a rare and pleasing occurrence. They spent their days lazing around outside, running the maids and serving girls ragged. They were there for five days before they had a single guest, and then one night Lisette awoke to the sound of a horse's hooves on the gravel out front. She went to the window and gasped, her hand going to her mouth. She shook the other two girls awake, startling them out of their slumber. "Help me get dressed," she hissed. "It's Armand. Hurry and help me. *Mon Dieu*, look at me—I'm a mess." Both girls scrambled out of bed while Lisette took a moment to watch him from behind the curtains, as his strong lithe body leapt from the horse and strode purposefully up the front stairs to bang on the front door, waking the maid, who was petrified by the sudden intrusion.

"It's Monsieur du Preix. Open up. *Vite. Vite.*" She felt a wave of relief and ran to the door, almost tripping on her disheveled skirts. He pushed past her, dropping his cape in her arms and shouting a command. "Stable my horse. He needs water and a blanket." More kindly, he whispered, "Please, hurry," taking the besotted maid into his confidence. "I don't want to be seen," and he rushed to the stairs, taking them two at a time where, at the top, he started calling Lisette's name in a loud whisper. She opened the door, and led him down the hall to the corner room, always made up for unexpected visitors. Closing the door quietly behind them, she turned as Armand grabbed her wrist, pulling her toward him, crushing his mouth on hers, tears streaming down his face. Her heart broke to see his pain and she caressed his head gently, murmuring soothing words in between kisses.

"Armand, you should not be here."

"I could not stay away. I had to see you. Lisette, it was so awful. Her pain was so terrible. I cannot stand the memories I carry from that night."

He was visibly distraught, so she held him to her, kissing away his tears. "*Shhh. Shhh.* There, there," speaking as she would to a child. "I am here, *mon chéri.* I am here." He led her to the bed, undressing her silently and then undressing himself. They crawled in together, making love with a hunger that had been left unsatisfied for far too long. He desperately tried to fill himself with her and after only a couple of hours he dressed quickly and left her lying there, more disconcerted than before. He longed to stay with her for the night but knew he had to be back in his home before dawn. He had come too far to let his plan slip now by any selfish indulgence on his part, and it was a hard two-hour ride back to safety.

His stable hand could be trusted and had readied his horse on many late night outings, dressing it down on his return, so this evening was nothing out of the ordinary for the *Monsieur.* He also knew his master would often visit *Madame de Rouler's Maison,* and who could blame him with a cold wife like he had. He crossed himself quickly, realizing too late he had been thinking ill of the dead. But he was not sorry to see her go, nor was any other living or breathing creature, he speculated. The household had been gossiping about it ever since the night of her death.

Cook had her own suspicions that Madame had tried to poison Monsieur, but her plan backfired. She had been acting strangely to him all night, and had been the one to request mushrooms with dinner. Monsieur almost died as well, which would have been catastrophic for all of them. He was loved and revered, and every last member of his staff supported his undying affection and loyalty to his wife when the enquiries had been made, and Cook had responded honestly, as she had no intention of trying to protect Madame. "No, there was nothing unusual, although Madame was acting strangely that evening before dinner. No, Monsieur never struck Madame. Another man with Madame? Unlikely, but possible. She came and went as she pleased."

In this way, her story corroborated with the others, and Monsieur was never suspected. It was determined to be a tragic accident, with private whispering about Madame's possible tampering. Seeing as she was the one dead, it was never pursued after the initial inquest.

Monsieur crept through the back door and up the back stairs, discarded his boots, and, fully clothed, fell heavily into bed. He stayed there past noon, when his valet came in to check on him, bringing wine and a plate of cold food. "Claude, I must speak to Juliette's father immediately. Please send him a note."

"Monsieur, are you sure that is wise?" Claude was concerned for his master and worried his guilt might be giving him second thoughts.

"I am sure. You will be happy with what we discuss, so do not worry." Then looking directly at him so he had his full attention, "You and I will never speak of this, to each other, or anyone. Agreed?"

"Agreed."

"Go along then. Fetch *le Duc* while I ready myself for our meeting."

"Duc, Sir, how are you managing?" Armand's tone was filled with concern as he shook the man's hand, clasping his other on top and patting it several times before releasing his grip.

He shook his head in response before he was able to utter, "Not well. Not well, at all." Remembering his son-in-law had also lost his wife, he remembered to ask at the last minute, "And you. How are you doing, Armand?"

Armand mimicked the old man's gesture with a shake of his head. "Not well, either, sir. It is why I have called you here on such short notice."

Le Duc was curious and bent his head in closer to hear his news. "*Duc*, this house is filled with Juliette's memory. I cannot look at a single ornament or picture without thinking of her. I can no longer eat in my own dining room, the tragedy too fresh in my mind. I have not slept since that horrible night and have burned all of our matrimonial linens, knowing I can never lie in them again." Armand was speaking a truth here that overlapped his other feelings and memories, but what he was saying was true to the letter, and *le Duc* felt great sympathy for the man. "I sleep on another floor, in the servants' quarters, to avoid any contact with her things. Sir, I feel I must move myself, and some of my staff to the country home for an unknown period of time. It is the only way I can remove myself from everything that was *her* and take some time to be alone with my thoughts. I hope this will not inconvenience you and your wife in any way, and that you will try to understand my motives."

"Juliette was lucky to have you, my son. She was a difficult child and was set in her ways, but you managed to tame her unruly spirit without breaking it. For that I will always be grateful. I know she was happy with you, for she confided in me just before you went off to the country. You have my blessing to go and take whatever time you may need. I'm sure you will arrange for someone to look after your affairs here in the city in your absence. May I ask, though, why the country house? It is where you spent your last days together and it, too, was her home?"

"If I may say, Sir, it was and yet it was not. I brought it with me into the marriage and she never grew fond of it. Most everything—the furnishings and tapestries, the art—were already there before we married. She went out of obligation, as her station required, to entertain in the country and have guests stay, which she did enjoy, to a point. In fact, we had a lovely weekend with our friends before... before she..." and Armand struggled to finish and said instead, "on our last visit. This is another reason I want to go. I think it will help ease my suffering." Armand truly was saddened by what happened. His wife had been a horrible woman but it was out of her own sadness, he was sure, and he felt great empathy for her while she was still living. He also felt her father had contributed to much of the dissatisfaction she felt for her life, giving in to her every whim and putting up with her tormenting as if it were normal behavior from a child and then later, an adult. He resented this man before him to some degree but could not blame him either. He knew enough about his life as well to see where the pattern began.

"Yes, you're right. I do remember her having a dislike to the place. I never realized it was so strong, though, but I understand now why you will feel better there. When do you plan on parting?" Now he was all business, recovered from the brief reminiscing.

"As soon as I take your leave, if I may. I do not want you to feel I am abandoning you and your wife, or our business dealings. As you can see I'm worn out and plan to ride out this afternoon so I can drop into bed for three days upon arriving. I will leave Cook behind, and a few of the others, and take my valet and horseman and that is all. The staff there will be able to accommodate my meagre needs while I am gone. If you give me your leave," *le Duc* nodding his affirmation again, "I shall be off and wish you *adieu*." They shook hands again and he left *le Duc* standing alone in the grand foyer to find his own way out.

After speaking to his staff, Armand had one more stop to make before he left. He took one of his spare horses and donned a nondescript cape from the back hall, ducking out quickly and unnoticed by his watchful servants. *La Maison de Rouler* was not far and he hoped he would catch Madame before his entourage left in the next hour or so. Still hooded, he knocked loudly and waited to be admitted. At first the young girl didn't recognize him and when her eyes lit up she started to say, "Oh, it's you Monsieur—" but he cut her off by placing his forefinger against his lips, saying, "*Shhhhhh*. I don't want anyone else to know I am here. I am still too distraught for small talk. Is Madame here? I would like to speak with her privately, if I could." He had always treated every one of them with respect and appreciation and got it back in kind on an occasion like this.

"*Oui, Monsieur*. She is here. I will take you to her. I am sure she will not mind being disturbed, under the circumstances," and she led him down the hall to her other *bureau* at the back of the *maison*, used strictly for her private work. Madame was surprised by the knock but not surprised when Armand entered, as she had been half expecting him.

She stood quickly, nodding to the girl, "That will be all" and held her arms high to take Armand into them. He accepted with relief and knew Madame would understand his mixed emotions. As if reading his mind, she said, "Armand, I am so sorry. You must be plagued with so many emotions at this time. I knew your wife well and to be candid, this is a mixed blessing for many, but for you I am sure it is doubly difficult. Please accept my condolences and my offer to help in any way you may need."

This was an exceptional woman standing before him and he leaned down to kiss her forehead affectionately. "My sincere thanks, Madame. It is why I am here."

She waited for the wine to arrive and when it did, took her place across from Armand and lifted her glass, toasting "to your health," which they said one after the other, Madame wondering if it had been a grossly inappropriate choice, but not hesitating for a moment. She sat waiting, wondering what he had in mind. She did not wait long before he began.

"Madame, this is what I would ask of you." He spoke at length of his request and the plan involved and when he was done, Madame was further amazed at his acumen and wisdom in this delicate situation. They never spoke of Juliette, but her suspicions were aroused more than once during their conversation, although not by anything that was said out of turn. More of a hunch, based on the culmination of all of his words and gestures. On his parting, she kissed his cheek and wished him safe travels.

Armand made it home in time to throw a few personal belongings on the luggage carriage and leave the remaining staff with final instructions. He decided to take the long bumpy carriage ride himself and have his horse ridden slowly by his horseman. They both needed a day off after yesterday's long ride. Instead of the usual two hours, it took them four, but Armand sat alone, undisturbed, throughout the day, drifting in and out of sleep. He still saw her face when he first closed his eyes, and he fought with himself to accept what he had done and move on. She could not have been happy, he knew. But was that justification to take someone's life? Of course not, but what was done was done. His guilt and remorse conflicted with his relief of her being removed from his life and he hoped some day he would be able to replace the former with the latter, or all of it would have been in vain.

He greeted the staff, apologizing for arriving with no warning, and asked to have a tray of bread and wine brought up to his room, where he would remain, undisturbed, the rest of the night. He knew this was a two-fold solution to the situation he had unwittingly forced upon them. First, it allowed him several hours to himself, which he craved desperately and could easily justify by today's journey and last week's tragedy, and second, it would give the staff until the morning to bustle around, scrambling to get everything ready for their master's surprise indefinite stay. There were few provisions in the house (he knew bread and wine were always safe bets) and he could almost feel the Cook running over a list in her head of what they would need to prepare for breakfast, what needed to be picked up at the market, how many for lunch tomorrow and God knows what else. The head maid would be doing the same and he had little interest in their questions—which would be unavoidable if he were downstairs in his *bureau*—so he did what was his right as master of his domain, and left them alone to do what they were all good at—their jobs. The only request he made was an inquiry as to whether they had had a chance to change his and Madame's sheets since they were here last, as he couldn't bear to sleep in them again with her smell lingering there. He was assured that yes, of course, they were all changed the next day, but did not feel insulted as they understood it was an important precaution to take and one that they would not want overlooked either, had they been in his difficult shoes.

Once in his room, he threw his clothes on the floor and put on his chemise, committing himself to staying put for the night. He poured a healthy glass of wine and turned the chair to face the window, which overlooked the back of the estate. It was beautiful here. He had always loved it and knew he had made a good decision in coming. He would be able to think here, and sort out his life. Every once in a while he would hear the frantic whispers in the hall and the commotion of what he had caused, but in this moment he did not care in the least. It was good for them to keep busy and feel important so no harm was being done. But he certainly caught them all off guard and it would be fun to see what breakfast would bring. Tomorrow morning he would go out for a long ride. It would feel good to be back on his horse for a leisurely tour with no schedule to keep. He planned to be out most of the day so he'd have to remember to tell Claude so he would be sure to warn the others. Otherwise, they'd be out looking for him by noon, he was sure. They were good to him, these people, and it would be a nice change for all of them to experience the new shift in power.

Chapter XXVII

The little *château* in the country that housed three beautiful women and their staff was also abuzz. Everyone was packing up to go, but Lisette was asked to stay behind. There was an important guest in the area who was well known and very, very rich, and who had asked Madame if they could possibly accommodate him. She explained there was little there, in way of support, but she would ensure one of the girls and a small staff would stay behind, and would be more than happy to attend to his needs. Madame had singled out Lisette as she had been on holiday "for long enough"—her exact words—and it was time to get back to work. Lisette asked who this gentleman was, if she could indeed call him that, dropping in on them in the middle of nowhere and expecting everyone to cater to his every whim. No one seemed to know, and Madame had not said, so she would have to improvise, which she detested. She detested everything at the moment and was tired of the endless serving of the 'greater sex', as she had once heard them referred to. Ha. She didn't know what was so great about them and found them all to be pains in the derrière more than anything.

Once she was left alone, she chose to take a stroll along the creek and sit by the rocks until she would need to return to start preparations for this evening's caller. She opened her cape, and, choosing a spot out of site from the house, laid it on the grass under a towering oak. She brushed the acorns away so they wouldn't jab into her backside and lay down under the partial shade, listening to the trickle of the creek and the incessant chirping of the birds until she drifted off into a lazy sleep. She was awoken by a dark shadow creeping across the path of the sun, and felt a sudden chill wash over her as she opened her eyes hesitantly and sat up. Her scream was muffled by a gloved hand, while his other motioned insistently for her to be quiet. She nodded mutely and when he removed his hand he quickly replaced it with his mouth, kissing her forcefully and throwing her off balance, forcing them both to fall back on the cape. When she finally was able to catch her breath, she screamed breathlessly again.

"Armand. How did you find me? When did you get here?" Her eyes were glistening with tears of joy and he abruptly pulled off his gloves, allowing him to brush them away with his bare hands.

"*Chérie*, you have alerted the entire country with your scream. Now I must leave before I am discovered."

She was horrified and looked fearfully at him. "No, please, you cannot leave me. I promise to be quiet. *Please,*" she begged, "do not go."

"I jest, *chérie*. I was hoping you would invite me in for a little bite, perhaps. I am starved." He began nibbling her ears and her neck, teasing her and pretending she would be his first course.

"Armand, I am sorry, but someone is expected here this evening. Someone important. You cannot come in. I am truly so sorry." Her anguished look spoke volumes.

"Someone is coming here? To see *you*?" his voice growing louder and his kisses stopping abruptly.

"*Oui, Monsieur*," came her quiet peep.

"Someone more important than *me*?"

"No one is more important than you, *mon chéri*. You know that. But this is something Madame has arranged and you know I must comply." She was almost begging with her eyes for him to understand.

"If there is no one more important than me, then I refuse to leave. Unless your mystery guest is someone I know. Someone we *both* know, perhaps? Hmm…" and he paused, rubbing his finger on his temple, "Perhaps…it is *moi.*"

At first Lisette did not understand, and then he saw the dawning on her face and he smiled his biggest smile while she started pounding her fists into his chest.

"You? It is *you* all along? And you did not tell me? Madame did not tell me? And I have been pining away for you all of these days, and it is *you?*" She was still pounding him with her fists, but losing strength as she started laughing in relief and then crying with the full comprehension of his words.

"*Oui, chérie*. I could not stay away from you any longer. I have lots to share with you and a few more surprises. Come. Let's go up to the house and get something to eat. The little bite I just had didn't seem to be enough." He nipped her ear as he jumped up and then ran back to the house, leaving her to grab her cape and follow as quickly as she

237

could. When she caught up she tugged on his sleeve to stop him. "Everyone knows?" she asked, before they entered the house.

"Not everyone. No one in my household knows, except Claude, of course. Madame knows, and the staff that is left here, but the other girls do not know. We are safe to act freely while we are here, *chérie*."

"How long are you staying? Just tonight? Please say you are staying longer than just tonight. I could not bear you leaving me twice in as many days."

"I will tell you everything once inside. Really, *chérie*, I must eat. And I mean real food, not code for 'ravish your body.' Sustenance. And *then* your body." He held her arm while they walked up the stairs and greeted the staff, who were obviously honored to have been part of the conspiracy. "You knew?" she chided them all. "And you didn't tell me? I can't believe no one told me, sulking as I have been all week." They were all happy to see her happy and took her scolds as the friendly camaraderie she had intended. They had prepared an extravagant lunch for the two of them, all set up and ready on the back terrace. Every now and again, Lisette would see how things had been planned and pains taken right under her nose, and she had been oblivious to it all. This had also been Madame's doing, she knew, and she was once again grateful to her long-standing mentor and friend.

They were sipping champagne and chatting amiably when Armand decided it was time to share the rest of his thoughts and schemes he had held inside for so long.

"*Chérie*, there are many things I want to discuss with you today and I want your full attention. No more joking and teasing. What I am about to say is genuine. Are you ready?" She looked scared and he added quickly, "No, no—it is nothing bad. In fact I think it is good, *chérie*." He took a breath before he continued, wanting to get his words just right. "We have been together now for some time, *non*? And I believe we have both developed a fondness for the other, would you agree?" Her smile and nod encouraged him to continue. "I am not a young man but then you are not exactly a young woman either." Watching her roll her eyes, he quickly added, "For someone in your profession, that is. I have spoken to Madame and if you are willing, I have asked her to release you from your contract and she has agreed."

He waited for some kind of response from her but she continued to sit, staring intently at him, willing him to go on. "I have asked that you may stay out here in this estate for one year, after which time I should like you to become my wife." He heard a catch of breath but needed to finish, so he pushed on. "*Chérie*, I am in love with you. I really, truly love you. I have since the first time we met, I believe. Somewhere between you pulling your knife on me to cut off my shirt and the next morning when we tenderly made love. It is a tragic event that allows us to be together, but I feel in a year's time the gossip and stories will have halted, freeing me to make my own choice, and that choice is irrevocably you, my love." He took a deep breath, smiled and now waited for her to come into his arms.

Instead, she sat back slowly, twisting a strand of silky hair between her fingers. "Hmm. That is a generous offer and I would like to give it some serious thought, if I may."

Armand was appalled at her gal and furious or devastated—he wasn't sure which—at her need to think on it at all. He had obviously misinterpreted her loving actions as sincere.

She saw the anger flash in his eyes and the torture she was putting him through and couldn't prolong it any longer. She leapt to her feet, jumped into his lap, and started kissing him everywhere, saying, "Yes, yes, yes" between each kiss. "Of course. Yes. I love you, too, *mon amour*. I really, truly do."

"You were playing with me?" Armand, still shocked at what had just happened, needed to make sure it was not still part of her game.

"Serves you right for sneaking up on me like that today. Don't you *ever* do that to me again, you hear? I have been *devastated* without you here, Armand. *De-va-sta-ted*. Two can play at that game, you brute." And she jumped from his lap and started running toward the garden, laughing and skipping, looking back over her shoulder to see Armand following in hot pursuit, laughing and shaking his head at his uncontrollable lover.

Chapter XXVIII

It seemed that life at *la Maison de Rouler* was starting to wind down. Madame was nearing fifty, and one of the richest women in Paris, and after all of these years, finally losing an appetite for her craft. The group of girls had gradually been both shrinking in number and growing in age as Madame took fewer and fewer new girls on. Paulette had expressed an interest in taking over, and she needed to give that some serious thought. Paulette had never gone the way of the courtesan but she knew more about the house now than Madame herself, living side by side with everyone and sharing the gossip and news. Now that Isabel's contract had been picked up by François and Lisette's bought out by Armand, there was little left for her to concern herself with and she started having visions of country life. Lisette would be marrying Armand soon and moving in with him, freeing up the *petit château* she loved so much. It would be the perfect place to end her days, hosting parties and growing fat from excesses, neither of which she had enjoyed during her life as Madame, with girls looking up to her for advice, expecting a worthy example. Yes, she would consider Paulette's offer seriously. Or maybe she wouldn't bother thinking on it at all and just hand it over. She certainly didn't need the income, and Paulette had dedicated her life to Madame's success. Time to live life differently. She stood before a blank canvas and could paint whatever she wanted. She felt a growing peace descend on her world.

"Paulette? Paulette? Lauren, go find Paulette for me please. It is urgent that I speak to her immediately," *before I lose my nerve.* She smiled to herself, closing her office door to wait with exhilaration at sharing the news and to see how her decision would change both their lives so dramatically.

François couldn't get enough of Isabel and she couldn't get enough of him. One had never seen a couple so in love. He had been dedicated to her unfailingly from their first meeting and it still moved her to remember his second place offer. She liked to tease him sometimes, reminding him that Armand was still first, but he didn't mind at all and respected the deep and meaningful friendship the two had fostered over the years. Maybe it was time he made an honest woman out of Isabel and married her, too, before someone else beat him to it. He smiled at the idea, knowing he was the only one for her.

When Madame finally left her post, handing the keys to an elated Paulette, many of the girls scattered to make their own way in the world. François took an apartment in an upscale neighborhood, where the neighbors were at first shocked by the whore who had moved in next door. Isabel took little interest in their small-mindedness, and found her own way in her new world, making new friends, some of them men, and rising up through their social circles. It didn't take her long to turn the tables. She was no longer referred to as a whore and in fact had an impeccable reputation as one of the finest hostesses in the city. Her lavish parties were sought after by all, and those who had scorned her now regretted their initial misjudgment. Some got up enough courage to approach her and apologize. Isabel was more than gracious, willing to pass it away with a wave of her hand, mentioning she was having a little gathering and would they like to come. She had a forgiving heart and even the women began to adore her.

Their lives became rich with good friends, love and laughter. He starting imagining little Isabels padding around their apartment, and it warmed his heart. There was also an abundance of money. François had entered into several business deals with Armand, first hearing about his story from Madame and then watching the way he treated Isabel and the other girls of the house. They had both done extremely well by each other and their friendship had strengthened with the years. He was standing for Armand at their wedding, which was an honor above all others.

As Isabel and François planned their future together they started talking about the inevitable. What would the other do when one of them died? How could they live without each other? François always had the same response. "Love of my life, we will never be apart. You may die. I may die. But I will always find you." And he kissed her lovingly to seal the promise.

"But how will I know it is you, my love?" Isabel wanted something concrete. Something that could quell her aching heart whenever she contemplated his death.

"That will be easy, *chérie*. I will ride up to you on a beautiful white horse and when you look into my eyes, you will know it is me."

With those words they both knew their love was eternal and she had nothing to fear.

Part VII

Chapter XXIX

Chloé was not looking forward to her dinner with Marc. What she really wanted to do was cancel. He was playing her, like all the others. His charm, his sweeping-her-off-her-feet gestures. She had had it with men. All this deceit. Arghhhh. What should she do? She was meant to be there in half an hour. She heard her phone beep—a text coming in— and glanced at the message. Marc. Probably canceling.

can't wait to c u ♥ marc.

I'm sure. She felt like crying, but pulled herself together. *To hell with it, I'm going.* She decided to wear the sexiest, sheerest dress she had and make him suffer all evening before she broke *her* promise and asked him how he felt about a 'change in direction'. Perfect. Now she could hardly wait to get over there. Her strappy sandals weren't the best choice for a quick getaway, but it would be worth it tonight. Thank God she didn't have to work tomorrow. The blisters would be too much.

At five to eight she rang the bell at his front door. With a swoosh of the door, and a bend at the knee, he welcomed her with, "Come in, my darling," like something out of a Dracula movie. She leaned in for the obligatory cheek kiss and then walked by him toward the dining room, looking for the wine. "You look ravishing." Marc was overcome by her beauty and stood with the door still open, all but gawking at her.

"I bet you say that to all the girls." *I bet you said it to the woman on your candle-lit porch last night, in fact.* She found the wine and asked if she could help herself to a glass by grabbing the bottle in one hand, glass in the other and pouring.

"Of course. Mi casa es tu casa. Chloé, come here and let me kiss you. I haven't seen you for what feels like ages…"

"Seventy-two hours, give or take," she interrupted.

"…like I said, *ages,* and I want to talk to you about something important. Right now. Before dinner. Before too much wine. Before I lose my nerve. Will you come over to the couch with me, please? Bring your wine and sit."

Here it comes, she thought.

"Chloé." He took a deep breath and looked straight into her eyes. "I'm just going to come out and say it and then I'll fill in the pieces after. Last night Sabine was here for dinner…"

"Sabine, my boss?" Now she was going to be really pissed if all along their little *friendship* turned out to be something else.

"Yes, Sabine. Anyway, I invited her over because I wanted to tell her about you and how we met and everything…"

"Wait. You invited Sabine for dinner last night so you could talk to her about *me?*" Oh. My. God. She was a complete idiot—again. Still.

"Yes, of course. We're good friends—you know that—and we get together a lot. I hope you don't mind, because she's really good in the advice department. Anyway, I told her how I felt about you after only knowing you for five minutes and she threatened to call you last night and haul you over here if I didn't call to do it myself, so here you are, and, well, I don't want to wait any longer to tell you… Chloé, why are you crying? I haven't even said anything yet."

"It's okay. I'll tell you after, okay? Go on. I'm okay."

"Well, what I wanted to say is this:" He took a deep breath and launched in. "I've fallen completely and madly in love with you. I've waited a lifetime to find you—maybe more—and I can't imagine living a moment of my life without you in it." He paused for a moment and hesitated, before going on. "I would ask you to marry me but really, marriage isn't my thing. But if it's something you want I would ask you right here, right now."

There had been only a handful of times in Chloé's life when she was left utterly and absolutely dumbfounded but this topped the list by a landslide. She had visions of banging her head against the coffee table like a mad woman, but instead, in a feeble attempt to keep her composure, she improvised. "Marc, I need a minute to catch my breath. You just said a mouthful." She didn't even know where to begin to attempt a recovery. "You talked this over with Sabine last night? Here, at your place?"

"Yeah, she was here quite late and by the time I told her, it was too late to call or I would have told you last night. Chloé, are you okay? I had it in my head that you would be excited by this or maybe feel the same way. I also realize you might not be there yet, which is okay, too, so this isn't about pressuring you into anything. You understand that, right?"

"Yes, of course." In that moment she knew a full confession was her only salvation. "Marc, I'm so sorry. I have a confession to make." A strange tinge started to color Marc's cheeks. He felt the first stirrings of nausea in his belly and marveled at the audacity of his assumption.

"Marc, wait. Listen before you get upset. I've been such a jerk. I walked over here last night to stop by to see you, thinking it would push me out of my comfort zone and hopefully be a nice surprise for you." She could see the look of confusion on his face. "I know. I never made it. I was coming up the street and saw the lights on the verandah. Then I got closer and saw you having dinner outside with some woman, with candles and wine—the whole romantic scene— and I jumped to all the wrong conclusions."

Marc's expression softened as the realization sank in of what she would have seen last night.

Chloé was desperate to continue. "Oh God, I'm such an idiot. Why do I do this to myself? You've just told me the most incredible thing I've heard in my life and I'm still recovering from the realization that you're not about to dump me. This 180-degree turn is too much to grapple with so quickly. Could we please try this again? Wait here. I'll be right back, okay?" She went out the front door, closed it, counted to five (ten was far too long) and then rang the doorbell. Marc opened it, without the previous flourish and Chloé kissed him on the cheek warmly. "Marc, it's so good to see you. I've thought of nothing else but you and our time together last weekend and I couldn't wait to come over tonight." Her eyes were brimming with tears and her smile was apologetic and so pathetic looking that he had no choice but to play along.

"Me, too. Come in. There's something really important I want to talk to you about." His words, although not enthusiastic, were still sincere.

"Me, too. Ladies first, okay?"

"Ladies first, then."

"Marc, I have been thinking of nothing else but you all week. And except for last night, when I experienced a moment of irrational insecurity, I have never felt like I have with you. I'm petrified to tell you I love you because it's such a significant word. But I do, Marc. I love you. I truly do. And I can't imagine a better way to spend my life than with you." Chloé was so scared. She'd almost blown this completely and had just laid her heart on the line. Her tears were fresh and rose from the depths of her core. She wanted to beg him to re-tell his news. Forget about what she said. But she bit her lip. Hard. She knew she owed him

247

a wait. She took a deep drink of her wine, enjoying the richness of it, distracting herself from what may come in his next words.

"Did you just say you loved me?"

"Yes, I did."

"Whoa. I didn't see that coming."

"Me neither."

"I guess that makes us even, then. Because, as you know, I love you too."

"I do know." She smiled with relief, her tears flowing freely now. "I can see it in your eyes." He leaned in to hold her close and a familiar feeling engulfed her as she wept in his arms with sheer joy and relief.

When Chloé's breathing became normal again, Marc had something more to add. "Chloé?"

"Yes."

"What do you think it feels like to have sex with someone when you really, truly love them?"

Fresh tears flowed but she couldn't hold back her smile and thought for a moment before replying. "I don't know but I think we should find out tonight."

Chapter XXX

Lunch with Nathan and Marc was intense. What Nathan shared was incredible. The fact that he had gone to a regression therapy session *in itself* was incredible. Sabine would have never guessed it and was so excited for him. She'd dabbled in reincarnation and found it fascinating but it wasn't something she felt the need to go into too deeply. It was so obviously clear to her that that was how life worked, so why would she want the details? Once in a while she caught a glimmer of something and chalked it up to one of her other lives lived. She didn't understand the notion that different time periods could be happening simultaneously, but she had read that on numerous occasions and found the notion fascinating. But Nathan's detailed recollection about his life, and Marc as his husband, and he killing him. Or her? That simply was too bizarre to grasp. Marc didn't seem that shocked when she thought about it. I guess there's a lot still to learn about Marc Bouchard. And now Nathan as well. This had taken incredible courage and she felt sheer relief that he was doing so much work to get his life back on track. Even though he'd had this amazing revelation, neither of them felt drawn to try to reconnect. It was as if she had been a catalyst in his life—and he in hers—to help each other get back on track.

But she was tired of only ever being someone else's catalyst. Maybe she needed to see Dr. Cameron as well to get to the root of some of her issues. She decided to get more details from Nathan and asked him if he would mind if she tagged along tomorrow when he went in for his session. It couldn't hurt and she was tired of being in limbo in her life.

Nathan thought it was a great idea and they rode together to the appointment, which felt a bit strange in light of the events leading up to his having to meet the doctor in the first place, but it felt good for them to talk to each other. They walked up the stairs, arm in arm, she entering first, feeling the warmth of the old Victorian home waft over her. She closed her eyes and breathed in the smell of the place, and then looked around at the old wood paneling and framing. It was intoxicating and it reminded her that she had to sell her condo and buy a character conversion or something. This was definitely more her thing.

Nate breezed in like he lived there, flirting with the receptionist, leaving Sabine to hang back and then take a seat in the comfortable waiting room. She picked up *Natural Home* magazine and then flipped through *Simple*. She loved how everyone was going organic and green. Back to the basics. Add a bit of luxe and that was the philosophy to live by as far as she was concerned. Nathan sat with her for a few minutes and then the door opened to reveal a rugged looking man with salt and pepper hair and an athletic build, dressed in jeans and a v-neck sweater in a gorgeous salmon cotton. He looked over at Nate, and then at Sabine. She smiled shyly and walked over to shake his hand while Nathan introduced them. As she reached out and connected with his hand a sharp shock jolted her and she laughed nervously, apologizing for the charge and muttering something about the carpets. He smiled, looking at her inquisitively before turning back to Nathan.

"This is Sabine. My ex, really. She tried to convince me ages ago to seek therapy, but I guess I just wasn't ready." His ribbing comment went over Sabine's head but brought a smile to James' lips. "She's pretty messed up, too," he added, which warranted a slug from Sabine. "And I wanted to introduce her to you. Sabine, Dr. C. Dr. C, Sabine. There, done. Let's get going, Doc. We have a lot to talk about."

The two men walked into the office and, before closing the door, James looked at Sabine in a disconcerting way. "A pleasure," he expressed, without taking his eyes from hers, and then the door closed, leaving her alone to wait. *I can only imagine what Nate told him about me,* she thought, as she searched for her place in the magazine, now curious about their previous conversations. She hoped she'd have a chance to defend herself if Nathan made her out to be the bad guy in this. It seemed important somehow. Then she realized the doctor probably already had him pegged and she instantly felt relieved.

At twenty after nine, the front door opened and Chloé waltzed in. "Howdy, Boss. What brings you to this part of town?" The two women embraced and Sabine mumbled "small world" under her breath. "Seriously, what brings you here? My image of you has been shattered if you have an appointment with Dr. Cameron. I thought you were completely and perfectly together."

"Well, I'm not, but I'm here with Nate. Not *here* with Nate. He told me about his experience and I'm interested to learn more and possibly explore it for myself."

"I'm still a bit leery, but honestly, it's hard to dispute. I had the most amazing session yesterday and would love to tell you about it. Are you game?" She hesitated just briefly, waiting for Sabine's nod, and then continued. "Oh, and by the way, I'm 'sick' this morning if anyone asks." Sabine rolled her eyes, and then encouraged her to go on. "Okay, picture this. 1700s, France. The time of one of the King Louis. I'm some royal courtesan and live in a mansion in Paris with a bunch of other whores, really. And my lover is married to an incorrigible woman. And so he murders her but everyone thinks it's an accident. Except me..." She looks at Sabine, who is gasping for breath. Sabine closes her eyes and then asks her to repeat what she just said. "Are you okay? You look kinda weird."

Sabine nodded for her to continue.

"I was saying that I was prostitute in France. There's this murder mystery that goes unsolved, kinda like Marc's book. Oh my God – I wonder if that's where all of these ideas came from. His book."

A chill ran up and down Sabine's spine and she went pale, but then began to collect her thoughts and arrange the pieces of the puzzle based on what Chloé had said, adding them gradually to Nathan's. The doctor must be amused by the close connection of two of his patients, if he was even aware of it yet. She needed a moment to work this out. Nathan was a woman. Nathan died a terrible death, murdered by her husband cum brother, Marc, who had 'coincidentally' just written a book set in the 1700s, France. (She was going to have to go home and read it again to see how closely it all tied in.) That would mean Chloé was...

"Oh, Chlo, you're not going to believe this." Before she could even begin to explain, the door opened and Nathan and Dr. Cameron came out, shaking hands and talking like old friends. "I'll tell you later," she said, and she kissed Chloé on the cheek, squeezing her hands "for good luck," turning to Nathan and the doctor. "How did it go, Doc? Any new revelations?" Sabine's smile was edgy. She had just learned something that the doctor probably hadn't deduced yet and she felt a bit cocky.

"So much, Sabine," was Nathan's reply. "I'll tell you all about it in the car."

"I learned a few things on my own that you both might find interesting." The men were intrigued and Sabine added, "Talk with Chloé and see if you can figure it out." And then casually, extending her hand, she said, "Nice meeting you, Dr. Cameron."

"It's James. And likewise, Sabine. Nathan? See you Monday. Hey Chloé. Wie geht es dir? Come on in." He led Chloé to the office, looking back over his shoulder to catch a glimpse of Sabine's elegant derriere leaving the building.

Sabine dropped Nate off at his condo, saying she needed to take care of a few things, but thanked him for today and yesterday and extended a hand if he needed help with any of this. "I'm sure you have a lot of questions and I might be able to answer some of them. Call me if you want, okay?" She was still unsure how to handle him but felt his confidence had been boosted since his therapy began and she was grateful to Dr. Cameron for his part in it all.

Back at her apartment she picked up the phone and called her realtor. "At the sound of the tone…"

"Julia? Get over here as soon as possible. I'm tired of my place and need a change. Let me know what you think it would sell for and let's talk about what's out there that would suit the new me. I love the water, but I'd like a bit of character. See what you can find, okay? Ciao." She set her phone down on the counter and then seconds later heard the vibration against the granite. Grabbing it, she answered, "Ciao, Baby. That was fast."

"Ciao a voi. Come va?"

It was a male's voice and not her realtor after all. "Who is this?"

"It's James, er, Dr. Cameron."

"How on earth did you get my cell number?"

"Nathan gave it to me. He thought it would be okay. Sabine, I think we need to meet. Soon. Today. What about lunch? Are you available?"

"For lunch, or generally?" She really was feeling cocky and even surprised herself at her boldness.

"Both, actually. But lunch first. I've already called Nathan and asked Chloé at our meeting if she could arrange it. She said her boss was a real pain in the ass but if no one was to say anything…"

"Ha, ha. Too drôle. I guess I can meet you for lunch, seeing as my assistant is M.I.A. and didn't have the courtesy to call to say she wouldn't be working today because of *personal problems*. What time and where?"

"I've made reservations at *Karma*. What do you think?"

"Fitting. I guess we'll soon find out, won't we? You might want to pick up a copy of Nathan's brother's book if you get the chance. It's *fascinating*. Ciao." And she clicked her phone off, feeling intrigued by what he might want and what the meeting might reveal.

Sabine, Nathan and Marc shared a cab, and Chloé was already there when they arrived. It was a warm October day and she had secured a table on the patio, street-side, already sipping on what looked like a margarita.

"Hiya," from Chloé, comfortably ensconced in her little niche she'd carved out for herself. Marc leaned over and kissed her passionately. Sabine and Nathan smiled at each other, eyes wide with partial surprise.

"I called your boss and told her what you said and she told me to tell you you're fired." Sabine leaned over and kissed her assistant warmly on the cheek.

"Oh, thank God. I've been wanting a change." Chloé simply shrugged her shoulders as if she hadn't a care in the world. "Switching subjects a bit, what do you think this is all about?" She raised her eyebrows up and down in mock suspense and Nathan laughed.

"I think that Dr. C has discovered something and wants to talk to us about it. Even though it's a bit unorthodox, both Chloé and I have agreed to discuss it with each other, and you two, of course, as it involves all of us." Nathan's answer revealed nothing and was all they would get out of him until the doctor arrived.

"I think you may be in for that change after all." Sabine hesitated before going on to explain where her thoughts were leading. "Do you want to hear what I think is going on?" They all looked at her, surprised that she might have insight into the mystery. But she wasn't deterred by their skepticism and continued without waiting for their answer. "Do you guys ever wonder what we are to each other? What I am to you, Chlo? And me to you, Nate? Or you to Nate? Or Marc? How we might be all connected in some intrinsic way."

"What do you mean?" Chloé found this stuff fascinating as a distraction but didn't take it seriously.

"Well, here we are, sitting all together under strange circumstances. I know all three of you yet you're only really just meeting. According to your sessions, Chlo, you lived in the 1700s in France and so did you two," glancing at both Marc and Nate. "Two of you have memories of a murder of a young woman, but from a different perspective, and the other wrote a novel about it. Think about it." They looked back at her with varying degrees of confusion and were trying to mull over what she said.

"Who were you, Nathan? I don't think you ever said?" Chloé was acting as if she would solve this in no time.

"I was a rich society *woman,* killed by my husband. Turns out that husband was Marc. Freaky, isn't it?"

253

"Not really. If you believe in this past life stuff, we've all been murdered or worse, been murderers. Not too surprising when you look at it that way." Chloé had it all figured out and was now contemplating her own experience with the doctor. "Turns out I was some high-class whore, and my lover was some rich guy with an annoying wife. Sabine, is this making any sense to you? Sabine...?"

Sabine wasn't paying attention. She had caught a glimpse of a flashy sports car pulling up across the street. "Uh, Nate? What kind of car is that?"

He squinted into the bright sun before answering. "The white one? A Ferrari."

They both watched as Dr. Cameron stepped out onto the sidewalk and strolled jauntily over to the restaurant.

"Figures. Ferrari. Symbol of a stallion. How fitting. Now I see where my 200 bucks has been going."

"*What did you say?*" Sabine spun around to look at Nate, meanwhile straining to see the symbol on the hood of the doctor's car. She was desperately trying to recall the conversation she'd had with her brother, but the details were blurry.

"About my 200 bucks?"

"No, the other part."

"The guy drives a white Ferrari, right? Have you noticed the symbol? It's a horse on its hind legs. Pretty sexy, wouldn't you agree? I'm sure that's why most men want to own a Ferrari. It's such a sexy car." Nathan was lost in car-world fantasy, already wondering if he should buy one for himself.

James sauntered across the street, heading toward them by the side patio entrance. He glanced over at their table, looking directly at Sabine. As he approached the table, he reached for her hand as if to shake it, brought it slowly to his lips and kissed it seductively.

"Nice seeing you again, Sabine," he whispered softly in her ear.

"Nice seeing you, too, James," was her breathy response, as she was having a hard time breathing with the sharp constriction in her chest.

He sat down beside her, without releasing her hand.

The other three looked at each other, hunching their shoulders in the universal gesture of "I have no idea what just happened," and broke into laughter.

Sabine just gazed up at him, ignoring the others, a tingling sensation starting to creep into her lips that slowly migrated over her face and neck. James just looked back at her and smiled, a knowing smile that was starting to knock her off her center. He could tell she was confused, but a light was slowly dawning in those beautiful amber eyes of hers and he continued to look into them for a few more moments before breaking the spell.

He smiled an almost wicked smile before turning to the others. "So," James began, addressing everyone at the table, "let's talk about France, shall we? I'd like to hear more about those two courtesans." Turning back to Sabine and holding her gaze with his twinkling eyes, he asked, "Shall we start with your thoughts, *chérie?*" He was going to enjoy helping her put the pieces together, if she hadn't already managed to do so on her own. *Mon Dieu*, he could hardly wait…